CW01573052

To Gordon,

Have a really enjoyable
read

Nigel

Nigel Wild is an author, journalist and business consultant. He lives in the Cotswolds with his wife Cathy, two gorgeous cats and a Triumph TR6.

NIGHTWALK

To Cathy

Nigel Wild

NIGHTWALK

AUSTIN MACAULEY

A CIP catalogue record for this title is
available from the British Library.

ISBN 978 1 84963 103 7

www.austinmacauley.com

First Published (2012)
Austin & Macauley Publishers Ltd.
25 Canada Square
Canary Wharf
London
E14 5LB

Printed & Bound in Great Britain

I would like to thank the following for their help and support:

The staff at the Imperial War Museum London, Richard Day, Curator of the Bugatti Trust, Kim Murray and Hannah Bealey at Austin & Macauley, Chris Hogan for all his advice and being my sounding board, my sons Tim and Richard and my wife Cathy, both my rock and my sternest critic.

Foreword

Fittingly, I started this book on holiday in France in 1997, when a week of torrential rain kept us housebound instead of cycling the local byways. By the time the rain had stopped, I had the synopsis, Chapter 1 and most of Chapter 2 under my belt.

English has always been far and away my best subject. My mother, God bless her, taught me to read fluently before I went to school; my grammar school was next to the public library and thanks to a long train journey each day, I devoured books at the rate of three or four a week. Even now, my bookshelves contain yellowing tomes marked 'Prize for English Essay'. My attempts to enter journalism after university proved fruitless, largely because the quiet and shy 21 year old I then was seemed unlikely to exhibit the chutzpah to doorstep. Despite this, my passion for writing remains undimmed and as well as the day job, I am now a freelance journalist.

After France, progress was steady, but personal circumstances caused writer's block and for almost two years, I stopped writing. I have always been fascinated by World War II history and following the adage to write about things you know, sought to weave a novel around a WWII theme. When the urge to take up my pen –well, mouse – returned, I realised that key to the problem was my lack of knowledge of SOE training methods and operations. The excellent staff at the Imperial War Museum at Elephant and Castle were more than helpful, and I left the former Bedlam armed with sheafs of information. Juliet Gardiner's beautifully researched book 'Wartime Britain' was a mine of information and essential reading for anyone seeking the detail of a country at war. Robert Gildea's 'Marianne in Chains' paints a similar picture of occupied France. Research is all part of the fun of writing. Richard Day, Curator of the Bugatti Trust, seriously enlarged my knowledge of the marque. The Daily Telegraph obituary column focuses on military figures and from one eulogy on a former SOE agent, I discovered the Lysander roll for exiting a moving aircraft. When I had almost finished the book, I was astonished to read an obituary on Jacques Poirier, an SOE agent. Unwittingly, my hero could be Jacques' clone. Frank Muir's 'A Kentish Lad' contained an unexpected bonus with his clear description of the parachute training school at Ringway. Plus, I have always been an Autolycus for facts, snapping up unconsidered trifles for later use. 'Dynamite' fishing I learned about from my maths teacher, a former commando.

I salute the extraordinary courage of the men and women of SOE, a courage very different to that of battlefield bravery. Agents lived for months, sometimes years under cover, using and remembering different persona and carrying volumes of information in their heads. The bigger the networks they created, the greater the chance of Gestapo infiltration or betrayal by an informer. The merest slip could be fatal. One newly landed agent was caught because he asked for café au lait in a bar; genuine residents knew that the Germans had all the milk and only café noir was on the menu.

The role model for Colonel, the hero's wire-haired fox terrier, was Humphrey, a family pet. Role model is perhaps the wrong phrase. Both share the endearing traits, but whilst Colonel's behaviour is impeccable, Humphrey never did a damn thing he was told and remained a lovable rascal until his death. I miss him still.

This is a novel spanning several generations and explores the gamut of human emotions but with love the most important. If despite my research there are errors, please excuse them, likewise my slight liberties with French geography.

The support and encouragement of all my family has been invaluable, especially my sons Richard and Tim, the latter himself a writer, but the key figure has been my wife Cathy, whose exhortations of 'This is so readable, I can't put it down, you've got to finish it' bolstered my sometimes flagging motivation.

'Readable' is my genre, that of Clive Cussler, Dick Francis and Nevile Shute, yarns that you just do not want to put down. I hope you take as much pleasure reading the book as I did writing it. Have a great read.

Nigel Wild

Chapter 1

The droning black shadows overhead at first excited no attention from the young Frenchman or his dog as they walked on the hills above Montluçon. Since early November, Guy Duplessis and his soulmate, the wire-haired fox terrier called Colonel, had become accustomed to the sight and sound of the Dornier bombers stationed at nearby Vichy.

Suddenly, Colonel began to growl, the visible rictus at his lips backed by a deep, menacing rumble in the throat which presaged danger. The rocky hillside on which they were standing lay bare and empty with not a soul in view. Where was the unseen danger? Then Guy looked up and his heart almost stopped beating in sheer terror. Normally, the Dorniers were at four or five thousand feet on the climbout. Now they were at less than two thousand feet. And the bomb doors gaped open, to reveal the savage cargo in Damoclesian suspension.

In two echelon formations astern, the planes flew menacingly towards the town.

Rooted to the spot, neither Guy nor Colonel moved a muscle, powerless to stop the impending carnage. Almost lazily, the bombs began to tumble from their bays and within seconds, the sleepy town became a hell's kitchen of noise and destruction. The air was rent with the whistle of falling ordnance, the roar of explosions, the crash of breaking glass and collapsing masonry and the crackle of fire. Soon, this cacophony was joined by the stammer of machine guns, the belly and tail gunners strafing those who ran from dying buildings. Eerily, the screams of the injured and dying keened through the intense welter of sound to rise towards the hills.

Despite his fear, Guy's brain was in overdrive and as the first bomb left its rack, he guessed the reason for the raid. Angered by the Nazi occupation of the Free Zone earlier in the month, the local Resistance had gone from passive to active mode. They got wind of an ammunition train and wired the track on an embankment so that the wheels would detonate the explosives hidden in the ballast. The Resistance intelligence missed that a troop train would precede the goods. Travelling at 60mph, the train hit the detonator, cartwheeling the engine down the embankment and scattering glowing coals amongst the grass. Tinder-dry from a hot summer and rainless autumn, the grass burst instantly into flame, to consume all the wooden carriages and their occupants which tumbled haplessly after the locomotive. Three hundred crack German troops had been killed or badly injured and the local Gestapo Kommandant, Obersturmbannführer Wägner, had been apoplectic with rage. One of the Resistance was caught, but when he died after a week of excruciating torture without saying a word, Wägner swore retribution on a grand scale. Fearing the usual rounding-up and shooting of local people, townsfolk kept off the streets. When nothing happened after a week, the inhabitants began to dread what the SS leader might have in store. Now the answer had come.

As Guy continued to watch, the local Catholic church received a direct hit, to implode with a rumble and a roar, its graceful spire jackknifing before crashing into the ruins below. A panoply of black smoke and embers began to spread over the rooftops.

The Duplessis villa stood at the edge of town, its red tiles distinctive among the grey slates of neighbouring houses and the rear gate of the garden almost touching the base of the ridge on which Guy and his chum were still transfixed. As Guy stared, a bomb tumbled from a Dornier to explode with shattering force in the street at the front of the Duplessis home. There was the flash of the explosion, the distinctive roof seemed to lift momentarily amid a cloud of dust and then Guy and dog were running as fast as they could towards their back gate. The clear of a November afternoon offered good visibility, but it was over a mile to that gate and the ground uneven. By the time Guy and Colonel reached home, the bombers were long gone. Somehow, the screams had stopped and the only sounds were the crackle of buildings ablaze and the bells of the fire engines.

Totally breathless, Guy paused for a minute or two in the garden to catch his wind. From the back, the house seemed normal and untouched, but as Guy approached the kitchen door, his sense of foreboding grew. The back door gave easily to his touch, but the door from the kitchen to the hall was very stiff and he practically had to wrench it open. The hallway running from front to back was like another world, a shambles of broken glass, furniture and ornaments. Pictures had been stripped from the walls, to lay in shreds of canvas and shards of glass. The pendant fitting in the hall ceiling hung gamely from just one wire and, devoid of lamps and shades, pirouetted gently in the draught. The front door lay neatly on the floor, blown clean off its hinges by the blast. Through the opening, the house opposite was clearly visible, its front elevation blown away and looking like a dolls house with the front open. A thick miasma of plaster dust hung in the air, the weak afternoon light dappling through the cloud.

Almost directly opposite the kitchen door, the door to the salon lay drunkenly askew, blown outwards by the explosion but still hanging by a thread from the top hinge. Fear and nausea gripped Guy, but with Colonel at his heels, he inched his way into the salon. Less than twenty minutes previously, the two rag dolls against the rear wall had been Guy's parents. The 500kg bomb had dropped exactly outside the bay window where Robert and Madeleine had been enjoying a Saturday evening glass of Sancerre. In a fraction of a second, the shock wave reduced their flesh and bones to a flaccid pulp, then hurled the twisted bodies to the far end of the room. Behind Guy, Colonel whickered softly, smelling and sensing the death before him, but afraid to approach the two lifeless figures.

Unable to take his eyes from his parents' corpses, Guy scarcely noticed the devastated room, furniture in matchwood, ornaments in smithereens, books now rent asunder into thousands of separate leaves, nor that the ceiling sagged dangerously, bereft of support from the bay window frame. Forcing his leaden limbs into action, the young man tiptoed up to Robert and Madeleine, seeing more clearly the myriad cuts on each inflicted by flying splinters. Very gingerly, he reached out and touched his mother's face, but recoiled sharply at the ghastly marshmallow feel under his fingertips.

As he stood, Guy's near reverie was broken by the sound of two German voices. Guy spoke good German and he could hear the two discussing looking in the bombed houses to see what valuables they could find. Instinctively, Guy stepped back through the hall and into the kitchen before the two soldiers came into view. He motioned Colonel to be quiet and the well-trained dog sank noiselessly to the kitchen floor.

The Germans agreed to split and meet again at their Mess later to compare spoils; the other soldier moved away into a nearby sidestreet. A tall Gefreiter or corporal crunched his way through the Duplessis front door opening and into the salon. Guy crept from his hiding place and peered round the salon door, to witness the Gefreiter bending over his mother's corpse and wrenching the wedding and engagement rings from her lifeless fingers.

At that instant, rage, grief and pain melded, to seize the young

Frenchman with an emotion of an intensity he had never before experienced. In one bound, he leapt across the rubble towards the German. Hearing Guy's footsteps, the soldier half-turned, but he was too late. Guy snatched the bayonet from the Gefreiter's scabbard and plunged it into the man's back with all his might. As he was later to discover, he hit the kidneys with deadly accuracy and the soldier folded silently to the floor.

As the enemy died, an icy shaft of realisation hit Guy. The occupiers would see the death as murder and it would not take an Hercule Poirot to deduce who had carried out the stabbing. For a moment, Guy's bowels turned to jelly and he almost turned and ran blindly away, but cold reason gripped him again and he began to plan his escape.

Guy decided to walk out of France. But in which direction? The Spanish border was 350 miles away and he did not know the country; Switzerland was nearer, but tales of refugees being turned back to France were becoming more frequent. The Normandy coast was around 350 miles and Guy knew that the fortified coastal zone was forbidden except to residents and those with special passes. The most persuasive reasons to choose the Channel route were that he knew the country in between and his Uncle Hubert lived in St Malo. The Channel coast it had to be, then a boat to England. The pair would have to walk at night and hide by day to evade discovery.

But before he could cut and run, Guy had to conceal the body and give himself a headstart. Moving the dead weight of a 12 stone corpse over rubble requires tremendous strength and at first, Guy found it impossible. The raw fear of being seen through the remnants of the bay window or still worse, that the Gefreiter's co-looter might put in a sudden and unexpected appearance, produced an almost manic burst of strength to drag the body into the kitchen. Lifting the rug and releasing the panel which hid the cellar door, Guy pushed the German through the trap. He frightened himself with the almost insouciance with which he pulled the bayonet out before tipping the body over the edge, to hit the cellar floor like a sack of potatoes. To Guy's amazement and relief, pressing the switch inside the trap of the small cellar produced light. The corpse was covered with an old groundsheet before Guy and his little dog locked themselves beneath the trap and began to pack.

The Duplessis family had been keen hillwalkers and owned a treasure trove of all the right kit. Into a rucksack went a very light but warm Finnish sleeping bag which packed down to almost nothing, a compass – a beautiful, luminous ex-Army model of his father's – a small pair of binoculars, Swiss Army knife, waterproof matches, a torch and batteries, snares, twine and a sewing kit. Maps were included – knowing the potential risk if found by the Nazis. A water-bottle and purifying tablets took care of liquid needs and a pannikin would serve as a combined kettle, saucepan and plate. From a well-hidden safe came 100,000 francs and 20 gold sovereigns which Guy stitched into the hem of his anorak the following day. For the terrier, there was a double sided steel dish. The inert, mute figure beneath the groundsheet was an ever-present reminder of imminent danger. Even the few minutes spent in its presence set every nerve and sinew jangling.

Straining to hear if there was anyone above, Guy inched open the trap. Darkness was falling and nothing seemed to be moving at all. A swift foray up the now rickety stairs allowed Guy to retrieve the minimal clothes he needed, just some woollen shirts, a spare pair of cord trousers, underwear and two sweaters, but several pairs of heavyweight socks and two pairs of gloves. Guy decided that his one fine pair of boots would have to do, he could not afford the extra weight of spares. Food was also minimal – a stock of pemmican acquired on a trip to the United States, some bread, cold meat, coffee, sugar and chocolate, plus a hip flask of brandy. Soap and a razor were necessaries: a small towel and a flat pack of toilet paper were little luxuries. Some sticking plasters for the inevitable blisters were a sudden inspiration. His excellent anorak, another Finnish item, would keep the man dry and the dog had a fleece-lined dark gabardine coat that also served as camouflage, as Colonel's predominantly white fur was quite visible in the dark.

Guy knew that on average, he could walk 12 miles per night on easy ground He should be able to make the coast by about the end of December if all went well.

Packing complete, still trembling fingers strapped Colonel into his coat. Turning to leave, Guy was gripped by a compulsion to look at his parents for the last time. He trod softly into the salon and lingered for a moment with the two figures, now almost invisible in the poor light. Then Guy and Colonel crept through the garden gate and onto the hill. For a brief moment, they were silhouetted by a flash of flame from a burning house, then man and dog were swallowed by the night.

Chapter 2

The first two nights were relatively easy, although Guy set a stiff pace to get as far away as possible using the walk 55/rest 5 routine for each hour. He knew the hills and helped by a dry night and a fitful moon, navigated his way up hill and down dale. Autumn had hung on for longer than usual and it was warmer than expected.

One early mistake was to try walking along a local D road, but when the pair only just hit the ditch before a German patrol hove into view, thereafter they stuck to the fields. Not unnaturally, Guy was tense, expecting a search party looking for the Gefreiter's killer, but when there was no sign of pursuit, he began to relax a little.

'Come on, Colonel.'

The little dog needed no second bidding and hopped onto the lap of his master who was perched on a tree stump. Colonel tucked his furry head under Guy's chin, Guy wrapped his arms around his beloved dog and for several minutes, the two communed silently but eloquently.

Although experienced at map-reading and navigation by day, Guy had never done so at night, so he practised the techniques on the ground he knew so well. Daylight navigation was easy because you had visual references, but at night, you had to be able to follow a course without them. It was rather like the difference between flying visually and then on instruments. At first, Guy could not keep on track and kept zig-zagging, but after a few hours, he could accurately set and hold a compass bearing and his chosen course.

As dawn approached, they headed for a remote cattle shed that Guy knew. A typical farm building, it contained some cattle pens and a hay store at one end. Guy prayed there would be no cattle in it, which would have meant someone coming to tend them, but to his intense relief, it was bare and empty. Even so, he approached cautiously, relying on his dog's sixth sense to warn him of any problems. But the terrier gave no signs.

'OK, boy, let's go in,' said Guy and they slid quietly into the empty, cold and shadowy barn.

As he shone his torch, Guy jumped at a sudden movement near

his feet. Two large brown rats shot out from the cattle pens and into the night. Colonel nearly shot after them, but stopped on command.

The very remoteness of the building meant that farmworkers often had to spend long hours there and a little fireplace had been constructed at one end. Some fir cones lay near the hearth and with some of the hay in the shed, soon produced a cheerful blaze. Once warmed by a pannikin of coffee shared with Colonel, Guy doused the fire and scattered the ashes in the bushes outside before taking cover in the top of the hay pile. No more rats appeared, to Guy's relief and Colonel's disappointment. The pair bedded down on the hay, Colonel snuggled contentedly against his master, and soon the pair were fast asleep.

About 3.30 in the afternoon, Guy awoke and had a careful scout round to see that all was clear, sweeping the immediate area. Nothing moved. The sweep was also useful to recce the ground ahead and plan their direction. As darkness fell, the little fire sprang to life again to warm man, dog and coffee to wash down a simple meal.

Guy checked his map by the light of the fire, calculating that one more night should see them through the hills and into more rolling farmland. Once again, all traces of the fire were scattered and not a clue remained from their visit.

'On y va, Colonel,' whispered Guy and they slid away from their shelter.

The night was absolutely clear, the bright pins that were stars twinkling in the velvety cushion of the night. A three-quarter moon bathed hills and valleys in a cold glow and Guy had to use the ground for cover and walk around the tops of hills to avoid being silhouetted against the skyline. Still in the 55/5 routine, the night was strenuous but uneventful, bringing the fugitives, as planned, to the edge of the hills. As cold moon retreated before dawn's slightly warmer tide, neither map nor eye could offer any shelter. A small fir coppice at the base of one hill was the only relief in an otherwise bare landscape.

Guy carefully lit a small fire in a clearing, having first dug a little firebreak ditch for safety. The last of the cold meat, some by now stale bread and some coffee were the evening repast before Guy made a hide of branches, complete with mattress. Now they shared the sleeping bag, glad of the mutual warmth man offered dog and vice versa.

Coming-to, Guy felt stiff and unrefreshed. A wind was by now whipping through the trees and there was the steady washing noise of rain on the branches. Whilst making a crude stew of pemmican and a bit of bread, he began to worry about replenishing his food. His ration-card was valid for another two weeks, but would have to be renewed at a mairie to legitimately buy food. If, as he believed, he was on a wanted list, he could end up being arrested.

Inspiration dawned when during one very wet night, he had almost tripped over a school roadsign. He had left the Lycee three years ago. In those years, he had physically changed not that much and could still pass unnoticed in a crowd of teenagers. If he happened to be around when the Lycee spilled its mob, Guy had seen that the Germans took little notice of the homeward bound pupils and he had never seen them check papers. Guy figured that if he used towns rather than villages where strangers would be noticed, he could mingle with the pupils as they left the Lycee and try to buy staple foods like bread, milk and cheese. Still, it would be a risky business, as practically everything was rationed. To buy food officially required a ration card issued by the local mairie complete with coloured stamps for the various staples. He would have to trust to luck, charm and paying over the odds. Greed in war-torn France was a powerful force.

Colonel in the van as always, they stumbled on through the night, to find shelter in a hayrick before first light. Progress had been slow, because thorn hedges between fields meant finding the gate every time rather than climbing over – and many of the gates were in seemingly impractical locations. Much of the ground was rough, impeding smooth progress. Stumbling on clods and tussocks in the darkness was a perennial hazard for Guy, although Colonel seemed totally unmoved by any such problems and trotted over any ground at an undiminished pace.

The country around the rick was bare and open, so a fire was out of the question. Frozen to the marrow, burying themselves in the rick was the only solution, to fall into an exhausted and fitful slumber. Before finding the rick, Guy had caught his foot in a rabbit burrow, so he set a couple of snares before retiring.

A weak afternoon sun spilled onto the rick, bringing reluctant life back to the sleepers. Dark and menacing clouds still scudded overhead, but the rain had stopped and the wind abated. Best of all, Guy espied a plump bunny in one of the snares and a small thicket that had not been visible the previous night. As evening fell, man, dog and bunny moved swiftly under cover, to dry out before a well-hidden blaze and dine on rabbit stew and coffee laced with brandy.

On the fifth night, Colonel saved their lives.

The weather had been cold but dry, allowing good progress. Guy had successfully used his plan to buy food in a small town and stocks had been replenished. Leaving Colonel and the rucksack well concealed, he had walked into town at just the right time and passed totally unnoticed amongst the townsfolk. Thankfully, he was not asked for a ration-card or any form of identity.

That fifth night was again dry, but an impenetrable blanket of cloud blotted out any kind of light from the moon and navigation had been from the luminous glow from his compass and walking into fences and hedges in the seemingly impenetrable blackness. So black was the night that although now practised at blind-flying, Guy was having difficulty keeping on track.

They were walking, Colonel slightly ahead, when the dog stopped as though suddenly frozen. Instinctively, Guy stopped too, then gingerly felt ahead with his walking stick. To his horror, the stick jabbed into nothing. Guy dropped to his knees then inched carefully forward, to find his hands clasping the edge of a drop, in that darkness a drop of unknown and unseen proportions. Even so, Guy tried to peer over the lip but could make out no detail at all.

Retreating a few yards, Guy turned left before he and Colonel warily started downhill using Colonel's senses and Guy's stick to skirt the drop. At the bottom of the hill they found some rusty machinery. They found it not because they saw it, but because the tip of Guy's stick hit steel. In that stillness, what was in reality a little 'plink' seemed to resound like the clang of a church bell. Once again, Guy and Colonel froze, terrified they would be discovered. When nothing happened, Guy began to run his fingers over the machine his stick had struck, trying to guess its purpose. Under his touch he found a maker's name embossed in the casting. To his somewhat wry amusement, the name was English and read 'Charles Ward Sheffield', but meant nothing to Guy. At that moment, a fortuitous flick of moonlight bathed the ground with light. The flick was so brief, it was like a flashbulb going off, but showed Guy he was at the entrance to a disused quarry, the surrounding area dotted with rotting hulks of heavy machinery, all large gearwheels and conveyor belts. That momentary illumination also revealed a sheer rock face towering 150 feet or more above them, a face that had so nearly claimed both their lives. Guy shuddered, not from the cold.

They did make progress that night but it was slow, trying to find gaps and gates in the dark and equally, trying to stay on course. With dawn threatening, it was yet another small wood for the day's shelter.

But what an uncomfortable day it was.

'Pierre, have you fed the chickens?'

The voice of the farmer's wife snapped Guy from his snooze. The pair had just bedded down in a hollow. Guy risked a quick recce to discover he had stopped near a farm and the farmer and his wife were going about their daily business literally yards away.

As quickly as he could, Guy concealed himself and Colonel in the hollow and covered themselves with leaves, then lay awake all day dreading that they might be found. The farm boasted two dogs, the standard chiens méchants seemingly beloved of French farmers. Fortunately, neither animal came anywhere near the wood that day. Lying there was both nerve-wracking and tiring and there was no chance to eat. Cold gnawed at them from the ground and penetrated their very marrow, as Guy did not risk opening up the sleeping bag.

The welcome dark of night seemed to take forever to arrive and when it came, two very stiff figures creaked silently away, both to steamily relieve their bursting bladders at the first opportunity. After a couple of miles they came upon a deep hollow in a copse, where Guy risked a small fire to boil water for coffee and they ate bread and cheese. Despite the paucity of the blaze, Colonel sat in front of it and leaned forward to get some heat into his chest, his nose pointing forward and a look of pleasure in his eyes at the longed-for warmth. The coffee seemed to sear down Guy's throat, its heat dissipating into his bones and doing at least something to counteract the chill.

Glowing embers illuminated the map sufficiently to plot a course before Guy wiped all traces of their presence and they decamped once more. Cloud hid the moon, but offered a mild glow and made navigation easier. Guy felt tired beyond all measure, cold, muscles creaking and aching and feet like lead. At that moment, he would have given almost anything for a decent meal and a warm bed. Despite his low spirits, he still watched with enormous pleasure as Colonel trotted ahead of him. As ever, the terrier's nose tracked the ground, searchingly instinctively for new smells. The two soft and silky ears both folded over at the top, flapping deliciously in unison with the dog's gait. And, to Guy's surprise, the sickle-shaped tail was vertical, indicating that Colonel was still having fun despite everything. The terrier especially loved piles of dry autumn leaves, ploughing them with his nose. Occasionally, he would stop in the middle of a deep pile and balancing on his forelegs, kick his back legs furiously, spraying leaves joyously in all directions.

The bond between Guy and Colonel, already strong, forged itself to tungsten-hard and they thought as one.

Another small town offered chance to bolster not only their meagre food stock but also to fill the water bottle from a tap rather than a stream.

'I haven't seen you before,' said the middle-aged woman behind the boulangerie counter.

'I just moved here yesterday,' came Guy's swift invention.

The woman nodded, new faces were a fact of war.

'Ration card?'

Guy proffered the required document, which the woman inspected suspiciously, then sold him two small loaves.

He rapidly escaped back to Colonel.

Ten miles further on, Guy saw a miracle.

It was a house.

No ordinary dwelling by a road, the tiny house was one up in size from a hut and set in a wood seemingly miles from anywhere. They were once again on their night walk and Guy stumbled on it by chance, doing his usual foray in a wood because dawn was nigh. Looking at the little building, Guy half expected Hansel and Gretel to come tripping out. A single-storey edifice, it had a cattle byre at one end and a combined bedroom, living room and kitchen at the other. Front and back doors were locked fast with heavy padlocks, both so rusty that they had clearly not been disturbed for ages, but Guy still looked around very carefully before tentatively approaching the building. The windows were intact and locked shut, but the trusty Swiss Army knife prised open a catch and they were in.

Before committing himself to the house as a resting place, Guy drew the thick hessian curtains still hanging at the windows, then left Colonel on guard whilst he checked the area. As dawn broke, he scanned the horizon with the small field glasses, but not a soul or a beast could be seen. Traversing the wood showed no well-used tracks that would indicate human traffic.

Satisfied, Guy rejoined his chum and took stock of his surroundings. The woodshed yielded kindling and logs for the cast-iron stove within. An upturned wooden bucket stood on the edge of a well which in turn offered clear, clean water. The inside of the hut smelt damp and musty. Furniture was sparse, a wooden table and chairs and a truckle bed still with its mattress. Not unexpectedly, the mattress was reeking damp. Almost throwing caution to the winds, Guy coaxed the stove to a roaring heat, then stood the mattress on edge in front of the blaze. Within seconds, a cloud of pungent steam arose from the bedding, but within an hour, it was bone dry. It was still none too clean and Guy wrinkled his nose at the odour still rife within the ticking. In the meantime, he had found an old tin bucket and filled with hot water, it became his bath and laundry. The luxury of a good shave with really hot water was followed by shirts and underwear getting a well-earned scrub before being hung over the backs of chairs near the fire.

Colonel thought the stove was manna from heaven, sat in front of the glowing logs and soaked up the warmth. It was so hot he became slightly light-headed, swaying forward until the fierce heat brought him sharply from his trance and he backed away.

One very useful find was an oil lamp. The clue to the lamp's presence had been in the woodshed, where there was a grime-encrusted drum of paraffin. Making the connection, Guy searched the darkest recesses of a large built-in cupboard near the stove. At first, he was dismayed to find that the mantle had crumbled, but he really thought God was on his side when a dusty box in the cupboard's even darker recesses yielded a new one.

Somehow, both Guy and Colonel sensed that this house was safe and relaxed in the warmth and comfort it offered.

As a stew, it was unlikely to rate a Michelin rosette, but the remaining pemmican, some ham, cheese, together with a turnip and two potatoes garnered from a field en route all melded together to form a delicious meal for both human and canine consumption.

Guy packed his now dry clothes and the rest of his kit into the rucksack in case they had to make a quick getaway. The stove was banked up and the damper set low. Warm, dry and sated, Guy and Colonel retired to bed.

The scratching of an owl's claws on the ridge tiles woke Guy with a start. His watch said 11 o'clock and opening the curtains a crack revealed night. They had slept for sixteen hours.

'Come on Colonel' whispered Guy and they slipped carefully out through the window to check the lie of the land.

Nothing but nothing stirred, the only slight noises were the sound of the owl winging away to hunt and the soughing of a gentle breeze through the trees.

With stove and lamp rekindled, the warm glow suffused the room once more.

'Excusez-moi, M'sieur'.

Colonel looked up at the sound of his master's voice.

'Would M'sieur object to a repeat of last night's menu?'

Colonel climbed onto one of the chairs and leaning forward, licked Guy's hand to indicate that any food would be gratefully received.

Realising that it would be virtually impossible to find such warmth and shelter again and that they were still desperately tired, Guy decided to risk another night and day in the house. It was a wise move.

Night fell again; time to move. Having found the stove with cold ashes in it, he left it that way. Some loose dust and cobwebs were spread on the furniture and lampglass, the lamp returned to is dusty recess, the windows opened to lose all the heat and water thrown over the mattress to dampen it again.

A sudden panic gripped Guy. Somehow, the warmth and protection offered by the hut seemed a mesmeric attraction and for an instant, he was tempted to stay longer. Then panic faded to be succeeded by steely resolve once more. With a last, lingering look at their haven, the duo set forth yet again on their long walk to freedom.

This was their eleventh night, which began dry, but a steady drizzle turned to hard rain, swiftly evaporating the warmth and euphoria from the little house. Shelter that day was another wood, to be followed by a (fortunately) dry ditch and a large hedge for the next two. The strength regained by their stopover in the hut faded rapidly, to be replaced by tiredness.

Guy had set his pace to arrive at a large town, where he attempted his ruse to buy provisions as his ration card had expired. The archetypal French market town, it had shops all round the square on which all main thoroughfares converged. Guy bought a loaf of black bread at the baker's using the same story as before; to his utter relief, it worked once again. He had checked that the mairie was not on the square, which could have blown his cover. Black bread lasted quite well compared to the traditional baguette, which went stale within hours.

All was quiet when Guy entered the boulangerie, but there was a queue and he emerged to find German patrols at all four corners of the square, checking papers. Raw, cold fear gripped his entrails and he stood rooted to the pavement; near panic-stricken, he could do nothing but stare, along with other people who had come out of the shops to see what was going on. Behind him, there was a click and a creak as the side door of the bakery opened and he found beside him a large man complete with floury apron and smelling of countless baguettes and croissants.

Without looking at Guy, the baker whispered out the side of his mouth 'Slide behind me and go into the bakery'.

Noiselessly and unseen, Guy did as he was bidden and slipped through the door, which was still ajar. Out of Guy's sight, the baker looked around once more and, seemingly content that he had seen enough, re-entered the bakery and shut the door.

'Come in here,' he said, pushing an ashen-faced Guy roughly into the bakery office. 'I don't want to know who you are, but I guess that you are on the run?'

Guy nodded dumbly.

'I saw you in the shop and I knew I didn't recognise you,' went on the baker.

He then reached in his desk and produced a bottle of marc, pouring Guy a generous measure. The fiery spirit almost took the young man's breath away. A little colour returned to his cheeks, but only for seconds, as the banging of a rifle butt on the door and 'Oufrez' announced that the Germans had widened their check.

'Quick, in here'.

The baker thrust Guy unceremoniously into the large bread oven.

'It's still warm, but I've finished baking today'.

The door clanged shut and Guy hauled his body into the farthest corner and lay, scarcely able to breathe in his fear. The baker's idea of warm was an understatement and within seconds, Guy began to sweat profusely.

Despite the thick iron door, Guy could make out sounds of German and poor French as the Boche checked out all papers. At one stage, he heard a soldier approaching the oven, but the wily baker diverted attention by offering the soldiers a bag of hot croissants. To the fugitive's barely contained relief, stomachs prevailed over duty. What seemed like hours later, the Wehrmacht troops moved on to the greengrocer's next door and then the chemist. Still Guy lay in concealment, by now close to heat exhaustion such was the residual temperature in the oven.

Eventually, the door clanged open, he was released and fell almost unconscious to the floor. A still bigger marc was pressed into his trembling hand, followed by a demi-baguette full of ham and French mustard. The baker sat mute, watching the impromptu meal being devoured, then checked outside to see the state of play.

'It's OK,' he said on his return 'the Boche have had their fun and gone, but I'll let you out the back way and give you a good route out of town'.

The grim inflection he gave the word 'fun' spoke volumes. Then he smiled at Guy.

'My instincts say you're OK. Just don't prove me wrong, will you?'

Guy smiled his acquiescence.

'I can't thank you enough for risking your neck for me,' he exclaimed numbly, suddenly overwhelmed both by his escape and the baker's kindness.

'Anything to outsmart those bastards,' came the rejoinder. 'And bonne chance,' he added, grasping Guy's right hand warmly with his own floury one, at the same time thrusting a packet of ham, charcuterie and ersatz coffee into Guy's left.

Following the directions given, Guy found himself weaving through a maze of narrow alleys and quiet streets until he reached the edge of town. Taking care to be unobserved, he regained his hiding place to be met by an ecstatic Colonel, who licked Guy's face in sheer joy. The dog feasted on some of the food Guy had bought and they settled down to slumber until nightfall.

Chapter 3

'Pass me the 12 mil' ring, Guy,' called Robert Duplessis from beneath the chassis of his Bugatti 35TC and accompanying his request with an outstretched and very greasy left paw.

It was 1932.

Robert's voice was rather muffled by his position, the pits at Monthléry were awash with noise and the 11 year old Guy was totally immersed in his own task.

'Guy, can you pass the me the 12 mil' ring?' repeated his father.

This time, Guy heard and selecting the spanner from the shadowboard behind his bench, slapped it into his father's palm rather as a theatre sister hands a scalpel to a surgeon.

Leaving Robert to tighten the front shackles, Guy turned back to his bench. Laid out on a white cloth were the surgically dissected components of the Bugatti's Zenith carburettor and for the third time that day, the boy was cleaning rusty muck from the float-chamber, jets and passages.

'Not again,' wailed a voice from behind.

Unheard, Robert had emerged from beneath the car and was watching his only son work his magic on things mechanical.

'Sorry, papa, you've picked up some really dirty fuel, we'll have to flush the tank.'

'Bugger,' remarked Robert feelingly, 'there's only 45 minutes before the race starts. And even if we flush the tank,' he continued, 'how do we know it's clean?'

Guy pondered.

'Some kind of fine filter, put fuel in the tank after we've cleaned it, drain some out through the filter and see if it runs clean?'

'What's in the tank now?' demanded Robert.

Guy leaned over and peered down the filler, then stuck in a metal rod.

'About 8 litres,' he advised.

Robert breathed a sigh of relief, as a full tank was over 90 litres and would have presented considerable difficulty in draining that much petrol in the time available.

'Find Gerard and Maurice and get the tank out,' ordered his father and strode off towards the back of the pit area.

Gerard was the manager of one of Robert's chain of car dealerships, Maurice a mechanic at the same garage. Both stalwarts comprised the pit crew.

As if on cue, Gerard and Maurice appeared from the other side of the Duplessis transporter carrying steaming mugs of coffee.

'No time for that,' said Guy and explained the problem.

In seconds, Gerard and Maurice were bent over the car. Guy's forte was carburettor tuning, his keen young ear unmatched when it came to tuning and balancing the instruments, but he was in awe of Gerard's mechanical skills. Gerard always chose exactly the right spanner by eye, and often the tools were a blur in his hand as he worked, always in the correct sequence to get the job done the fastest way. Tall and heavily built with enormous hands, he had started with Robert as an apprentice, but showed business acumen as well as surprising deftness and worked his way up to manager. Gerard loved racing with a passion and was more than content to spend his summer weekends at race circuits across France to support his boss. Maurice in contrast was dapper, but shared his larger copain's love of racing. His speciality was gearboxes, which he stripped and rebuilt with consummate skill.

Whilst the pair removed the tank, Guy reassembled the carburettor and inserting it carefully through the open panel in the lower bodywork, bolted it back onto the base of the supercharger.

Robert strode purposefully towards his Delahaye. He paused only to wipe his hands briefly on his overalls before opening the boot and rummaging through his wife Madeleine's suitcase. Madeleine was nowhere to be seen and was somewhere up in the stands with her friend Charlotte, who was painting a watercolour of the scene. 'Travelling light' was a phrase totally absent from his wife's dictionary and Robert was once again flabbergasted at the amount of clothing she had packed for the weekend, mostly suitable for a grand ball rather than a dusty racetrack. Her overkill was actually in his favour this time, as there were numerous pairs of silk stockings. Robert grabbed 3 pairs and shot off back to his racer.

By the time Robert was back at the pits, the tank was almost out. Gerard and Maurice swirled the remaining fuel around, then inverted the tank and drained it into an empty churn. Robert had stretched a stocking over the neck of the churn to gauge how dirty the petrol was – it was filthy. It took fifteen minutes of washing, swirling and draining before the vital fluid ran clean and a further fifteen to remount and fill the tank.

As soon as everything was in place, Maurice cranked the motor to life and ran it at a very fast idle to warm it up. Doctor Guy then checked his Zenith patient, adjusting and listening, blipping the throttle to hear the engine and clean the plugs. With three minutes to go before the grid formed and now on hard racing plugs, the Bugatti once again sang pure and powerful.

As his father moved off towards the start, Guy slowly wiped his tools and his hands, drinking in the panorama he found so magnetic. It was a heady mixture of sights, sounds and smells. Racing cars in their national colours – the blue of France, the dark green of England, the fiery red of Italy. The sounds were an orchestra of many parts, the whine of cams and chains, the slightly higher note of superchargers, the growls of gearboxes and axles, all topped with the visceral screams of racing engines being revved towards the red line and full power. Hot odours of rubber, metal, petrol, leather, overlaid with the sweet smell of the castor oil based racing lubricants. Guy was in heaven.

Robert had qualified 8th, but made a good start and soon worked his way up to 6th. In absolute terms, he was doing really well. The heyday of his car had been the 1920s and by 1930, the Bugatti was just about yesterday's car. For all that, the 35TC was Robert's favourite car and in his hands on a twisty circuit, it could outpace the newer machinery. Mindful of the last-gasp effort to make the grid, Robert's ear was tuned for the slightest hint of trouble. The car ran like a watch, hammering round the famed banking like an arrow. The Alfas and Auto-Unions were making the pace, but Robert clung gamely to his position. His well-drilled crew performed impeccably at pit-stops and with 30 laps to go, he was still 6th.

Flat out at 125mph on the banking, he saw the left front tyre suddenly balloon and then shred on its rim. Instantly, the 35TC slewed sideways towards the top of the banking, the stench of hot rubber filling the air and the magnesium wheel rim clattering harshly on the rough concrete. By now Robert had the car on full opposite lock to avoid being dragged over the edge, but the rim of the banking was coming at him at excruciating speed and beyond that rim, tall pine trees and a precipitous drop. Sweating in desperation, he released a little lock then reapplied it. With the left rear wheel actually half over the banking rim, tyres shrilling, heart hammering, he wrested back control and drove back to the pits.

Entering his pit, shredded rubber flapping and rim clanking, he stood up in his seat and gesticulated wildly at the faulty wheel, bellowing 'No time, no time, just change that one!'

Gerard and Maurice were on it in a trice and moving like automatons, had a fresh wheel on in 30 seconds. As Gerard whipped the quick-lift jack out of the way, Robert dropped the clutch, buried the throttle and screamed out of the pits, peppering his crew with small stones and leaving them choking on a wreath of rubber smoke.

With the field quite strung out, the blowout had dropped him to 11th. At that moment, a strange spark within Robert burst into life and he began to drive as never before. Guy had long admired his father's car control, his ability to drift and slide the car, but this was a father he had never yet seen, a man on another planet. This was a skilled racing driver using every ounce of power, every modicum of grip, every inch of the road. His drifts were balletic, millimetre perfect, his gearchanges rifle-bolt precise, his braking on the brink but never beyond.

Robert caught 8th, 9th and 10th place men so deep in a battle of their own that their first glimpse of Robert was as he outbraked them into a tight right-hander. He slipstreamed both 7th and 6th off the banking on successive laps; now he was up to 5th. His pit signal suddenly indicated he was 4th, a message that became clear when he spotted the stricken Alfa motionless at the trackside, the power of its engine once more too much for its gearbox.

Fourth place was held by a 35TC virtually identical to Robert's and by a driver Robert's equal. Now it was man 'gainst man in identical machinery. There were only twelve laps to go. Inch by inch, Robert whittled down the ten-second gap to his rival until he could touch the flowing tail of the car in front, but try as he might, he could not outwit its pilot, Pierre Duchesne. Looking for a way round, Robert noticed that Pierre braked fractionally earlier than himself into one particular left-hander. On two successive laps, Robert tried to overtake at this bend and failed. They were now on the last lap. Robert saw that his only hope lay in carrying more speed into the left-hander than Pierre, overtaking him on the outside and thus gaining the racing line for the next corner. He glued himself to Pierre's tail, engines howling and crackling, the two men oblivious to anything else at Monthléry save their duel. As they rushed towards the left-hander, Pierre braked at his usual spot. Timing his move to the centimetre, Robert flicked his car to the right. For the second time in less than an hour, Robert found himself completely sideways. Out of sight of the battling

Bugattis, another Alfa had split its oil tank on the approach to the left-hander, leaving a fine, invisible but lethal slick in its wake.

In a trice, Robert was on the grass and oil drum markers were looming wickedly fast, but God was obviously a Robert Duplessis fan that day. With bone dry grass and gravelly topsoil, Robert suddenly found traction, the chequered flag and the laurels for third place. Driving past the pits, he could see Guy, Gerard and Maurice leaping and hollering with joy and when he drove into his pit, Madeleine, Charlotte and his pit crew were dancing a kind of ring a ring o' roses in celebration. Completely ignoring his oil-soaked overalls and his coal miner face, Madeleine rushed up to her man and smothered him with kisses. Much champagne flowed that evening and looking at the shining faces of his family and friends, Robert felt himself a truly lucky man.

*

'Well,' said the Duc du Plessis taking a sip of his red wine 'you know my situation.'

'You mean, you may be a duke but you have to earn a living,' replied Simon. 'I take it you didn't escape with much?'

'What we stood up in, a few gold coins and some of Anne-Marie's baubles,' replied the duke. 'Not a great deal really.'

'What did you leave behind?' enquired Simon.

'A beautiful chateau in the Loire, 600 acres of farmland and vineyards, a stable block full of thoroughbreds and an extremely healthy bank account,' came the reply. 'One of the servants managed to get to us just ahead of the mob and we just took what we could and ran for it. We managed to hide in Paris for a while, then slipped across the border and made it here.'

'Here' was a small tavern in Gembioux, a village in the Austrian Netherlands, destined to become Belgium in the early 19th century, but now under French control. Simon was the landlord and he and the duke were alone in the bar.

'Makes you think, though,' continued the duke. 'Retaining your head on your shoulders suddenly assumes a distinct je ne sais quoi! You've told nobody who we really are?'

Simon shook his head.

'You're just William and Anne-Marie Plessis. You trained for anything, William?'

'Riding to hounds, bit of farming, making wine – I had staff to do all the work.'

Simon looked skywards for inspiration.

'Old Julien is retiring to live with his brother up north somewhere. How about a bit of weaving?'

Seeing William's rather blank look he went on 'You know Julien – oldish chap, quite short, big thighs.'

William remembered, especially the thighs, developed by years of pounding the loom.

'The old boy wants to sell his loom and his cottage. He's due in any time for his usual, why not have a chat?'

Julien duly appeared, Simon effected introductions and the following day, William went to see the loom, a large and well-kept affair in a back room of the cottage. They agreed a price, to include three months of lessons before Julien hung up his boots.

At the end of his first day, William went back to Anne-Marie almost in tears.

'I'll never get the hang of it,' he said, 'Julien makes it look so easy, the shuttle glides across and he keeps the rhythm up for hours. I'm all hands and feet, no coordination. And some of the patterns – they're just so complicated.'

Anne-Marie looked kindly at her husband, an amused grin puckering her lips.

'He's been a weaver all his life, he's a lot fitter than you and you can't expect to learn fifty years of experience in one day. Keep at it, my love.'

After two weeks, William had the glimmerings of success. His flabby thigh muscles became stronger by the day and he was beginning to pick up the rhythm, his legs working the loom whilst his hands plied the shuttle.

'Well, I suppose you'll do.'

Coming from Julien after the months of hard training, that was the ultimate compliment. William, Anne-Marie and Julien were sharing a farewell bottle of wine in the local. Somehow, the one bottle had become three and to use the French vernacular, Julien was beurré. He leaned conspiratorially towards William, opening his mouth to reveal both a dentist's nightmare and a bad case of halitosis.

'And what's your advertising slogan going to be, your grace – Liberté, Egalité, Qualité?' he cackled. 'Don't worry, I'm concentrating on retirement' he added. 'Best of luck.'

With that he rose unsteadily to his feet. The adieus of his friends ringing in his ears and weaving a distinctly different pattern to his usual, he lurched out of the door and into retirement.

The sale had included some cloth patterns, but William was amazed and delighted when Anne-Marie produced a sketch block containing some very stylish designs that she had drawn up whilst her husband was learning his craft. Then William realised that he should not have been surprised – the tasteful furnishings and décor of the chateau had been entirely masterminded by Anne-Marie. Her eye for colour was superb.

By earning a steady crust weaving stout worsted for the equally stout local burghers, William was able to invest in the materials for Anne-Marie's finer cloths.

People liked the Plessis cloths, they really liked them and the business flourished. After three years, they were employing ten weavers and William gave up working a loom to run the business.

A key market was England where they had an agent, Joshua Ordish.

'The cloth business is booming,' remarked Joshua on one of his regular visits. 'Why don't you move to England and set up there?'

Joshua lived in Yorkshire. William and Anne-Marie took one look at the county and fell instantly in love with it, moving to a comfortable house just outside Halifax. With Joshua's contacts, they established a new cloth-making enterprise called Tissus du Plessis at Joshua's suggestion.

'The English are terrible snobs, they just love a sniff of aristocracy!'

To begin with, weaving was done on manual looms, but William grasped the Industrial Revolution firmly to his bosom and mechanised with the new Jacquard models which used punched cards to weave the pattern. As his was a growing business, he employed more and more staff, thus avoiding the riots suffered by other industrialists from workers claiming that the new-fangled machines put them out of their jobs.

In 1798, Anne-Marie's interests switched to motherhood when their only son William was born. The younger William proved equally adept as his father and continued modernisation and mechanisation. His own and only son, also William, was not in the same mould. 'Sturdy and steady' his father called him. Lacking the customary du Plessis spark, he ran the business rather like a caretaker.

The final 'Just William' and again an only son, let out his first birth cry in 1863, but his mother breathed her last twenty minutes after he was born. Fortunately, the creative spark had skipped a generation and once he had learned the ropes, William junior began to pressure his father into modernising. The old man was immovable and the business began to slide. By now much of the machinery was old, creaky and unreliable; breakdowns were so frequent that the younger man often felt there were more looms being fixed than running. Spares were no longer stocked by the manufacturers, which meant having them made by a local engineering firm at vast cost.

Deliveries were late and the crunch came when du Plessis lost a valuable Army contract. William stormed home and confronted his father. It was like talking to the wall and William retired to bed in despair.

Salvation came at 6am the following morning, when the housekeeper panted into his bedroom shouting 'Come at once Mr William, come at once, it's your father!'

William hurried to the paternal bedroom. There lay his father, serene but cold. Like his machinery, his 57 year old heart had suffered a breakdown, this one terminal.

*

'Margaret, come and sit in the box, I need to talk to you.'

The machine-minder started at William's hand on her shoulder. The orchestra of shafts, pulleys, belts and cogs transmitting power to the looms played at a constant and deafening crescendo, accompanied by a cacophony of myriad shuttles flying between the warps. Even if you bellowed at the top of your voice, you were unlikely to be heard. All the minders were expert lip-readers.

Fearfully, Margaret sat down in the box opposite William and he closed the door. The 'box' was one of William's innovations. Made of wood and insulated with a thick layer of kapok, the box's one small window was a double-glazed affair of heavy glass. With the door shut, the box insulated the two occupants from the noise and allowed a normal conversation. Each machine room had several boxes along one side.

'Margaret, that's the second time this week I've caught you without your ear-muffs, isn't it?' enquired the mill owner sternly.

Margaret nodded mutely, well aware that to be caught without the muffs even once was a sacking offence. The muffs were another of William's brainwaves. Even though Decibel meters were long into the future, he had noticed how many retired and long-service staff suffered hearing problems. Many were profoundly or completely deaf.

By experimenting with cotton and kapok, he had developed a crude form of ear defenders and insisted staff wear them. Many were scornful that the constant noise damaged their hearing, so he was forced to make it a sacking offence not to wear the protection.

'Margaret,' said William carefully 'I've no doubt that in years to come, machinery will become much quieter, but for now, we have to accept that deafening racket out there.'

He gestured towards the machine room.

'I don't want my staff deaf. Wear the muffs, it's your last chance. Next time...'

He drew his finger meaningfully across his throat.

*

'I feel almost guilty,' admitted William to Constance, his fiancée. 'Father's funeral was just yesterday and here I am poring over my business plan to modernise. I feel ashamed too, that we went to bed on a row over this very plan.'

Constance, just two years younger than her fiancé, was a Brigadier's daughter. Reared in the rather harsh environment of the Army, she was made of stern stuff and had little time for sentimentality. Being a Yorkshire lass though, she did clearly understand the value of 'brass'.

'You tried for years to make the Old Man see sense,' she remarked, using William senior's familiar nickname. 'You have to modernise, William, you just have to. If you don't, Tissus du Plessis will go bankrupt and you'll destroy the livelihoods of hundreds of people. Go to it, William.'

William did indeed go to it. Du Plessis was a cash-rich company, self-funding a carefully honed re-equipment programme and setting aside capital reserves each year to finance the next phase.

Now freed from the parental yoke, William made sweeping changes.

The looms were the latest and best in the Jacquard range, but with one important modification – the safety link. In the Victorian industrial scene, safety was a joke. All that mattered was production and life was held cheap. Far too often, William had helped to extricate maimed workers or corpses from machinery that had started without warning although apparently switched off and made safe. The links, locked and unlocked with a special key held only by the shop foremen, were sited such that even if the machinery accidentally started during removal or replacement, the operative's fingers and hands were not drawn into the works or crushed. Once withdrawn, a link was locked into a rack at the front of the loom and only foremen had keys. All removals and replacements were made against signatures – or an 'X' – from the foreman and the minder in the machine log. Each link had a serial number, entered in the machine log. Spare links were locked in the machine room office and any changes followed the same logging procedure. Working on looms with the link in situ or changes without following the procedures resulted in instant dismissal.

Overalls with tight-fitting sleeves, caps or bonnets with hair tucked in, a ban on ties and jewellery, ear protection all then followed. Changing rooms with lockers were built and to the staff's intense surprise and initial suspicion, hot showers. The Victorians seldom washed and the thought of showering after a long, sweaty shift never entered their heads. William and Constance bathed daily and the thought of having that outer skin of muck so common amongst their contemporaries made them shudder.

'Look,' said William addressing his workers, 'just try showering regularly after your shift and see how you feel about it.'

Within weeks, 99% of the staff were converts. Not only did the machine rooms' regular atmosphere of BO improve markedly, but staff health improved as well. It was not long before William found women sneaking their children in for a much-needed wash. At first he turned a blind eye, but as numbers multiplied, he built a family bath-house.

The next innovation was a staff canteen. Everyone was entitled to one free meal per shift and for most, William guessed it was probably their only solid nourishment each day. Each machine room would shut down in rotation at the midpoint of the shift and these shutdowns gave a bonus of allowing maintenance to be carried out. Each minder had two ten minute tea breaks per shift as well.

'Mr Goss, Loom 18 needs help.'

The foreman peered through the window of the control room, spotted the red metal flag that had appeared above No 18. Quickly chalking '18' against his name on the stateboard, he descended the stairs into the machine room. All the machine rooms had identical set-ups, a control room overlooking the machines. In the room sat two foremen and four machine minders. If a minder had a problem with a loom, he or she pulled a lever which raised a red flag; if the minder needed to go to the toilet, a similar lever raised a white flag and one of the minders from the control room would substitute for a few minutes. All the minders spent a shift in the control room in rotation and provided two kept watch, the rest were free to chat or knit, insulated from the clamour down below. It was a highly prized perk and one of the punishments for lateness or sloppy work was to be denied one or more shifts in the control room.

With the increasing success of the business, new pay rates were introduced, including a profit-related bonus.

'What are those, William?' asked the new Mrs Duplessis.

It was 1888. William had changed the family name by deed poll to Duplessis just before marrying Constance.

William looked up from the plans on his desk.

'That, my darling, is the new family medical and dental centre,' came the reply.

Constance pretended to shield her eyes from imaginary glare.

'I can't see anything for the reflection from your halo,' she teased.

William just grinned.

'Apart from the humanitarian angle, it makes good business sense,' he argued. 'Most of the staff can't afford a proper doctor, so simple complaints either linger on or turn into something more serious. We often employ several members of the same family, so they pass on whatever they've got to the rest of the family and then I'm several workers short instead of just one.'

*

'Gentlemen, gentlemen, may I have your attention.'

William tapped the side of his cognac balloon with his knife to attract attention and rose to his feet. The atmosphere was a mixture of cognac fumes and the smoke of expensive Havanas as William surveyed the twenty or so local mill owners gathered around his dining table.

'Gentlemen, I've asked you here because I know that you're unhappy with my ideas for building housing and amenities for my workers.'

A chorus of rhubarb noises indicated that his fellow industrialists did indeed object.

'See here, Duplessis,' grumbled John Ordish, pronouncing William's surname 'Duplessiss', 'it's bad enough you paying'em above the odds and giving 'em free meals and baths and medicines, but this is too much. We keep losing staff to your mill and now my lot

41

are demanding the same conditions or they say they'll strike. You'll ruin us all with your tomfool liberal ideas.'

John Ordish was the grandson of Joshua Ordish. He ran a large mill and his embonpoint and a ruddy complexion bore testimony to his success, characteristics shared with a number of his fellows around the table. Within seconds, Ordish was supported by a chorus around the table, all baying against William.

William let the chorus sing for a while, then called once more for silence.

'Right,' he said, 'perhaps you'll be good enough to open the envelopes my butler has just placed before you.'

Each owner had a large brown envelope with his name inscribed in a neat copperplate hand and the exhortation 'Please do not open until requested.' There were two sheets of paper inside each envelope. The first sheet contained a graph.

'The brown line represents the output from my mill and the blue line is the average of the outputs from all your mills,' explained William, 'bearing in mind that your businesses all differ in terms of size and the type of machinery in use.'

John Ordish was at it again.

'Where the hell did you get your information about our production figures?' he spluttered angrily.

'Ways and means, ways and means,' smiled William.

'If you look,' said William, 'my production was way below your average when I took over from my father. You can see a large increase when I re-equipped, but then the figure climbs steadily. Currently, we're 38% above your average and that's a steady-state figure, not simply a one-off peak.'

His words were like turning a switch. The rhubarb dissent just stopped.

'38%?' said another owner, 'your figures can't be right, surely?'

'They are, they're 100%,' countered William. 'My philanthropy as you term it not only pays for itself, it pays dividends. Look at the second sheet.'

There was much rustling of paper.

'Those figures are my accident, sickness, absenteeism and labour turnover figures against yours. As you can see, I come out clearly ahead in every category.'

The rhubarb had started again, but now distinctly in William's favour.

'Gentlemen, the beginning of this century saw the Industrial

Revolution and we are beginning to see another. The working man is no longer content to live in a hovel, scrape a living and die in the poverty to which he was born. He wants a decent wage, a decent standard of living and why not? Make no mistake, the trade unions are beginning to flex their muscles. Either we pre-empt the situation or have it forced upon us and I know which I prefer. And,' added William, 'if it makes all of you richer in the process....'

Much like Joseph Cadbury and Lord Lever, William did create his model village, complete with a school, a church, a pub, a community centre and a Co-Op. He did not, however, attempt to emulate The Port Sunlight art gallery.

1889 saw the birth of Robert, and William's first son was followed by Henry three years later. They were to remain William's only issue, as Constance almost died giving birth to Henry and was advised against having further children.

Robert was strong on commonsense and sporting ability, weak academically: Henry abhorred any kind of physical activity but was exceptionally bright. Whilst Robert captained the 1st XI at cricket, the 1st XV at rugger and was the handsome captain of the tennis team, Henry waltzed through school picking up innumerable prizes on the way. The major problem was that the brothers hated each other's guts.

'Give that back, that's my tennis racket!' came the enraged yell of the ten-year old Robert to his younger sibling.

William, trying to have a quiet snooze in the warmth of a summer Sunday afternoon, sighed inwardly but ignored the altercation. Nothing he had tried, from straight talking to wallopings had the slightest effect on the long-running war. Sending the brothers to separate boarding schools ensured peace during term-time, but within minutes of the two arriving home for school holidays, battle-royal would commence. As the boys grew older, they would often spend parts of their holidays with friends. Typically though, Robert would be sailing on a friend's yacht or touring with them in their new car, Henry would be at a classics summer school improving his Greek and Latin. Needless to say, William actively encouraged (and paid for) any activity that kept the warriors at bay.

Robert entered the family business in 1907 straight from school, spurning university. By now a handsome, dashing young man, he took to business like the proverbial duck to water. At his own request, he started at the bottom and worked in every department. Within months, he came forward with practical and practicable ideas for greater efficiencies and enhanced profitability. Very much a people person, the staff loved him because he had no side nor any qualms about getting his hands dirty alongside them. When not at work, he pursued a coterie of pretty girlfriends, played all kinds of sport with verve and skill and raced the new-fangled car in England and France, picking up fluent French along the way.

Henry – surprise, surprise – crowned his academic reign at Eton with a scholarship to Oxford to read Greats. Even in vacations he was rarely seen at home and travelled extensively throughout Europe. The occasional postcard from Greece or Germany or Czechoslovakia was the only indication that he was still alive and well. Nine out of ten cards requested William to telegraph funds to some foreign bank. Barely was the ink dry on his inevitable First than the dry scholar entered the Civil Service, using a succession of faces as stepping-stones on his inexorable march towards the top echelons.

Apart from the fact that Henry cared little for anyone but himself and regarded his father's payment of his university expenses as his birthright, he bitterly resented what he saw as blatant favouritism towards Robert. Truth to tell, William had recognised almost immediately that the cause of the friction between his sons was Henry's mean spirit and selfishness. William had always wanted to cut the dash now done so effortlessly by his eldest progeny, but lacked the savoir-faire. Now William funded Robert's increasingly successful motor racing in an era when cars were incessantly unreliable and needed constant and costly fettling. Henry's generous allowance continued for many years after he joined the Civil Service, but that cut no ice with Henry, who considered he was getting a raw deal.

*

'Father, I'm going to join up.'

Sitting opposite his father at his generous desk, Robert saw the hurt in his parent's eyes at the pronouncement. It was October 1914 and already war-fever and patriotism had gripped the British Isles, with queues outside recruitment offices.

'Well, your mother's a soldier's daughter as you know,' said William, 'but I can't pretend for a moment that I want any son of mine to risk perishing in the Flanders mud. Have you spoken to your mother?'

Robert nodded mutely then added 'She thinks I should.'

William sucked in air, then resolutely straightened his shoulders.

'God be with you son, you'd better get down to the recruiting office whilst there are still spare places.'

He smiled wanly at his own rather feeble joke.

*

'Try it again, Corporal Bennett,' came Robert's voice from the bowels of the Thornycroft truck.

Wearily, the NCO swung the crank, to be rewarded by the rumble of the engine starting reluctantly to life. Robert straightened and grinned at Bennett, who grinned back.

'Not quite looking at yer parade best, Captain Duplessis,' he said. 'Hands like a Yorkshire miner, not to mention a greasy stripe all across yer left cheek!'

Somewhat to Robert's surprise, the Army decided to make use of his talents and put him in charge of mechanical transport at the front line. Robert saw his beloved France from a very different viewpoint as he struggled to keep crude and unreliable lorries running with few spares and often up to their axles and beyond in the mud of the Somme. Despite it being infra dig for an officer to get his hands dirty, he often did so as he worked his mechanical magic coaxing yet another stubborn truck back to life.

Day after day, his MT squadron moved ammunition and supplies towards the front. The never-ending return cargoes were grim, bodies and frequently just bits of bodies that had somehow been recovered from the mud and the barbed wire. Alone in his room at the Mess, Robert would weep at the unspeakable horrors he witnessed, seeing thousands slaughtered uselessly to gain a few yards of ground, only to lose it again scant hours later in a counter-offensive.

Constance Duplessis had often tended the wounded and dying at various battles and instinctively sensed her son's ordeal. On his leaves, she would organise visits by relatives and a few parties, briefing all the guests in advance not to ask directly about the war. Sensibly, she and William left Robert to do what he wanted to do for the majority of the time; Robert walked the moors and woodlands of his native Yorkshire, savouring the tranquillity before the next bloodbath.

'Ca va bien?'

Robert struggled to open his eyes, to be met by the prettiest pair of green eyes he had ever espied.

'Oui, mademoiselle, ca va bien, merci.'

He was lying. Actually, he felt as if he had been run over by

45

several of his own trucks. His right leg hurt like hell and the whole of the right side of his body was on fire. Struggling to focus, he looked around to find he was in a field hospital, a panorama of stretchers, bandages and blood accompanied by the moaning and screaming of the wounded and dying.

'What happened to me?' he enquired of the green eyes in French.

'You were hit by a whizz-bang,' replied the eyes. 'Your right leg is broken and you are peppered with shrapnel on your right side.'

The Army surgeons set his leg and did a fine job of metal detection with the larger pieces of the shell, but Robert had to undergo further surgery once he was shipped back to Blighty to recover. By then, he and green eyes – one Madeleine – were head over heels in love. Following his return to the front, they spent all their spare time together and married in the Spring of 1919.

The wedding, held in Madeleine's home town of Dinard in Brittany, was a riotous affair. Despite the ancestry, William spoke no French, but Constance had picked up some on her travels and a couple of Robert's Army friends were comfortable in the language, so non-French speaking guests were kept very much part of the party; Henry thankfully made his excuses.

*

Esme Loddon, Sir William's secretary, was poised on the edge of her swivel chair, muscles tensed ready to spring into action at the summons she knew would come ever since she had placed today's copy of The Thunderer on her boss's desk. William had received a knighthood for his services to the weaving industry and the war effort.

'Miss Loddon,' came the stentorian bellow from the new knight, 'find Mister Robert AT ONCE.'

Robert had his own copy of The Times and had been expecting the call.

'What is the meaning of this, what is the meaning?' demanded his father, more suffused with rage than Robert had ever seen him and stabbing his forefinger at a banner headline which read 'Former officer seeks to indict generals for war crimes.'

'It's treason, that's what it is, treason' roared William. 'And besides, we have huge contracts with the Army and the Navy which we just cannot afford to lose.'

Robert gazed steadily at his father then began to speak, at first quietly then with increasing volume and fervour.

'Do you know how many men died in the War, Father?'

His father shook his head.

'Ten million. Ten MILLION,' replied his son. 'The cream of England's manhood gone and do you know why?'

Before his father could reply, Robert continued.

'Because we fought a 20th century war using 19th century tactics, that's why. There were significant developments in the War – the submarine at sea, the aircraft, the tank and the widespread use of the machine gun. Future wars will be very, very different, but for us poor bloody infantry, it was the machine gun. There we were, scrapping over a few yards of muddy ground between the Allied and German trenches. We'd go over the top at dawn and a few machine-gunners who didn't even have to be very accurate would hose us with bullets and cut practically everyone to pieces within seconds.'

Robert was growing more emotional by the second, tears welling up in his eyes.

'The Jerries would counter-attack and we would do the same to them and that's all we did throughout the whole bloody war, it was totally, totally futile. The Pals battalions would go off to France thinking it was huge fun and singing 'It's a long way to Tipperary' and thousands of them would be dead within minutes of beginning their first assault. Some of them couldn't take it and cracked, so we lined 'em up and shot them for cowardice. You could understand the generals getting it wrong to start with, but when they just carried on the same hopeless tactics year after year and ordered continual and certain slaughter of their own men sitting safe in their field HQs miles away from the action, that was too much.'

Robert paused for a moment and his father wisely sat mute, sensing more to come.

'When I came home on leave I said nothing because I needed peace and quiet to gather enough courage to go back and face it all again. There were times I almost couldn't. I used to walk on the moors and some of the soil up there is the same as France and when it was wet, it smelt just like the trenches. And when it happened, I started to shake and cry and even wet myself at the uncontrollable fear that smell brought to mind.'

'I was lucky, I survived.'

Robert was now sobbing uncontrollably.

'But I saw the flower of English man wither on stems of barbed wire. THAT'S why I want to prosecute. It wasn't war, it was wanton murder.'

William sat silent and stunned. Never had he seen his normally extrovert and fun-loving son exhibit such depth of emotion, nor to be so eloquent and poetic. William rose and placed his hand on his son's shoulder. The silent gesture spoke volumes of both love and sudden understanding.

'Do what your conscience tells you is right, Robert.'

Robert did try to pursue the generals, but it was in vain. Ex-rankers supported his cause, but England was still a society obsessed with class and the Establishment. The clout he sought from his fellow officers who had suffered the same and worse never came. 'We beat Jerry and won the war, doncha know' was the attitude, and cars, parties and flappers were the most pressing items on the 1920s agenda. Robert was not a popular man.

Robert and Madeleine had settled outside Halifax and Robert tried once again to immerse himself in the business. His wife's halting English became absolutely fluent and accentless and so good was she at the language, she wrote a cookery column for the Halifax Mercury.

Increasingly, Robert was disillusioned and found cloth-making boring and irksome. In 1921, whilst racing in France, Robert saw a garage for sale and bought it. A month later, Robert and Madeleine returned to her homeland for good; in 1926, Robert took French citizenship. In the meantime, one garage became a chain with agencies for Peugeot, Citroen and Renault. As the business expanded, luxury makes such as Hotchkiss, Delahaye and Bugatti were added.

The Duplessis establishments were years ahead of their time in facilities and customer service. Most garages of the era were little better than blacksmiths shops, dirty and junk-riddled. Les Garages Duplessis were modern, well-equipped and immaculately kept. Mechanics were trained at the factory on particular makes and Robert also introduced while-you-wait servicing. In those days, the wait was rather longer, but allowed some hours for shopping, an aperitif and a leisurely lunch. While Madame et Monsieur tackled foie gras and a crisp Meursault, a team of fitters and cleaners tackled engine, transmission, brakes and body. The rejuvenated car was returned to its rejuvenated and delighted owners, ready once more to motor the dusty roads of France.

Madeleine's father ran a moderately prosperous seed-merchants, complete with a small fleet of trucks. Armand never fully recovered from a gas attack in the trenches and died in 1928. Robert bought the company from Armand's widow Josephine and retaining the seed-merchants, expanded the haulage side into a much larger operation.

Almost all the Duplessis garages were on the outskirts of town, so Robert built a depot at the rear of each one to warehouse goods and service the trucks. Well ahead of Norbert Dentressangle and Eddie Stobart, Robert insisted on immaculate trucks and immaculate drivers. Neither was easy – French roads were dirty and dusty and the average camioniste more interested in Disque Bleu and vin rouge than looking his best. After Robert sacked a few lazy and untidy drivers, the message got through and he got his way.

Rather like the stagecoach system of old, Robert established long haul routes by changing over drivers at the depots and fettling vehicles before the next leg. By the mid-1930s, Transports Duplessis was one of the biggest hauliers in France.

Guy arrived in 1921, a happy event marred by a birth so difficult that Madeleine was advised it should be her last.

Robert was one very proud father, especially when he found young Guy a chip off the old block. Wealth generated by the business funded Robert's motorsport and he raced Bentleys, Alfas and Bugattis, in fact anything fast. Guy just adored the heady sights and sounds of racing and by the age of ten, was a highly-skilled mechanic. The boy grew tall and by twelve, could reach the pedals, so his father taught him to drive. Graduating from Bebe Peugeot to Alfa and Bugatti, by fifteen he could drift the cars like an ancien pilote.

In Montluçon, the Duplessis were known as 'les bilingues'. The affectionate nickname had been bestowed by the locals because of the family's determination – some said near obsession – with preserving the language and culture of Robert's native England and that of his wife and adopted country. Guy was called Guy because it could be pronounced both the French and English way.

Outside the home and when friends came to call, the Duplessis spoke French: when alone, they spoke English. In the summer, the family would host garden parties English-style and encourage their guests to speak English. The extensive family library contained as many English books as French.

Keen that his son should learn other languages, Robert found a lady from Alsace fluent in both French and German. Young and with a keen ear, by his teens Guy spoke pretty good German.

Robert liked to keep his hand in on the transport side and would often drive one of the lorries in place of its regular chauffeur. In school holidays, Guy rode shotgun and learned every highway and byway of central and northern France.

*

'Look Guy, look!'

Robert's voice dragged Guy from his reverie in the passenger seat of the truck. It was a stiflingly hot July afternoon, the heat shimmered from the tarmac in great waves of convection and even with the windows open, the cab was like an oven.

The truck squealed to a halt opposite a sign saying 'Wire-haired fox terrier pups for sale'. Of the four quivering bundles inside the old playpen, Guy fell headlong for a brown and white one, which was soon asleep in a box beside his new young master. True to form, the dog was christened Colonel, as the name could be pronounced the French and English way and because of his little white beard.

'Guy, fox-terriers are notoriously hard to train,' said Robert, 'they have minds of their own.'

'OK papa,' acknowledged Guy, 'I'll have to work at it.'

But dog and boy formed an instant bond. Guy spent at least an hour a day training Colonel and within a year, the pair were almost telepathic, the dog responding to Guy's body language before he uttered a word. Naturally, Colonel responded to commands in both languages. At night, the terrier slept in Guy's room, officially on the floor but invariably dawn found him at the end of the bed. Since fox terriers shed almost no hair, he was indulged.

*

'Robert, would you lend me some money to open a restaurant?' asked Madeleine over Saturday breakfast one morning.

Robert nearly choked on his croissant in surprise. He was used to his wife's passion for cooking, her French and English library of cookery books lining the walls of the huge kitchen, of rarely knowing what was for supper but that it would be delicious. It was the suddenness that shook him, that his up-to-now happy to be a housewife and spouse should want to branch out.

'Tell me more,' said Robert, now regaining his usual sang-froid.

'Old Jabby is selling up his bookshop and I want to convert it to a restaurant.'

Robert had visited Jabby's emporium many times, as the old boy found and kept cookery books for Madeleine, but the shop itself was relatively small and would cater for only a few covers.

'Isn't it rather small?' enquired Robert.

'Downstairs, yes – that would be the bar – but upstairs is big and there is plenty of space to convert the storerooms at the back to kitchens. Come and see.'

Before the remains of his croissant could be consumed, Robert found himself in his wife's car speeding towards the other side of town.

Jabby, whilst old, looked older than he really was, but he had read many of his books and was a keen wit and raconteur. Robert had spent many a happy hour swapping anecdotes with Jabby whilst Madeleine scoured the bookshelves. The premises were exactly as Madeleine described them, spot on. She insisted on a proper business arrangement, a loan to buy the property, equip and staff it. Originally for five years, the loan was repaid in three.

The cuisine reflected a foot in both British and French camps. Finding a good chef who knew French cookery was not too difficult, but Madeleine wanted someone who knew how to cook British food. His name was Jean-Luc. Tall and lean, he was no advert for his profession, but had spent five years in the bowels of London hotels. He cooked British dishes beautifully, he could even make good tea. He spoke English, which would prove a help with the students from Angleterre that Madeleine planned to use as waiters and waitresses in summer, but it was still rather fractured, rusty and spoken with the Cockney accents of the chefs who had been his teachers.

To help Jean-Luc improve his English, Madeleine and Robert would hold meetings in English, translating where there was a problem. One afternoon, they were reviewing progress. Jean-Luc was having problems with one of the new ranges and the suppliers were trying to wash their hands of the whole thing. Jean-Luc was poring over the contract, hoping to find a clause on which to nail the suppliers.

'Alors,' he said, 'alors!'

Robert and Madeleine looked up. Jean-Luc's eyes gleamed, he had obviously found something.

Stabbing one finger excitedly at the page he exclaimed in English, 'We've got zem by ze short and curlies!'

He never understood why Robert and Madeleine dissolved into helpless and uncontrollable laughter.

Jean-Luc had a kind side which he tried to hide, as no self-respecting French chef could be anything other than a tyrant. When Guy first visited Madeleine's as the restaurant was called, Jean-Luc took one glance at Colonel and said menacingly 'Keep that bloody pooch out of my kitchens or…' and drew his finger across his throat.

Guy suddenly noticed that whenever he went to his mother's restaurant, Colonel would silently go missing, to reappear shortly looking smug. The next time, Guy appeared not to notice Colonel slope off, but quietly followed into the corridor that led to the kitchen.

'Ah, Colonel mon ami.'

It was Jean-Luc's voice. Peering surreptitiously round the door, Guy saw Colonel being fed some very juicy morsels.

'Now monsieur, hop it before your master notices and thinks I've gone soft.'

Guy whizzed back to his seat before an almost grinning terrier reappeared.

*

'Messieurs, dames.'

Yves le Cheminant, restaurant critic of Le Monde and town resident was making his speech at the opening. His kind words were propitious and from Day One, the mix of cuisines worked. Jambon or jellied eels, ragout or roast beef, crème caramel or custard, it was excellent fare. Locals and tourists loved the place and many a student learned service and the language during summer months.

*

'Darling, I'm home.' Robert shut the front door against the chill of a December Thursday evening and shook snowflakes from his collar.

'There's a telegram for you,' came Madeleine's voice from the villa's kitchen, accompanied by the usual delicious odours of the evening meal.

Robert opened the telegram. It was in English. 'Mater and pater dead. Funeral at St Anselm's Tuesday 12th at 2pm. Henry.' Robert stared at the yellow form, at once devastated by his parents death and at the same time, angry that Henry did not have the compassion to phone. Almost idly, Robert also saw red at the stupid and incongruous use of the Latin.

Sensing that something was wrong, Madeleine was by her husband's side and then Guy appeared downstairs. Now aged nine, he had visited his grandparents many times and was particularly close to his grandfather.

*

'How many Fred?' asked the Fire Chief, indicating the rows of corpses in the theatre foyer and suddenly weary.

His deputy wiped his soot-streaked face with the sleeve of his uniform, sucked the end of his pencil and rechecked his arithmetic.

'Eighty-three by my reckoning, including those in there.'

The fireman's hand indicated some charred and unrecognisable figures in the front rows of the stalls, just visible through the doors.

The stench of fire and smoke, overladen with that sickly-sweet odour given off by burnt flesh, was everywhere. Death was all around. Water was still draining into the orchestra pit, which resembled a swimming pool.

It was the beginning of the second act of, with macabre appropriateness, The Sacred Flame. The safety curtain was raised and the sudden draught stoked the small fire in the scenery on the prompt side of the stage. Within seconds, it was a raging blaze. Before anyone could move, a huge fireball leapt out from the stage, devouring eighteen of the audience in the front rows of the stalls.

A second later, the panic-stricken audience stampeded for the exits. High in the stalls, William and Constance, on a weekend break to London, also tried to flee. Constance had an arthritic right hip and unsteady on her feet, fell underfoot in the melee.

'Help me William, help me!'

Her terrified screams were the last words she ever uttered. In vain, William tried to pull her up but was also engulfed and the couple died together, suffocated by the crowd.

Robert and his family journeyed to Halifax, arriving on Monday and booking into the Grand Hotel. Leaving Madeleine and Guy to settle in, Robert took a cab to his parents' mansion outside the town. He was greeted by Eric and Mary Thornthwaite, the couple who had looked after his parents and the house. William and Constance lived quite simply, bringing in caterers for any functions, so Eric was butler, chauffeur and general factotum, leaving Mary as head cook and bottle-washer.

'Where's Mr Henry?' asked Robert.

'Gone back to London, he'll be here tomorrow for the funeral, sir,' replied Eric.

The Thornthwaites, still visibly shaken by events, expressed their condolences to Robert and explained the fire in the theatre.

St Anselm's was in central Halifax and at two o'clock two hearses, drawn by pairs of jet black and gleaming horses, clip-clopped to a halt outside. Tendrils of steam rose into the crisp air as the horses snorted and exhaled, the harsh sound breaking an otherwise complete hush. It was as though all of Halifax had come to a halt at this funereal moment. Robert and his family, accompanied for once by Henry, stood silent and stock-still as the pall-bearers carried the identical mahogany coffins to the nave. The church was packed. Local dignitaries and fellow businessmen of William's paid tribute to the couple and the immense amount they had done for the town and its people. Then it was outside, to that heart-rending moment when the coffins were laid to rest in the family vault and Robert felt his heart would break. Madeleine and Guy were in tears, scarcely able to believe that Robert's parents were gone. Staff who had worked for Duplessis all their lives wept, stunned by the deaths.

The wake had been arranged at a local hotel and Robert found himself talking to people he had rarely seen in years. Henry deigned to speak to his brother, although it was not what might be termed a warm conversation. As they spoke, they were joined by Rhys Chapman, the family solicitor. Rhys had been only ten when he moved with his colliery overseer father from their native valleys to a Yorkshire pit, but his soft lilt was undimmed.

'The reading of the will is at my office tomorrow at 10am,' said Rhys. 'You are both named as executors.'

Rhys's office was crowded. William had made a number of bequests to staff, but left the residue of his estate to Robert and Henry in equal shares.

'I need to speak to you both once everyone else has left,' explained Rhys.

The door closed, leaving only the three men seated around the desk.

Rhys looked suddenly uncomfortable, fiddling nervously with the albert on his watch. Robert and Henry waited in silence for Rhys to begin.

'For one of the finest businessmen I've ever known, your late father could be remarkably short-sighted,' began Rhys, holding up his hand when he saw Henry about to speak. 'What I mean is that your father was a very rich man and for years, I tried to persuade him to put his money into trusts and the like, but he never would. Said it was morbid, even though he saw sense in making a will. 'I'm afraid,' said Rhys, 'that death duties are massive. The sale of the house will not make even a dent in it, you'll have to sell the business to pay off the duties.'

Henry had sat there without saying a word so far, but going steadily redder in the face as he realised the implications of the solicitor's explanation.

'You mean,' said Henry, suffused with anger and suddenly finding his tongue, 'that the silly old bastard has sold my birthright?'

At that moment, Robert had never loathed his brother more and only by superhuman effort restrained himself from grabbing Henry by his miserable throat and squeezing the life out of him.

Rhys Chapman was normally as mild as his Welsh accent, but when he spoke, the icy steel in his voice brought shivers down Robert's spine.

'You really are the most self-centred, mean and obnoxious man I have ever met, Henry,' said Rhys. 'Even your father commented on the increasing frequency of your visits as he and Constance grew older. Called it you sizing them up for their coffins.'

At this, Henry actually blushed.

'Despite your behaviour, you have still been left half the estate,' continued Rhys, 'but before your parents are even cold in the ground, you are vilifying your father's memory. Do you have a heart, is there any blood in your veins or just ice?'

There was a pregnant pause.

'I already have a buyer for the business who has agreed to pay the market rate and will run it in the same way your father did. Even after paying the duties, there will be plenty to buy you your country estate, it just won't be quite as grandiose as you no doubt expected.'

His Welsh accent accentuated and elongated the syllables of the word 'grandiose'.

Henry swiftly recovered his composure.

'No doubt you legal vultures will take a large share,' he riposted. 'Kindly pay whatever pittance is left into that account at Coutts.' 'And', turning towards his brother, 'doubtless your share will be put in the petty cash tin?'

With that, he threw the piece of paper with his account number onto the desk and swept out to some doubtless more pressing Whitehall imperative.

'Sherry, Robert? Dry, isn't it?'

The question broke the heavy silence that followed Henry's exit.

It was not until they were sipping their sherry that Rhys spoke once again.

'How did a wonderful couple like your father and mother ever manage to engender an unmitigated little shit like that?' he opined.

Robert had never heard so much as a 'damn' from Rhys's normally God-fearing lips before, so he understood clearly the depth of the man's feelings.

For half an hour, they discussed the estate. Rhys promised to draw up a power of attorney so that he could deal with Robert's duties as executor and have his clerk bring it round to The Grand that evening for signature. Robert also made arrangements for Rhys to create trusts for Madeleine and Guy with much of the money, then transfer the balance to the business account with Credit Lyonnais.

Guy had been deeply affected by the deaths and the funeral. To lift his spirits, his parents took him to London and let him loose for an hour in that boys' wonderland called Gamages toy department. It was a considerably happier Guy that emerged carrying several model cars of his favourite makes and a Swiss Army knife with countless blades. Whilst Madeleine toured couturiers and milliners, Guy and Robert ate a splendid lunch in the Savoy Grill. The following morning, groaning with various parcels, they caught the boat train home.

With no relatives in England save the noxious Henry, the Duplessis visits dwindled to nothing.

*

By mid-1939, the smell of impending war was everywhere. The Duplessis listened to French and English broadcasts and Guy monitored the German stations. Robert guessed clearly what was imminent and began to make contingency plans. He moved most of his money to England, retaining enough to run the businesses. Through the seed-merchants, he owned a number of large barns and secreted the Alfa 8C2900 in one and the Bugatti 35TC in another. He and Guy were the only ones who knew the cars' locations, hidden behind false walls. Both cars were placed on axle-stands, the oil pumped around each engine and the bodies heavily waxed. The false walls were a work of art, taking several days for each one; painting the walls with a mixture of cow urine and coffee made them look as though they had stood there for years.

Guessing that an English connection might serve them ill, the Duplessis walled up anything English with the cars and spoke nothing but French. Madeleine's menu changed overnight to French provincial. And the locals, unbidden, shut up like clams about 'les bilingues'.

Chapter 4

On the fifteenth night, Guy broke his ankle.

Of all the nights thus far, this was the foulest weather by a long margin. A screaming gale drove before it lashing rain that alternated with sleet. The icy spicules drove mercilessly into Guy's face, which numbed under the freezing impact; equally icy rivulets of water trickled down his neck. He and Colonel were soaked to the skin, their clothing moulded to their bodies like wet shrouds. Both now felt that warm little house a million miles away and both wondered if they could actually get any colder. Trudging along, Guy struggled to put one foot in front of another and the now horizontal dog's tail bore mute but emphatic testimony to his view of the status quo.

They were sliding their way down a steep muddy bank so wet they were virtually out of control. Unseen by Guy, a root arched out of the soil like a miniature but deadly croquet hoop. In a trice, Guy's left foot locked under the hoop and he arced forward under his own weight. For a micro-second, he stabbed ineffectually in front of him with his stick in a vain attempt to regain his balance. The final thing he remembered was a resounding crack as his ankle broke and a searing bolt of agonising pain so intense that he was unconscious before he hit the ground.

Guy was brought back to reality by a violent, throbbing pain and he groaned in agony at its intensity. Colonel was beside him, whimpering anxiously and nuzzling him to get up. But how? Guy's foot, he could tell, was at a gruesome angle to his left leg. The least movement intensified the screaming agony and actually freeing himself was to prove an Herculean task. For at least an hour, he tried to lever himself upright using his stick, which had fallen beyond reach but which Colonel retrieved. In the soft mud, it was hopeless. After about twenty attempts, Guy was exhausted by the effort and the pain, tears streaming down his cheeks.

The answer lay in his rucksack. Slowly, he peeled the bag from his back, then found the Swiss Army knife and began to saw through the root. Four inches of green wood presented a challenge to a proper saw, let alone a three-inch blade and it took an hour to cut just one side. Guy tried to swing the root away from his ankle, but the root stubbornly refused to relinquish its hold on him. Pausing for a breather, he set to on the other side and found that for some reason, the sap was less and progress quicker. At long last he was free and with enormous difficulty, eventually pulled himself to his feet.

Before struggling upright, Guy had risked his torch to check the map. Half a mile away was a farm. Could he make it?

It took 2 ½ hours of searing torment to drag himself to the farm. Despite the cold and the rain, he was sweating profusely from the shock. Time after time, he had to stop and let the pain subside. Twice he slipped and fell over and had to force himself to his feet again, every sinew tortured and pushed to the limit. Sometimes he wondered if death would not provide a merciful release, but the anxious face of his companion pushed him on. Still the icy rain lashed down.

Moving at snail's pace, he finally gained the farmyard. The farm dog heard the sound of Guy's tap-tapping and smelt Colonel's scent; he began to bark. Guy dragged his limp body towards the front door. By now, he was delirious, the combination of biting cold, pain and shock had almost drained every ounce of strength he had left. Those thirty yards across the yard seemed like thirty miles. At last he reached the front door. Gratefully, he leaned against the dark wood and raising the knocker, crashed it against its plate. Nothing happened. Summoning up his final reserves, he knocked again. For a moment, there was nothing, then a window above the door opened to reveal a torch shining above the menacing barrels of a 12 bore.

'What the hell do you want?' demanded a gruff male voice whose owner was as yet unseen.

Weakly, Guy explained.

'Please, please help me,' he beseeched.

His tone obviously did the trick. Within seconds, he heard the sound of footsteps on the stairs. As the front door swung open to admit him, he fell onto the hall floor in a dead faint.

Guy came to, finding himself lying on a bed in the spare room. He had been undressed and wrapped in a large, heavy blanket. His ankle still hurt like hell, but the farmer's wife had enveloped the joint in cold wet towels to reduce the swelling. Colonel was sitting on a chair at the side of the bed, misery written all over him at the plight of his beloved master. The farmer and his wife were staring down at him.

'Well, son,' remarked the farmer unequivocally, 'you're in the shit, aren't you?'

Guy nodded, still too shocked to take it all in.

'Well,' said the farmer again.

Even in his pain, Guy began to wonder if every sentence was preceded by 'Well.'

'My name is Jean-Marc and this is my wife Marie-Anne,' indicating the well-built and rather anxious applier of cold towels.

'Don't worry,' went on Jean-Marc, 'there's many here would sell their grandmother to the Boche, but not us.'

His nose wrinkled in distaste at the very thought.

'We hate them.'

'They shot our son,' added Marie-Anne by way of explanation.

'Tomorrow, I'll fetch the doctor,' continued Jean-Marc, 'but we have to be very careful, he's watched all the time in case he's tending wounded airmen. In the meantime, try a very large brandy and some sleeping pills.'

Even in his distress, Guy thought the prescription one to make any doctor wince, but he was past caring and took his impromptu medicine. Fortunately, it did the trick and he lapsed into grateful slumber.

The doctor appeared the next morning. Like most doctors left behind in rural practice, he was elderly and greying, the young ones having been taken elsewhere to look after the Germans.

Gently, he felt Guy's broken ankle. Gentle he might have been, but Guy jumped at every touch.

'You,' said the doctor, 'are an incredibly lucky young man. From what you've told me, I would have expected a complicated fracture, but yours is a clean break. If you do what you're told, you'll be fit to walk again in about 5-6 weeks.'

The doctor turned to his bag, producing a cloth and a bottle of clear liquid.

'Anaesthetic,' he explained.

Enlisting Marie-Anne as his nurse for the day, he poured some ether onto the cloth and applied it gently to the young man's nose and mouth. Soon the patient's steady breathing announced he was under and the doctor manipulated the broken joint back into position and plastered it. Marie-Anne kept Guy under by applying more anaesthetic when needed.

Felling muzzy, Guy came back to life. He felt sick and very weak; his ankle throbbed but certainly appeared to be more the way it should be.

'I'll try and get back to see you soon,' explained the doctor, 'but you probably know that the Germans take an unhealthy interest in where I go.'

The doctor laughed at his own pun, then packed his bag and left.

The next two weeks were uncomfortable for the patient, who felt acutely embarrassed at being so dependent and having to be helped on to the commode. Gradually, his ankle began to knit and the shock and pain subsided.

Jean-Marc and Marie-Anne were kindness itself, nothing was too much trouble. They fed Guy and Colonel royally, looking after Guy as though he were their own dead son and taking Colonel out for his constitutional after dark so that he was not seen by anyone else.

Reading became Guy's saviour. He had always devoured books and surprisingly, the Gounon library was quite extensive, featuring Proust as well as romans policiers. By the third week, he could put careful weight on the ankle, which was just as well. The farm was raided by the Germans.

Looking for a British airman seen to hit the silk about five miles away but who could not be found, house to house searches were organised.

Fearing such an event, the Gounons had kept Guy's bedroom clear at all times, taking away every empty cup, plate and glass and returning the commode to their own room across the corridor. Hearing the Germans approach, Marie-Anne helped Guy and Colonel into an attic room, where she released a hidden catch and a wardrobe swung round on invisible hinges to reveal a small room behind. The wardrobe clicked shut after Guy and Colonel.

Below him, Guy could hear the Germans searching, noisily turning over furniture, hurling open cupboard doors and rooting through drawers.

'Steady, Private Schumann,' Guy heard a voice say, as a crash from below spelt the demise of one of Marie-Anne's Limoges vases. 'You're supposed to be searching, not wrecking the place.'

'Bloody French,' said Schumann, 'I'd shoot the lot given half a chance.'

Gradually, Guy's eyes became accustomed to the darkness and he could see light leaking through gaps between the tiles. Eventually, he could see a good deal. A good deal, he was amazed to find, included a cache of weapons, some plasticine-like material and a small case containing a radio transmitter. He also became aware of the penetrating cold and laughed at the irony of hiding from the Germans a second time in diametrically opposed temperatures. The patrol worked its way upstairs and for the second time, Guy felt the gut-wrenching fear of discovery. They searched the attic, opening the doors of the wardrobe. Guy froze. The hairs on the Colonel's back grew stiff with fear, too.

'There's bugger all in here, let's search the outbuildings,' said the same voice that had chided Private Schumann.

'OK, Sarge,' came the reply and to Guy's intense relief, a clatter of boots announced the patrol moving downstairs and into the yard.

Almost immediately, there was a howl from Schumann as the farm dog left a deep impression of his opinion of the invaders on the private's right buttock. The soldier had to be restrained from shooting the dog on the spot, but the incident unnerved the patrol and within minutes, the sound of wheezy engines and grating gears signalled their departure.

Guy sat in the hidey-hole shivering from cold and tension and at the same time, humbled by the extraordinary risks taken by his hosts.

Half an hour later, they came and helped him back to bed. A bowl of steaming broth restored his circulation and a sleep his vim and vigour.

Recovery was swift and two weeks later, the doctor pronounced Guy fit to travel. He now had fresh clothes provided by Jean-Marc and Marie-Anne, as he approximated to their son in height and build. With a rucksack bulging with provisions from the farm, Guy said goodbye. There was an enormous lump in his throat as he did so, he simply could not express his gratitude for all the help and kindness and the risks they had taken.

'See you after the war,' said Jean-Marc.

Marie-Anne just dissolved into floods of tears and hugged Guy as though she never wanted to let him go.

With a last wave, Guy turned his back on the farm and pointed his compass towards the Channel coast.

The broken ankle had thrown his timetable completely awry. By now it was January and a pretty cold one at that. Guy feared it would snow and not only slow his progress, but make him visible against its whiteness and he would leave tracks to mark his passage. Fortunately, there were some flurries, but nothing more sinister than that.

The cold was far from ideal for a healing ankle. Guy's pace already reflected his injury and the cold seeped into the joint and made it ache interminably. Rest stops became more frequent and progress slowed.

The other problem facing them was that by now, they were in the most heavily occupied zone of France, where military establishments abounded.

After the raid on the farm, Guy and the Gounons had a real heart to heart. By mutual consent, all Guy ever told Jean-Marc and Marie-Anne was that he was trying to reach the coast and find a boat to England. He never told them where he came from, nor any of the details of his parents' death and killing the soldier. Both sides understood clearly that what you did not know, you could not tell. In his pursuit of covering his tracks, Guy had regularly burnt his maps once he was sure he would not have to backtrack. He also guessed that the Gounons had searched his rucksack soon after he arrived.

With the Gounons' Resistance involvement revealed, Jean-Marc explained that one of their major tasks was intelligence-gathering and produced a hand-drawn map detailing a large number of German military installations between the farm and the Channel coast. Night after night, Guy would study the map, committing the contents firmly to memory before returning it to his host. Guy risked asking whether their son's death had any bearing on their Resistance activities.

'Indirectly,' came Marie-Anne's reply. 'Our group attacked a supply convoy and the following day, the Germans rounded up twenty people and shot them. Alex just happened to be in town at the wrong moment and became one of the twenty.'

Even after a year, the memory was still a raw wound and her voice faltered as she explained what had happened.

The Allies made constant attacks on the Germans by day and by night. Inevitably, some of the aircraft were shot down and the Germans would search for aircrew who had either baled-out or survived a crash-landing. If there been any sort of air raid the night before Guy reached an area, he had to be doubly careful not to run into patrols and search parties. He also realised that buying food openly was too risky and he would have to eke out the rations the Gounons had given him until he reached safety.

The other difficulty was that the locations given on the map he had studied so carefully were not 100% accurate and his own navigation was not perfect either. On two occasions, Colonel's acute senses had prevented them stumbling into a barracks and an airfield. A hasty retreat and regroup each time had proved wise counsel.

The combination of raw cold, poor shelter and meagre rations began to tell, as did the tension of always being on the qui vive and little sleep. Skirting German emplacements just added to the distance and Guy wondered if they would ever reach the coast, let alone England. Not for the first time, he felt young, scared and totally alone.

The now telltale signs of Colonel as rigid as Lot's wife with his teeth slightly bared alerted Guy that they had almost walked into the Germans again. According to Guy's map, there should be nothing here, but the flare of a match, the smell of cigarette smoke and German voices told otherwise.

'God help us if the Warrant Officer sees us,' said a voice. 'He'll have our balls, especially with all that petrol we're guarding.'

Before there was a chance for any kind of emasculation, the drone of heavy aero-engines cut through the silence and air raid sirens began to wail.

'Oh shit, Tommy's after our fuel again,' said another voice.

By now, the planes were nearer and searchlights began to probe the sky, trying to cone aircraft in their beams. There were sounds of activity from the soldiers near Guy and the next second, a diesel generator rattled into life powering yet another searchlight. The side-wash from the powerful beam showed that Guy had nearly walked into a combined searchlight and gun emplacement. The gunnery team concentrated on trying to find the attacking bombers and locking on to an approaching Wellington, they began to fire.

Guy made certain they were all concentrating on their ack-ack duties before beating a steady retreat, glancing over his shoulder from time to time.

The Wellingtons began dropping their loads. The first three aircraft undershot their target but the fourth was either accurate or lucky and a stick of incendiaries straddled two large petrol tanks and set them ablaze. A thick column of orange flame, suffused with black smoke, leapt skywards and even far away as he was, Guy could feel the heat from the fire.

The impromptu pathfinder flare was a gift to the RAF, illuminating the fuel dump as though it were daylight. Wave after wave of bombs fell and soon, millions of gallons of high-octane petrol were blazing fiercely. The final wave signalled the dump's coup de grace and with a sound like a monumental thunderclap, it blew up.

At that moment, Guy had his back to the fire and the next thing he recalled was being slammed by a hot and gaseous tidal wave that hurled him through the air like an autumn leaf. His stick was torn from his grasp and his rucksack from his back as he spun end over end above the ground.

He mused later how far he would have travelled had his flight not been arrested prematurely by a tall but very thorny hedge. Curiously too, he recalled wondering if these were his last moments before death. Guy struck the hedge upside down and backwards before tumbling to the ground dazed, deafened, shocked and bleeding. As he lay gasping and breathless, further waves of searingly hot gas passed overhead until the explosion faded slowly away.

Like a small mountain rescue dog, Colonel came panting up to Guy. Being so low to the ground, the terrier had missed the blast and was totally unharmed.

Groggily, Guy sat up and checked himself over. The blood was actually very little, just the backs of his hands and one ear cut by the thorns. No bones seemed broken and Guy rose stiffly to his feet. His head was ringing. Colonel bounded off, to return seconds later with the walking stick. The lurid glow made it easy to spot the rucksack, which lay intact some 50 feet away. Knowing where he had been standing previously, Guy saw he had been thrown about 100 feet into the hedge.

The scene at the dump was pandemonium. Above the roar and crackle of the flames could be heard the screams of the troops burned by the holocaust. Wailing sirens and fire engines were everywhere in fruitless attempts to quell the inferno. Burning fuel streamed in molten rivers from ruptured tanks and into every stream, gully and crevice. Roads in the site were impassable, covered in impenetrable walls of scorching flame. Every vehicle and every building in the vicinity was alight too, adding to the heat, the noise and the Dantian chaos. The gun emplacement near Guy was no more. Bizarrely, the searchlight was still working, but its beam pointed almost vertically at a sky now devoid of aircraft. The ack-ack guns were intact but now morbidly stilled; their crew was also stilled but by no means intact, charred beyond recognition by the giant flame-thrower that had engulfed them. So denuded of flesh and blackened were the corpses sprawled over the sandbag parapet that they appeared almost Lowryesque.

Guy was simultaneously fascinated and repulsed by the sight so clearly illumined by the flames that no binoculars were necessary. The air reeked of petrol fumes and the sweet aroma of burning human flesh.

Without warning, Guy was violently sick and despite little in his stomach, retched and gagged for several minutes before the spasm passed. When it did, he began to shake uncontrollably then burst into tears, realising how for the second time in six weeks, he had cheated death by a hair's breadth.

Gounon rations had included refilling his brandy flask and a very stiff measure did much to revive the corpuscles. For several minutes, he and Colonel hugged each other like lost souls. First thoughts were to hide until all the kerfuffle died down, until Guy worked out that the commotion presented a golden opportunity to move unnoticed. Fighting fires and scraping up human remains would keep the Germans busy for quite a few hours.

Guy could see a box of K-rations still intact within the emplacement. They say that the instinct for survival is strong, but to even approach the gun-pit took every ounce of courage Guy possessed and he felt like a grave robber. Trying and failing to ignore the stench of burnt flesh, he retched and gagged as he purloined tinned rations of cheese, sugar, coffee and bully-beef.

With rucksack bulging, Guy and Colonel headed west then north. Crossing roads took some care because of emergency traffic, but otherwise they walked unmolested. By morning, the fire was just a distant plume of smoke on the horizon.

Much to Guy's astonishment, his ankle stopped aching and although it grumbled from time to time, it never really troubled him again.

Five days later, Guy lay concealed on a hilltop, watching a checkpoint on a road leading into the coastal zone.

Chapter 5

Those five days had been a nightmare. Now in a heavily occupied zone, Guy was constantly encountering military establishments, from barracks to checkpoints. His mental map was useless, as none of them were on it. Colonel saved their bacon time and again, his keen nose for Les Boches now razor-sharp. Finding somewhere to sleep was not easy either and Guy was terrified he would wake up to find himself staring at the wrong end of a Schmeisser. Colonel innately sensed Guy's tension and was as strung-out as his master.

Carefully analysing the slant of the winter sun to ensure it did not reflect off the lens, Guy peered through his field glasses at the checkpoint.

Teutonic ordnung was very much in evidence. Any vehicle was stopped, searched in every crevice and its papers scrutinised for the slightest imperfection. One Wehrmacht truck, loaded with civilians that Guy surmised correctly were Todt workers building the Channel defences, was turned back because its papers were not in order. Its driver was hauled from the cab and soundly bollocked by the Feldwebel at the checkpoint. An hour later, it returned with the right dockets and was allowed through.

For two days, Guy surreptitiously worked his way up and down the border to the restricted zone, but saw only repeat performances of the watertight security. Coils of barbed wire stretched for miles, making any thought of sidestepping the checkpoints impossible. Irregular patrols by officers and NCOs on the checkpoints ensured that nobody but nobody was going to fall down on the job.

Sleep became virtually impossible, such was Guy's fear of capture and his ragged nerves became even more frayed.

Inspiration dawned when Guy managed to work his way further west. Watching the countryside through his glasses, he spied what appeared to be a ship's mast moving slowly north through the fields. Waiting until dark, he moved towards where he had seen the mast and was rewarded by the moon glinting off the water of a canal, a canal unmarked on his map. Those glinting waters of the Canal D'Ille et de Rance he knew instinctively offered his route to the coast.

Dawn found the duo hunkered down in a hide but at a good vantage point overlooking the canal lock that led into the restricted zone. The lock was festooned with barbed wire and swarming with grey-green uniforms. All barges entering the lock were searched rigorously. Canal traffic in both directions was heavy, laden barges down to the gunwales with war materials going north, the same barges with much greater freeboard coming south.

Guy himself retreated south under cover of darkness and found a spot where the bargees moored for the night before entering the lock just after dawn the next day. When a fresh batch of five barges appeared that afternoon, Guy scanned each captain and his craft, trying to guess which was the best one to approach. His choice was actually quite simple, as only one bargee navigated single-handed.

Darkness settled its blanket once more over the Brittany landscape. Taking every smidgen of courage he had, Guy motioned Colonel to accompany him, crept silently onto the barge and tapped gently on the cabin door. Nothing happened, so he tapped again.

This time, the door was opened a crack and a gruff voice demanded 'Who the hell's there?'

'Please let me in,' replied Guy, 'and I'll explain.'

Instantly, the light in the cabin went out, the door was flung open and Guy found himself dragged roughly inside.

The light clicked on again. Guy found himself looking at a strongly-built man in a blue fisherman-type sweater and dungarees, both garments rather oily and in need of a wash. The face could be described as raffish and lived–in. Lined and weather-beaten by hours spent outdoors, the rough and florid complexion made it difficult to guess the man's age, which was probably between 40 and 50. In some horror, the young man stared fascinated at the bargee's right ear, the top half of which was missing as though sliced off by a scalpel. Small, gimlet eyes bored into Guy's very soul through the fug of tobacco smoke that was the atmosphere in the cabin, a stifling atmosphere fuelled by a roaring stove in one corner and the pipe jammed firmly into the sailor's mouth.

Following Guy's fixated stare at his ear, the man grinned wolfishly.

'Cost me a five-stretch in Rennes, that,' he cackled.

Sensing Guy wanted the whole story, he continued.

'Dutch bargee had the hots for my wife. I warned him off, but I came home one afternoon to find him just putting his pants on and my wife still naked in our bed. He grabbed a knife from his belt and went for me – that's how I lost this.'

His fingers brushed across the top half of the ear.

'What happened?' quizzed Guy, eager to find out the answer and dreading it at the same time.

The bargee cackled again and made a sweeping movement of his right hand towards his groin.

'Sings with the Amsterdam Boys' Choir now!' came the rejoinder.

Seeing Guy look aghast, he said, 'Don't feel too sorry for him – I got five years for grievous bodily harm and lost my wife into the bargain. Been a bachelor ever since.'

'Well,' continued the bargee, 'what do you want, young'un?'

'This canal leads into the restricted zone, right?' quizzed Guy.

A nod and a puff on the pipe indicated this was indeed so.

'Will you smuggle me in there?'

The eyes narrowed, the bargee took a long draw on his pipe and fixed Guy with a quizzical look.

'What makes you think I want to get myself shot, young feller?' he enquired. 'Nobody but nobody gets in there unless the Germans say so.'

A wave towards north accompanied the sentence.

'They search every boat with a toothcomb before we enter and then carry out spot checks along the canal and the Rance itself and then again in St Malo harbour. You can't get a bilge-rat into St Malo unless it's got a pass.'

'Why do you want to get there anyway, huh?'

'I have a friend in St Malo who will help me get to England,' replied Guy, not wanting to give the whole truth. 'I just want to fight the Nazis, my parents were killed in a Nazi air raid,' he explained simply.

'Well, son, you'll need a bit more meat on your bones for that,' exclaimed the boatman, eyeing Guy's meagre frame and pallid complexion and surmising accurately that his young visitor had been living on starvation rations of late.

'And what's he going to be, the regimental mascot?'

Colonel chose the opportune moment to look his most appealing and was rewarded by a pat from the bargee's horny hand.

Guy seized the moment.

'I can pay,' and matched the words with one of his twenty sovereigns gleaming in his open palm.

A similar gleam came into the sailor's eyes. He took the coin and tested it with his teeth.

'How many?'

'Ten when I get on board and ten more at St Malo.'

The bargee's gleam brightened visibly.

'OK, but no pooch, sorry, it's risky enough with you. One bark and we're done for.'

Guys sinews became steely.

'Where I go, the dog goes. He is impeccably trained and behaved, he'll never make a sound.'

For the next five minutes, Guy put Colonel through his paces until the bargee, Guillaume, was 100% satisfied that what Guy claimed was true.

'You can't spend the night here, be back at 5.30 tomorrow morning and for Christ's sake make sure you're not seen!'

Man and terrier spent a cold and uncomfortable night and prompt at 5.30, tapped once again on the cabin door.

Guillaume admitted them and locked the door. He thrust a mug of ersatz coffee into Guy's hand. It tasted awful, but sent a ray or two of warmth into the young Frenchman.

'Right,' said Guillaume. 'Where you're going to be is colder than a witch's tit and you're going to be there hours, so put all your warm clothing on and once you're inside, get yourself and the hound into your sleeping bag.'

Guy did as he was bidden and dressed himself in two pairs of trousers and all the sweaters he had in his rucksack. Colonel was already in his little coat.

While Guy was getting kitted-up, Guillaume poured the rest of the coffee into a Thermos and added a generous measure of rotgut brandy from a bottle in the cuddy.

Silently, the boatman led them through a door into the hold which was stacked high with the sacks of cement he was transporting from Rennes. The hold was a bit like a tent, the loadspace covered with a tightly sheeted tarpaulin cover over a frame running the length of the hold.

They squeezed their way past the sacks along the port side and stopped just short of the bow. Guillaume produced a screwdriver from his dungarees and removed six countersunk screws holding a plate covering part of the bulwark space. He lowered the plate noiselessly to the deck to reveal a dank void. Three planks sat atop the thwarts that both kept the hull in shape and supported the deck. A smell of manky bilge water and diesel hit Guy.

Guillaume motioned the pair to lie on the planks.

'If you need to go,' he whispered, 'just pee into the bilges.'

Guy and Colonel got into the sleeping bag and zipped it shut. Guillaume replaced the plate and screwed it home. Unseen and unheard by Guy, he took some dirt and cement dust and smeared them over the screw heads to conceal the witness marks and round the gaps between the plate and its neighbours. By the time he had finished, the plate looked as though it had been undisturbed for years.

Ten minutes later, the barge's diesel rumbled into life and Guy heard the sounds of both mooring ropes being cast off and thrown over the bitts, followed by the soft lapping sound of water over hull as the vessel lumbered towards the lock.

Guillaume had also donated a small torch and Guy flicked it on briefly to survey his surroundings. They were grim.

The planks were all that stopped himself and Colonel from falling into the bilges. With the plate screwed home, the foul air became even fouler and the smell from bilge water and diesel was overpowering. Their hidey-hole was below water level and in the cold of winter, the inside of the hull was rimed with a coating of ice. Before the engine started, all was quiet and Guy could hear rats splashing away in the murk below.

He also realised that should anything happen to Guillaume, he and Colonel would be entombed and he began to shake with the mere thought of it. It reminded him of the Great Eastern. During the ironclad's construction, a worker had been in the space between the inner and outer hulls and out of sight of his mates. The riveters had placed the final plate over the outer hull. Unheard through the thick steel, the man was entombed. Years later, his skeleton was found and his untimely death blamed for the jinx that had plagued the mighty vessel from its launch.

About thirty minutes later, the diesel slowed to an idle, then the vessel bumped into the lock chamber. A clatter of jackboots and German voices announced the boarding party, which combed the boat from stem to stern. At one stage, Guy found himself separated from the enemy by only a steel plate and shrank involuntarily further into his sleeping bag as if this would distance him further from the soldiers.

After several minutes of rushing water, the lock gates creaked open, the engine note rose and the barge continued its voyage up the canal.

The search procedure was repeated at each lock and despite his companion's impeccable behaviour, Guy trembled lest the dog have an off moment and give the game away. But Colonel was as good as gold.

Initially buoyed up by the coffee and brandy, Guy did not feel the cold, but as time went on, the damp miasma seeped deeper and deeper into his flesh and bones. He had thought that the cold he experienced when he broke his ankle was the ultimate, but it was as nothing to being in this dank tomb. He and Colonel gave each other warmth, but as the hours ticked by, their body temperatures dropped steadily.

The barge came to a halt again at yet another lock. When it left the lock, the slight rolling motion indicated that they were now in the Rance itself. The boat chugged on, then the diesel's revs increased as the barge headed into the tide coming upriver. The nearer to St Malo they got, the stronger the tide and the greater the roll. Almost poisoned by the foul atmosphere and fumes, Guy felt increasingly queasy, then finally threw up into the bilges, retching and gagging for several minutes until he calmed down again.

By now, all the coffee and brandy had gone. The moving river was far colder than the canal and despite continually rubbing his body and the dog's, both were beginning to succumb to hypothermia and drift into unconsciousness. Remembering his survival training, Guy fought against going to sleep, knowing that he would never awake.

Still the diesel rumbled on. Guy looked yet again at his watch, convinced it must have been at least an hour since he last did so, but found it was really ten minutes. Would he and Colonel ever emerge from their refrigerator and if so, would they do so alive?

At long last, the engine slowed as Guillaume turned to starboard and stopped at the harbour boom. His papers were checked, the boat searched once again and then he was given a berth number for overnight mooring.

The boom was lifted and much revving and bumping later, the barge was moored snugly for the night. The sound of feet told the now delirious Guy that Guillaume was approaching. The bargee knelt on the deck and whispered 'Give it a few minutes to make sure they don't come back for some reason and I'll let you out.'

Ten minutes, the plate was removed and for a second, Guillaume thought he had two corpses on his boat. A slight movement from man and hound indicated at least some vital signs, so Guillaume snatched Colonel from the sleeping bag and set him down in front of the cabin stove. Returning to the bow, he hauled Guy and sleeping bag onto the deck and half carried, half dragged him into the cabin. Colonel was already better for the warmth and making small movements as he sought the heat.

Guy's body temperature was so low, he felt like ice. Quickly, Guillaume stripped the young man of all his clothes and began to rub him vigorously. His efforts were rewarded by a tinge of colour as the circulation increased.

'Guy, Guy, are you OK?' he begged anxiously.

A muffled groan showed that life was still extant. Reaching up, the boatman grabbed the rotgut and prising Guy's lips apart, forced some of the raw spirit down his throat. Gasping and gagging at the fiery liquid, Guy came back to life.

Guillaume continued the massage, pausing only to give the dog a slurp of rotgut as well. By now, Colonel's coat was steaming and his usual doggy grin was returning.

It took over forty-five minutes of rubbing and rotgut before Guy was anywhere near normal again and when he put his now warm clothes back on, his fingers could barely cope with any buttons or fasteners. The warm clothes were manna to a hypothermic and another fifteen minutes saw still more improvement.

'Right,' said Guillaume, 'the sentry's patrol up and down the hard takes him four minutes and ten seconds.'

He grinned mischievously.

'The German passion for strict order has its advantages at times.'

'Put Colonel in your rucksack as you've told me and when I give the signal, walk twenty metres to the right and you'll find a loose board in the fence. Where are you headed?'

'Rue Quatorze Juillet,' replied Guy.

'Turn left at the fence, right when you reach the road and second on the left after about 200 metres.'

As promised, Guy had given the bargee ten sovereigns before the voyage and now produced ten more.

'I don't want any more of your money, young'un,' said Guillaume, suddenly overcome by remorse at Guy's near death. 'God be with you, you deserve some luck.'

'Take them, please,' implored Guy and thrust the coins into the older man's hand.

Reluctantly, Guillaume accepted the money, then prepared to monitor the sentry's movements. He turned off the cabin light and slid noiselessly on deck. Guy popped Colonel into the rucksack, something that he had done countless times over the years. Colonel just adored snuggling down inside the warm bag.

Hidden behind the opposite side of the wheelhouse to the dock, Guillaume kept watch on the sentry, letting him make two forays up and down before he was satisfied that his original timing was correct.

'OK Guy, NOW!'

With a last wave, Guy slipped onto the dock and hidden immediately in the darkness, tiptoed over to the fence. At first, he could not find the board. Panic set in, especially as he could hear the footfalls of the sentry nearing the end of his beat. Scrabbling noiselessly a little further to the right, his agitated fingers located the board and swung it clear. In an instant, he was the other side of the fence.

He made his way to the road and turned right, trying to look as though this was familiar ground and that he was part of it. Almost immediately, he met some German soldiers coming the other way, but they were full of beer and bonhomie and never even glanced at him.

The 200 metres to the Rue Quatorze Juillet seemed more like 200 kilometres, but after an eternity, he turned left and started to look for Bar Hugo. The creaking of a sign above his head drew his attention. It read 'Bar Hugo'.

Guy cautiously opened the front door and walked in. His uncle was drawing demi-pressions for his only two customers, both local fishermen.

Hugo's aplomb and insouciance were incredible, his white knuckles around the beer pump handle the only visible sign of his shock.

'Supper's on, Guy,' said Hugo in a voice devoid of any kind of drama and indicating vaguely towards the door marked 'Privé' as if Guy was a frequent visitor.

Guy slipped through the door into a darkened corridor, than spotting a crack of light under another door to the left, opened it and entered his aunt's kitchen.

*

'Good afternoon, I am Hugo Montauban. I am here to see Monsieur Albert Beaumont for the position of Head Chef.'

Heloise Beaumont looked up from the accounts ledger. 'Looked up' was an apt phrase, Hugo was 6' 5", 19 stone and just towered above her. Although well-cut and of good quality, his suit stretched over him so tightly that it seemed he would burst out of it at any moment. To Heloise, he looked like a giant bear that had outgrown its skin.

Motioning him to take a seat, Heloise said, 'I'll just fetch my father,' and disappeared into the back office.

An hour later, Albert offered Hugo the job. Hugo had been apprenticed in the Georges Cinq in Paris, a pedigree he used to good effect as he worked around France, Switzerland, Italy and England, always in top class hotels or restaurants. Apart from French, he spoke at least a smattering of German, Italian and English, the latter he spoke quite well.

Hugo agreed to start right away and have the rest of his belongings sent over from his lodgings in Deauville where he had been working.

'What happened to the previous Head Chef?' he enquired of Albert.

'He became an alcoholic. We've been flat out renovating the hotel for the past year and I simply have not had the time to keep a proper eye on things,' replied Albert, shrugging his shoulders and a little shamefaced. 'I did warn him several times to keep his drinking to off-duty hours, but last week I found him spark-out at his desk and he had to go. I'm afraid the kitchen's not quite up to snuff at the moment,' he added.

'Not quite up to snuff' was putting it mildly. Albert took Hugo into the kitchens and the chef was assailed instantly by that smell that screams 'dirty kitchen', an aroma of congealed fat, food lumps baked hard onto stoves and a floor in desperate need of a good scrub. Not only that, Hugo saw to his dismay the telltale signs of mouse droppings.

The brigade of six was preparing the evening meal. Albert introduced Hugo to Martin, the deputy.

'Right,' said Hugo, 'you carry on organising dinner and I'll watch how it's done.'

Four of the brigade were essentially good chefs, but two were a disaster waiting to happen. Slack and slovenly, both had obviously been drinking and their breath smelt like the inside of a wine cave.

As service progressed, Hugo wandered round taking it all in. The larders were as dirty as the kitchens and swarming with flies, and the vegetable larder stank of rotting vegetation. Hugo swiftly binned the offending items, wrinkling his nose as he did so.

By midnight, dinner service was over. The chefs made very little effort to clean the kitchens properly until Hugo gathered them together and in extremely basic French, told them exactly what he thought of the operation.

Within two weeks the kitchens had been deep-cleaned, the two useless chefs replaced and some discipline instilled into the brigade. Hugo now stalked his domain like a king, a posture that irritated Heloise, who thought him arrogant.

Heloise walked into the kitchen, wandered around as if checking what was happening and then made a beeline for the hollandaise sauce that had just been prepared.

'Can I help you, mademoiselle?' enquired Hugo.

Heloise made no reply, but dipped one finger into the hollandaise and tasted it.

'It's rancid!' she exclaimed.

The usual clamour of a busy kitchen was stilled in a moment.

'I beg your pardon?' riposted Hugo.

'It's rancid,' she repeated.

Hugo flushed. The veins on his muscular neck began to stand out in anger and for a moment, Martin who was nearest thought his boss might pick up the owner's daughter and physically eject her from his beloved kitchens.

'Three weeks ago, mademoiselle, I might well have agreed with you, but hollandaise in any kitchen run by Hugo Montauban is NEVER rancid.'

He tasted the sauce.

'It's perfect,' he said.

The faces of the brigade were a study. To enter the Head Chef's empire and criticise him was breach of etiquette enough, to do so in front of his brigade was unforgivable. Without replying, Heloise turned on her heel and walked off.

From then on, Heloise and Hugo were at each other's throats, with Hugo always on the defensive against the hotel proprietor's daughter and deputy. She criticised his menus, his food presentation, his rosters, in fact anything and everything he did.

It was one o'clock on a Sunday morning. Heloise stepped out onto the terrace to savour the warmth of a tranquil July night and draw breath from a frantic Saturday night. All the guests had long since retired, she was quite alone. Despite her antagonism towards Hugo, he had swiftly turned round the kitchens and the hotel cuisine, bringing back customers that had deserted the hotel and producing a table that had non-residents queuing up to dine.

She was leaning quietly against the terrace balustrade, drinking in the air, when she found herself picked up like a doll, swung round and

75

crushed in Hugo's bear-like grip. His lips fastened on hers. For a moment, Heloise tried to resist, then kissed him back just as ardently as he was kissing her.

Albert was not amused. He liked and admired his Head Chef and champion amateur wrestler, but strictly as a Head Chef and not a potential suitor for his daughter. Albert had designs on making a match between Heloise and Pierre Fabre, the son of another local hotelier. Whilst Heloise liked Pierre as a friend, he did not excite her corpuscles one iota.

Trying everything he could to part the couple, Albert interfered with their romance as often as he could. The strain on the relationship caused the rows to flare up again and it all came to a head one night at a dinner dance.

Hugo and Heloise had taken the night off to enjoy a dinner dance at the Hotel Metropole in Dinard. One of the guests, a tall and willowy brunette, was almost wearing a most revealing dress which flaunted acres of snowy bosom. The cleavage was impossible to miss and Heloise accused Hugo of ogling the display. A fierce row developed. Hugo stormed out of the hotel, leaving Heloise to find her own way home.

The following morning, Hugo was packed and gone.

Just as he had instantly disapproved of the relationship, now Albert instantly regretted his interference. The normally bright, chirpy Heloise whose interpersonal skills and charm made the hotel so welcoming, now became morose and withdrawn. Her usual warmth with guests was replaced by a cool, almost icy detachment.

Albert secretly tried to find Hugo, ringing all his hotel and restaurant contacts, but in vain. Wherever the chef had gone, he was not to be found.

Albert decided not to replace Hugo for the time being, hoping beyond hope for his swift return.

It was late September, two o'clock in the morning. Once again, Heloise was on the terrace. It was one of those warm, balmy nights that often come just before Autumn. A clear sky was bedecked with stars, the moon created small flecks of light on a sea mildly agitated by the merest zephyr, which also brought with it the fragrance of bougainvillaea. She stared out towards the Channel but saw nothing, engrossed in her own thoughts. She was far away when a huge pair of muscular arms encircled her waist and a voice in her left ear murmured 'Will you marry me, Heloise my darling?'

The right paw opened to reveal a tiny velvet-covered box, which in its turn opened to reveal an emerald and turquoise engagement ring. Heloise just buried her face in Hugo's chest and cried with happiness, nodding her acceptance when he asked her once again for her hand. The ring fitted perfectly.

*

The crack of gavel on block signified the speech by the father of the bride, resplendent in tails but perspiring in the heat of an exceptional May.

'Mes chers amis,' began Albert, 'today is a day of enormous happiness, the day my daughter Heloise marries Hugo. No man could ask for a better daughter, no man could ask for a finer son-in-law.' Albert's well-prepared speech moved on smoothly, the obligatory references to his offspring's childhood adventures and faux pas not only expected by the guests, but joyfully indulged as well.

'Today is actually a double occasion.'

At these words, all ears pricked up.

'Not only is my daughter's wedding, it is also the day I retire.'

Both Heloise and Hugo started, astounded by the unexpected announcement. Albert had given not the slightest inkling to anyone.

'It is more than about time I sat on the cliffs and painted the sea and the scenery, something I never seem to have had time to do running this hotel,' said Albert somewhat wistfully. 'And so, my children…'

He turned beaming towards the happy couple.

'I have a slightly bigger present for you.'

With that, he produced from his inner pocket a legal-looking envelope.

'Monsieur et Madame Montauban, I present you with the title deeds to this hotel.'

Heloise and Hugo could scarcely speak, let alone move, shaken to the core by the unexpected turn of events. Then they were laughing and crying at the same time, hugging Albert, whose own eyes were suddenly moist. It was an intimate family moment in a very public family occasion.

The already joyous celebration was lifted instantly to another plane, the champagne flowed even faster and the dancing and merrymaking went on into the wee small hours.

Albert did indeed retire to his cottage and now with the time to relax, developed into a highly competent watercolour artist.

Hugo and Heloise continued to develop the hotel. With Hugo in charge of food and Heloise the accommodation, the business prospered. The restaurant became a favourite table for hotel guests and non-residents alike and was packed every night during the season.

It was on one such night that Hugo entered the annals of St Malo folklore. It was August, one of those evenings that combined heat with humidity and caused frayed tempers. Heloise was bringing the accounts up to date when Charles, the maitre d', appeared at her office door looking flushed and apprehensive.

'Madame, one of the guests at Table 10 is drunk and causing trouble. He is demanding another bottle of wine and I have refused to serve him because he is so drunk, but he won't take no for an answer.'

Heloise strode briskly to the restaurant, pausing only to check the man's name on the bookings as she passed the desk. The room was packed with French and British diners, all now agog at the scene before them.

Charles was not exaggerating. The man was clearly very drunk, heavily flushed, wild-eyed and his expensive tie askew. In his late 20s, he offered an air of great wealth, but at the same time, appeared to view all his fellow guests as mere peasants fortunate enough to dine in the same restaurant as his exalted self. His female companion was pretty enough, let down by a somewhat vacant air.

'Monsieur LaSalle, I am Madame Montauban, what appears to be the problem?'

'I wanna 'nother bottle of the Bordeaux.'

LaSalle's high-class speech was slurred and his hand waved vapidly at the empty bottle of fine wine, the second he and his lady friend had consumed that evening.

'Monsieur,' began Heloise in her most coaxing tone, 'you and your companion have dined well and enjoyed an excellent vintage, but perhaps another bottle might be just a little too much, non?'

Her words, intended to be soothing, had exactly the opposite effect.

LaSalle, determined not to back down in front of his lady, swayed groggily to his feet and punctuating his words with a forefinger stabbing towards Heloise's chest, he yelled, 'I told you, I wanna 'nother bottle, you stupid, useless cow. Now move your fat arse and do as I say, or you'll be sorry.'

He accompanied the final words with a drunken lunge towards Heloise and for a moment, she feared he might hit her.

There was a resounding crash as Hugo came through the door

from the kitchen with such force it seemed it would tear from its hinges. Nostrils flared in rage, it would have surprised no one if flames had spurted dragon-like from Hugo's nose. Storming across the dining room and without breaking step, he grabbed LaSalle round the waist and tucking him under his arm like a piglet, continued at speed towards the dining room doors. The man was no lightweight, but Hugo carried him as though he were a gossamer.

Charles was just in time to open the door before Hugo used the guest's head as a battering ram. At unabated speed, Hugo carried the man through the open main doors, down the steps and dumped him unceremoniously in the gutter. Without a word, Hugo spun on his heel and marched back into the hotel. Looking to neither right nor left as he entered the dining room and totally ignoring the standing ovation from the diners, he crashed once more into his domain.

LaSalle's girlfriend had been making ineffectual twittering noises accompanied by equally useless hand gestures in a vain attempt to calm her boyfriend. Seeing his rapid and undignified removal, she burst into tears and rushed to the sanctuary of the Ladies.

'Charles, complimentary liqueurs all round,' ordered Heloise 'and get a taxi pronto.'

Heloise went to find the sobbing girl, not a difficult task, as her sobs could be heard across the hotel foyer. She was sitting in front of the mirror, eyes already puffy from crying and twin black runnels of mascara running either side of her nose.

'I'm s-s-so s-s-sorry,' she blurted. 'Martin is a really nice chap when he's sober and a perfect gentleman, but he gets silly with drink.'

'He's done this before then?'

A tearful nod agreed this was so.

'He's barred from two top restaurants in Paris because of it.'

'I can't control him when he's like that and I do love him so.'

At this, the floodgates opened once again.

Heloise waited until the flood had abated.

'You have to make a choice, then,' she advised. 'Either he learns to behave himself or perhaps you have to think twice about staying with him.'

The shocked look she received in reply proved her remark had hit home and hard.

The girl rummaged in her purse.

'I'll settle our bill,' she said.

'There's no charge and the taxi home is on us too, provided you promise not to bring Martin here again.'

An acquiescing nod was followed by structural facial repairs, by which time the taxi was sitting waiting.

Martin LaSalle had sobered up rapidly at being forcibly ejected and dumped in the gutter. He was perched miserably on the low wall at the front of the hotel, his smart jacket looking ruffled and dusty and his tie still askew.

Helped by his girlfriend, he poured himself groggily into the taxi and the Citroen ground away into the evening, twin yellow beams probing the road ahead towards the exclusive St Brieuc Hotel along the coast.

Heloise sighed deeply and returned to her accounts.

When the Germans invaded in 1940 and put the coastal strip off limits, they also requisitioned the hotel as an Officers' Mess. Hugo bought a small bar-tabac cheap and with Heloise, the two Hs, as they were known in the family, hunkered down to sit out the war.

When Guy walked into the kitchen, his aunt had her back towards him stirring a fish stew on the wood-burning range. The delicious smell hit Guy like a hammer blow and he realised how long it had been since his last meal.

Hearing the door open, Heloise swung round, letting out a strangled cry at seeing her nephew. Then she hugged him to her, wondering not only why he was there, but why he looked so gaunt and pale, with worry lines etched across his young forehead.

Guy had set his rucksack on the floor and there was now whining and scrabbling from within as Colonel heard and smelt one of his most favourite people. Released, the little dog leapt into Heloise's arms and there was much hugging and joyful licking, the stumpy tail a blur of delight.

Sensing that this was not the moment to interrogate Guy, Heloise enquired 'I expect you'd both like some food?'

Guy nodded. A bowl of the stew for Guy was accompanied by similar for Colonel, bolstered by some bread in the doggy version. Guy ate his like a starving dingo, his spoon moving with the speed and precision of a mechanical shovel. Colonel scoffed his just as fast, then settled in front of the range and fell asleep, emitting tiny snores from one end and little pops from the other.

'More, Guy?'

It was a silly question. Whilst the young man was consuming the second bowl, Heloise went upstairs to make up his bed. When she re-entered the kitchen, Guy was also sound asleep, head thrown back and his fingers clenched rigidly around the bowl and the spoon. Gently,

Heloise prised the digits free from the bowl and the utensil.

When the bar shut, Hugo came through and the couple ate, silently watching their nephew. Asleep, the deep lines on his face began to soften and now warm and well fed, the blueness in his face receded. Nonetheless, the two Hs could see clearly the pain and suffering still in that face.

As she cleared away, Heloise dropped a spoon in the pot sink and the harsh clatter brought Guy instantly awake. Disorientated by his unfamiliar surroundings, a wild and desperate look came into his eyes and he gripped the arms of his chair and made as if to spring up and escape.

'It's OK, Guy, you're safe,' said Hugo soothingly.

Guy came to properly and started to relax. Hugo offered him a glass of red wine and as the liquor hit him, the tension in his young frame lessened visibly.

'Do you want to tell us about it, Guy?'

Guy looked at Hugo and began his story.

'Maman and Papa are dead, killed in a reprisal air raid,' he said. 'I saw the bomb burst in front of the house and ran like mad home, but they had been killed instantly. Then a couple of Germans came to loot. They split up outside the house and one came into the lounge. I had hidden in the kitchen and looked round the lounge door to see the soldier stealing Maman's rings. I stabbed him to death with his own bayonet,' he added simply.

Guy recounted how he had concealed the corpse in the cellar and decided to walk to St Malo in the hope that his uncle could help him get to England.

'When did you set out Guy?' enquired Hugo.

'Late November,' came the reply.

Hugo did a mental calculation. 'Why has it taken you so long, I'd have thought no more than 4-5 weeks?'

Guy explained his broken ankle, the kindness of the Gounons and how he had so nearly been discovered in the raid on the farmhouse.

Hugo replenished all the wine glasses and Guy continued his tale. Hugo and Heloise learned of nearly falling over the quarry cliff, the little house, that stifling bakery oven, the horrors of the explosions at the fuel dump and finally, being entombed in the icy bulwark of the barge.

Initially, the words came as a trickle, then a flood and finally a torrent, those words which told so graphically of the sorrow, the hurt, the fear, the cold and the pain of his experiences. It was a catharsis, opening the floodgates of long pent-up and stifled emotion. Hugo and Heloise were fighting back the tears, remembering with love Robert and Hugo's sister Madeleine.

When it was over, Guy let out a long sigh and began to droop once more. Colonel had by this time awoken from his slumbers and the pair moved to the spare room. The unaccustomed luxury of a real bed, a warm and inviting feather quilt was manna from heaven and the pair fell instantly asleep, Colonel snuggled against his master.

Guy and Colonel remained hidden in the house for almost ten days, Colonel being allowed out only at night.

Feeling once again warm and safe, even if temporarily, Guy relaxed. Heloise fed him as well as she could, fish predominating the menu, but it was good wholesome fare and the gaunt skeletons of man and dog began to fill out and turn pink (at least, the human one did).

Hugo's passion was sea-fishing, thus he knew every fisherman within a twenty mile radius.

After a week, he announced that, 'It would be tomorrow night at 8.30'.

Prompt at 8.30, a wheezy Renault van stopped at the rear gate. Hugo, Guy and Colonel were waiting.

Forewarned about the dog, the fisherman driving the van said to Guy, 'Put your hound in your rucksack,' then opened the rear doors of the vehicle.

Guy's nose was assailed by the odour of stale fish, tar and fishing nets and his eyes met a wall of fishboxes stacked to the rear of the load platform.

Swiftly the fisherman and Hugo removed boxes to reveal a hiding place within a pile of nets. Having said au revoir to a tearful Heloise, Guy paused only momentarily to hug his uncle then climbed inside. The van moved off and bumped its way over the cobbles to the harbour entrance. Guttural voices were followed by the van doors being opened, but the familiar sight of the fishboxes and the rank smell meant no search. The doors slammed and the van motored on down the dock and bumped to a halt. Once more the doors were opened and fishboxes and gear offloaded on to the waiting trawler. Well concealed, Guy waited in trepidation.

Yet again, he could just make out the clatter of boots as the soldiers checked the trawler over, then moved on to the next boat. Seconds later, the fisherman came for Guy and with a whispered 'Quickly, quickly,' whisked him onto the boat and into the cuddy whilst the soldiers were below on the next boat.

Minutes later, the tock-tock of many diesels started and the little flotilla manoeuvred past the now open harbour boom and out into the English Channel.

Once clear of the harbour, Guy released Colonel from the rucksack and sat awaiting events. The night was fairly cold and a touch misty, the sea with an uneasy swell that reminded Guy of his trip in the barge. The cuddy stank of diesel, bilgewater, old fish and countless Disque Bleu.

An hour later, he heard the trawler shoot its nets and the motion of the boat steadied with the stabilising drag on its stern. The fisherman who had driven Guy to the dock appeared in the hatchway and beckoned to Guy to come on deck. Wrapped in his warm parka and Colonel likewise, the pair were glad of some fresh air. An occasional E-boat flashed past at speed, but Guy looked just like the rest of the crew and the little dog was invisible below the taffrail.

Guy noticed the trawler gradually edging north to become the boat that was farthest from the French coast. Twenty minutes later, a signalling lamp flashed from the north and was answered with a torch by one of the crew. Another trawler identical to Guy's hove out of the mist and began to draw alongside.

'Quickly, pooch in the bag and when I say jump, jump,' commanded Guy's fisherman friend.

Guy did as he was bidden and as the vessels bumped alongside one another, he jumped across the rails. Willing hands drew him inboard as other hands threw packages onto the deck of the French boat. Then just as swiftly, the trawlers parted and Guy's new conveyance began to edge back from whence it came.

Guy was put in the wheelhouse, where he sat on the floor and let Colonel out of the bag. Once out of sight of the little fleet, the helmsman pressed a hidden catch to reveal another set of engine controls. Turning the ignition key and pressing the starter brought forth a sound Guy knew in an instant.

'Bugatti,' exclaimed Guy.

'Nothing but the best,' replied the man in French and shutting down the tock-tock.

With that, he cracked open the throttle, the engine note deepened and the stubby vessel began to cut through the water at a speed indecent for such a craft.

Some hours and with the registration changed to the 'FH' of Falmouth, the boat neared the English coast. The Bugatti was switched off and the tock-tock restarted. After a check by the picket boat at the mouth of the estuary, the boat sailed on up the Helford River. Once into a quiet reach, the trawler swung to port, aiming for a large wooden boathouse. A quick request in English over the radio and the doors slid back to allow the vessel to motor straight in and moor against the dock.

Once the trawler was secured, the crew disembarked, taking Guy and his dog with them to a small cottage opposite the boathouse. It was still pitch black, a gentle wind sighing through the trees, but with faint fingers of a winter dawn beginning to peep over the estuary.

'OK,' said one of the crew in English, 'eggy bakes all round?'

The volunteer chef received nods of approval and with the help of a monster frying pan, produced hot breakfast for all washed down with thick white china mugs of strong tea. With his blood sugar level approaching something near normal, Guy's spirits began to rise appreciably. He had just swigged the last of his second mug of tea when a car drew up outside. Seconds later, a man dressed in a British warm and a ratting cap strode into the kitchen.

Somewhere in his 40s, athletic and fit, he radiated hidden energy.

'Lionel,' he announced to Guy and proffering his hand.

Guy shook hands, discovering that from then on, everybody had a first name but never a surname.

'We'd best get started, it's a long trip, so come on,' indicating to Guy to follow him.

Guy paused only to thank his rescuers in English.

'Think nothing of it, best of luck,' came the reply from the helmsman.

Guy walked behind Lionel to a dark green Rover on civilian plates. They set off, the wartime headlights making little way against the darkness. Fortunately, the car possessed a heater and with Colonel on his lap, Guy dozed. Dawn broke gradually and as it lightened, so Lionel increased speed, rolling through Devon and Somerset and into Wiltshire. Around noon they stopped at a pub, where Lionel treated Guy to his first pint of British beer and a cheese sandwich rather like a doorstep. Guy liked the warm, frothy liquid so different to the lagers of his native France. As dusk threatened, they drew into the outskirts of London.

Lionel navigated confidently through a leafy suburb and stopped at the gates to a substantial mansion visible through the trees that surrounded it. A sentry in civilian clothes checked Lionel's pass, then opened the portals to admit them.

The Rover crunched over a long gravel drive, pulling to a halt in front of the substantial porch.

'Come with me,' ordered Lionel and ushered Guy inside.

A male receptionist checked a list and looking up, said, 'Room 34'.

Lionel strode ahead, Guy and Colonel in his wake. Room 34 was a comfortable bedroom, complete with en suite bathroom and a telephone. Lionel picked up the handset and muttered into it. Almost immediately, a man appeared.

'Freddie will take care of Colonel, won't you Freddie?' said Lionel in a jocular tone. 'You and I have to meet someone.'

Suddenly, Guy was mortally afraid for reasons he could not explain. He was not worried about Colonel, who took immediately to Freddie.

Lionel strode off once more, taking Guy to a room in the cellars. The room stank of sweat, although how anyone sweated in the sub-zero temperature was mystery. A long table at one end complete with chairs and a lonely single wooden chair in the middle of the room were the sole furniture. The room also reeked of fear.

'Give me your watch, sit down and wait.'

Guy did as he was told, taking the single chair indicated. Now he was petrified, especially when he turned on hearing the door shut to find himself completely alone.

He was not alone for long, nor for countless hours to come. Four men entered by another door in the corner and sat down facing Guy. No sooner had they sat down than they began firing questions at him with machine-gun like rapidity.

'Tell us about the reprisal raid.'

'What is the name of the church in the centre of Montluçon?'

'Tell us the name of the local Gestapo commander.'

And so it went on, in both French and English, with frequent shifts of language, even in mid-sentence, trying to catch him out. If they asked a question in one language and he answered in the other, they screamed at him in the other language. The same questions were repeated over and over again in an attempt to trip him, questions about France, its geography, his knowledge of the roads and départements, questions about England and his grandparents and Halifax and London and God knows what else.

Periodically, his interrogators changed and he was allowed black coffee and to visit the toilet. If he fell asleep, they threw icy water over him and slapped his face. Some of his interrogators shouted questions in German. Guy lost track of time completely. He was so tired and bamboozled, he would have sworn black was white if he thought it would end this torture, but sensing the importance of what was happening, he clung on grimly.

On and on and on it went, eventually as Guy was to discover, for 72 hours. At one stage, a man came in and examined the soles of Guy's feet.

Just as Guy felt he could take no more, the lights were turned on and his inquisitors got up and left. Guy sat rigid, cold, exhausted, frightened, his brain totally scrambled. The door clicked and he swivelled in his chair to find Lionel standing next to him. The young man stared woodenly at him and uttered words that had never yet passed his lips.

'You fucking cunt,' he snarled through clenched teeth.

Lionel stared impassively at him, not seeming to acknowledge Guy's words, but replied 'What did you expect? You're the perfect double.'

Guy was still bemused and looked it.

'Look at it from our angle – totally bilingual French/English, good German, tremendous knowledge of France and a good knowledge of Britain. Absolutely perfect for a double.'

Seeing Guy's quizzical look, he explained, 'double agent'. 'Old Fritz has become too damn smart lately at infiltrating quislings.'

Guy had naively assumed he would be accepted as genuine without question and had never expected such a monumental grilling.

A sudden thought entered Guy's buzzing head.

'Why did you check the soles of my feet?' he demanded.

'Simple, if you had walked as far as you claimed, you would have callouses on your soles – and you did. Had a woman some months back who claimed to have done what you did. Cover story was cast-iron, couldn't break it. Then one of the boys had the nous to inspect her feet, smooth as a baby's bum. She's in Holloway awaiting the rope.'

Guy shivered at the mere idea.

'What's the time?'

'Half past seven on Thursday morning, you've been here three days. Breakfast time.'

He took Guy up to a dining room, empty save a small dog perched on a chair looking as if he just needed a napkin. Guy hugged Colonel delightedly. Freddie appeared with plates of bacon and eggs, including a portion for Colonel.

'Smashing dog that sir,' he remarked to Guy, 'we got on a treat, didn't we?' addressing this remark to Colonel and ruffling the soft hair on top of the dog's head. Colonel gave his usual doggy grin.

They were on to their second cup of tea each before Lionel admitted the true reason for the interrogation.

Seeing Guy's equilibrium returning, he looked him straight in the eye and said, 'We want you to become an agent for us and return to France.'

Silencing Guy's reply with his hand, he went on, 'We'll keep you well away from your home area and in any case, it doesn't matter.'

Guy looked puzzled.

'Do you remember smelling gas when you were packing up to leave?'

So preoccupied had Guy been with his escape, he had not remembered such a detail until now.

'Yes,' he replied, 'I do recall it now you ask.'

'The bombing cracked a gas main and about half an hour after you left, there was one hell of an explosion, flattened your house, next door and the two opposite. Entombed your soldier and neither the Germans nor your townsfolk have touched the rubble since.'

Catching the look of horror at the word 'entombed' and the tears beginning to well, he put an arm round Guy's shoulders.

'Not exactly a Christian burial for your folks, I know.'

Guy nodded, his mind back at the wrecked salon and the rag dolls that had been his parents.

'Do you want to do your bit?' asked Lionel.

Guy suddenly found a reserve of energy he did not know he had and nodded his assent vigorously.

Breakfast over, Guy hit the sack to sleep the clock round. The following morning, he breakfasted with Lionel once more before being taken to an office to complete and sign forms, have his photo taken and swear allegiance to the King.

'Welcome to the British Army and F Section of SOE, Lieutenant Duplessis,' grinned Lionel.

Chapter 6

'What now?' enquired Guy, now seated in the Rover as it headed west.

'You need a bit of peace and time off, so I'm taking you to a friend outside Exeter, Jack Welch. Jack runs a farm,' explained Lionel.

The Rover purred on into the pale of a winter's morning, pausing in Exeter itself for Lionel to introduce Guy to the manager of Lloyds Bank so that he could open an account for his military salary.

Ten miles north of Exeter, Lionel swung the Rover onto a narrow track. Half a mile later, Guy was shaking hands with Jack and Mary Welch.

'You are a welcome sight, Guy,' remarked Jack. 'My two tractors are very sick, I'm still in the horse-drawn era and the nearest garage is Exeter. My two land girls just know how to drive them, no more. Lionel says you're a pretty handy mechanic?'

Guy acknowledged this was indeed so.

Over tea, Jack introduced Guy to the two land girls, Letitia and Esme, just saying Guy was on extended leave from the Army and would be helping out for a few weeks. Letitia was from Borehamwood and British middle-class to the roots of her auburn hair. She insisted on being called Letitia not Letty – to her, diminutives of names were common. Esme hailed from Bethnal Green which she pronounced 'Befnal Green'. Knowing that being called Letty was a sure-fire way to wind up her workmate, Esme missed no opportunity to do so, but Letitia knew it was just teasing and ignored her. Both girls had been in the Land Army about a year and were townies still learning about country life, but they were cheerful and willing and worked long hours on the mixed arable and dairy spread.

Everyone took instantly to Colonel, even the rather scratchy collie that Jack used to round up the sheep.

Dawn was still some way distant when the farm woke to life the next morning. After tea and toast, Jack led Guy to a barn containing the tractors and a plethora of farm machinery. One end of the barn had been partitioned off, with large double doors in the centre of the partition. Jack opened one door.

'Norman used to keep all the machines in order, but he's in the Western Desert somewhere with REME.'

The partitioned off area was a workshop, but not just any workshop, it was a peach. Above benches on one side hung row upon row of spanners and tools, all with their sizes marked above each one. A lathe and a pillar drill stood at one end of the benches and various cupboards held workshop manuals on all the tractors and machinery, more tools including special tools and enough spares to practically rebuild any item on the farm.

There was even a flexible pipe hanging from the ceiling to fit over a tractor's vertical exhaust and let the fumes escape when running the engine in the workshop.

In one corner stood a stove, so mechanicking would be a warm and comfortable occupation.

A fine layer of dust announced that the workshop had been disused for some time.

'Norman did his apprenticeship at Rolls Royce,' added Jack on seeing the look of wonderment on Guy's face. 'I'll leave you to it.'

Much to Colonel's delight, Guy's first priority was to fire up the stove. The initial warm glow soon transformed into a radiant heat, cutting through the numbing chill and lifting spirits as well as temperatures. Colonel snugged down on a piece of sacking in front of the grate to doze and keep an eye on the proceedings.

A wander round the workshop revealed a switch marked 'compressor' and pressing it brought the familiar chunter of the air tank being filled. The air delivery line ran on three sides of the workshop, with take-off points at regular intervals. Under a tarpaulin in one corner sat a paraffin-powered steam cleaner. At first reluctant to fire after months of disuse, Guy eventually coaxed it to life and left it to warm whilst he cleaned up the shop. Norman's Rolls Royce days were evidenced by two pairs of overalls with the RR logo on the breast. They seemed about the right size for Guy, so he hung them in front of the stove to air.

Now set up, Guy went back into the barn proper and looked at the tractors. They looked like Fergusons but were badged Ford. Guy had queried this with Jack, who explained that the machines were Fergusons produced under licence by Ford in the US. Far from a pretty sight, they were caked so heavily in mud that the Ford grey paint was all but invisible. The engines of both were coated in a jacket of black, oily dirt. They shrieked neglect and a dire need for some expert TLC.

Guy started each one in turn. Neither started easily, but one was definitely very poorly; the other he judged needed simply a good service and some adjustment. He drove the latter around the farm for twenty minutes, warming it up so that he could switch from petrol to TVO, a kind of paraffin-based fuel that was cheaper than petrol. The cold engine was started on petrol, then switched to TVO using a changeover lever.

Leaving the engine running, he stopped the Ford outside the barn and fetched the steam cleaner, removing so much mud and muck that the vehicle seemed to rise on its tyres at being relieved of the encrustation. He cleaned the engine too, taking care to keep the steam wand away from the ignition system.

Guy parked the tractor in the workshop. Both sets of overalls were now aired, so he put one on. He and Norman might have shared the same height, but the absent mechanic was far more corpulent and the overalls bellied and sagged. A handy leather belt hanging on the back of one door was put to good effect to reduce the sag, but Guy still felt like Monsieur Bibendum.

A plentiful supply of oil stood on a rack, with filters on a shelf above. Guy removed the sump plug, but instead of a stream of oil, hot black gloop slurped into the drain can. Accompanying the almost slurry was that acrid stench familiar to mechanics the world over of old and burnt oil. What had once been Mr Tecalemit's finest had to be gouged from the filter bowl with a screwdriver. Guy looked for flushing oil to clean out the engine's internals, but ace mech Norman always changed the oil in good time, so had no need of such a liquid. All Guy could do was fill the sump with fresh oil.

Next he tackled the ignition system, renewing all the components and retiming the engine. Then it was the fuel system. What a mess. The glass filter bowl was full of black sludge, likewise the pump and carburettor. It was like Monthléry all over again. As was his wont, Guy returned all the parts to clinical cleanliness, then looked for the source of the muck. He did not have to look far, the TVO tank was a murky mess when he shone a torch into it. Draining the TVO, he used the steam wand to clear the inside and leaving the tank to dry, went outside to the bulk tank. Although fitted with a sludge drain at the back, the tank had been put on its trestles level instead of tilted backwards, so any lees flowed into the tanks of the tractors. Running off some fuel through a cloth filter showed it was pretty filthy.

Re-entering the workshop, Guy refilled the TVO tank from a can using the obviously-ignored filter funnel he found under the bulk tank, fitted the flexi over the exhaust and started the engine, adjusting the carburettor to achieve a nice tickover. The engine purred.

'Elevenses,' announced Jack's cheerful voice. So absorbed had Guy been in his task that time had just flown by. A large mug of tea and a thick wedge of walnut cake did wonders for the inner man and soon he was fettling the engine some more. At first slightly clumsy through not wielding a spanner in months, Guy's touch soon returned and he felt comfortable with himself.

He adjusted the clutch, then began to sort out the brakes, which had pulled badly to one side on his test drive. A monster screw jack and a steel trestle allowed him, with Jack's help, to remove each rear wheel in turn to strip and rebuild the brakes. Needless to say, there were replacement brake shoes in the spares cupboard. It took until tea-time to finish everything and the young mechanic's test drive was in the dark. The war regulations slits in the headlamps did little to illuminate the way ahead, but Guy chuntered around for half an hour. The Ford was A-OK.

The evening meal around a big table in the farmhouse kitchen was a convivial affair, although initially, all that could be heard was a gentle hissing from the range and the intake of vegetable broth. Some home-cured ham with potatoes followed and Guy realised suddenly that he was dog-tired. In the dawn to dusk culture of the farm, early to bed was a way of life in wartime and the next thing was the tinny alarm clock by his bed announcing 5.00am.

Guy dragged himself into a cold dawn, heavy with a sense of foreboding. He had an instinct that the second tractor was going to be very difficult and he was spot on. He stared at that grey machine and with almost x-ray vision, saw into that engine and the problems that lay within. When eventually coaxed reluctantly into life, the engine coughed and misfired on at least one cylinder, spouting ominous clouds of blue oil smoke from the exhaust stack. Leaving it to warm up, Guy delighted Colonel by lighting the stove before taking the errant Ford for a test drive. Even when warm, it still misfired and shuddered, so Guy took it into the workshop and repeated the disciplines of yesterday. One worrying sign was a fanbelt so slack, it bellied from the pulleys as the revs rose; on examination, the belt was cracked in three places and held together only by its canvas backing.

Removing the plugs showed 1, 3 and 4 to be white, evidence of a very weak mixture, whilst No 2 was oiled up and not firing. The fuel system was totally clogged and the main jet in the carburettor almost completely blocked. All in all, that the engine even ran was a miracle. Draining the oil produced a thinner than expected liquid reeking of petrol and TVO.

With all new bits and everything adjusted correctly, the engine was yet very sick and the blue pall of smoke from the exhaust undiminished. Sighing, Guy switched off and spent an hour or two on replacing worn steering joints and various other jobs whilst the engine cooled.

Jack's head and 'Elevenses' were yet again quite timely. Guy talked to him about the problems he foresaw and even Jack's non-mechanical mind could anticipate trouble ahead.

Teabreak over, Guy set about removing the cylinder head. It was like lifting the lid on Pandora's box. The weak mixture and the loose fanbelt had made the engine run too hot. The tops of three of the pistons were blue from overheating but still serviceable; No 2 piston was beyond redemption; two cracks at angles to one another had become a triangular hole in the crown the size of a penny. The oil smoke and misfiring were explained. The cylinder head was coked with a white encrustation. All four exhaust valves were wrecked. Two of them looked as if a giant had used them as lollipops and eaten chunks out the edges. Guy dumped the head in a bath of TVO to soften the deposits and sat down with the workshop manual.

The holed piston had to be replaced and naturally, Norman's stock included several piston sets, the necessary valves, bearings and gaskets...

Guy was perched beneath the engine when soft fur and a wet nose in his right ear announced a cuddle break. Much as they had done on the long walk through France, they sat for several minutes with Colonel on Guy's lap, his soft head tucked beneath Guy's chin. Time stood still and the war and smelly tractor engines no longer existed. Then it was back to that oily motor .

Fortified by lunch of soup, bread and cheese, Guy renewed his efforts. Once more, Guy was lost in the therapy of doing something he loved and unseen by him, the lines of worry and strain began to soften on his young forehead. By late afternoon, he had bolted home the sump and filled it with fresh oil.

Colonel was fast asleep in front of the stove, nose twitching and little squealing noises indicating that he was probably in hot pursuit of a juicy rabbit. Guy tickled the soft pink ears, but the little hound was out to the wide.

Hauling the cylinder head from its bath, Guy blew off all the surfaces with the airline and got stuck into the wearisome task of decoking. An old wood chisel proved just the right tool and the scraping began. Some deposits were so tough, it required a mallet as well as the chisel to remove them. Jack's cheery head and 'Supper' came at the precise moment the final speck of carbon succumbed.

Colonel was on his feet in a flash and tracker-dogged his way at some speed towards the fragrance wafting from the kitchen.

Esme giggled, pointing towards a streak of dirt that Guy had missed when cleaning up.

'Ow's it goin' then, maestro?' she enquired.

'It should be running again by tomorrow lunchtime,' replied the Frenchman, 'but she'll need running in.'

Letitia nodded, while Esme stared at him blankly.

'Wot's runnin in?' came the inevitable question.

A sudden realisation hit Guy.

'Do you have a driving licence?'

Esme shook her head.

'She does,' nodding towards Letitia, 'me, I'm an East-Ender, we scarce go' money for food and rent, never mind a mo'or. I go all over The Smoke on the bus or the Tube, the tractor's the only thing I ever druv.'

'The surfaces of new mechanical parts aren't perfect,' explained Guy, 'they have bits that stick out called high-spots, so you run the engine gently for a while to let the parts bed down gradually. If you don't, you can seize up the engine because it overheats.'

Esme was impressed.

'Cor, you don'arf know a lot for a young'un,' she said.

Privately, Guy wondered at the girl's lack of knowledge – had she never seen a 'Running In' sticker in a car's rear screen?

Within seconds of his head touching the pillow, Guy was crashed until dawn.

Much as he loved things mechanical, that certain smell of old oil and greasy parts hit him in a wave when he entered the workshop, but the cheery glow from the stove rapidly dispelled both the cold and the pong.

New valves, recut seats, valves lapped in, head cleaned. Now he was getting somewhere. Gently, he dropped the head over its retaining studs, torqued it down and set the valve clearances. Fingers tightly crossed, he hit the starter and was rewarded instantly by the throb of an engine on all four cylinders. Colonel looked up to see his master with a grin from ear to ear and trotted across to offer a lick of congratulation.

With the engine warm, Guy retorqued the head and set off for a test drive, his canine navigator perched on the passenger seat on one wing, fur rippling in the breeze. They bumped over to where Jack, Letitia and Esme were putting in some new fencing.

'Hmm,' remarked Jack, suitably impressed at yet another gleaming machine, 'two patients back to health in three days. Thank you, Dr Guy. I'd celebrate with champagne, but lentil soup is all I can offer!'

'You all need to know how to service and maintain the tractors and machinery,' remarked Guy over lunch, 'because I'll be going back to the Army soon. Let me fettle everything, then I'll teach you the basics.'

Jack nodded approvingly.

Over the next couple of weeks, Guy stripped and reassembled every item of machinery, blessing Norman for his meticulous set-up with all the manuals, as for Guy, many were new territory. Colonel was not quite so keen on this, as most items could not be hauled into the workshop and had to be worked on in the draughty barn. Being a canny dog though, he always managed to find a perch in a sheltered spot.

On the Friday, Guy moved some corn stooks in one corner of the barn and was startled to find a headlamp protruding through the stack. Further access was impeded by the thresher, so his next move was to ask Jack when the latter strode back for lunch.

'Oh, the Bradford, you mean?' said his host. 'It wouldn't start one day, I couldn't figure it out, so I pushed it into the barn. I keep it taxed and insured so I can claim petrol for it,' he grinned mischievously.

'What's a Bradford?' asked Guy.

'A Jowett van,' came the response.

Guy hauled the thresher out of the way and exhumed the van. Using the battery from Jack's Hillman, he tried to start it, but it was dead. The cause was soon found, the drive to the distributor had sheared, or rather the pin holding the gear to the shaft.

Offering prayers of thanks to Norman, Guy swiftly turned a new pin on the lathe using a piece of 6 inch nail. With the distributor working and timed, the Jowett rumbled to life. By midday on Saturday, the Jowett had joined the ranks of the those revived by Guy Duplessis.

'Right, Chief Engineer, time to enjoy yourself.'

Guy looked up from his tea.

'There's a dance every Saturday night in the Exeter Guildhall,' offered Jack. 'Why don't you take the Bradford and go into town?'

Firmly wrapped against the cold, Guy headed the little van into the night. The Bradford boasted a heater, but even at full bore, it wafted mere vestiges of warmth to the cab occupants. Driving along the twisting lanes was not easy either, as the mere slits of light demanded by blackout regulations did not encourage fast driving.

Guy had a rough idea where to find the Guildhall and parking the Bradford in a sidestreet nearby, navigated both to and inside the municipal building. A number of people, mostly in uniform, were standing around in the foyer and the sounds of strict tempo could be heard through the double doors at the rear. Guy pushed open a door and entered.

Three things hit him at once. The first was the band giving it all they had got; the second was the babel of sound from several hundred people talking and laughing; the third was an almost impenetrable blanket of cigarette smoke stretching from the ceiling down to nearly head height.

The dance had been going for an hour and was now in full swing. The five-piece band was giving its rendition of 'Blue Moon', the dance floor was heaving with Saturday night revellers determined to have a good time or bust in the attempt. What little air remained was overwhelmed by the cigarette fug and the smell of British beer was almost overpowering.

Guy elbowed his way to the bar through British, French, Belgian, American and Polish uniforms of every service and both sexes and ordered a pint. Once again, he found himself drawn to this frothy and almost warm liquid and he spent a quarter of an hour or so just sipping his pint and surveying the scene. It was indeed a babel, a wide variety of languages and accents competing with each other in an oft vain attempt to be heard, let alone understood.

He vaguely remembered his dancing lessons, when as a gawky youth he had tangoed and waltzed with equally gauche teenage girls from his Lycée. He was downing the last of the Devenish, when he was grabbed unceremoniously by a blonde Wren and hauled onto the dance floor. Thawed a little by the beer, he tangoed not badly and waltzed quite well, but a valeta proved too much and he returned to the bar. The Wren and her gang were made of sterner stuff and Guy found himself drawn into their party.

''Aven't seen you 'ere before,' remarked blondie. 'I'm Doris, that's Maisie, Sally and Moira,' waving her hand over her companions.

'Guy, I'm on leave,' explained Guy.

'Lucky bugger, wish I was,' was the slightly tart response of Sally, a tall and pretty girl who looked so outwardly demure that rude words never left her lips.

Guy plucked up his courage.

'Would you like to dance, Sally?'

It was a foxtrot, another in the Duplessis can-dance repertoire, so Guy acquitted himself well.

'There's Larry,' cooed Doris, seeing a rather pimply youth in Royal Navy bellbottoms sidling past. 'Ere, Larry, come an' join the party.'

Larry duly obliged and for an hour or so, they drank and danced and discussed the fortunes of war. Beer flowed, with Guy somewhat nonplussed to find women quaffing pints. Where he came from, ladies drank wine.

The girls announced suddenly that they had to get back to camp and left. Guy wandered towards the bar and struggled in the crush to get served. Pint in hand, he was moving towards a corner to observe the scene. From nowhere, a private three sheets to the wind crashed into Guy's back. In horror, Guy watched as in slow-motion, the top third of his pint detached itself from his glass and arced with pin-point accuracy into the lap of a ATS lieutenant. Completely oblivious to the havoc he had just caused, the private careered drunkenly into the melee and out of sight.

'I'm s-s-so sorry, it was that oaf crashing into me.'

Crimson with embarrassment, Guy proffered his clean hanky and stammered his apologies. The ATS girl looked up and laughed.

'Par for the course here on a Saturday,' she commented, then used Guy's hanky and her own to swab off the worst.

Whilst she was cleaning her skirt, Guy looked at her and liked what he saw immensely. Slim, medium height, an oval face, very kissable lips. Dark hair in a chignon, coupled with light green eyes with little flecks and smile lines at the corners. The ATS uniform usually looked shapeless and unflattering on even the prettiest girl, but it really looked good on her. She had small hands and short fingers and Guy felt almost guilty as he checked to see that there were no rings.

Swabbing over, the girl stood up and surveyed the rather damp stain.

'Looks as though I've wet myself!' she commented, completely unabashed at such a direct remark. 'Angela Walker.' She proffered a hand.

'Guy Duplessis. Can I buy you a drink to say sorry?'

'Half of bitter,' said Angela, 'but in a glass, not on my skirt!'

Leaving the remains of his beer with Angela for safe keeping, Guy fought his way to the counter and managed to return with most of the half pint still in the glass.

The noise level had by now risen to the cacophonous and the fug was sinking steadily lower. Guy indicated with his hand that they should move outside and Angela nodded acquiescence. The double doors to the foyer swinging to behind them was like turning a switch. The noise suddenly abated, the hot and sweaty atmosphere was replaced by cool, clear air. Finding a place to sit was easy as by this hour, the foyer was almost deserted. They deposited themselves on a carved oak bench bearing a plaque in remembrance to some former municipal worthy.

Sipping his drink, Guy looked at Angela and found himself abruptly uncomfortable under her clear and direct gaze as she summed up her companion. British clothes had been substituted for Guy's French ones, but he still exuded a slightly Continental air, notwithstanding his faultless and accentless southern English.

A faint pink tinge in Angela's cheeks acknowledged Guy's discomfort at being put under her microscope.

'I'm in charge of a whole bunch of ATS girls based at one of the Army camps here,' she volunteered, 'been in Exeter two years.' 'You?'

Instinctively, Guy knew he could trust her, but still came out with his cover story, carefully rehearsed with Lionel until he was word-perfect.

'Lieutenant Duplessis at your service.'

He half-rose and gave a tiny mock bow.

'I'm from Halifax originally, just on a few weeks leave and staying with friends about ten miles away. Jack's a farmer still firmly entrenched in the shire horse era, I've been fixing up his tractors.'

He smiled ruefully at his oil-stained cuticles.

'Hmm, you don't sound like a Yorkshire tyke,' commented Angela, knowing instinctively he was lying.

The poster on the foyer wall declaring that 'Careless talk costs lives' was a stark reminder for her not to enquire further.

'Went to school in Epsom, lass, so my vowels are straw boater rather than cloth cap,' he joked.

The more he looked at Angela, the more Guy felt a powerful attraction. Despite the music hall image of every French male as some lusty Lothario, the reality was that most young men of Guy's age were as unversed in the art of courting as their British counterparts. Guy had been out on a few dates with local girls, but apart from a bit of furtive groping in the back row, he had no sexual experience.

For the second time that night, Guy plucked up his courage.

'Angela, would you like to come out with me next Saturday night?'

'I thought you'd never ask,' she teased and instantly regretted the joke as Guy blushed to the roots of his hair.

'Can I give you a lift back to camp?'

Angela nodded vigorously. Parking their empty glasses under the bench, they strolled into the chill night and back to the van. Guided by Angela, Guy picked his way carefully through dark and empty streets to the camp three miles outside town. When fifty yards from the gates, Angela motioned him to stop.

'I like to keep my private life private,' she explained as he braked to a halt.

For a brief second, their eyes met across the cab, then her trim figure was gone and moving swiftly towards the waiting sentry boxes.

Guy navigated his way back into Exeter and after a few wrong turns, remembered the road to the farm. Suddenly, he was on Cloud 9, the mere thought of next Saturday offering an as yet unexplained frisson of pleasure.

The tinny alarm penetrated the tunnels of sleep, Sunday was yet another working day.

With one tractor now fit for hard duty, Jack taught Guy how to plough. Clad in his Finnish parka and one of Jack's ratting caps, Guy set his teeth against a horizontal sleet and moved slowly up and down the field, the screaming of gulls that had appeared from nowhere an incessant accompaniment to the throbbing of the engine. Muffled in his little coat, Colonel was curled up on the passenger seat, back to the wind and nose in paws. Dark clouds carrying the sleet and threatening snow raced across the Devon skyline and despite the cold, Guy felt relaxed and at peace with himself. Meal breaks had to be taken outdoors as the field was quite far from the house. Easing his body stiffly from the seat, Guy sat with his back to a wall to shelter from the wind and shared his flask of soup and his sandwiches with the ever-peckish terrier.

Lunch over, the pair had a ten minute stroll to restore circulation before cranking the engine to life once more. As darkness began to settle over the hills, Guy surveyed his day's work, delighted to find that his initial wavy lines were now arrow-straight. He rumbled back to a warm fire, supper and his bed.

Ploughing was followed by chain-harrowing, then seeding. The tractor-mounted drill made the job so much easier and Guy blessed Harry Ferguson and his ingenious system. By now, the young officer's strained pallor had left, a ruddy glow suffused his cheeks and the plain but nourishing food was returning weight to his spare frame.

To Guy, Saturday was an endless day, but at last he parked the tractor and put on what Esme called his 'gladrags' ready for his date.

'Cor, Jack,' remarked Esme as Guy walked into the kitchen spruced-up and ready to go. 'Oo's this 'andsome fella, 'ain't seem 'im before?'

'Got an 'ot date darlin'?' she enquired of Guy and was rewarded with yet another Duplessis blush that answered her question in one.

'Leave the poor chap be, Esme,' remonstrated Mary.

Totally unfazed, Esme just cackled and rose to switch on the huge wireless in one corner of the room.

Once again, he wound carefully through the lanes and with accurate dead reckoning, found a parking slot outside the cinema where he had arranged to meet Angela. Scarcely had he set the handbrake than Angela appeared, huddled in her greatcoat for protection against the biting wind. Guy was out of the van in a trice and arm in arm, they exchanged the cold of the street for the warmth of the auditorium.

The film was some war epic starring Audie Murphy, but Guy scarcely noticed the screen, so happy was he to be sitting beside Angela. Innately, he sensed that she felt just the same and it was not long before her tiny hand crept into his broad paw.

The film over, they followed the pungent and inviting aroma of fish and chips to a shop fifty yards away. The temperature had dropped still further while they had been in the cinema, the wind keening down the narrow street and knifing through Angela's coat and Guy's anorak to their very bones. Gasping from the cold, they reached the sanctuary of the batter-laden heat of the chip shop.

Two ladies, obviously sisters and clad in identical turbans exuding the scent of their trade, presided at the zinc counter. Behind them, four large fryers crackled with hot oil, pumping a torrid haze into the shop and hissing as the fish were immersed.

'Yes, my duck?'

'Rock salmon and chips and...?' Guy looked enquiringly at Angela.

'The same please, Guy.'

They took their supper, tastefully gift-wrapped in yesterday's Daily Mirror and ran for cover in the Jowett, giggling like children.

The cab stank of fish and chips, salt and vinegar. Guy and Angela licked their fingers like cats washing their paws and wiped off the final remains with the newspaper.

'Funny, isn't it,' said Angela, 'that fish and chips only tastes really good out of newspaper?'

She looked across at Guy, who nodded agreement, blissfully happy.

Unbidden, Guy started the engine and motored out to a country pub he had spotted when returning Angela to camp the previous week. The pub offered a blazing fire and a well-kept bitter. Clutching their glasses, the couple found seats next to a foursome of French army NCOs, who were chattering away about the goings-on in France.

Guy's rapt attention as he hung on their every word hit Angela like a slap in the face. That he clearly understood and empathised with them was equally obvious. He suddenly came to, realising that Angela was staring at him intently. Yet again, Angela witnessed the Duplessis blush. Seeing that the snug had just emptied, Guy took Angela's elbow and guided her to its privacy.

They sat down beside one another and for a few seconds there was silence as Guy collected himself and his thoughts. What he was about to do was against everything Lionel had drummed into him, but somehow his trust of Angela was complete and utter. Sensing his misgivings, a small hand once more crept into his. The closeness of Angela, the soft fragrance of her skin, her very proximity buoyed up his courage and he began to speak.

'As you've noticed, I speak French as well as English because my father was English and my mother French, I'm completely bilingual English/French.'

Angela made no comment, but her face and a little squeeze invited Guy to continue.

Slowly, in almost a déjà vu of the discussion with the two Hs in St Malo, Guy recounted the tale of the raid, the death of his parents and how he had stabbed the German. Several times he had to pause, sipping his beer to bolster his train of thought. Angela sat mute, sensing more to come and unwilling to break the spell. Guy recounted his escape through France, the horrors, the fear, the loneliness. When he was finished, there was both a silence and a new, unspoken bond between them.

Angela was the first to break the silence.

'They want you to go back as an agent, don't they?'

A nod. At that moment, they fell hopelessly in love.

Guy drove slowly back towards the camp, but stopped well before and out of sight of the sentries. He and Angela gazed at each other for a mere second, then they were in each other's arms, mouths locked one against the other. Guy could taste her lipstick, taste the deliciousness of her. He stroked the fragrant cheeks, nuzzled her ear, ran his fingers through her hair. Angela responded with deep-seated passion, stroking his head in her turn and they were as one.

In the next two weeks, the couple met as often as they could and as time and duties would allow. Neither had ever been so happy. Angela recounted growing up in Worthing with her parents and an older sister Joyce, such a joyful, carefree childhood.

'Where's Joyce now?' asked Guy.

'She's in the ATS, too, based up in Glasgow, driving 3-tonners, we rarely see each other.'

'Daddy's in the Home Guard, works for Barclays by day and totes a Lee-Enfield by night, Mummy's in the WVS.'

One Saturday evening, Angela came out to the farm to be warmly welcomed into the bosom of the Welch family. Colonel thought she was the bee's knees and declared undying friendship by plonking himself firmly on her lap and refusing to move. Angela returned the affection, stroking the little dog and tickling his ears.

On Sunday evening, Guy came in for supper to find Jack sitting alone in the kitchen looking uncomfortable and glum. He avoided Guy's eyes.

Jack cleared his throat.

'Lionel rang earlier, he's coming for you a week tomorrow.'

Guy's heart seemed to miss a beat. It was like going to the dentist – you managed to put it out of your mind and pretend it was not going to happen until the very moment you caught that first whiff of mouthwash and ether.

'What time?' he asked.

'Ten Ack Emma,' came the gruff reply, then Jack was gone, too embarrassed to stay longer.

Guy managed to get a message to Angela to ring him. An hour later, the phone jingled in the hall and Guy shot towards it as though jet-propelled.

'Darling, I'm going away a week tomorrow and I don't know when I'll be back.'

A mere fraction of silence, but a fraction more telling than many thousand words.

'So soon?'

Guy could hear the catch in Angela's throat.

Scarcely believing he was hearing himself, Guy went on, 'I'd like us to go away together next weekend, can you wangle a 48?'

There was a touch of breathlessness in her reply that spoke of love and longing and passion yet to come.

'I'll sweet-talk Colonel Grumpy, I'm sure I can fix it. Where are we going?'

'I rather thought you'd have a better idea of that than I would' chuckled Guy, 'I'm the foreigner, remember!'

'I know a nice little hotel in Lyme Regis, the Hart and Hind. I'll check it out and call you.'

An hour later, Angela rang with her 48, a booking at the Hart and Hind and some transport. Much as Jack was willing to lend the Jowett, he was short of petrol and the tractors had to come first.

Late morning next Saturday found Guy and Colonel at the farm gate awaiting Angela's arrival. They heard her coming long before she hove into view, the staccato hammer of a misfire bouncing off the banks of the lane as she negotiated the hill. Guy opened the gate to admit the Morris 8, which braked to stop in front of the farmhouse.

Angela alighted from the little car leaving the engine running, to find Guy creased up with laughter.

'What's so funny?'

Still laughing, Guy pointed at the car. So bad was the misfire, the Morris was bouncing on its springs in unison with the uneven firing and looked for all the world like a clown's car in a circus.

'Well,' remarked Guy, 'we're not going to get very far in that, my love, are we? Come on.'

Loading Angela and Colonel into the car, he drove round to the workshop and parking inside, left the engine running and opened the bonnet. In the otherwise dark room, his face and upper body were bathed in a cold blue St Elmo's fire as myriad sparks played hopscotch around the high tension leads and a rivulet of high voltage fire cascaded down a track mark in the distributor cap.

Captivated, Angela watched as her man deftly replaced the faulty leads from a roll of new cable and cleaned up the film of dirt on the plug tops and distributor. The engine ran almost as it should, but even after scraping the track mark with a file tang, Guy could not stop the current tracking down the cap. Inspiration came as he looked up from the engine bay and saw his lady's beautifully applied pink nail varnish.

'Have you got your nail varnish with you?'

Angela clamped her arms firmly around her handbag and hugged it to her in a defensive gesture as though Guy might snatch it from her grasp.

'Do you know how difficult it is getting nail varnish in wartime? Why do you want it, anyway?'

'I only need a smidgen,' replied Guy soothingly.

Reluctantly, Angela delved into her bag and produced the precious bottle. Guy removed the brush, wiped it on the neck of the bottle to reduce the amount of liquid, then carefully painted the remainder down the track mark.

'Right,' he said, returning the varnish to its rightful owner, 'just give it five minutes to dry.'

Sure enough, the trick worked and the now four-cylinder Morris bore away towards Lyme Regis with Guy at the wheel and Colonel ensconced on Angela's comfortable lap.

They drove slowly through the Devon lanes, savouring each other's company, sometimes chattering like excited schoolchildren but often tootling along in companionable and silent togetherness. Angela was glad of Colonel, the Morris had no heater. Despite her thick tweed coat, his hot doggy body was a welcome source of heat in the chill.

The landlord of the Lamb and Flag in the aptly named Beer smiled indulgently at the lovers as he served them Palmers ale and cheese sandwiches. They had eyes solely for each other and were almost oblivious to anyone or anything else around them.

After lunch, they sauntered along the coast, stopped for a long walk and let Colonel work off his excess energy. Beautiful as the coastline was, it was marred by barbed wire, tank traps and gun emplacements. Every lane that pre-war, had led to some glorious beach was now barred and 'Danger – Mines' notices proliferated. As darkness set in, they rolled into Lyme Regis.

The Hart and Hind lay in Church Street, a black and white structure that had stood since Elizabethan times. Guy slipped the car under the archway that led to the car park. Angela once more dived into her handbag and almost coyly, slipped a slightly too big wedding ring on her finger. She caught Guy's amused grin and had the grace to blush.

'We don't want to be thrown out now, do we?' she mocked.

The Reception was deserted. Guy rang the brass bell. The hotel had that smell peculiar to so many such establishments, an indefinable mixture of carpets, polish, old bacon and eggs and last night's beer.

Frances Smithson appeared from the back office and suppressed a smirk as Guy signed the register as Mr and Mrs Duplessis. Frances had seen many an assignation during her career, none more so than in this wretched war and she could tell an unmarried couple at a hundred paces. The number of Smiths that had registered at the hotel since 1940 far outnumbered all those in the London telephone book. Frances' view was simple, who was she to deny couples a little happiness when it might be their last?

Angela and Guy accompanied Frances to the room.

'Sorry about the cold, just put the gas fire on an hour before bed,' she advised. 'Dinner's at 7.00, I managed to get some lamb yesterday. Your dog is well-behaved, isn't he?'

Colonel did his party-piece soulful look and immediately melted the landlady's heart. The door clicked shut behind her.

Almost frightened that they were alone, the couple moved slowly into each other's arms, kissing and hugging themselves into confident mode before unpacking. The room even boasted an en suite bathroom, but as befitted everything in WWII, the water was cold.

Whilst waiting at Reception, Guy had picked up the crackle of an open fire, so they took themselves downstairs to thaw out over a couple of pints of Palmers for Guy and G&Ts for Angela. Colonel sprawled across the hearth and toasted his belly. The trio appeared to be the only guests.

Guy sat and looked yet again at Angela, basking in the glow of love and companionship. His lady was dressed simply in a dark green needlecord skirt and matching high-necked jumper. Her dark, straight hair framed her face and tiny gold droplet earrings were her only jewellery apart from the ill-fitting gold band on her third finger. She looked gorgeous.

'Dinner.' Frances' head appeared round the door of the bar. 'Would you like some wine?'

That she had any of the precious and scarce commodity was a miracle, but she produced a bottle of half-decent claret to accompany the tender and juicy roast lamb. Apple pie and Devon cream followed and the meal was rounded off with some local cheese and home-made biscuits. Good ol' Colonel was hauled off to the kitchens, from whence he returned some time later burping and grinning like a

Cheshire cat.

Feeling distinctly stuffed, Angela and Guy retired once more to the bar to let their meal settle over a couple of whiskies. Alone once more, they sat and gazed adoringly into each other's eyes and let the world go by. Guy remembered to light the gas fire in the bedroom in good time.

At about ten, they slipped unseen from the bar and headed for their room. Exhausted by his truly strenuous day, Colonel leapt on to the armchair and was in the land of Nod in seconds.

Guy moved towards the door and switched off the main light, leaving only the soft glow of the bedside lamp. Shyly, he pulled Angela towards him, cupping his hands on her bottom and pressing her closer. He was conscious of his own breath quickening and felt hers quickening too as the desire rose in both their bodies. Their mouths locked together and great waves of excitement and love and passion welled up in both of them.

Gently, Guy pressed Angela back onto the bed. His right hand slid beneath her sweater to caress and fondle her warm, firm breasts. Reaching behind her, he fumbled inexpertly with the catch of her bra. Angela obligingly arched her back a little to allow him more space. Even so, the catch continued to defy him until all of a sudden, it was free and the lacy garment was loose around Angela's shoulders. She sat up, sliding the green sweater over her head. As she did so, the bra fell to reveal sweet, white rounded breasts like young apples. Her small, dark nipples were erect and hard with desire.

Guy pressed her back down, kissing her with fiery intensity, his right hand teasing her nipples and stroking her whiteness. Ardently, she responded, sliding her own hand inside his trousers and marvelling at his hardness. Then she felt his touch inside her skirt, his fingers rippling over her nylons to find the softness of her inner thighs above. She moaned as he caressed her through the lace of her panties.

Desire was running through them both like a furnace. Sitting up, they helped each other to undress until Guy was naked and Angela was clad only in stockings and suspenders. Suffused with love, Guy found her. His touch was electric and Angela began to pant and moan under his delicious fingers.

'Now Guy, now' she whispered.

Slowly, carefully, he entered her and she let out a little cry as he took her virginity, then they were writhing in the glorious flames of a red-hot ardour as they rose higher and higher. Their climax was thunderous and incandescent, a long cry of ecstasy from Angela and an equal, near vulpine howl from Guy evidence of their mutual and intense satisfaction.

Exhausted, they collapsed into each other's arms, then snuggled beneath the eiderdown to slumber in a warm and loving embrace.

Twice more that night they loved and coupled, giggling as they found one another under the protective bedclothes, not daring to venture outside into the bedroom's frosty chill.

Dawn came to Lyme Regis and they were lovers once more, sleepy, sensuous, relaxed sex, finding joy one in the other.

Breakfast was at nine. At eight, Guy risked the savage iciness of the room to swiftly kindle the gas fire before leaping back under the goose feathers and the softness of Angela's arms.

Venturing into the bathroom, they found it unexpectedly warm from the heated towel-rail supplied by the hot water system. Scarcely believing their luck, they ran a bath and luxuriated in its radiance. Angela bathed first, then stood at the basin applying her makeup. Guy had never been a bath lounger and after a fairly swift dunk and a wash, sat on the edge of the bath behind her and facing the basin mirror. Angela, deeply immersed in the intricacies of mascara, could see him watching her and smiled. She saw his eyes, warm and love-filled, hit by a thunderbolt of imminent and uncontrollable desire. Then he was against her, cupping her breasts with his hands and his rock-hard erection pressing into the cleft in her buttocks.

Softly, he lowered her to the floor and took her. The million-volt electricity that surged between them peaked still once more and seconds later, they exploded into a breathless time-warp where time and the Second World War stood rock-still.

Resuming their respective places at basin and bath, Angela looked in the mirror to see an amused grin on Guy's face.

'And what,' she enquired in mock anger, 'is so damn funny?'

Guy pointed at her behind.

'Your bum has a tile pattern on it!'

His reward was a cold and soaking flannel, hurled with deadly accuracy.

They descended for breakfast, almost like a honeymoon couple after their wedding night, sure that their passion was writ large all over them. It was and Frances was hard-pressed to stay cool and professional when lading out the bacon and eggs and tea. It was patently obvious that she could have served them cardboard and vinegar, they were so lost in each other, they would not have noticed any difference.

'We want to go walking, can we leave the car in your car park?' enquired Guy as he settled the bill.

'Of course,' replied Frances, 'would you like some sandwiches?'

Guy and Angela nodded vigorously.

Swaddled against the rigour, they strode out on the hills above Lyme Regis, striding first north over springy turf then east towards Charmouth. The day was steely-grey after a hoar frost, a cloudless and even sky their panoply above a frozen and iron-hard ground. A light inshore breeze played on their cheeks and lips, adding to the chill factor but somehow welcome. That breeze brought with it the tang of sea and salt, of rotting seaweed, of tar, of that plethora of scents that epitomise being at the seaside.

Basking in each other's love, the couple were absorbed in themselves, the weather was of no consequence. They walked slowly hand in hand, savouring the companionship and the moment. Colonel raced first ahead then circling back, covering four times their distance. In seventh heaven in the still frosty grass, he snow-ploughed its whiteness with his nose, spraying a wake of icy droplets to either side of his nostrils and kicking up his heels in absolute delight.

Angela and Guy came to a halt at the top of the hill overlooking Charmouth. An old, splintered but relatively intact wooden bench stood on the summit and they sank on to this wintry seat and gazed out to sea. Two British destroyers glided eastwards across the slightly popply waters, black smudges from their grey funnels distinct against the uncertain horizon. Otherwise, there was nothing between the lovers and the coast of France.

Guy looked to see Angela staring hard out to sea as if willing the French coast to be visible over that horizon so that she could destroy it and prevent him going there. Knowing intuitively her exact thoughts, he drew Angela close to him, hugging, comforting, stroking her hair, kissing the top of her head. Thus they sat for half an hour in total silence and total communication.

Hot soup from the hotel's flask was followed by sandwiches from the previous night's lamb and two apples. There was even a separate little paquet for Colonel, marked with his name.

Half an hour of downhill brought them into Charmouth just before closing time and a pub whose fire reminded them of how cold it really was outside and how bitter beer can warm the cockles.

A hint of dusk was clearly apparent as they wended their way back to the Hart and Hind to return the flask and collect the Morris. This time, there was no meandering the lanes, the direct route to the farm was their agenda.

The journey was an almost completely silent one, thought waves saying everything they needed to say. Sensing the atmosphere, Colonel sat on Angela's lap, leaning his little body and head against her welcoming softness and giving her hand tiny licks from time to time.

All too soon, they were back at the farm. Guy climbed from the driving seat, willing this moment to last to the end of time and knowing it would not. Angela stood beside him, then they were in each other's arms, crushing, desperate, lip-pushing kisses, weeping uncontrollably at this unbearable parting.

'Take care Guy and come back to me safe.'

Angela's voice was but a whisper, sibilant and penetrating for all that. Guy nodded, too overcome to speak. Then Angela broke suddenly from his embrace and racing to the car, let out the clutch without a backward glance. Eyes filled with hot salty tears, she narrowly missed the gatepost on her way out, then she was gone.

For a long moment, Guy stood, hearing the little car descending the hill, the burble of its tiny engine somehow Angela's voice still talking to him. Then the sound was swallowed up in the lanes and complete silence reigned. Above him, a clear sky dappled with the merest speckles of starlight and nothing at all was moving. He could have been alone in a vast desert and at that moment, he did feel utterly alone and very afraid.

Colonel pawed his leg, indicating that he wanted a cuddle. Gathering the little bundle in his arms, Guy picked up his bag and walked slowly towards the farmhouse.

Chapter 7

Ten Ack Emma precisely. Lionel was as punctual as ever.

'Now Colonel, Mary will look after you and Angela will come to visit when she can, so be good until I return, huh?'

Making sure that Letitia and Esme were out of the way by sending them to the far side of the farm, Jack and Mary stood in the yard to say their goodbyes.

Jack thrust out one calloused mitt.

'Best of luck Guy, don't let the bastards grind you down.'

Mary could not speak, she just grabbed Colonel and kissed Guy warmly on both cheeks. Guy could not utter a word, afraid to open his mouth in case he broke down. Returning Mary's embrace and Jack's firm shake, he jumped into the car. Lionel shot off and was round the gate and out of sight before Guy had a chance to look back.

Once more the Rover headed east. Snow flurries blew intermittently across the windscreen and the vestiges of an icy sun peeped occasionally through the sleet. The car droned on. Toward late afternoon, Guy recognised the distinctive ferns and brackens of the New Forest and it was not long before Lionel was turning into the gates of a mansion. The sentry checked his pass, then raised the pole barrier. The Rover crunched up a long gravel drive and rolled to a stop opposite the main doors.

'OK,' said Lionel, 'this is where it all begins. You won't see me for quite a while, I'll introduce you to Simon.'

He pronounced Simon the French way.

Grabbing his bags, Guy trailed Lionel into the cool, dark hall. Alerted by the gate sentry, Simon was waiting for them. Dressed in British army fatigues with no badges of rank, Simon was somewhere in his forties, dapper, a little plump. Bald apart from a dark cowlick of hair brushed back over his pate, his only other facial hair was a droopy moustache hanging disconsolately over his upper lip. He stared at the world through bottle-bottom lenses in wire frames.

Before Simon uttered a syllable, Guy pegged him immediately as reeking 'French' and thought he looked like a university professor. Though he never actually found out, Guy was spot on. In peacetime,

Simon was indeed a professor of history at the Sorbonne.

Lionel introduced them in English.

'I'll leave you now, Guy, best of luck.'

Then Lionel was gone.

'OK, your codename from now on is Martin,' explained Simon rapidly in French, 'and you answer to no other. I'll introduce you to the other five on the course at dinner. Many of your instructors speak only English and you will have to speak English to them, but otherwise, speak, eat, drink, sleep, live only French. I'll show you to your room.'

He led Guy up the grand staircase to the second floor and opened the door to a comfortable room.

'Dinner's at seven, dining room is first right at the bottom of the stairs.'

Slowly, Guy unpacked and took in his surroundings. The house was probably late Georgian, all fine oak panelling and dark wood. His room was quite large, about fifteen feet square, with an ancient wooden bed complete with embroidered counterpane. A couple of stuffed armchairs, a heavy oak wardrobe and a writing table completed the furnishings. In one corner, a basin with hot and cold running water. Unpacking over, Guy ventured into the corridor and soon found a toilet and a bathroom, the latter's bath a Victorian monstrosity with huge claw feet and massive taps.

Regaining his room, Guy tested the basin, finding really hot water and freshened up before going downstairs on the dot of seven.

Three of his fellow would-be agents, two male and one female, were already sipping sherry and deep in conversation with Simon about the state of the war in France. Simon effected introductions. The girl's codename was Lysette, the two men Charles and Yves. Shortly they were joined by another man, introduced as Jean-Luc and another girl, Marianne.

Dinner was anything but French, a decidedly lumpy shepherd's pie followed by rice pudding. Guy was starving, so would have cheerfully eaten anything. As he chewed through the gristly meat, he observed his companions.

The most striking was undoubtedly Lysette, an absolutely stunning brunette in her twenties of medium height and a lissom figure to die for, complemented by perfect teeth and cherry-red lips that needed no lipstick. She looked terribly out of place, a soirée or a salon seemed rather more her style.

Marianne was brunette too, but everything about her was stubby.

Short and strongly built for a woman, she had short legs, short arms and short, spatulate fingers. Guy judged her to be around thirty.

Two of the men, Charles and Yves, were nondescript, thirty-ish, both with brown hair, medium build. They looked as if they could wear each other's clothes.

Jean-Luc was about the same height as Guy, but built like the proverbial brick shed. A square head sat on a short, bull-like neck, powerful shoulders and a muscular frame. Huge hands with fingers like bananas and Guy shuddered inwardly as he visualised them squeezing the life out of some errant German in months to come. 'Rugby man?' mused Guy. Unbeknown to Guy, Jean-Luc played prop forward for his local club.

Lysette, he could tell was English, as was Yves. Both spoke fluent French, but Guy's keen ear could detect the English accents. Charles he judged was from the Midi, Jean-Luc from Brittany and Marianne from somewhere near Paris.

Simon attracted their attention.

'Let me yet again repeat that you must not quiz each other about your true identities nor use anything but your codenames. Apart from when you have to, think French all the time.' He added dryly, 'Your lives will depend on it and so will the lives of your colleagues. After dinner, we will go to the stores and get you kitted up. You will be here about three weeks for basic training, squarebashing and PT to get you fit.'

'Let's go.'

Obediently, they followed him to a Nissen hut in the grounds, where they were issued with fatigues, shirts, underwear, socks, boots and combat clothing plus a tin hat and a gas mask. They were given PT clothing too, huge pairs of shorts of fabric so stiff that Guy feared the crutch might neuter him the first time he made any kind of movement.

'Good night, messieurs, dames, reveille's at 5am.'

Simon disappeared into the frosty night.

Guy was roused from a long tunnel of sleep by an insistent knocking at his bedroom door. Struggling to remember where he was, he heard a voice say, 'Outside the front door in PT kit in ten minutes.' Guy squeezed into shorts and PT vest, groping his way downstairs to be joined in quick succession by the other five. The shorts did feel impossibly stiff and the morning impossibly cold. An army PTI in a tracksuit appeared through the front door.

'Right, a nice five mile cross-country run to get those slack muscles working.' So saying, he set off at an impossible pace and apart from Jean-Luc, they wheezed after him.

Within seconds, razor-sharp daggers of icy air were slicing past Guy's oesophagus and stabbing him continually in the lungs, which could not inhale fast enough to supply his heaving chest. His legs felt like lead and refused to do what he told them and he staggered drunkenly along, wondering why the hell he had agreed to this. It was small consolation that the super-fit Jean-Luc apart, his fellows were in similar if not worse distress.

'Move that idle arse, Mr Martin sir,' bellowed the PTI from behind his left ear. In agony, Guy tried to comply.

After about ten minutes he found a modicum of second wind, but the forty-five minutes or so to complete the run were a living hell. As they approached the house once more, the PTI wheeled right towards another Nissen hut and they found themselves in the gym. If it were at all possible, the inside of the unheated hut was colder than the outside, but the PTI saw to it that nobody got hypothermia through inactivity. A brisk hour's running, jumping, vaulting and climbing ropes kept the corpuscles working. Even Jean-Luc was looking a little pale.

After a brief respite for ablutions, lumpy porridge, cardboard toast and tea the consistency of lubricant, they were told to don combat gear and join four other similar courses out on the parade square. For two hours, an RSM whose eyes were almost invisible beneath the peak of his cap screamed instructions and epithets in equal numbers, at various times calling into doubt their sanity, intelligence and parenthood.

Zombie-like, they collapsed into a classroom in the main house for a lecture on map-reading, followed by another on German aircraft recognition. Lunch was as big a culinary disaster as breakfast, then it was more drill, the assault course and a final burst of PT before they were allowed to stagger to their rooms. Fortunately, there were also shower rooms that Guy had missed, so they were able to wash away some of the cares of the day before descending to the bar. A couple of pints did much to restore flagging spirits, but dinner was inevitably thoroughly noxious, macaroni cheese with suet pudding as the coup de grace.

After three days, Guy was totally and utterly miserable. There was not a single bone, muscle or sinew in his body that was not screaming for mercy. He missed Angela with an ache that was physical and on several occasions, he had reached out his hand when in bed to ruffle Colonel's head normally propped against his knee to find nothing there.

As they entered the second week, the little group was beginning to shake down. Jean-Luc was the physical bear, who completed the assault course twice as fast as everyone else, then ran back to help those less capable. Marianne's unflinching diet of thirty Gauloises a day had done serious mischief to her breathing, so hard physical exercise was anathema. What she lacked in fitness, she made up for in brain, having a prodigious memory for aircraft silhouettes, armoured vehicles or German uniforms. Charles and Yves were excellent navigators and being dumped in some unfamiliar terrain at dead of night with just a map, a compass and several rendezvous points to make before dawn proved no obstacle.

Despite never having fired a gun in her life, Lysette was a natural shot. Within ten minutes of being shown how to handle a Lee-Enfield, she had grasped range and windage. Whenever there was rifle practice, she would sniff the wind, then instinctively offset the muzzle to score bull after bull.

True to his mechanical instincts, Guy shone at stripping and reassembling weapons, often doing a Jean-Luc for his fellows who managed to get bolts, springs and firing pins in a dreadful tangle.

By the end of three weeks, they were all a great deal fitter, even Marianne who, reconciled to the fact that fags and fitness were strange bedfellows, gave up the weed entirely.

On Friday evening, Simon took them to one side before dinner.

'OK,' he said, 'you've all done well enough to move on to the next stage. Coach leaves here 0700 tomorrow for Southampton station, we're going up to Scotland.'

As if to mock them, dinner was a very respectable roast beef with all the trimmings and a trifle itself three parts pissed on the sherry in it.

The west coast of Scotland has a reputation for a mild climate, but someone had forgotten to remind the weather of what it was supposed to be.

For five wet, raw and unforgettable weeks, they learned unarmed combat and silent killing, boat handling, shooting with pistols and sub-machine guns, using and field-stripping British, German and American weapons and elementary Morse. When shown how to kill with a knife, Guy realised that unwittingly, he had stabbed the Gefreiter in exactly the vital spot.

Much of the course was devoted to explosives and Guy was reacquainted with the curious substance he had seen in the Gounon's attic all those months ago.

'Right, can I have your attention?'

Their explosives instructor paused only to lift a thick rope of a putty-like substance from around his neck before continuing.

'This is plastic explosive, very powerful but very safe unless fired with a detonator.'

To prove his point, he laid the rope on the desk in front of him and hefting a 2lb lump hammer from behind the desk, smashed it down on the explosive. Everyone else in the room tensed ready to fling themselves floorwards at the certain Armageddon, but barring a large square crater in the plastic, nothing had changed.

Guy had been briefed on the explosives man by the Commando sergeant who taught silent killing.

'Shit-hot sir, shit-hot, our Mr Rogers, but nothing less than 110% effort from everybody will satisfy him.'

The room of the large Scottish country house in which they sat was pretty cold, but Guy soon forgot the chill, fascinated and absorbed by Daniel Rogers' teaching and fired by the instructor's obvious enthusiasm and love of his craft.

'The beauty of this stuff is that you can carry it concealed by moulding it inside say, your suitcase. When you reach your target, you can shape it round the crucial points so it becomes that much more effective.'

Daniel was getting into his stride.

'Detonators.'

He stuck a hand inside his left breast pocket and dug out a slim metal tube which he waved at his audience.

'Pencil detonator, chemical, varying time delays according to type.'

Laying the detonator on the desktop, he reached down and produced a black, square box with a handle protruding from the top which he proceeded to lift and twist sharply.

'Electric.'

Rummaging in the desk's middle drawer, he displayed yet another type, a clockwork timer.

'OK, now for some practical work,' said Daniel, 'we're off to the beach.'

The dozen would-be explosives experts piled into a waiting 3-tonner outside and bumped their way along a rutted and stony track which meandered down through the cliffs. The beautiful and once deserted sands were no longer deserted, their beauty defiled by the

114

hulks of various British and German tanks, AFVs and self-propelled guns.

For two hours, Daniel first explained then demonstrated how to use plastic to its best effect, the weak points of each kind of vehicle and how to make the most of the least explosive. Joined by another instructor, the agents then tried it for themselves, plastering the grey material like some lethal modelling clay around tracks and gun barrels, then setting it off using a variety of detonators.

Some of the class incurred Daniel's wrath because they simply did not listen to what they were told, but Guy had found his metier and took great satisfaction in blowing large lumps off the hulks using only a modicum of material.

Once they had learned how to wreck armoured vehicles, they moved on to railways, detonating old carriages, trucks and lengths of track at a nearby disused siding.

They were walking back from the sidings along a woodland path flanking a shallow river.

'Hmm,' remarked Daniel as they passed a pool, 'I think a nice bit of salmon would go down well Ron, don't you?'

His fellow instructor said not a word and Guy's curiosity as to how they would catch any fish without tackle was soon rewarded when Ron dug into his rucksack, kneaded a tiny lump of plastic into a ball and plugged in a detonator. Plastic lobbed into the pool, a dullish thud, then three fair-sized fish floated the surface. Willing hands used osier braches to pull their prize to shore.

'Not sure the laird would approve of our dynamite fishing,' grinned Ron.

At this, a strange light appeared in Daniel's eyes.

'His lairdship can go fuck himself,' he declared stoutly, 'there's a war on'.

If Guy was delighted with his skills with explosives, he was sorely disappointed with his Morse. For a man so deft, he became all fingers and thumbs and whilst his fellows progressed to a steady stream of dits and dahs, he could manage only a staccato, ragged transmission. The instructor, a CPO naval telegraphist, was fortunately a man of immense patience. Time and again, he demonstrated to Guy how to hold the Morse key and operate it. Much like his forebear with the loom, Guy felt he would never master it as he watched the key come alive in the Navy NCO's hand.

'Just let it come to you, sir,' advised his mentor, 'don't tense up, that's the secret.'

Guy tried once more, but it was as if he was wearing a boxing glove, so inept was he.

Two days later, he sat once more in front of the Morse key. At first, it was the same story, a hesitant, unsteady 'hand'. Guy stopped, took a few deep breaths and let his body go limp for a few moments. Then he tried again. On the other side of the room, the ever-patient telegraphist had his back to Guy and had been sighing inwardly at the haphazard rattle from the young man's key. Now he spun round, amazed and delighted at the even and regular notes of Guy's Morse.

'Told you sir, just let it come to you, didn't I?'

He was answered by a wide Duplessis grin.

*

'OK girls and boys, time to put all those new-found skills to good use. You're going to mount a mock attack.'

Once again, Simon was briefing them, huddled around a huge log fire in the Scottish mansion. He handed each of them a large brown envelope.

'Details in your envelope, you'll have until tomorrow night to work out a plan, then we take the train south, attack's that night. Nobody must leave this house from now on and all the doors are guarded, but you'll be able to rehearse in the grounds, bonne nuit.'

Yves was the first to speak after Simon's departing back disappeared through the oak doors of the lounge and the lock clicked shut.

'Can I suggest we each read what's in our envelopes, then decide what we want to do?'

Nods of assent were followed by the rustling of paper and furrowed brows for the next half hour.

As if on cue, they all looked up. Guy raised his hand.

'I don't know about you, but I need time to absorb all this, make some notes and come up with some suggestions. Can we meet here again at 6am tomorrow and start pulling it all together?'

More nods, then bed.

Once more, Guy stared at the sheets in front of him on the counterpane. One of the sheets contained a layout of some docks, where they were he did not know. The objective of their raid was to destroy the pumping mechanisms of the large dry-dock at the eastern end of the complex. The briefing sheets were very comprehensive, complete with scales, guard rosters and frequencies, photographs of

116

the pump houses and machinery and a weather forecast. With considerable relief, Guy noted it would be well below freezing, snow flurries and completely overcast. Because these details were patently real, every sheet was numbered and stamped 'Top Secret'.

Dawn was scarcely thinking about making a start when they reassembled in the lounge, but the fire had been laid after they had retired and a cheerful blaze soon raised temperatures and spirits. An armed guard appeared as they came downstairs and once they were all inside the lounge, they heard the lock click. A blackboard, chalk, paper and pencils, even a stopwatch had been provided in their absence and soon the air hummed with ideas. The briefing notes had specified a landward approach.

In essence, the plan they hatched was simple. Climb the dock walls at a conveniently low point near the main gate, a point sheltered from view where the wall turned at right angles, work eastwards using the cover of warehouses and timing the guards, then split into two pairs, one per pumphouse, with Jean-Luc and Yves as sentries. The rules allowed for knocking guards out, but nothing rougher. Guy and Marianne on Pumphouse 1, Lysette and Charles on No 2. Each pair contained one native English speaker as they guessed correctly that the guards might have strong regional accents.

Simon appeared about elevenish to see how they were progressing and to advise them of the pile of kit in the hall to mock up the attack zone. With their scheme committed to memory, they used string and pegs to recreate the docks near the assault course, whose wall conveniently served as just that for the rehearsal. Time after time, they ran through their paces, with Jean-Luc and Yves as observers and timekeepers. All too soon, they were ordered to dismantle the mock-up and on returning to the lounge, found Simon first counting, then shredding and burning all their papers. Two MPs, one male and one female, strip-searched each in turn to ensure nothing incriminating was still in their possession.

The weather forecast had been right. The wind screamed over Birkenhead docks, whipping snow and sleet in their faces and penetrating every loose stitch in their battledress. Despite a towelling scarf around his neck, Guy shivered as yet another icy rivulet coursed between his shoulder blades. Cold it might have been, but it provided perfect cover for a raid. Apart from the sound of the wind itself, rattling doors, windows and roof panels drowned out any inadvertent noises from the attackers. As a bonus, guards were far more intent on keeping warm than serving His Majesty.

Stealthily, the six glided over the wall and hugging the walls of the buildings, slid rapidly towards their targets. Despite the inclement weather, the mobile guards patrolled ceaselessly, but the timings in the briefing notes were spot on and after a fraught half hour, Guy and co were ready to pick the locks of their respective pumphouses. But it was then that the decision to have a native English speaker on each pair proved invaluable. Even Guy found the impenetrable Scouse accent almost impossible to understand, but he did grasp that chummy was dying for a slash and was coming round to where Marianne was in full lock-pick mode to relieve Mafeking. Pausing only to check that Jean-Luc and Yves were out of sight, Guy grabbed Marianne's elbow and rushed her in the opposite direction to the bladder-emptier and round the corner of the pumphouse. Heart hammering, Guy prayed that Mafeking would return from whence he came; he did.

Marianne and Guy eased inside the pumphouse and relocked the door. Unable to show a light, they had memorised the photographs of the interior and worked their way down the steel staircase by touch. The pumphouse reeked of cold steel machinery, oil and slightly manky water. Once at the bottom of the steps, they felt their way around the giant pumps, put two dots of white paint to signify where they would have packed explosives and crept up to the exit once more. Hearing nothing, they slid noiselessly through the door, locked it and looked around for Jean-Luc. Jean-Luc greeted them like long-lost brothers and together they found Yves, but there was no sign of Lysette and Charles. Leaving the others in concealment, Guy tried the door, but found it locked. He rejoined his fellows. After what seemed like an age, in reality three minutes, Jean-Luc's keen ear detected the sound of the pick-lock even above the howling wind and within seconds, six attackers were on their way out. Once again, an errant sentry came within inches of them and Guy was convinced the sound of his heart must give them away, but the man passed by oblivious to the nearness of their presence.

The day after the mock raid found them in a remote corner of Ringway airfield, with Lysette dangling in a parachute harness from the arm of the simulator frame and being lowered swiftly towards the ground to learn how to land without breaking anything.

When they had all learned to forward roll, adjust their rigging lines and do their safety checks, it was time for their first practice jump. As the DC3 rolled towards the runway threshold, a clammy knot of fear tightened in Guy's stomach. Looking at his fellow parachuting virgins, he was not alone in his trepidation. Having flown a number of times when going on holiday, Guy was of the immutable opinion that the only way to exit an aircraft was by a set of steps.

The Dak bellowed its way to jumping altitude, the cheery Flight Sergeant despatcher using the climbout to make sure his protégés were safely buckled in, then attaching the static lines to each one. A waved hand from the co-pilot indicated that they were coming to the dropping zone. The despatcher unlatched a door near the tail and above the roar of the slipstream, indicated that they should line up. Anybody having second thoughts stood no chance. The despatcher just hurled each pupil out the door with nary a second's pause between bodies.

There was a mighty snatch of crutch straps and a loud crack, then Guy was floating above Tatton Park, relieved and delighted to find he was not to die just yet. More drops followed, including night-drops from a Whitley bomber, an aircraft in common use for agent work. To Guy's relief, all the jumps were static line and his 'chute worked perfectly every time.

Before leaving Ringway, they were all taught the Lysander roll. The high-winged monoplane used to deliver and collect agents had a ladder permanently attached to the port side. If the pilot was forced to make a quick landing and getaway, his passenger had to leap from a moving aeroplane – hence the roll. Quite a few bruises and a sprained ankle for Marianne later, they were all quite proficient.

Green ferns and golden brackens of the New Forest welcomed them back to the south of England, to yet another country pile at East Boldre. Suddenly it was all terribly serious. Clandestine techniques, walking round in Southampton and London spotting and losing tails, when to change addresses, how to conceal a personality.

Guy found himself in the dentist's chair having his fillings inspected. All of his were the real French McCoy, but the Brits had all theirs changed for French amalgams and so did Jean-Luc, having had one new filling since fleeing to Britain.

Lysette had a new coiffure every bit as soignée as her old, but clearly French not British.

Being totally and utterly French in every way was drummed into them like a catechism. One evening, they were sitting at dinner when Simon, once more their mentor, held up his hand.

'There's something wrong, what is it?' he demanded.

Guy thought he knew.

'Lysette and Yves aren't eating the French way?'

'Exactement!' came Simon's rejoinder. 'They'll spot you a mile off and for Christ's sake, remember that the French authorities sympathetic to the Germans outnumber the Germans.'

Another morning, Simon announced dictation and dictated a shortish passage in French. Guy immediately clicked that it contained numbers and common French abbreviations. Simon collected their papers and pinned them to a board. He scanned the writings and satisfied with the content of each one, pulled the board centre stage. Guy's, Charles, Marianne's and Jean-Luc's appeared very much alike, but the totally British round hands of Lysette's and Yves' stuck out like a sore thumb against the other three's cursive continental script. Intensive lessons for Lysette and Yves in writing French-style followed.

Despite Simon's fiat not to talk about themselves to each other, there was inevitably some chatter, from which Guy learned that F Section was supposed to recruit only French-speaking British nationals, with French citizens going to the Gaullists. Someone, somewhere, had pulled some strings to recruit Guy and three of his fellows. Or ignored the rules.

They learned codes and deciphering, how to memorise and use a poem as authentication, how they would be assigned an operator who could recognise their Morse 'hand' and be able to tell if they were transmitting under duress.

At 3am one morning, Guy found himself hauled from his bed, bundled down to a freezing cellar and interrogated by two SS officers in uniform on the cover story he had learned that afternoon. Although tense and nervous, he kept his cool and was unshakeable, despite the test bringing immediate and stark memories of the drubbing he had received on arrival in Britain. They kept at it for eight long hours, switching to English at times to try and catch him out, but he stuck resolutely to French and gave nothing away.

Totally drained by his ordeal, Guy fell into bed and slept the clock round, but was dragged from his reverie by the familiar face of Lionel at the end of his bed. The officer's presence brought an immediate sense of foreboding. In response to Guy's quizzical eyebrow, Lionel came straight to the point.

'Normally, you'd have a spot of leave before going live, but we just don't have the time. You're ready now and we have a problem in the Le Mans area. The local network was blown ten days ago, got everyone but one cell.' Lionel paused, a very pregnant pause. 'We think there could be a Quisling still in what's left of the reseau. We need you to get in there, recreate things and try and winkle out any traitor.'

Still it did not make sense to Guy. Sure, a blown reseau was problem, but a delay of a few days or even weeks would make little difference.

'So, why the rush Lionel?'

'Well, you know that SOP is that you have ID and ration card, but you keep moving address and nobody knows your real name and where you live?'

A nod.

'Well, because of your background and circumstances in Le Mans, we have a unique opportunity to infiltrate you into a real job that allows you to wander around freely. You know the seed industry and André Lavallois in Le Mans runs a seed merchants and flour millers. His salesman left a month ago. On our instructions, André has been making and taking fake phone calls in the hearing of his staff and agreed with you to start immediately. We debated this long and hard, but we feel that having you legitimately embedded outweighs the risks of you being openly known. My only advice is that you should only ever take part in live operations if you feel the risk is justified.'

'When?'

'Tomorrow night, parachute drop.'

He saw Guy wince.

'Not your favourite, is it? Oh, by the way, I'll be your handler, so learn your poem for me.'

Guy drifted back to sleep, to be woken the next morning by a cup of strong black coffee, swiftly followed by breakfast on a tray.

The batman came to clear the tray and said, 'Once you're dressed, please go to the RT room, Sir.'

Guy did as he was bidden and was asked to record his 'hand' in Morse once more for his operator. Then Lionel appeared and spent six hours briefing him on his mission and the lie of the land. Guy had memorised a poem by Keats, which he passed to Lionel. What happened next was a bit like the dentist's waiting room. Guy was taken to a room, ordered to strip naked and handed a dressing gown, then led to another room containing his French clothes and possessions. Alone once more, he dressed, feeling strange to be in French clothes for the first time in ages. A small suitcase on the bed held his personal effects. Another case held a radio.

A guard led Guy downstairs, where Simon sat with Lionel and together, they checked Guy's papers, possessions and radio and ensured one last time that he carried nothing out of place.

'Bonne chance,' came from Simon, then he was gone.

Silently, Guy and Lionel climbed into the staff car, which ground away towards RAF Tangmere. The guard at the gate was expecting them and after checking Lionel's ID, waved them through. The driver made straight for dispersal. Gleaming dully in the light of a jumper's moon, the silhouette of a Halifax stood out against the night sky. As the car approached, the starboard engines rumbled to life, swiftly followed by the port, steadying to an even idle as the engineer adjusted the controls. Lionel spoke briefly.

'There'll be others aboard tonight, bit of a school bus job. Speak to nobody. Good luck, I know you won't spoil the show.'

He gripped Guy's hand momentarily, then turned away and climbed back in the car, which immediately pulled away.

The whirling propellers peppered Guy with frost-flecks as he clambered into the dank fuselage, then the jump-master latched the door and spoke quickly into his headset. The Halifax carried out cross-wind power checks, then lumbered towards the threshold of the runway. On parachute jump seats inside the dimly-lit bomber sat three men, all dressed in French clothes and carrying small cases. They smiled to accord Guy's presence, but instructed to say nothing, exchanged not a word. Parcels containing various items for all the agents were stacked in the fuselage, ready to be dropped with each man.

The plane smelt exactly like the DC3 used on the training jumps, metallic, vaguely damp and with a strong odour of hydraulic oil. A cold knot of terror gnawed at Guy's stomach at the thought of jumping and his bowels shook. The bomber stopped on the threshold as the pilot wound it up against the brakes. Every rivet and sinew of the airframe shook and vibrated, the noise was deafening. Brakes off, rolling, gathering pace, then merciful peace as the beast unstuck and started to climb gently. Soon, the throttles were eased and the plane made French landfall at low level.

Guy was first out. With ten minutes to go, the jump-master fed Guy a rum hot-toddy, then attached his 'chute, cinching the straps, attaching a static line and hooking on a bag containing both cases so that the bags would dangle below Guy's feet and give warning of touchdown. The jump would be from 400 feet to keep the Halifax below German radar. The jump-master's headset crackled. He held up five fingers to Guy to indicate five minutes, then one finger, before opening the fuselage door and checking Guy's static line once more.

Guy's mind was in a turmoil. Shit-scared of jumping, shit-scared of returning to the land from which he had escaped barely weeks ago, or so it seemed. A red light illuminated on the panel by the door and the jump-master ushered him towards the noise and the slipstream and the nothingness that lay beyond. Petrified and numb with fear, Guy was powerless to resist. At the green light, Guy was propelled unceremoniously into the night. A crack above his head and a jerk on his genitals announced that there was yet life and that cleared his head. Looking down, he could see the flares of the dropping zone rushing towards him, the parcels gently dropping earthwards and steered his canopy to make a perfect drop. As he hit the deck, the flares were extinguished and a group of people ran over to help him.

Willing hands divested him of his parachute, which was swiftly buried.

'Bienvenu en France.'

He was now Christophe Courcy, employed at the local seed merchants, an excellent cover as he knew the business back to front and it gave him carte blanche to talk to almost everyone in an agricultural community without arousing suspicion. His field codename was now Michel. As manna from heaven, there truly was a vacancy at the seed-merchants, as the previous incumbent had moved back south.

He was bundled into the back of a Peugeot van and driven to a farm.

Farmer Albert led him into a warm kitchen and introduced him to his wife Sylvie. Guy had not realised how cold and stiff he had become, cramped in the Halifax's tomb-like fuselage, the rigor only partially relieved by the rum before his descent through a spring night's chill. Sylvie proffered a steaming mug of central heating.

'Thanks,' mumbled Guy, clamping his mitts around the hot earthenware.

The ersatz coffee tasted, well, of not much at all, but its fire rekindled the circulation.

'You'll be here until tomorrow afternoon, then I'll take you down the line to catch a train for Le Mans,' explained Albert. 'We'd better hide that,' pointing to the attaché case which held the vital radio.

Albert led the way upstairs to the loft, where a panel with a concealed latch sprang open to reveal a hidey-hole. The case was locked away, then Sylvie showed Guy to a bedroom which if anything, seemed marginally icier than the fuselage of the Halifax. A thick goose-feather duvet looked tantalisingly inviting and dog-tired, Guy stripped to his undies, climbed beneath the goose feathers and was dead to the world.

A weak and pallid sun beamed a chink of light through the heavy curtains, announcing that once more, night had become day. The narrow beam aimed itself unerringly at Guy's right eye, dragging him from the depths. For a moment he lay there, with unfamiliar sights and aromas teasing his memory as to his location. Then his brain cleared and he was instantly awake and on the qui vive for anything untoward. But only the lowing of cattle in the byre and the distant clink of Albert's pail as he fed his beasts broke the winter still. Guy's watch proclaimed 9.30am.

The bedroom was still at meat-preserving temperature, evidenced by Guy's breath turning to vapour as he exhaled. Spring in this part of France was obviously rather late. Quitting the warm snugness of the duvet took more than a little courage, but Guy jumped swiftly into his clothes. Considering the short time he had spent wearing English garments, he was amazed to find how strange it was to be clad in French clothes again. Unsure of what to do, he eased open the bedroom door and peeked out. The landing was clear, so he peered over the banister and strained his ears to hear any sounds. The farmhouse was large with thick stone walls, but he could just make out traces of movement from what he guessed to be the kitchen. As if reading his thoughts and dead on cue, Sylvie appeared carrying a mug of coffee in one hand and a tin ewer of hot water in the other. Unseen by Sylvie, Guy slid back into his room.

'Bonjour, you slept well?'

'Rather,' replied Guy, 'it was a long night.'

'Some coffee, and hot water for shaving. Please come down to the kitchen when you are ready, there's only Albert and myself here, so there's no one to ask questions about who you are.'

The bitter but scaldingly hot brew pumped some life into his veins, then Guy poured the water into a bowl on the washstand and made his toilet. Clean and refreshed, he made for the kitchen, where Albert and Sylvie were tucking into eggs and bread.

'Sit you down.'

Albert indicated the spare place at table. Discovering he was ravenous, Guy made short work of his ration of the meal.

'OK,' said Albert, 'here's the drill. You are supposed to be arriving in Le Mans by train this afternoon from Dijon. I'll hide you in the van, then drive you to Nogent. It's a busy station, so we'll infiltrate you on to the train from Chartres when it stops, complete with a genuine ticket from Dijon in case anybody checks. Then it's about half an hour to Le Mans, where you'll be met by your new employer, André Lavallois. Tall, sandy-haired chap, small 'tache, drives a black Citroen. We'll leave about 2.30, don't go outside in the meantime.'

Guy did as he was bidden and spent an anxious morning waiting for the off, finding he was incredibly nervous at what was to come.

Fortified by some vegetable broth, he once again found himself being concealed in a van with his kit and his radio, then bumping along rough country lanes for what seemed hours, until the hiss of escaping steam and clanking of conrods announced Nogent station. Albert knew his ground well and parked where the van could not be overlooked. Without turning his head, Albert spoke softly but clearly.

'I'll come round the back and unlatch the doors. When I say 'Go', slide out the van and slip on to the platform via the wicket gate.'

At this point, Guy's stomach began to gyrate and the cold, stark terror that he had known on his march to freedom gripped his intestines once more. He took several deep breaths and waited for Albert's command. It was actually about a minute, but seemed like an aeon before 'Go' penetrated through the closed doors, then Guy was out and through the gate in a trice. The farmer's timing was impeccable. Hidden in the crowd, Guy passed unnoticed by the German sentries.

A shrill whistle from the guard was answered by a deeper note from the engine, then the train was away, wheels spinning momentarily on the damp and worn track. Guy settled in a seat in the last coach, facing the engine so that he had early warning of anyone entering the carriage who might pose a threat. He was lucky, there were no searches on the train.

Forty-five minutes later, the train fussed into Le Mans station. Guy alighted to join the queue of passengers being checked and scrutinised by two Wehrmacht soldiers, who assiduously scanned his ticket and papers, then let him go. Although the radio was concealed in his suitcase, he somehow felt that suitcase transparent, but he escaped any search. He breathed a huge inward sigh of relief.

Spotting André Lavallois proved no problem, his being the only private car amongst the gas-powered taxis with balloon-like structures on their roofs.

Guy walked over to greet André, saying sotto voce, 'The smell of wine is heavenly.'

'Only in Bordeaux,' came the equally soft but correct reply to his password challenge.

'André.'

'Christophe.'

Unbidden, André hefted Guy's case and stowed it in the boot. Guy was pleased to find that the Citroen had a heater and sank back into the leather as the car wound its way through a labyrinth of streets and into the countryside.

'I'll introduce the staff and explain the set-up once we reach the office,' said André, 'but I never talk anything but business at work. The staff are not at all involved and you'll see that our neighbours and visitors might just hear the wrong thing.'

The road began to climb and after about two miles, began to run parallel to a wooded area protected by an airfield fence; the fence was largely intact, but rusty through neglect. As the Citroen rounded a left-hand bend, a Nazi flag stood out proudly in the breeze. Below the flag, two sentries stood alert, guarding the entrance to a military installation.

'Local Wehrmacht barracks,' mouthed André, 'our neighbours.'

Half a mile further on, André swung the Citroen left along a lane, the continuing fence showed he was skirting the airfield. Two hundred yards more, then the car turned left through a gap cut in the fence and bumped over a pierced-steel plate trackway laid between the road and the perimeter track. The trackway was directly in line with the runway threshold and as they turned left yet again towards a dark green hangar, Guy could see the runway heading numbers painted on the concrete and fresh tyre marks indicating recent aircraft movement. Despite the gathering dusk, he could see the runway disappearing over the brow of the hill they had just climbed in the car.

The hangar stood like thousands of others the world over, a nondescript, wide, tall structure with a concrete dispersal apron at the front. Huge sliding doors complete with crank handles and outrigger tracks permitted full-width opening for aircraft with big wingspans. The paint was a distinctly passé camouflage green. Equally faded tricolours were stencilled on each door, together with the barely visible lettering of some long defunct French Air Force Squadron. To avoid unnecessary cranking for other than aircraft, a truck-size pair of doors had been installed on the right-hand side and André drove straight through the open portals. Greying light from the high windows on both sides striated through a myriad of particles of flour dust from the milling operations and despite an obviously well-run set-up, a fine coating of flour covered every surface.

André drew up by the door to the office, climbed out and

motioned to Guy to do likewise. Guy did so, shivering in the chilly hangar after the warmth of the Citroen. At first glance, the building seemed unoccupied, but the clink of studded boots on steel ladders drew the eyes to three men ascending towards the galleries below the windows. Once on the galleries, they unrolled thick canvas blackout blinds to allow the lighting to be switched on.

André took Guy into the office, a brick pod on the side of the hangar. When André pulled open the steel door leading into the pod, Guy was quite surprised to be met by a current of air. Seeing Guy's startled look, André showed him the basic but effective airlock that kept dust out of the office. Two fans in the ceiling of a wooden vestibule maintained positive pressure and by the simple expedient of closing the outer door before opening the inner, 'flouring' of the office was minimised. A switch on the inner door cut the fans momentarily to prevent a draught in the office.

'Yolande, I'd like you to meet Christophe Courcy, our new salesman,' said André, introducing a dark and slightly gypsyish-looking woman in her forties. Black straight hair, a Romany hue to the skin and white teeth were matched by a full skirt in some patterned fabric and chunky bracelet and earrings. Once slim, she was now a little fatter in middle age, but she was still what British men would term a 'looker' and would yet attract glances from admiring males as she passed.

'Enchantée, M Courcy.'

The accent was somewhere down south, Spanish border country, but soft and gentle. The teeth flashed as she spoke.

'Yolande is my accountant, secretary and general factotum, knows all the customers and has impeccable systems so she knows where to find everything. How long is it now, Yolande?'

Yolande pondered for a second.

'Twelve and a half years, André,' came the reply, complete with the mere trace of a secretive smile and matters mutually understood but unspoken.

The use of André's christian name instead of the more usual M Lavallois prompted Guy to speculate at some deeper relationship, either now or in the past.

'That's yours.' André pointed at a slightly battered desk in one corner of the office. 'You and I share the car, it's strictly business, petrol is like gold dust. We also share a bike, so when one of us has the car, the other uses muscle power. Come and meet the lads.'

The office sported a small coke stove and was comfortably warm.

Instinctively, Guy snuggled further into the collar of his wool coat as they exited the airlock. By now, small floodlights illuminated the lower areas of the hangar and the 'lads' as André termed them were moving sacks of flour onto racks ready for collection. 'Lads' was indeed a euphemism, as none of them would see 45 again. Luc and Matthieu were the labour, Fréderic the miller and his elderly assistant, Gaspard. Both sported dusty overalls that had that smell reminiscent of the kind baker who had hidden Guy in the bread oven all those months ago. Luc was short, slightly chubby, balding, just a trace of mousy brown hair still provided the vestiges of a tonsure. Muscular forearms and big shoulders told of a stronger and perhaps fitter man than first glance might suggest. Matthieu was a whippet of a man, tall and spare, but with strong physique and not an ounce of spare flesh. When in the coming months Guy came to watch Matthieu and Luc hefting sacks of flour or grain, he realised they were both pretty fit men.

Fréderic reminded Guy of the way children draw a cat, a small blob for the head and a bigger blob for the body. How anyone could maintain such an obese figure with the rigours of wartime rationing Guy did not know, but Fréderic managed it. Perhaps he used some of his own product to bake copious loaves and keep up his carbohydrate intake? Gaspard was, well, old and wizened, but still with a twinkle in his eye.

André made introductions.

'You'll be with Fréderic and Gaspard for a couple of days learning about milling, then I'll leave you to the tender mercies of Luc and Matthieu for a few days. Now I'll show you around.'

Before André could fulfil his promise, the large electric bell above the office door clanged. Luc walked over to the double doors, now closed for blackout. He pushed them open to reveal a Wehrmacht Hanomag truck, which drove in and reversed up to the mill's loading bay. The German driver presented a docket and having scanned it, Luc and Matthieu pretty much filled the truck with sacks of flour. The driver signed the docket, grated into first gear and drew out of the hangar in a haze of blue and oily exhaust fumes.

Sensing Guy's unspoken question, André explained.

'We supply all the local garrisons with flour, so we see German lorries here most days.'

He grinned wolfishly.

'When they first invaded, the Germans came here with a fleet of trucks and requisitioned ton upon ton of flour. When I protested, they stuck a gun in my face and threatened to blow my head off. As soon as they left, I stormed off to the Area Commandant and demanded an audience. I told him that if his men came stealing again, they would find the doors locked, the cupboard bare and my business closed for the duration. The Commandant blustered and tried to tell me it was war.'

'How the hell do you think I obtained the grain for the flour?' I asked him. 'By paying farmers for it, that's how. You take it without payment and then I'll have not a sou to pay for more, or the costs of milling it, so I'll close. Take your choice. Give him his due,' continued André, 'the next day one of his quartermasters appeared here and set up a contract. Needless to say, the price is rock-bottom, but it does allow me a modest profit.'

'Right, the guided tour, we'll start with the milling operation. I'm the largest flour mill on these parts, so most of the local farmers sell to me. They drive their lorries or trailers on to the weighbridge over there.' His hand swept towards the giant scales directly in line with the double doors. 'All the trucks and trailers have to display a clearly legible tare plate so we can calculate the load and we do percentage checks of the empty ones as they leave.'

It was that wolfish grin again. 'Few years ago, one farmer thought he'd try a flanker. When you've been at it as long as I have, you get a feel for the weight of a load just by looking at it and this chap's loads were consistently heavier than I felt they should be. He was running a shuttle service with two lorries and when we weighed them empty, they were 250kg heavier than their plated weights. When we had a look underneath, he'd welded lengths of railway line inside the chassis members. The cunning sod knew we'd probably check the weights early on, then take things on trust when the harvest was in full swing, so he'd waited a few days until things got busy before he upped the ante. He was also smart enough not to put too much weight on the trucks because he knew that would blow the gaff right away. We reckoned he'd have pulled in about 10% more income if we hadn't spotted his little game. And I paid him as if all his loads were faked, so for those that were genuine in the beginning, he lost out.'

The actual milling operation occupied the right hand side of the hangar. A large grain drier on the extreme right was flanked by a number of huge silos. A hopper allowed sacks or loose grain to be offloaded, then pulled skywards by augers to a manifold along the top of the drier and silos. Wet grain could be pumped straight into the drier and once dry, another auger pushed it up to the manifold once more. Electric paddles were opened to let the grain drop into the designated silo. To pull grain into the mill, Fréderic had a panel controlling low-level paddles and augers so that he could select what he wanted. André first took Guy into Fréderic's dusty kingdom, then led him down the loading bay steps and made for the seed stores. Monster steel racks five storeys high stretched towards the top of the hangar, each storey designed to hold two layers of 50kg sacks yet still allow a man to stand upright on the top layer. A railway track ran either side of the four rack towers, curving round the end of each one like a 'S'. On the track sat a tower hoist. André and Guy climbed into the control cabin of the hoist and Guy was shown how it all worked. The floor of the hoist was divided into two platforms that could be extended either side of the hoist like a drawbridge. Each platform held twenty 50kg bags. By setting the hoist to the height of a trailer or truck, seed bags could be easily offloaded onto the platforms. Buttons marked '1a', '1b' etc automatically took the hoist to the desired level. Safety fences on the racks were then lowered and each platform extended in turn to permit Luc or Matthieu to slide each bag into place with minimal effort. Using twenty bags as the standard simplified stock checks.

To load the seeds, the whole process was reversed and a swivelling and extendable chute was used to slide seed bags into place using gravity.

To move the hoist, big rubber tyred wheels powered by electric motors bore against the concrete floor. Flanged wheels like castors that swivelled on the corners kept the hoist in position and cantilevered arms at the top ended in wheels sitting in a U–shaped trough to prevent the hoist leaning inwards or outwards. Safety detents prevented any movement of the hoist when either platform was extended. A spring-loaded arm like a tram's atop the hoist connected to an electric catenary.

André was obviously very proud of his state of the art set-up.

'I did it not only to cut down labour costs but also because I've seen far too many people in this trade crippled with back problems and I wanted to minimise the risks,' he explained to Guy. 'I got this lot really cheaply. A big seed merchant in St Nazaire went bust just after ordering this, so I picked it up for a third of the cost in the liquidation sale when it was still en route from the US.'

Numerous plates marked 'Roberts Inc, Little Bend, Illinois' showed the origins of this technical tour de force.

Descending from the hoist, André pointed towards one corner of the hangar.

'Our rodent control staff,' he said, 'Alphonse, Minou and Minouche.'

Alphonse was a rangy terrier whose responsibility was any rats, the two tortoiseshell moggies took care of the mice. As Guy was to discover, little if any of the prey was eaten and the first to open up in the mornings had to perform morgue duty on the neatly laid out rows of rats and mice deposited by the team.

'Electricity is critical,' remarked Guy.

'Too right,' came the reply. 'Come and look.'

A door in one corner of the hangar opened to reveal a chunky diesel generator left there by the French Air Force.

'We can run for 48 hours if we have to, never had to use it for more than 6 hours though, even in wartime,' commented André.

'OK, messieurs, dames, home time.'

Within minutes, all the staff had gone, leaving André and Guy alone.

'You're lodging with me, Christophe, hop in.'

Chapter 8

The Citroen coasted downhill to save petrol, rolling silently past the Wehrmacht barracks on the edge of the airfield. Guy was bursting to ask more questions, but instinctively held back until they reached André's imposing maison de maitre, where André produced a bottle of wine which they supped companiably whilst André prepared dinner.

'I never talk about anything in the hangar other than work.' André was busy stirring a rabbit stew. 'As I said, the staff know nothing about my outside activities.'

'Even Yolande?'

The back of the chef's neck went crimson.

'Sorry,' went on Guy, 'but I have to know. If you're sleeping with Yolande, then she's bound to pick up on all sorts of things. The last reseau was blown and what people don't know, they can't tell.'

Discomfited, André became slightly aggressive.

'Yolande is completely trustworthy, I've known her for years and I never even hint at my Resistance activities. We've warmed each other's beds since 1936. My wife died from pneumonia in 1935. Usually, I go to Yolande's place, it's a cottage in a quiet country lane, so none of the nosy parkers in town see what's going on. I'll make sure to stick to that, it's easy now because you're lodging here and I can make you the excuse.'

'OK, but be very, very careful,' was Guy's rejoinder.

'The other reason for not talking about the Resistance at work is in case any of the Germans accidentally overhear something through the hangar walls. They may be steel, but the sound carries.' 'Also', continued André, 'we've heard of the Nazis embedding microphones at installations like mine to pick up any juicy titbits. We can do without that.'

'Tell me how the last reseau was blown,' demanded Guy.

'Simple, a paid quisling, a Frenchman who valued his pocket far above his countrymen. One Dominic Legrand, or should I say, the late Dominic Legrand. He infiltrated the reseau, worked his way to a position where he knew almost all the cells, then spilt the beans. The

Boche spirited him away down south somewhere, but one of our guys happened to catch sight of him. I gather he's playing a harp now.'

'So André, where do you fit in?'

'I was in the one cell Dominic knew nothing about, so I and some others escaped. The other poor sods were executed right away or sent to concentration camps.'

The Frenchman shuddered involuntarily, a look of intense pain came over his features and he waved his hands in a kind of helpless gesture.

'I asked London for an agent to build a new network. Welcome to France!'

The words were accompanied by a little mock bow.

'Any ideas where to start?'

'You're a seed and fertiliser salesman, so that gives you a great excuse to be practically anywhere. No doubt you'll genuinely get lost trying to find some of the farms, but that's another plus – you can plead being lost if you need to. I'm sending you out with Luc and Matthieu on their delivery rounds and as part of your job, you'll have to do deliveries. Plenty of scope for seeing what's going on, blend in with the scenery and meet people who might well want to join the cause. You can drive a truck?'

Guy nodded, adding, 'I'm pretty handy with engines and vehicles.'

This brought a smile of approval from André.

'Thank God, we could do with someone to fix'em from time to time.'

It was Guy again.

'What's with the garrison, our neighbours?'

'Wehrmacht as you saw, regular soldiers doing patrols and keeping order. The CO is Major Wippelmann, not a bad chap, quite good French. Drops in from time to time, he'll want the SP from you when he meets you.'

'And the airfield? Seems to be in use?'

André nodded.

'We call it the letters and legover service.'

That wolfish grin played on his lips once more.

'Supplies of most things are by road or rail and road, but to keep up the morale, there's a once a week flight doing a mail run. Plus it takes a few soldiers at a time over to Rennes and they get a week's local leave, complete with a brothel the Boche have created. The plane comes in every Friday, but the times vary depending on what's going on. There are no runway lights, the pilot just uses his landing lights if it's dark. There must be a radio in the barracks, the Germans always turn up when the aircraft is on approach. With all those trees and the hill in between, they certainly can't see the plane even in daylight.'

Guy's mind was already going twenty to the dozen, he could see some mileage in having an active runway just yards from André's hangar. Emergency only, but ver-r-r-y useful indeed.

Guy's mind switched back to the trucks and deliveries.

'How often will you want me to do deliveries?'

'Once or twice a month, why?'

'Could be just the thing for my sked.'

'Sked' referred to Guy's regular radio contact with England.

'If I hide the radio near the business, I can pick it up and conceal it in the truck, then transmit somewhere well away from home and a different place every time to fool the RDF.'

The Germans had an excellent RDF system for tracing spy transmitters. Ground and mobile stations for triangulating the source and in towns, even people in civilian clothes with miniature detectors directing them towards the rogue transmissions. Their favourite trick was to identify a block of flats and then turn off the electricity supply. If the transmission stopped, they knew they had hit the target and would raid all the flats in search of the radio. If Guy used the lorry battery as his power source, then he could meet his sked out in the countryside, where he could see or hear anyone approaching and with no giveaway loss of mains power to worry him. Plus, if he chose the right spot, he could hide the long aerial in bushes or trees. At this idea, André looked a bit askance, but conceded that short transmissions from a variety of locations would make tracking more difficult. The risk of the radio being discovered in a search was a constant threat to any agent.

'I thought these radios needed mains power?'

André raised one quizzical eyebrow, knowing of the German trick of cutting mains power to isolate a transmission site.

'Latest version, works off its own 6v battery as well,' came Guy's rejoinder.

'And one key thing, André…'

'Yes?'

'You are the only one to know that I have a radio. If the question ever comes up and you can't avoid an answer, say that I have a radio op in the area, but as this a need to know, you haven't a clue as to who it is. OK?'

134

'OK.'

'Then what about the staff of Lavallois et Cie, André?'

'You mean as part of the reseau? Luc and Matthieu might be interested and Yolande has often commented that she'd like some way of having a crack at the Germans, so possibly, yes. Fréderic and Gaspard, probably not. They're both getting on and I think just want to sit out the war. I've nothing concrete to back that up, just a gut feel. Problem is, if we involve some, how do we keep it away from the others? Needs thought, that, because so far, I have been the only Resistanceard of Lavallois. Having Germans in at all sorts of times to collect flour is a constant threat of them seeing or hearing something incriminating, but the other side of the coin is that they are less inclined to suspect a place they visit frequently and without warning. Hmmm…'

Guy found he was still tired, the red wine had a soporific effect and he suddenly found his head lolling.

'Shuteye, methinks, Christophe?'

Guy nodded. The radio was carefully hidden beneath a log pile in the cellar, then it was sack time. Only minutes later, or so it seemed, the alarm clanged and he was back in the Citroen and heading out of town.

The inside of the hangar was nail-bitingly cold and clouds of steamy breath emanated from each person like an aura. Luc was on morgue duty, four rats and six mice being the night's tally. The bodies were removed, then taken far away from the hangar for disposal to avoid attracting foxes and other vermin. Then everyone warmed up in the office with some almost coffee and Matthieu lit the stove. Guy perched on the corner of his desk and looked around. Yolande had everything in apple-pie order, banks of files all neatly labelled and in chronological order. Her desk was impeccable. Guy made a mental note to keep his patch tidy, as he sensed that disorder was a sure way to get into Yolande's bad books.

'Right, Christophe, you're with Fréderic and Gaspard today and tomorrow to learn about milling.'

This remark was accompanied by some overalls of about the right size from a stock in a corner cupboard; the approximation of their fit took Guy's thoughts back to Jack's farm, Angela and Colonel. For an instant, the young agent's thoughts were two hundred miles north and he turned quickly to wipe a small tear from his eye.

Guy followed the two out of the office and into the mill, itself a separate building within the hangar. Guy knew the seed business to a

T, but flour was just something you bought from the baker's in different varieties according to the type of bread or pastry you wanted to bake. The next two days were a revelation. Because of the war, the number of varieties had diminished to one for baguettes, one for Pain de Campagne, a wholemeal and one for croissants. This was the first part of Guy's lesson, backed up by examples of each.

'Rub it through your hands,' urged Fréderic, 'then you'll be able to distinguish each type by touch. I can literally do it with my eyes shut.'

The inside of the mill was no warmer than the hangar, at least until the machinery started and the heat from the friction punched the temperature up a couple of degrees, so Guy's hands were not at their most sensitive. But he could tell the differences and in a blind test a few minutes later, scored 9 out of 10.

'It's rare just to mill a flour from just one type of wheat,' continued Fréderic, 'most are a blend and like any winemaker, the skill is in the blending.'

Climbing up to the platform containing his control panel, he brought three kinds of wheat from the silos into the gristing box. The platform stood above the box so that Fréderic could gauge exactly the right amount of each and also check for any impurities that might have been missed by the magnet and sieves on the delivery pipe. Fréderic had already consulted his order sheet and like all good craftsmen, gauged by eye exactly how much wheat to draw into the gristing box. First he agitated the paddles to mix the grains, then a core sampler was dipped in and the sample rubbed between his fingers to feel the moisture content.

'Mmm, bit dry,' was followed by dampening the mix with a hose before setting the grinding rollers and pumping the mix into the mill. After ten seconds, Fréderic halted the machinery and ran his touch test on the flour. Satisfied, he started the process once more and left the mill to its own devices.

'Spring warmer, Christophe?'

Having lit a small coke stove in the cuddy that served as an office, Fréderic set a kettle on top and he, Guy and Gaspard shared a mug apiece of acorn coffee laced with a drop of what passed for brandy but was closer to meths.

There was a thud as the mill automatically stopped. Fréderic drained the last of the bitter brew, then led Guy back outside the cuddy to the hopper containing the ground flour. A quick test to see that it met his standards, then he, Guy and Gaspard bagged the flour in white 25kg sacks and moved it to the loading dock on a conveyor for stacking. With Gaspard loading and Guy and Fréderic stacking, it all moved quite swiftly.

Hard physical work was the only way to combat the insidious chill of the hangar. Like many such buildings, it was colder inside than outside and Guy was by nature a summer sunshine man for whom winter was anathema. Under Fréderic's skilled guidance, he learned how to mill every kind of flour on offer, restoring his circulation at regular intervals heaving sacks of flour.

The lunch break brought a welcome respite and the comforting fug of Yolande's office. Spotting a dog-lover at a hundred metres, Alphonse somehow managed to inveigle his way into the office, where the tried and trusted ploy of resting his chin on Guy's knee and gazing at him soulfully produced a few titbits from Guy's paquet.

Throughout the day, there was a steady stream of vehicles, from Wehrmacht and Luftwaffe trucks to battered vans driven by local bakers and Guy was kept busy assisting with the loading and checking requisition dockets.

They reached the maison de maitre and unbidden, Guy began preparing supper. André was pleased, it was nice to have someone else cook for you and even with the meagre wartime rations, Guy made a good fist of a stew and dumplings French style. The sight of food reminded André.

'You've got a valid ration card, I take it?'

'I have,' said Guy, 'London's forgers are pretty good now.'

André inspected it and agreed it looked truly pukka.

André made a quick call to Yolande to explain why they would be late the following morning.

Guy cleared his throat. 'I've got a sked in two days.'

'Oh shit, must you? Yes, I know you must, but we have to do it well away from here, or your new face and fresh transmissions… What time?'

'1700.'

'Right, we will visit one of my major customers about 30kms away and you can transmit out in the country somewhere.'

The ration card was immediately put to good use in the local shops before the two men wended their way up to the hangar, where Guy spent yet another day learning how to be a miller. Apart from the cold, two things struck Guy. The first was that despite the machinery being modern and well kept, a fine pall of flour dust leaked everywhere, coating every surface and cranny in a grey-white patina.

Surfaces, nooks and crannies encompassed clothes, eyes, ears and noses. Even a mouthful of coffee brought a top dressing of flour dust. That dust hung in the air, a permanent suspension. No wonder every Miller in Great Britain was a 'Dusty'. Guy found himself sneezing and the racking coughs of both Fréderic and Gaspard told of a lifetime's inhalations.

'Why don't you wear dust masks?' enquired our innocent.

The withering looks he got in return gave him a clear and unequivocal answer. The second was that the British phrase 'the daily grind' summed up this occupation to a T. Terminally boring to a man of Guy's quick intellect, the only palliative became hard work, trying to be Canute to a never-ending stream of flour, countless sacks and vehicles to be loaded.

On loading duties once more, Guy swung round from the stack to find his face almost reflected in the highly polished leather of a pair of boots. As Guy straightened, the heels of the polished leather clicked sharply together.

'Major Wippelmann. Your papers, please.'

Trim, cleanshaven, somewhere in his thirties, Major Wippelmann was immaculately dressed in feldgrau, knife-edge creases, tie dead-centre, cap squarely on his head. Guy unbuttoned his overalls, reached inside his jacket and proffered the documents. Silently and with deliberation, the German officer scrutinised each and every page. Satisfied with this aspect, he began questioning.

'Where are you from?'

It was the start of an interrogation. Although heavily accented, the French was good, grammatically correct. Instantly, Guy was back in that freezing cellar at the training school being grilled by the two pretend Nazis. As then, he switched immediately into another mode, a mode as icy as the hangar in which he now faced the enemy. For twenty minutes, the relentless questioning continued, but Guy remained unfazed, answering coolly. He knew not only that his story was rock solid, but that any checks by the Nazis would confirm his replies and bona fides. The French intelligence officer that had both composed the cover story and coached Guy to be word perfect was especially proud of this particular effort.

'One of my finest, I have to say,' he confided in Guy.

To which the reply had been, 'I bloody well hope so, my life depends on it.'

'Thank you.'

The heels clicked once more as Wippelmann returned the papers. Spinning on one gleaming heel, Herr Major marched briskly into the office to question André. But Guy and André were one step ahead, having spent some fruitful time on that first evening going over and over Guy's cover to ensure that it all matched and there were no gaps. A further twenty minutes passed before the officer strode back to his kubelwagen parked outside. A brief spurt of revs from the air-cooled engine, then he was gone.

By then, Guy and his colleagues were back at work. Such checks were commonplace in wartime and excited neither comment nor attention. Inwardly, Guy let out an enormous sigh of relief, but knowing he would be checked and tested again by the conquerors.

The rest of the day seemed to drag interminably, but at last it was home time once more. Guy waited until they were well past the Wehrmacht barracks before he spoke.

'How did Wippelmann know about me so soon?'

That mirthless grin again.

'His sentries. Our major's troops not only think they're the bee's knees, they are the bee's knees. They're trained to observe and report anything different or out of the ordinary and there I was with a passenger in the car two days on the trot when normally I travel alone. They might have only glimpsed you in the dark the first day, but they got a really good look at you in the daylight this morning. They'd have reported that, in fact when I looked in my mirror after passing the barracks, I saw one of the guards going back to the guardpost. I'll bet he was ringing Herr Major about you. It's said that not even a mouse farts round here without Wippelmann knowing – and which way its arse was facing at the time. Any of his troops screw up, they not only cop for extra sentry duties, but they miss out on one legover run, too. It was Wippelmann's idea to add the legover part to the existing mail run and he knows damn well the power of sex. Also, Wippelmann likes to keep one step ahead of the Abwehr and the SD, it's a matter of personal pride.'

André offered himself as duty chef. Perhaps competent cook was nearer the mark, the famed culinary skills of the French not having rubbed off on André, but then filling the void took priority over gastronomy.

'Where are we going tomorrow?'

The cook answered without turning from the stove.

'We're off to see Simon Gauthier, he farms about 40kms from here. Simon is my oldest customer and my biggest. A good proportion of our stock will be delivered to Simon. In every sense, it pays to keep him sweet, but he's a really nice chap, you'll like him.'

Guy spent yet another bone-chilling morning, this time with Luc and Matthieu, climbing up and down the racks of seeds and fertilisers and learning the types and quantities in stock. Plus, despite the best efforts of what Luc termed the RAT – the Rodent Assassination Team – a few still managed to overcome the rat guards on every stanchion, munch into the abundance of tasty fodder on the shelving and create nests in the sacks. Luc and Matthieu systematically checked all the stock bag by bag, removing damaged ones and rebagging salvageable items. Both men carried heavy sticks and any rodent caught in flagrante was immediately despatched to the hereafter.

Around 2pm, Guy and André rolled off in the Citroen, the radio still hidden under the spare wheel where they had concealed it that morning under cover of André's garage. One very useful thing Guy had found on the Citroen's dashboard was a two-pin accessory socket, complete with plug which he had wired to the radio's power lead. This had several advantages. First, connecting and disconnecting power was quick and did not entail lifting the bonnet. Second, it avoided witness marks on the car's battery terminals from crocodile clips, marks that might be a giveaway to a sharp-eyed German. Last but not least, there were identical sockets in both Lavallois trucks. The greater capacity of the car or truck batteries would make life easier and avoid the problem of a flat battery in the radio at a vital moment.

André and Guy rolled companiably through the countryside with Guy driving and André navigating. It was some time since Guy had driven a Citroen with its idiosyncratic gear lever protruding down from the dash, but in a few miles he found his sea-legs and André sat back to admire the young agent's smooth style. Guy drove ahead, judging the bends and adjusting speed with delicate use of the throttle. In this way he kept his momentum, rarely touched the brakes and eked every possible kilometre from the scarce fuel.

Sensing he was being watched, Guy merely said, 'My father was a racing driver, he taught me.'

Something had been nagging at Guy like an itch and he just had to scratch it.

'Why did you put me with Fréderic and Gaspard for two days? I could have learned enough in one, you're not looking for me to be a miller.'

'What do you think of my judgement of them?' was the somewhat unlikely reply.

Guy clicked at once to their conversation of the first evening, when he had asked about potential recruits from chez Lavallois. He grinned.

'So, OK, there's method in your madness. And I do agree with you, both just want to sit out the war and with their chests, I can't see them hiking across country with a backpack anyway. I'll reserve my views on Luc and Matthieu until I know them better.'

Simon Gauthier was indeed a nice chap, although his tweeds would have been more at home among the banks and braes than northern France. Ruddy, weather-beaten cheeks and a slightly rolling gait from walking across rough ground were telltale signs of his profession.

'So, who's your young assistant?' was Simon's greeting to André.

André introduced Guy. With Spring planting on the horizon, the talk rapidly turned to Simon's requirements and Guy made careful notes of the quantities on order. With wartime petrol rationing, transport was to be a mix of Lavallois trucks and Gauthier vehicles.

Somehow, Guy sensed Simon was ill at ease – his shuffling from foot to foot and dropping his gaze without warning were clear signs. Also, it was abundantly clear that Simon was trying to sum up Guy.

'Whilst you're here, there's something I'd like you to see, André.'

It was a command, not an invitation. As bidden, André and Guy followed Simon through the farmyard and into a large barn. Checking to see that they were not being watched, Simon led the way into the barn and up a ladder. The trio found themselves staring at a wall of corn stooks, but Simon tugged a few of the stooks away and gestured them to follow him through the gap he had created. Two seconds later, they stood inside a room created within the stooks, a room dimly lit by an oil lamp whose glow revealed a British airman lying sleeping on a mattress on the rough floor. Pilot's wings and a single broad ring announced a pilot and a rank of Flying Officer. Even without the telltale signs, the whizzo-prang moustache was a dead giveaway. Somewhere in his late teens or early twenties, the young man's natural complexion was overtaken by a pallor and a thin film of perspiration that spoke of shock and pain.

Guy's heart began to hammer. He had been warned in training that exactly this kind of thing would happen and he would have to decide on his feet what to do and whether to reveal that he spoke English.

'Parachuted from a bomber three nights ago, right leg's broken,' came from Simon.

André whispered urgently in Guy's ear. 'Trust Simon, I've known him 30 years.'

Guy took a deep breath, then addressed the injured pilot in slow French. The pilot waved his hands helplessly, indicating that he understood not a word. It was shit or bust time.

'How are you feeling?' asked Guy in English.

'Fucking terrible, my leg hurts like hell. You Resistance?'

Guy nodded.

'What's your name?'

'Peter Lewis, Flying Officer, 7691743, Royal Air Force.'

At this, the airman reached inside his collar and locating the dog tags, pulled them clear so that Guy could read them. Even this minor effort brought a pained look to Peter's eyes and yet more perspiration. Guy squatted and read the tags in the dim light, the engraved letters and numbers confirming the wearer's identity. Again, Guy breathed deeply, knowing that the aircrew were drilled to give name, rank and service number only, no matter who was asking the questions.

'We have to know you're genuine, so you have to tell me where you are from and where you were headed.'

'No way,' replied Peter, 'if you're genuine, you'll know the drill as well as I do.'

A naturally kind person, Guy struggled to say what he had to say next.

'This country's choc-a-bloc with Nazi plants and I certainly wouldn't put it past them to break your leg under anaesthetic so that you looked the genuine article. Now, either you give me some gen or we'll leave you there to get gangrene. What's it to be?'

At this, Peter Lewis realised that if he really wanted to see Blighty again, he had to do as he was asked.

'I was the pilot of a Lancaster out of Harwell.'

Seeing Guy's slightly blank expression, he added 'Oxfordshire.' 'We dropped our load and were on the home run. Because we're at Harwell and the flak around here is less, I take a detour going home. Port inner seized up just into France, so I was already on three. We were jumped by an FW190, killed the tail gunner and the mid-upper gunner too. Nav got a bullet in the leg. The port outer caught fire and it spread to the wing, so I told the boys to bail out. They'd just gone when I lost the 190 in some cloud and the fire suddenly went out. I thought I could limp home on two, at least as far as the coast, when I came out the cloud and there was chummy in the 190 again. He hammered some more cannon shells into the port wing and it caught fire again. I jumped, but I hit a tree on the way down and broke my leg.'

'And what were your registration letters?'

'Able Baker – AB.'

'Simon, can we get any medical help?'

'Doctor's coming in the morning, he's been laid up with pneumonia. I had a gentle feel of the leg, seems like a clean break of the lower leg, so I strapped it up with a splint.'

Guy softly felt the limb, but even his delicate touch brought moans from the British airman.

'OK, doctor's here tomorrow, he'll set it in plaster, just take it easy, there's a good chap. Right, Pete, we'll be back and Simon will take very good care of you.'

With that, the trio left Peter Lewis to sleep once more and carefully rebuilt the stook wall that concealed the pilot.

'Who found him and when?' asked Guy of Simon.

'Georges was out feeding some of the sheep. He heard the gunfire, then a few minutes later, he found our man sitting next to a big old oak. Georges put him under the empty feed sacks and dragged him back here. We normally use the room that Peter's in to hide things we don't want the Germans to pinch.'

Simon's nose wrinkled in disgust at this thought of the enemy.

'Georges has been with me for years.' The quizzical eyebrow aimed towards André brought an affirmatory nod. 'He'll not give anything away.'

'Have you hidden British airmen before?'

'No,' replied Simon, 'he's the first.'

'André and I will try to get him down the line once he's fit, but I'd guess he'll be hors de combat for five or six weeks. Can you keep him hidden that long?'

'I guess so,' was the reply, 'but I've places to move him to once that leg's set.' Guy was remembering his own broken limb not all that many miles from here and not that long ago.

'And,' added Guy, 'once he's got over his injury, get him to lose that moustache, it screams British from a hundred metres.'

Simon nodded.

By now it was dark. Guy waited until they were well clear of the farm gates before he opened his mouth.

'Wasn't quite what you and I expected, was it?'

Out of the corner of his eye, Guy saw his passenger nodding in assent.

'I've known Simon all my life, we were at school together, so I'm not surprised at what he's done – anything to get at the Boche, he hates'em even more than I do,' was André's rejoinder.

'I take it there is a line? enquired Guy.

'Yes, I've used it a few times before and all but one got to Spain.'

'Good,' came from the young driver, 'but keep the details to yourself, what Simon doesn't know he can't tell.'

He heard the sigh from André and Guy reached out to pat André comfortingly on the shoulder.

'It's a bugger, this war, isn't it? Keeping things from a lifelong friend, it's not natural.'

Guy smiled.

'There's a wartime poster in England, it says, 'Be like Dad, keep Mum.'

Even for a bilingual, Guy struggled to translate the vernacular into French, but André's chuckle told him he had succeeded.

A mile further on, André indicated to Guy to turn right into a narrow lane leading into a small forest. Parking out of sight of the road, Guy rapidly assembled his radio and at precisely 1700, started his maiden sked. Guy found himself trembling, frightened beyond all measure that his fingers would not obey him and his Morse would be hopeless. His fears were groundless and in less than a minute, had reported safe arrival and contact and requested a check on Flying Officer Lewis for his next sked in ten days. London had no instructions. With a sigh of utter relief, he signed off, packed up the set and resumed the drive home.

The next day was rather more comfortable work-wise, spent in the office learning about the clients and the paperwork system. Initial impressions had been right, Yolande was a top flight administrator. The ranks of box-files were in immaculate order, with one alphabetical series and one chronological series. Client details were held on rolodexes meticulously updated. Like all good administrators, she could lay hands on papers, letters, invoices and delivery notes within seconds. Guy also set to work to learn the railway and bus timetables, with wartime petrol shortages, his longer trips would be by train or bus, carrying the ancient bike to travel between the stations and the farms. The office was warm and muggy and come the afternoon, Guy found himself in a reverie, his mind on Angela, Colonel, that smell of the warm kitchen on the Exeter farm. Almost blushing, he realised that his thoughts were very erotic as he remembered Angela standing naked in the bathroom in Lyme Regis.

Embarrassed, he blew his nose and returned to the timetable.

Guy being Guy, he had a look at the famous bike. Sound and solid, it looked as though it had been built from spare lengths of gas-pipe and it weighed a ton. Although generally in good order, it needed some TLC, especially the brakes. Squeezing the levers produced little in the way of retardation and Guy was not about to lose his manhood against the crossbar on some of the steep hills that abounded. A well-stocked bench in one corner offered tools and an oilcan so 'Auntie', as Guy christened the machine, was given a thorough fettling. By adjusting the cable on the Peugeot 3-speed gears, he regained all three instead of just the top two. The brakes now worked fortissimo and screeched Auntie to a respectable halt at the end of a test-run in the hangar. André watched the mechanicking and just grinned.

'You can move on to the trucks when you're ready,' was his only and laconic comment.

As they bowled companiably home that night, André revealed he had taken a phone call from Simon. Using the agreed code phrase 'I confirm the order for wheat', Simon advised that the doctor had fixed up Flying Officer Lewis. André would start the process of moving the pilot once his bona fides were confirmed by the RAF and he was fit enough to travel. Knowing that the last leg into Spain meant tough climbing in deep snow, André would want to be a hundred percent sure of Peter Lewis's fitness before sending him down the line.

'It's Friday night' announced the head of Lavallois et Cie, 'we'll have a meal in the Auberge St Honoré, and you can meet one of the reseau, François Duhamel. He owns the hotel and he's the head chef – a bloody good one, too. I won't reveal your true identity just yet, let you size him up first.'

The auberge was about 10 minutes' walk from chez André on a side road off the main street. A typically French stone building, it was covered in creeper and had a steep tiled roof. Large hooks on the wall showed that in summer, hanging baskets adorned the front wall. André pushed open the front door and slid past the inner curtain, closely followed by Guy. It was like turning a switch, the calm of a quiet suburban street became instantly the hubbub of France enjoying herself on a Friday night. There was an almost imperceptible tempering of the enjoyment with four of the twenty tables occupied by German officers, otherwise, it was business as usual.

The large single room with tiled floor doubled as restaurant and bar. Against the rear wall, a bar counter ran almost the entire length of the room, with the swing doors to the kitchen at the right hand end.

The right hand end of the room was set out for dining, with check cloths and matching napkins on the tables; the remaining tables were bare just for drinkers, but even as Guy and André entered, a brightly coloured nappe was being used to convert from drinking to dining. A well-polished upright piano occupied the left hand corner of the room. The atmosphere was a mix of good food, wine, beer, French and German cigarette smoke and a soupçon of oxygen. Smoking was one thing about his country that vexed Guy. Neither he nor his parents had ever smoked, but recognised that they were in a tiny minority in a land addicted to Gitanes, Disque Bleu and Caporal. Apart from the Germans, the clientele were a classless and eclectic mix of workmen in slacks, open-neck shirts and berets to middle class France in some quite modish garb. Conversation level was just below a dull roar. Two young waitresses scurried between tables and behind the bar, a lady was kept fully occupied quenching thirsts.

André and Guy found a couple about to leave one of the four-seat tables and took their places. Remembering his training to always sit where you could see as much of what was happening as possible, Guy sat at the cloth-covered table so that he faced down the room. To his left were four Germans engrossed in their meal and talking in low tones.

As if on cue, patron François walked through the kitchen door as he came back into the restaurant and spotting André, came straight over to greet his old friend.

'François, this is Christophe Courcy.'

'Welcome, welcome. You'll take a drink with me?' enquired François. 'Marie-Claire, two glasses of house red if you please.'

The lady behind the bar obliged.

François was only medium height, but thickset and muscular. Dressed in traditional chef's dog's-tooth check trousers, white apron and chef's hat, he exuded considerable presence. Whatever ills beset François in WWII, starvation was not one of them and his bulky frame contained more fat than it should. Compared to the grey-faced and skeletal appearance of a nation at war, he stood out like a beacon. One other facet of François was a huge aura of garlic, an aura so powerful that Guy smelt him at least six or eight feet before he reached their table. Not for nothing was la belle France renowned for her love of garlic and many of her citizens ate so much that it permeated through their skins, but François was clearly a serious addict. He smelt like a Metro station but with ten times the intensity. As Guy was to discover, that addiction was to prove a problem. He was something of a ringer for his Uncle Hugo, barring the garlic.

'I recommend the goat ragout,' opined mine host.

'Two goat ragout and a bottle of red,' came André's concurrence.

As they waited for their order, Guy watched a very professional set-up in operation. When François walked back to the kitchen, the open door revealed a spotless and tidy cuisine. François and all his staff constantly scanned the room to observe progress and body language – that half turn in the chair or a head beginning to look around – appearing at the table at precisely the right time but without making the guests feel rushed or pressured. Not for the St Honoré that fatal disease called waiter's blindness, when at precisely the moment you wanted service, the waiter or waitress seemed determined to look anywhere but in your direction. Marie-Claire had a highly-tuned radar set and whenever one of the waitresses or François was at the bar, would point them in the right direction if they had missed anything. François himself floated between kitchen and restaurant, supervising the standard of food and presentation within and standard of service without.

The kitchen door closed a little slowly on its spring and as the chef was re-entering from yet another foray, he let forth a thunderous fart, accompanied by a number of smaller aftershocks. The two kitchen staff turned not a hair, so obviously they were accustomed to such outbursts.

Just as François watched his customers' body language, so Guy scrutinised François'. With his compatriots, the patron was open and friendly, with the Germans, he changed. Aside from the fact that he spoke more slowly to be understood, a subtle stiffening of the back and a coolness in his tone gave evidence of his distaste for the invaders. The changes were too miniscule to be noticed by the Boche, but to a native Frenchman like Guy, these traits shouted 'I'm doing this because I have to, but I wish you bastards in hell'.

The nearby Germans had finished their meal and were slurping large brandies. Tongues loosened by the alcohol and to overcome the noise level, their speech had become louder. Remembering Norman's teachings, Guy began surreptitiously to earwig their conversation.

*

Ah, Norman, he was quite something else. All the other SOE instructors wore flannel bags, open-neck shirts and fairisle sweaters; Norman wore one of a collection of navy chalk-stripe suits, stiff collar and a red bow-tie. A fresh red or white carnation adorned his buttonhole daily. A hawk-like nose and a shock of curly grey hair gave him a raffish appearance and his cut-glass accent was so high up and far back, even Guy found him difficult to comprehend.

'I'm a linguistics expert and I'm here to teach you how to listen,' was his opening salvo and seeing the looks of astonishment on his audience's faces, he continued, 'I see you think the old duffer's off his trolley, what?'

He pronounced it 'duffah'.

'Right, we'll start with a little experiment. Who speaks fluent English?'

Guy's was one of three hands to go up.

'OK, come next door.'

In the next room were four tables. Two contained three instructors each, two were empty. Norman directed Guy and Jean-Luc to sit at one table facing the other empty one. The remaining students then sat at the second table, but all facing Guy and Jean-Luc.

'Martin and Jean-Luc, I want you to listen in to the conversations at both tables, then give me a resume of each one at the end. OK?'

Norman motioned with his hand towards the instructors and both sets began animated conversations. One group was discussing life at a particular Army camp, how remote it was, how badly the stores was run and the price of drinks in the officers' mess. Their conversation was riddled with slang and Army acronyms. The second group was debating investment in antiques and trying to predict whether furniture or silver would give the best return. After a couple of minutes, Norman stilled both debates and turned to Jean-Luc.

'This group were talking about antiques – furniture and silver? – but I did not understand why they were talking about them.'

Jean-Luc waved towards his right.

'This group about the Army – but that is all I understood.'

'Martin?'

Guy gave a brief but highly accurate resume of both conversations. Norman turned to the watching agents.

'What did you see?'

'Martin just sat there without moving a muscle, but it was obvious Jean-Luc was straining to hear what was said,' volunteered Lysette.

The group returned to the classroom.

'Okaaay,' drawled Norman, 'this is the problem you are all going to face. Did you know that we hear only 50% of what is said? Our brain fills in the blanks because it is our native language.'

Norman turned to the blackboard.

'For example, if I say 'Dover Strait' or 'home straight', a native English speaker's brain automatically knows the context and the spelling.'

He wrote both on the board for the benefit of the native French.

'If you don't speak the language fluently, you need to hear 75% or more to make sense of it. You'll be listening to Germans speaking with strong regional accents, peppering their speech with abbreviations and acronyms and in many cases, they'll be half-cut and slurring their words.'

'What is half-cut?' demanded Charles.

'Beurré,' interceded Guy helpfully.

'The other problem is that you're trying to listen to a group in conversation and you don't understand the language well enough to filter. If you are addressed directly, one-to-one and can watch the speaker's lips, you may well understand quite well. Martin is fluent in English, so he can tune in and out of conversations even if he only hears a few words or phrases.'

'And,' went on Norman, 'you'll have just the problem we've seen with Jean-Luc – straining to listen and it being very obvious that he's listening. Do that and you'll attract exactly the kind of attention you're trying to avoid.'

Over the next few days, Norman taught them how to listen without it being obvious – inclining the head towards the conversation, tensing up when you thought you were missing a vital bit.

'Your facial expression gives most away,' taught Norman, 'so try and sit to one side or with your back to the conversation and where nobody else overlooks you. For Christ's sake don't write anything down – I know that's obvious, but sometimes the obvious is not the obvious.'

As part of the course, Norman had lists of German Army, Navy and Air Force slang and abbreviations which they all had to learn for a test at the end.

'Another tip, nothing to do with how to listen.'

It was Norman again.

'The Germans often designate certain bars and cafes off-limits either to officers, NCOs or other ranks so that one doesn't mix with the other and they can all relax over a beer or a meal. You'll find that even where there are no specific orders, there will be unspoken rules about such and such a bar being only for ordinary soldiers or airmen or officers. If you want to pick up interesting information, your best

149

bet is the soldiers' bars and cafés. They will chatter about what to them are quite ordinary things without realising the significance of such intelligence to the jigsaw-puzzle of information. And,' he went on, 'they are far more likely to get – beurré?' He grinned at Guy.' And shoot their mouths off.'

*

As he sipped his drink from the patron, Guy listened in whilst chatting to André, but the Germans were talking about home. One was going on leave back to Düsseldorf in a few days and his companions asked him to carry letters to their families and phone wives on their behalf, all run-of-the mill, uninteresting stuff.

'Voila, messieurs.'

It was François with their ragout. As expected, the goat content was distinctly lacking, but compensated by plenty of vegetables. André had been right, François was a true chef who could summon flavours buried deep within the food and the whole dish was excellent. Washed down with a bottle of vin du pays, it put a much rosier glow on the evening. A marc apiece added the finishing touch.

They were halfway through the meal when Marie-Claire forsook her optics for ivories, switching on a small microphone as she took her seat at the piano. As if by magic, the room stilled in an instant. Caressing the keys, Marie-Claire began to schmooze her way through a medley of classical and ballads, slipping seamlessly from one tune to the next. She was undoubtedly a very good pianist, technically near faultless, but to Guy the performance was cold and lacked soul. Pulling the microphone closer, Marie-Claire launched into a few patriotic French songs. She had a melodious, slightly throaty delivery and the husky tunes touched the nerves of some of the French customers, who joined in. The Germans glowered but otherwise did nothing. Guy smiled inwardly at this neat two fingers to the occupiers. Somehow, Guy sensed an air of expectancy in the audience.

With ten minutes to go in the half hour set, Marie-Claire riffed her right hand across the keyboard to announce an upbeat, driving jazz tune. Within seconds, the whole restaurant was rocking, with toes and fingers – including German ones – tapping in time with the rhythm. As for Marie-Claire, she took on another persona. From the calm songstress, she moved up another two gears, eyes flashing and fingers flying across the keys. She was in heaven and her performance reflected it. With thunderous applause and cries of 'Encore' and

'Noch einmal' ringing in her ears, Marie-Claire resumed her station at the bar.

Alcohol-induced slumbers meant Guy had a good night's shut-eye and by mutual consent, both he and André had what the French called a grâce matinée – a lie-in – on Saturday morning, followed by a leisurely breakfast of coffee and fresh croissants from the local bakery. Of all the things Guy missed during wartime, it was real coffee. The acorn ersatz brew was bitter and taste of nothing at all. Breakfast over and the washing up done, both men donned their femme de menage hats and did housework and their smalls. Their reward to themselves was a pression or two, encore chez François. Chez François was André's suggestion and instinctively, Guy knew it was so he could size up the chef once more.

There were only French in the bar at midday and there was that intangible sense of greater freedom in the absence of the Germans. With just a few customers, the patron was alone behind the counter, Marie-Claire and the waitresses were not in evidence. Marie-Claire was Madame Duhamel, a fact confirmed to Guy by André. The conversation was punctuated at frequent intervals by encores of the earth-shattering farts witnessed on the previous evening. Not only were the eruptions malodorous, they were also extremely loud. The cause was not difficult to find. François kept a small bag of garlic cloves by the bar and at regular intervals, he would peel one and eat it raw much as anyone else would eat a chocolate. It seemed that François was like a petomane from the old music-halls, able to control his anal artillery in public but giving it free rein in private. By 2pm, Guy and André were the only customers left. Fifteen minutes earlier, François had disappeared into the kitchen to prepare a snack for them.

'What do you think, Guy?'

'He's OK,' was the reply. 'I watched him last night and to me, he shrieked his hatred of the Boche.'

A slow smile spread across André's face.

'Great, shall we call a meeting of the reseau?'

Yet again, a panic gripped Guy. Just as you felt you were safe with the people who knew your secret identity, you were forced to widen that knowledge, plunging once more into the unknown.

'François, we need to have a chat,' said André.

François merely nodded before locking up and resuming his place behind the counter.

'So, André?'

'Christophe is an agent, sent here to rekindle the local reseau.'

Guy could sense the chef weighing him up before deciding to accept him.

'I'd like a meeting of all the cell tomorrow night before curfew,' continued André.

'I'll fix it, warehouse at 1900?'

François raised one eyebrow and received assent. André and Guy walked slightly unsteadily home before sleeping off the pressions in front of the fire.

Guy awoke slightly stiff and with that sour taste in the mouth that comes from sleeping off booze in the armchair. André was out to the wide, his mouth agape and loud snores coming from it. The fire was almost out, but Guy quietly revived it with judicious poking and a couple of fresh logs. Then he rooted round in the cupboard and began to make supper. He was interrupted by the phone, it was Yolande for André. Guy woke the recumbent figure and called him to the phone. A few minutes later, André stuck his head round the kitchen door and announced that he was off to see Yolande, so dinner for one, Salisbury. André had a second bike in his garage, yet another sit up and beg model, on which he creaked off for a night's amour. Guy settled down to a single repast, then listened to some records before retiring to his bed.

The lover reappeared mid-morning on Sunday, the satisfied grin on his lips silent testimony to the passions of the previous night. He had some news for Guy.

'Yolande was talking again about having a go at the Boche and asked me if I knew anybody in the Resistance. I said I'd ask around, but I gave nothing away and I swear she does not suspect you.'

'Let's see how tonight goes,' replied Guy, 'then I can give some thought to Yolande.'

Guy wanted to get the lie of the land for Le Mans, so after lunch, he and André walked for three hours around the woods and fields. As they walked, Guy quizzed André about François and Marie-Claire.

'Is François into some kind of sport – he's a big feller?' asked Guy.

'Was,' came the correction, 'weightlifting. Reasonably successful amateur, there's a few cups and medals on his sideboard. Gave it up when he moved here six years ago.'

'François hails from Le Touquet. He did his apprenticeship at one of the big casinos. He wasn't allowed to gamble at his own place, but that didn't stop him doing it elsewhere. When he got fed up with losing all his money at the tables, he moved on. Worked abroad, even did a stint at Baden-Baden in a posh spa hotel, but that was in the early Thirties, when the brownshirts and the Hitlerjugend were stirring things up. François was sickened by what was happening and moved on again. Good thing is, he speaks reasonable German, but keeps that very quiet so that he can eavesdrop on Jerry's conversations. He's brought me a few tasty morsels in his time.'

'And Marie-Claire?'

'She was born and raised here, very strong musical talent. She studied classical piano at the Brussels Conservatoire, but she'll be the first one to tell you that she knew she would never be good enough for the concert platform. She went to a jazz club one night and got hooked. Playing jazz was far more exciting than Chopin etudes. She told me that the Principal of the Conservatoire was a real killjoy. For him, if it wasn't Beethoven, it didn't exist. One night, she and her mates were having a jam session in one of the practice rooms. Old Prinny was passing and heard her giving the Bechstein rocks. She got a severe telling-off for playing 'heathen music' and told if she did it again, she'd be for the chop. When she graduated, she took a job as a music teacher at a girls' school in Lyon and played piano with a jazz combo in the evenings. François was in town for a competition and he and some of his pals went to her club. He fancied her, bought her a drink in the interval and the rest is history.'

'How come they ended up back here?'

'Pure serendipity,' was André's response. 'They were on holiday and came back to see Marie-Claire's parents. François decided to go over to Le Touquet to catch up with some old mates and promised Marie-Claire that he wouldn't gamble. But the lure of the roulette table was too much and he had a flutter. For once it was his lucky night and he was on a roll. He had the sense to quit while he was ahead and walked out of the casino with a fat cheque. Back here, Marie-Claire heard that the Auberge was up for sale. The old boy that owned it had let it run to rack and ruin. It was dirty, the food was bloody awful and he drank the profits. A heart attack made him an invalid, so he needed to sell. When François came back with his cheque, he got a sound bollocking for breaking his word, then hauled round the corner to view the Auberge. They bought it, did it up and have a great business. Don't let the simple décor fool you – in peacetime, François has produced some truly spectacular cuisine. I've yet to eat better and that includes Paris'

A light meal prepared by André, then it was time to meet the cell. The warehouse was a derelict building on the other side of town, but surrounded by other buildings so that approaching it was easier than across open ground. Nonetheless, Guy and André did all the usual tricks to check that they were unobserved. Before leaving for the rendezvous, André had given Guy a rundown on the remaining five members. Alain was a mechanic at the Citroen garage, Edouard worked at the mairie on building control, Pierre was a dentist, Christel was a nurse and Gabriel a truck driver.

Guy had been unequivocal.

'All kosher, no reason to suspect any of them? Remember, I'm exposing myself here. The last thing I need is to be blown by a Quisling.'

André was at first shocked by Guy's vehemence, but immediately saw the potential problems. He reassured Guy that there was no cause to suspect anyone and that as far as he knew, none of the reseau had family interned in concentration camps. Threatening to execute family was a favourite ploy of the Gestapo in recruiting informers.

At the appointed hour, they were standing in the warehouse, whose boarded-up windows allowed a lamp to be lit. One by one, the other network members slid quietly into the building and the meeting began. Guy introduced himself and explained his role in recruiting new members, gathering intelligence and organising sabotage and resistance. Alain revealed that by the nature of his job, he had access to a variety of vehicles; Edouard being in the mairie was in a position to hear what was going on; Pierre treated German as well as French patients and kept an eye on new uniforms and regiments in the area; Christel also looked after Germans in the local hospital and listened in to the chatter when visitors were clustered round a German's bed, but as her German was very weak, she did not tend to garner much; Gabriel was in a position to see much from his cab and logged the details of military installations and gun emplacements.

'What we need is more recruits to the cause,' explained Guy, 'so if any of you have any ideas, I'll see each of you separately at the end of the meeting.'

Sure enough, each one had an idea – a customer at the garage, a pal at the mairie, another patient, a fellow nurse, a mechanic at the lorry depot. A key question on each potential member was their political allegiance, as Guy had been well-briefed on the Communists and their separate agenda. Only Gabriel's man was a red, but according to Gabriel, devoted to loosening France from Herr Hitler's implacable grip. Gabriel was insistent that his mate's politics would not get in the way.

Arranging to meet again in a week's time, Guy and André wended their way back to the maison de maitre, where they made plans for the coming week. Luc was due out on a flour delivery run on Monday morning and Guy would ride shotgun.

'That will give me a good excuse to look over the trucks when we get back, ostensibly to check them, but really to see if there's a good spot to conceal the radio,' remarked Guy.

The first task that Monday morning was to ward off the cold by loading sacks of flour before setting off with Luc around the district's bakers. Luc was a terrible driver who grated the gears, had no sense of anticipation and hammered the brakes. Guy found himself wincing at every gearchange and after the third dropoff, suggested he drive in order to familiarise himself with the vehicle. Despite Luc's best efforts, the Renault was still in generally good order, except that the wartime merde called petrol did nothing for the health of the engine. After a few miles, Guy was double-declutching smoothly and silently up and down the crash box and quite enjoying the drive. He met a number of bakers, storing away mental notes of those who might be brought into the Resistance. They stopped at a service station for petrol and Guy spotted and swiftly bought two dust-covered tins of Redex lying on a back shelf.

Just after lunch, the pair rolled back into the hangar. A quick snack, then Guy donned his overalls once more and armed himself from the well-equipped bench. He serviced the fuel, ignition and cooling systems, removing half a sand dune from each carburettor and cleaning the jets with a bristle from the yard broom. Then he took one truck outside, parked nose into the wind, and removing the air cleaner, he wound up the tickover and trickled Redex into the carburettor intake. A dense cloud of pungent blue smoke poured from the exhaust to be swiftly followed by lumps of carbon and gum from the cylinder head and valves. A couple of minutes later, a small carpet of black lumps had fallen to the ground below the exhaust pipe. When turned down to normal, the truck ticked over more smoothly and the throttle response was distinctly sharper. Guy repeated his trick before diving under each chassis. By now, Luc and Matthieu has lost interest and gone inside, precisely as Guy had hoped. The underside of both lorries was pretty black, which suited Guy admirably. At the point where the forward end of the body met the back of the cab, he found an ideal hidey-hole for the radio. To see it meant crawling right under the chassis and with a strong light, so it would pass a standard roadside inspection but not a thorough search. It also meant that if he had to hide or dump the radio in a hurry, it was the work of but seconds to do so, rather than concealing it beneath a load of heavy, bulky sacks.

André had left early to see his lawyer, so Guy had to bike home on Auntie. This suited his book admirably, as on the way back with Luc, he had spotted the remains of a cottage on a side road. He blessed the extra height of the lorry's cab, as the cottage was invisible from the Citroen. The cottage was a wreck, only three walls standing and a few rafters scant testimony to the roof that had long since gone. What had drawn Guy was that the chimney wall had survived and with it the fireplace. Knowing French construction methods, Guy reached carefully inside the fireplace and sure enough, there was a shelf above the stone lintel. Countless rainstorms had washed down the gaunt stack, cleansing it of soot that might be a giveaway if disturbed or deposited on Guy's hands. Under cover of darkness the next evening, Guy and André wrapped the radio in oilcloth and deposited it in its new hiding place.

Chapter 9

Now three weeks had somehow passed. To say Guy felt easier or more comfortable with his alias and his clandestine role would be wrong, but there was a certain familiarity now with his situation and the day to day routine.

It was lunchtime, Guy at his desk with his paquet, absorbed in the local paper. Alphonse had, comme d'habitude, wormed his way into the office and with his appealing look, head on knee repertoire, was being duly rewarded with the odd snippet. Yolande too was seated behind her ancient Remington, André was out.

Thus absorbed, Guy did not see what Yolande was up to, except his subconscious could detect pen on paper, but it did not register.

Lunch over, Yolande went out to the hangar and Guy stood up to stretch his legs and let Alphonse out. Glancing at Yolande's desktop, he spotted what looked like a sketch pad and the subconscious clicked into the sound he had heard.

Opening the pad, the topmost drawing was a pen and ink rendition of Guy and Alphonse, capturing beautifully the soulful look in the dog's eyes and a tiny ray of sunshine spilling over the animal's back. Like all natural artists, Yolande had the gift of creating a likeness in a few deft strokes.

Guy leafed through the pad. It contained stunning vignettes of life at Lavallois et Cie, Luc and Matthieu loading a truck; Fréderic and Gaspard, complete with floury overalls, filling sacks; one of the cats, mouse in mouth. These were such powerful drawings, breathing life and movement into the very paper. You could feel Luc and Matthieu's energy as they swung heavy sacks; you could smell the flour dusting Fréderic and Gaspard's overalls; the cat drawing exhibited the look of triumph in the eyes to perfection, the proud whiskers, the cock of the tail.

Absorbed, Guy did not hear Yolande return and started guiltily as she came round the desk.

Blushing, he proffered an apology.

'Sorry, I should have asked…'

Yolande was completely unfazed.

'Not at all, be my guest. Do you like them?'

'Wow, I'd say so,' replied Guy in genuine admiration. 'You're extremely gifted. Have you had any training?'

'My art teacher at school in Perpignan helped me and was very supportive. Other than that, no.'

'I've never seen you sketching, apart from today. How do you do it?'

'I take a mental photo of a scene, then draw it while it's still fresh.'

'Yolande, you've missed your vocation, truly you have.'

As someone whose artistic talents registered well below zero, Guy envied a gift he would never possess.

And when he thought about it, Yolande's handwriting was itself very beautiful, a flowing, flowery script: Guy's resembled a drunken spider's.

*

Three weeks later, André came home with some bad news.

'Hubert is dead, had a heart attack last night, just keeled over. Only 56, never had a health problem to my knowledge. Bloody shame.'

Sad as he was at Hubert's sudden demise, Guy clicked immediately the problem. Hubert was an excellent forger and worked for the line creating false documents for British airmen. Supplied by Auguste, a local printer, with the real McCoy of blank ID cards and ration documents, Hubert performed miracles. His documents were indistinguishable from the real thing. Rubber stamps fashioned using the genuine article 'borrowed' one night from the Prefecture de Police as patterns, the equally genuine ink, smudges and artificial ageing, Hubert incorporated all the nuances that fooled even a close inspection.

The line was controlled by Sybille, a retired civil servant who lived in Issoudun. Guy had been introduced to Sybille as part of his network. Greying, hair always in a bun, soberly dressed, Sybille looked as if butter wouldn't melt in her mouth. Plus, she was a lady you would pass in the street and never remember, a key attribute in a trade like hers. Sybille had a well-developed relay system that took airmen south, then over the Spanish border. Long it might have been, but it was far safer than trying to smuggle escapees out across the Channel. With the increasing level of military activity in La Manche, it could be like Piccadilly Circus, even at night.

With the war now far advanced, air raids on Germany intensified and with them, a commensurate increase in the number of downed aircrew.

Now, there was not only Peter Lewis holed up with Simon, but six more like him from a crippled Lancaster and two Hurricanes spread around various farms in the area. The Gestapo put 110% in trying to locate these Terrorflieger as part of their propaganda efforts. Getting them out of the region quickly was vital.

Peter was still an invalid, although now able to walk with a stick. Three or four weeks would see him fit to go down the line. The four Lancaster crew and the Hurricane pilots were all hale and hearty.

Guy was two steps ahead of André's thought processes.

'You want Yolande to take over as the forger, don't you?'

André was dumbstruck at Guy's prescience.

'How the hell did you know that?'

'Because I know about her artistic skills, she drew me and Alphonse the other day and I had a look through her sketch pad.'

'Ah.'

The hairs on the back of Guy's neck were struggling to tell him something, but at the same time, the need for a good forger was paramount and beggars could not be choosers. Guy comforted himself with the thought that André and Yolande had worked together for years, that they were long-term lovers, that André knew Yolande far better than he did.

That evening, André invited Yolande for dinner chez Lavallois, with Guy as volunteer chef. Guy had already made up his mind to cook French style, even though he had learned various cuisines through his mother.

Dinner was roast leg of beef, obtained on the marché noir from one of André's many farmer friends. While the majority of town dwellers suffered food shortages and long queues, farmers generally did not. Much of their meat and produce was under requisition by the occupiers, but the agricultural community had become past masters at underdeclaring their output. This satisfied two desires. One was the pragmatic need to fill bellies; the other was the inbuilt French urge to put one over on authority.

Stuffed with garlic, accompanied by an assortment of vegetables from the identical source to the beef, the meat was slow-roasted. The aromas as le chef did his thing in the kitchen set the olfactory nerves twitching in anticipation of delights to come. The nerves were right:

pink, juicy and tender, the beef just fell off the bone, the vegetables had that slight crunch. Bliss, sheer bliss.

André waited until tarte tatin had been consumed and the plimsoll line on the second bottle of red was well on its way south before he tackled the matter in hand.

Adroitly, he steered the conversation round to the war.

Yolande picked on the problems with food.

'We shouldn't have to sneak around to get meat like this,' she exclaimed, pointing to the remains of the leg. 'The bloody Boche are starving us while they live off the fat of the land – our land, to be precise. How long before we're rid of them and their strutting up and down like turkeycocks?'

'Yolande, you've often said you'd like to help the Resistance if you got the chance?'

André fired his opening salvo.

'Definitely!'

'Well, you can.'

Yolande's dark pupils dilated visibly, clearly her lover's words came as a complete surprise. Then she looked at both André and Guy and it clicked.

'You're an agent, aren't you?' she directed at Guy.

He nodded.

'And you, André, what have you been keeping back from me for so long?'

Her tone was accusatory.

'Yolande, I've been part of the Resistance a while, but I didn't want to involve you, this war's bad enough without exposing you unnecessarily.'

Yolande made as if to speak, but André silenced her with a gesture.

'Yes, I know, I know, you've said to me several times that you'd like to do your bit, but I really was in a cleft stick and so I erred on the side of caution and safety for you.'

'So, what's behind the change of heart?'

'The number of Allied airmen crash-landing or baling out is rising all the time, we need another forger to help with false documents. It really is a problem we need to solve and right now.'

This was part of the pre-arranged dialogue that he had agreed with Guy. Although Yolande did not know either Hubert or his activities, the overwhelming need for watertight security and need to know obligated telling Yolande as little as possible about the escape line.

Yolande's brain was patently in think mode.

'What do I have to do, André?'

'We'll supply all the cards and that sort of thing, but we're desperate for your artist's skills. The cards have got to pass muster on the spot-checks and at places like railway stations. Very often, we give the lads Dutch or Flemish nationality to excuse their lack of French. Plus, you have to make the cards look as though they've been issued in various parts of France. It means hiding the materials in your house so you can do this during the evening.'

At this, Yolande's nose wrinkled, but she nodded in agreement.

Then another thought struck her.

'Are any of the other staff at Lavallois involved?'

'No, and they're not going to be,' said Guy at his firmest. 'And the cardinal rule is that we never, ever breathe a word of this at work.'

Responding to the woman's furrowed brow and slightly puzzled look, he went on, 'We have everyone and his brother calling on us and the Boche will be well aware of the golden opportunity that offers as an information exchange. Or, the SD might have some of our customers on their payroll as informers. They may well have the place bugged for all we know.'

'I see.'

There was a great deal said and meant in those two little words.

'And you, Christophe?'

'The other cardinal rule is that what you don't know, you can't tell. You and everyone else get told exactly what they need to know and no more, it's the safest for all of us, because the Boche are too damned smart at infiltrating networks. I'm here to organise and command, that's all you need to know.'

This produced a mutinous look from Yolande, but Guy's expression and tone left no room for argument.

Everyone helped clear away. André and Yolande retired to André's bed to doubtless expunge some passion. Guy poured himself a brandy and spent twenty minutes contemplating his navel before climbing the stairs to bed.

Yolande assumed Hubert's mantle as if it had been tailor-made for her. A bit of practice and she was turning out work the equal if not better than her dead predecessor's. She had a gift, a touch. Not only that, she could work at speed and three or four sets of documents would appear after only a couple of evenings' work.

Sybille in turn responded by sending escapees down the line at a previously unheard of rate, but it was like the widow's cruse, as fast as one batch travelled south, so a new one would materialise.

Of necessity, Yolande and Sybille had been introduced, but the leader of the line was the only person in it that Yolande knew.

A month went by. Guy went off on a selling trip for several days, travelling by train, bus and Auntie. Late one afternoon, he cycled back to the hangar. Parking the bike against the steel wall, he strolled through the airlock into the office. André sat there, quite alone.

A pang of anxiety struck Guy.

'No Yolande today?'

'She's taken a few days holiday.'

André's reply was accompanied by a conspiratorial wink to indicate that Guy should ask no questions.

Scarcely able to contain his curiosity, Guy nonetheless held his tongue until they reached the maison de maitre.

'Where's Yolande?'

He was surprised to hear himself bark the question like an RSM on parade.

'Easy, easy, Christophe.'

André was reacting to Guy's obvious tone.

'The lady that was supposed to take Peter Lewis down the line got knocked over by a Boche truck last night, broken ankle and bruises, she's in hospital. We had to get him out on schedule, so Yolande's taken him as far as Limoges.'

Guy was aghast.

'André, are you completely gaga? Yolande's irreplaceable as our forger and you risk her on a courier run?'

André threw up his arms in a gesture of futility and defence combined.

'Yeah, yeah, it's OK for you, Mr High and Mighty. You weren't sitting here up shit creek without a paddle. Peter had to go and there was nobody else available, all the other girls are on runs. It was Yolande or nobody. Sorry, but it was my decision and I made it.'

For two days, Guy sweated. Using the telephone was out of the question, all the lines were tapped, so unless a call could have innocent codewords in an otherwise normal conversation, it was asking for trouble.

At the end of the second day, Guy and André drove home. The silence between them fizzed. Unbidden, Guy made supper. At nine o'clock, André could take no more and drove off towards Yolande's little cottage. With the unreliability of the French transport system in wartime, anything could happen and frequently did.

At 1030, Guy heard the sound of the Citroen approaching. Unable to contain his impatience, he met André at the front door. The look on the man's face told him all he wanted to know.

'She's back, safe and sound. Went without a hitch, our man's on the second leg.'

Guy knew that the line operated by delivering escapees to houses, where they would spend a night before being taken further down south by a second courier, who handed them over to a group on the Spanish border. From there, they would be taken by Spanish guides up and over the Pyrenees, frequently up to their waists and beyond in snow. Even if they made it, there was always the chance of being spotted by the Guardia Civil and incarcerated in some flea-riddled Spanish jail. The British Consulate usually managed to spring them, oft by oiling the wheels with baksheesh, then smuggling them out via Portugal or Gibraltar. A 'home run', as it was known, could take months.

*

By 1943, France and in particular, France's mood, had changed totally since the German invasion in May 1940.

The defeat of the well-equipped and well-trained French army came as a hammer blow to the whole nation and left an open wound that would take decades to heal.

As the tidal wave of the Nazi onslaught swept westwards over the northern two thirds of France, reactions in towns and cities varied. Some communities resisted, only to suffer casualties and damage from bombardment; others, knowing or fearing such calamity and that any opposition was but to delay the inevitable, declared themselves 'open' and let the Germans in without firing a shot.

Perhaps anxious to dispel any reputation for brutality that might still linger from World War I, the German military established good contact with local officials and set up control and administration systems that accorded French local government and justice systems a large degree of autonomy. At the same time, the occupiers made it clear that resistance would not be tolerated and had designated hostages in the event of a problem.

By and large, the French took the view that working with rather than against the Boche made life easier and allowed them to carry on as normal a life as wartime would permit. For some, the inducement was hard cash. Industrialists were awarded contracts to supply the Nazi war machine. For others, it was a rampant black market, feeding an unceasing demand from the invaders and well-heeled French for luxury goods.

Rocking the boat was not on the agenda, to the extent that anyone resisting might be shopped by their own.

The pivotal moment that ignited the beginnings of resistance came in October 1941, when a Communist trio from Paris assassinated the Military Governor of Nantes, Lieutenant-Colonel Hotz. On Hitler's direct orders, 48 hostages were executed and only pressure from many quarters prevented 50 more sharing the same fate.

The executions shook France to its very core, the stark realisation that this was no benign occupation, but a savage and unforgiving enemy. Before long, the Gestapo took over control from the firm but fair military, instilling a brutish regime. Deportations to concentration camps increased for both Jews and non-Jews, food and other essentials like electricity decreased as the war deepened. The Free Zone was taken over by the occupiers in 1942 and in 1943, they introduced the STO, the Service du Travail Obligatoire, essentially forced labour to work in factories in Germany. Many young men became réfractaires, draft-dodgers, who hid from the authorities.

The French nation had gradually come to realise that the occupation had to end and the initial resistance to the Resistance had become at worst tacit support and at best real help and assistance. France wanted the hated Boche out and the sooner the better.

Nonetheless, acts of sabotage and resistance had to be well-considered. In the Unoccupied Zone prior to November 1942, SOE had a 'no bangs' rule for fear of upsetting the applecart and triggering an occupation.

In the Occupied Zone, SOE's primary role was to organise an underground ready to spring into action after D-Day, to harry and hinder the Germans from repelling the Allied invasion. Any sabotage was mainly limited to economic and industrial; attacking and killing German forces would bring swift and terminal retribution on the local populace.

Communications were a prime target for saboteurs. Roads, railways, canals, telephone lines were all on the hit list and none more so than the railways.

The need to move large amounts of men and materiel over long distances made the rail network a vital artery of the German war effort. Their relentless fortification of the Channel coast drew an equally relentless stream of trains laden with construction materials, heavy weapons and munitions: the Hun knew full well that an Allied invasion was but a matter of time.

*

'I need a word, Christophe.'

The whispered request at the regular meeting of the reseau was from Jean-Marie, a fitter and machinist in the local railway works in Le Mans.

Jean-Marie was in his forties, a tall, slim and actually quite elegant man whose elegance was spoilt by hands yellow with oil stains, dirty fingernails and black cuticles from his profession. He smelt permanently of cutting oil, a sweet yet pungent odour.

As everyone else bade goodnight and set off home, Guy and Jean-Marie sat down to talk.

'You know that Le Mans is an important junction in the rail network?'

Guy nodded.

'Did you also know that our workshops are one of the biggest for miles? We employ 350 men. St Nazaire's are about the same size. They're the nearest and that's 200km. They're flat out all the time, no spare capacity. If ours were knocked out, it would be a helluva blow to old Fritz.'

The Le Mans workshops were in a roundhouse, a building resembling a ring doughnut with a section cut away. Locomotives entered and left through this section. When entering, an engine would stop on a big turntable in the middle, then be rotated to line up with its designated shed and driven inside.

Guy had seen the roundhouse from a nearby road, but until Jean-Marie had been recruited, he had no intelligence on what lay within.

'Tell me more.'

Accompanying his words with a rough diagram on a piece of paper, Jean-Marie explained the layout.

'There are twelve sheds. Eight are for routine maintenance and the middle four are major servicing bays. Each of the middle bays has a gantry crane to lift off boilers or even detach whole engines from their bogies. At the back of those bays are machine and heat treatment shops. There's nothing we can't do in there. We re-tube boilers, repair wheels and machine new parts from scratch, all the major overhaul stuff.'

'And of course, there's the turntable. Smash that and the whole place grinds to a halt. They lock big freight locos in there at night, too.'

'Kay,' said Guy, thinking quickly and with a gleam in his eye. 'What about the building itself, can we have a go at that?'

Jean-Marie smiled.

'Not unless you've got access to high explosive. The sheds were put up in 1890, true Victorian brick outhouse standard, three layers of stone, masses of cast-iron. The RAF might be able to do something if they managed to hit it, but not thee and me.'

'Guards, Jean-Marie?'

'Actually quite a small patrol and they do checks inside about every couple of hours. I know that because I've done the odd night shift. The inside patrols stop about 4.30am when the firing crews come in to get all the boilers going.'

'How do we get in?'

'There's various doors at the back. We're not supposed to have keys, but I do.'

He indicated a door at the western end of the roundhouse.

'Inside's totally open-plan, so once you're in, you can get anywhere.'

'I'd like a recce, first of the guards' routine, then get inside for a look-see,' said Guy.

'Tomorrow night, Jean-Marie?'

A nod, then swiftly a flame from Jean-Marie's Zippo as he burnt his little drawing to ashes.

The following night, Guy and the railwayman were hunched between some carriages in the sidings, night-glasses trained on the roundhouse. Sure enough, the guards patrolled around the building, leaving time gaps sufficient to gain entry or exit. The inside checks were at about two-hourly intervals, but varied by up to fifteen minutes either side – some Germans had begun to learn about ordnung equalling predictability. Except one thing was predictable, they always seemed to use the western door to enter and the eastern to leave.

'Jean-Marie, what happens if they come in while we're there?'

'The guards don't like going in the pits under the locos, so if they do come in, we'll duck into a pit.'

The next two nights were crystal-clear with a bright moon, but on the third, rain and sleet swept across the Sarthe. Just right.

Dressed in overalls and berets and wearing rubber-soled shoes, Guy and Jean-Marie once more found themselves in the marshalling yards. They crept closer and closer to the western end of the sheds, watching an inside check take place. Several minutes passed before the clang of the steel door at the eastern end of the roundhouse announced the patrol's exit.

Seizing a gap, the pair were across the tracks, to silently ease their way in and shut the door without making a sound.

Jean-Marie had spent his entire working life in the sheds and knew his way around blindfold.

The air reeked of soot, of coal, of oil, of wisps of steam, of warm metal and cold metal. Even a blind man would have known exactly where he was. The floor was gritty underfoot with ash and dirt. Pieces of locomotives and whole axles were everywhere. Accustomed to the dark, Guy could make out the huge bulk of the freight locos, some still warm. From Guy's right came a loud clang and he jumped like a startled rabbit.

'Easy, easy.' Jean-Marie's hand was on his shoulder. 'Just a boiler cooling off, but don't touch any engine that's warm.'

Jean-Marie's voice was a sibilant hiss.

'They retain heat for hours, you could get seriously burned if you touch the wrong bit.'

Treading like cats with butter on their paws, the two inched their way to the machine shops. Huge doors offered access to large engine parts, but an unlocked personal door served for humans.

His father's garage at Montluçon had a machine shop for engine rebuilds and Guy was no slouch with lathe or milling machine, but what he had used were as Meccano to these giants. Despite the dark, Guy could see the faceplate of a monster lathe. Huge endmills, horizontal and vertical borers, it was like being Lilliputian in Gulliver's travels.

'If we sabotage all these, could they be replaced?'

'I hardly think so.'

Jean-Marie's reply was a chuckle.

'The lathe is used for repairing and truing driving wheels. It was made by a company called Patterson's in Milwaukee. Right now, I can't see Fritz picking up the phone and saying "Guten Tag, Chuck, can I have a new lathe please?" Besides, all these things are made to order and that takes months. Then they're shipped in sections, assembled on site, then commissioned. More months. The milling machines are Swiss, the borers come from Sweden. Hard to say whether they'd sell the Germans new kit, but it wouldn't be quick, even if they did.'

'You must also remember that all this stuff is years old. It's built to last and the bearings can be adjusted to take up wear. There's been no re-equipping in my time and that's twenty-five years. So whether there's any spares out there is anybody's guess.'

They went carefully back into the main sheds and Jean-Marie showed Guy the cranes, substantial girders with electric gantries overhead.

Listening first for any signs of activity, they descended a stone staircase and entered the tunnel leading to the turntable. Safe from prying eyes, Jean-Marie switched on a torch and they entered the machinery chamber. Steam-driven from the central boiler that doubled as the heat-treatment forge, the mechanisms were as massive as the engines they transported. The support frame for the turntable rotated on a ring of steel roller bearings. The central shaft that located the turntable would have needed more explosive than Guy could muster, but if they blew the bearing ring and the supports on the frame, plus the steam-driven mechanism, that would cripple the whole shebang.

Time to retreat.

Watches were checked. They had actually been there only half an hour, but with the tension, it seemed far longer and there was always the threat of the outside patrols. Standing on a box at one grimy window, Jean-Marie watched the soldiers do their rounds before slipping the lock on the door.

Next evening, Guy and Jean-Marie sat down at the latter's home to flesh out a plan.

'As I see it ,'began Guy, 'we have three targets – the machine and heat treatment shops, the locos and the turntable. You have to be part of it, Jean-Marie, we need your inside knowledge and your ability to navigate around in the dark. I suggest you head the machine shop party and I run the turntable side. Then you lead us round the cranes and the locos.'

All that day, Guy had been focusing on how big a group to take and decided on a total of seven including himself. He would take one man to help him mine the turntable, leaving Jean-Marie to pack explosive around all the most sensitive points on the machinery, including the furnace. After that, all six would place charges and time-pencils on the crane supports and the left-hand cylinder and conrod of each steam engine. Daniel Rogers had dinned into his pupils that the art of sabotage meant wrecking the same component of a number of machines to prevent cannibalisation. The seventh man was lookout, essential to warn Guy and his companion down in the turntable pit if anything went wrong.

The fitter nodded.

'So, how long to do the job?'

'Fifteen minutes for the turntable, then we help you finish off the two shops, so I calculate half an hour, then on to the cranes and engines. Maximum of an hour. What's your view?'

'You're explosives trained, but it sounds good.'

'Who then, Christophe?'

For fifteen minutes, they tossed around various names before settling on five they felt right for the job, younger and more nimble resistants who could crawl around in the pits and pack the plastic from the reverse side, out of sight. The weather appeared set foul, so two nights later, they sat down with the commando and briefed them. Guy had some plastic and a pencil fuse, which he used to demonstrate how to putty it around objects, then plant and arm the fuse. Jean-Marie briefed them on the key points on the machines.

All the team were locals and knew the roundhouse, in fact one had made deliveries there. A diagram of the layout was used for briefing and the many questions answered.

Each man was issued with overalls, beret and rubber-soled shoes.

'When do we go?' enquired Honoré, Guy's co-saboteur on the turntable.

'Tomorrow night, here's the rendezvous. Be there at 0100.'

Guy's finger indicated the spot on a local map.

Rain and sleet were once more in evidence as they stood at the RV, dividing up plastic and fuses.

'Synchronise watches. On y va.'

Hugging the cover of wagons and carriages, they inched towards the western door, stopping only to observe the inside patrol for timing before cracking the door.

Now sure of his ground, Guy led Honoré downstairs and into the pit. They were halfway through packing explosives around the mechanism, when Honoré caught sight of three torch flashes from the other end of the tunnel. It could mean only one thing, that the inside patrol had entered.

'Christ, is this it?'

Guy's mind was in a turmoil, his heart was hammering and sweat beads stood out on his forehead. They simply did not know if the patrol included the pit.

With nowhere to go, the pair moved back into the darkest recesses of the chamber and turned to face the wall.

Upstairs, Jean-Marie led his group swiftly and noiselessly across the shed and into the deepest pit, where they too crouched, faces covered, blood pressures soaring.

Much to their surprise, they heard only two sets of boots. What was going on?

Crouched in the loco pit, the saboteurs were frozen with fear, scarcely daring to breathe.

The two pairs of boots crunched nearer and nearer, the sound seeming almost deafening to the anguished ears in the pit.

Down beneath the turntable, Guy and Honoré were bereft of thought, unable to hear or know what was happening above.

Had Jean-Marie or any of his fellows spoken German, they would have heard one the soldiers say, 'I dropped my brandy flask here somewhere. I told the sergeant it was my lighter.'

The two continued. The patrols used only torches to avoid any lights showing to possible aircraft raids and shone the beams on the floor where they had walked.

'Found it!'

The soldiers retreated the way they had come.

Five sets of French lungs breathed out in unison.

Instructed by Jean-Marie, the lookout walked down to the turntable pit to give the all-clear.

Time fuses primed, Guy and Honoré joined the others.

'Why did they come back?' demanded Honoré, still at high doe.

'One of them seemed to have dropped something on his last patrol,' explained Jean-Marie. 'He found it and they went back the way they'd come.'

'Jesus!' remarked Honoré with feeling, 'I thought that was our lot!'

With adrenaline at a peak, the party moved swiftly, laying charges on not only the crane supports, but also the gantries and motors as well. Led by Jean-Marie, plastic was packed behind loco cylinders and conrods.

Guy's estimate of an hour was spot on. Before unlocking the western door and making good their escape, Guy scratched the wards of the lock with one of his picks to divert suspicion from an inside job.

*

Unable to hang around to see the results, the commando split and went home. It was several days before Guy could visit a dead letter drop to pick up a coded message from Jean-Marie. Trembling, he decoded the note.

170

Half an hour after the raiding party had decamped, the charges went off. Every loco was disabled to await new cylinders and conrods; all the cranes collapsed; the machine shops were now totally useless, with little or no hope of spares for months if not years and the turntable would require a total rebuild from scratch.

Success!

Chapter 10

A constant problem for the Resistance was finding secure hiding places for their weapons and equipment. The Boche were nothing if not assiduous at snap searches of buildings and there was always the risk of betrayal from some Frenchman or Frenchwoman short of a few centimes in wartime. Farm buildings and barns were a favourite target for searches, since these offered the most likely and often remote hidey-holes for arms caches and downed airmen.

The afternoon was chilly, a light breeze brought a smell of impending frost. The cows in a field to Guy's left munched gently at the dank grass. Even the birds seemed to have hibernated and the total silence of the countryside was palpable. It reminded Guy of the days he had shared with Colonel on Jack's farm and for a moment, his heart and mind were back in Devon, aching to tickle those pink ears.

Now about eight miles from Le Mans, Guy suddenly realised he needed to pee. Not being of the customary Gallic ilk that turning your back to the passing traffic, sparse as it was, constituted modesty, Guy looked for a side turning. After another quarter mile, he found a sideroad to the right, a ribbon of brown and irregular tarmac spiralling downhill between some tall hedges. Over the top of the hedge to his left, he could see the scar of a stone quarry and about a hundred yards further down, braked to a halt in the bellmouth of a gateway leading into the workings. The rusty wire fence to either side of the gateway, the undisturbed surface of the track leading into the quarry and a sign so devoid of paint as to be illegible bore witness to the workings being disused for some considerable period. The track looked quite smooth and free from the sharp flints that could shred the Citroen's rubber. On impulse, Guy backed up and swung through the entrance.

The roadway might have been smooth, but it was very steep, curving downhill to the left and disappearing behind a rock wall. Gingerly, Guy crept down in second gear, ever conscious of the drop to his right. As he rounded the bend, huge lumps of rock became visible on the quarry floor, plus various rusty bits of machinery including a conveyor belt. Also visible, tucked hard against the rock face to his left, was a single storey building with steel plate walls, a corrugated iron roof and metal-framed windows. A dusty concrete apron at the front provided a car park and Guy stopped outside the double doors leading inside the building. Having relieved the inner man, he started to explore.

The inside was very dark and the small windows so grime-encrusted, nothing was visible. The double doors were secured with a padlock, hasp and staple, the former so rusty, nothing short of dynamite was going to shift it. All the windows were intact and Guy thought it prudent not to break any glass. Being metal framed, the windows' catches could not be slid with a knife blade. Luckily he found that on one of the windows to the side, much of the putty to one pane had cracked and fallen out. The trusty Swiss knife swiftly got rid of the rest, then the knife blade was used to ease the glass from its seating. Reaching inside, Guy swung the lever catch and creaked the casement outwards on its rusty hinges. Seconds later, he was inside.

Skylights allowed a certain amount of light to spill in somewhat murky shafts, but the panoply of dust visible on each one formed a highly effective filter. Adjusting his eyes to the gloom, Guy could see large steel worktables, various saws and cutting machinery. Above his head stood a travelling crane on a sturdy gantry. Everywhere was covered in a patina of grey dust and his footsteps scrunched as he walked on the gritty floor. To his surprise, some blocks of stone still lay on the worktables, one block even had a power saw yet embedded in the half-completed cut. Hammers, cold chisels and a variety of stoneworking handtools were strewn around on tables and benches, just abandoned where they lay. The whole thing had a Marie Celeste feeling, as though the occupants had done a moonlight flit. In the far right hand corner stood an office created from plywood, its entrance door clinging on by the one hinge still intact. Guy strolled inside, to find only two cheap wooden desks and a couple of chairs. Like everything else, the furniture was almost invisible beneath a coating of grey dust and no papers of any kind were visible. A block and chain tackle lay in one corner. A calendar for 1932 was pinned to a cork notice board. It showed what appeared to be the Bridge of Sighs in Venice. The name on the calendar was Bernadini et Fils. Were they the quarry's former owners, pondered Guy.

As he parked, Guy had seen that the left hand steel wall of the building was tight against the rock face, in fact set into it so that an outcrop hid any view of the narrow fissure. Now as he wandered the inside of the workshop, he gazed at the left hand wall. At first glance, it appeared normal, but instinct said something was not quite comme il faut. Each of the steel sheets forming the walls was securely welded to a substantial angle iron frame, with the frames' vertical sections bolted together. At the top, the frames were bolted to the underside of an I-girder supported on cast iron pillars; at the bottom, rag bolts held the lower edges against the concrete base. Substantial it certainly was, draughtproof it was not and daylight shone through innumerable gaps where steel did not fit exactly against steel. The breeze excited little dust eddies across the floor.

Then it hit Guy what had attracted his attention. The wall section in the front left hand corner was not only bolted to its right hand neighbour, but was also welded in two places near top and bottom. Although rusty, the welds seemed fresher than any other fixings on the structure. The four rag bolts in the bottom edge were completely missing, as were the bolts in the top edge. Intrigued, Guy attempted to peer at the left side frame, but it was in virtual darkness. Swiftly, Guy returned to the Citroen for a torch, which he shone on the frame. At first sight, all that was visible were the heads of large bolts, one each at top and bottom, but very faint semicircular witness marks on the adjoining frame showed that the wall section had pivoted outwards at some time. Pointing the torch upwards confirmed similar marks at the top.

A rickety but serviceable stepladder stood against the wall of the office. Guy helped himself to ladder, club hammer and cold chisel. Checking that no one was around, he climbed the ladder and attacked the upper weld. Tempered for stone not steel, the chisel rapidly blunted and he used up two chisels on each of the welds. Lacking a spanner, the chisels came in handy for loosening the four nuts and bolts and some oil courtesy of the Citroen's dipstick made an awkward task of freeing the nuts completely rather easier. Nonetheless, it took nearly an hour to release the right edge.

The problem now was to get a sufficient handhold on the section to be able to pull it outwards. Then Guy remembered the block and tackle, but how to secure it? Inspecting a cross strut revealed a hole near the right hand end suitable to take one of the securing bolts. One of the worktables nearby had steel legs, so he hooked one end of the mechanism to the bolt and one to a leg, then started hauling. Initially, absolutely nothing happened except the sweat began to pour off him and the blood began to pound in his ears. The young man backed off and drew some deep breaths before bracing his feet against the worktable leg for more purchase. Still nothing. Now despairing, Guy looked around for some means of increasing the leverage. Propped against the opposite wall lay a four foot crowbar, obviously for moving stone blocks around. Wrapping the free end of the chain around the crowbar, he jammed the crowbar's toe against the table leg and hauled lustily. For a second, nothing moved, then with a bang and a screech of metal as the rust bond between the two sections let go, the wall panel swung free with such a start that Guy lost his balance and fell flat on his back. Winded, he lay there, thankful that the hefty crowbar had swung to one side and missed him on its way floorwards.

Regaining his breath, Guy picked up the torch and shone it towards whatever lay behind the pivoting wall section. The light revealed the mouth of a tunnel, in origin a natural opening, but clearly modified so that the arch at the top had been squared off. The marks from a pneumatic chisel were patently obvious. The alteration was such as to allow quite a large vehicle through, with the vertical face either side of the entrance accurately dressed to allow the steel wall to sit just a few millimetres away, effectively blocking any view of the cave mouth. Guy started walking down the tunnel into the pitch blackness.

He had advanced about thirty feet when he let out a piercing scream of sheer terror as the beam picked out four eyes staring at him. Except they did not, in fact those eyes had not stared at anything for a good many years. Before him were four eyeless sockets, the sockets belonging to two skeletons sitting on the ground with their backs against a large grey van. In the centre of each forehead, the entry hole for a large calibre bullet told how they had met their unfortunate end. Regaining his composure, Guy moved towards the bodies, starting as a number of rats scuttled past him and out of the cave. Apart from the bones, everything else in the way of flesh and clothing had long since been devoured by vermin. Even the leather boots had gone, only some plastic buttons remained, sitting by the brass buckles of each corpse's belt. Around each clavicle sat a brass dog tag on a chain. Fascinated, Guy read the identities. Both corpses were male, one Paul Gauvain, one a Paul Montigny. Their former employer was also identified, Banque de la Seine and each tag contained a serial number, presumably the employee number for each man. The grey van bore no markings, but was fitted with substantial rear springs and twin-wheel rear axle. Inside the van lay a pile of smallish wooden boxes that were immediately identifiable as bullion boxes. Casting his light around, Guy saw a small furnace and crucible, the latter with traces of gold still visible. So here was a crime scene, a bullion robbery resulting in the murders of the two van drivers. The perpetrators, well Bernadini et

Fils had a great deal of explaining to do. Being hard-headed, Guy recognised that he had discovered a superb hidey-hole for the Resistance, provided he got rid of the two bodies to prevent awkward questions. The cave was almost circular, about thirty feet in diameter and twelve feet high. But despite his delight at his find, Guy's natural curiosity wanted to know the story behind the robbery and the deaths.

He waited until he and André were well into their main course before he broached the subject of the quarry and the hidden cave. At his words, a light came on in André's eyes.

'So *that's* what happened!' he exclaimed. 'I'll tell you the story. The quarry was owned by Marco Bernadini and his sons. They were stonemasons, arrived here in 1919, Marco told us they came from somewhere in southern Italy, I don't remember the name of the town. It started off with Marco, then his four sons turned up soon afterwards. Marco said he was widowed, so no Signora Bernadini. With the devastation caused by the war, so many buildings were damaged, especially the churches and the Bernadinis were very good. About a year after they came, Marco found the quarry site and bought it. The stone was just right for the local buildings. Marco spoke quite reasonable French, but all the sons didn't, what they did speak was really rough and so heavily accented, they were pretty unintelligible. They spoke Italian to one another and never employed anyone else, so French was unimportant. From time to time, two or three of them would disappear for a couple of months at a time. Marco's explanation was that they still picked up jobs in Italy and that's where they'd gone. Now I wonder what mischief they were really up to.'

André paused.

'So what about the bullion?' enquired Guy.

'I got the lowdown from the local Police chief,' explained André. 'October '32, the Banque de la Seine bought a lot of bullion from a New York bank and had it shipped to Le Havre on a liner. Problem was, a mother and father of all storms blew down the Channel for a week and the liner had to run for cover in Brest. The insurance was very specific, the bullion was covered by the shipping line until the liner reached France, so once it docked in Brest, it was down to the bank. They laid on an undercover operation to move it to Paris and they were so paranoid about secrecy, not even the Police were told. Instead, they used an unmarked van with two drivers, who had to go direct from the docks in Brest to Paris without stopping except for fuel. As security, there were number of checkpoints along the way, manned by bank staff in unmarked cars. The van was allowed a certain amount of lateness depending on the distance from the last checkpoint, the estimated traffic in towns and refuelling. If the van ran over its lateness, the observer had to inform the Police. The van failed to make the checkpoint east of Laval and the bank's man called the cavalry. They combed the whole area and never found a vestige of anything. What you've uncovered shows the Bernadinis as the thieves –and murderers too, for that matter.'

'I remember that in the Winter of '32, I passed two of the Bernadini trucks going south, each with some large blocks of stone on the back. I happened to see old man Bernadini in a local post office and he said they'd picked up a large contract in Italy and they were all going down there for several months. That was the last I ever saw of Marco and any of his sons. Nobody ever made any connection because we were used to the Bernadinis disappearing and by then the trail was cold anyway. My guess is that those stone blocks had been hollowed out and were many times more valuable than anyone could have ever imagined. Hmm, wonder if the Bernadinis are still in Italy – doubt it somehow. Anyway, nothing will bring back those two poor sods and if we want to use the cave, we'll just have to keep quiet about what you've found. If we hide the skeletons elsewhere and burn the boxes, the van will just be an unidentified vehicle. I think the secret can remain hidden until after the war, don't you? Well done, Christophe.'

A couple of days later, the pair returned to the quarry armed with two large wooden crates, picks and shovels. They packed a camera and flash as well, to record the exact scene before they moved the evidence. Once again, the lane was deserted as Guy rolled carefully downhill and stopped outside the workshop. André could see the tension on Guy's face for what they were about to do and gave his shoulder a reassuring squeeze.

'OK, let's do it, Christophe.'

Woodenly, Guy climbed from the truck they had brought along and repeated his trick with the window pane. Once inside, they picked up a large hammer and chisel and returned to the outside of the double doors. Taking the chisel firmly in one hand, Guy put the cutting edge against the top of the rusty padlock and whacked the chisel with all his might. After five heavy blows, the padlock succumbed. André felt in his jacket pocket and withdrew another padlock, which he looked at admiringly.

'Not bad, even though I do say so myself,' he smirked.

He was referring to the artificial rusting he and Guy had created on the exterior of the lock by packing the internals with thick grease, then immersing the ensemble in vinegar and salt water. A coating of the local quarry dust completed the disguise to perfection.

Now with access to the workshop, they hefted the two crates inside. Guy retrieved the stepladder from where he had replaced it and using spanners, swiftly unscrewed the bolts securing the pivoting wall section. This time, pulling the wall outwards was easier, but it still took the extra leverage of the block and tackle to crack open the panel. As the steel moved outwards, Guy shivered again and felt himself gripped by a horrible nausea. He gagged for few seconds, then got a grip on himself and in concert with André, walked once more into the crypt.

'Right, I'll record all this.' André's voice contained a false briskness to hide his own disquiet.

Moving carefully so as not to disturb the scene, André took over half a roll of film. He started with an overall covering shot of the scene, then moved on to the two skeletons, recording their positions, followed by close-ups of the dog tags. He also took pictures of the entry and exit holes in the van where the bullets had passed through. Surprisingly, the bullion van was not armoured and the projectiles had passed straight through the vehicle's sides to splatter against the rock face behind.

'Now for the inside of the van and the registration plates,' muttered André, carefully retrieving yet another spent flashbulb from the cave floor.

Pictures of the small furnace and crucible were next before André rewound the film and sealed it into a canister using insulation tape.

'Where are we going to put all this lot, I wonder?' mused André.

Checking the coast was clear, they scouted round outside and found a sort of cave at the back of the quarry caused by the blasting. Knowing what they had to do next, neither man was keen to return to the scene of death, but drawing deep breaths, they forced themselves back inside. Each skeleton was laid carefully in its crate so that it was as intact as possible, then the lids were nailed down and the impromptu coffins laid to rest in the cave, accompanied by the furnace and crucible. One coffin contained the film and the van's plates. There was yet space for the bullion boxes, which saved them burning the evidence. A cairn of small and medium rocks sealed off the entrance.

Glad it was all over, they swung the wall section back into place. But it was not yet over. Guy's eye had been drawn to the swivelling panel because it lacked bolts top and bottom. Inspecting the other panels revealed that some were missing their full complement of bolts, so by purloining fasteners from the darker corners of other sections, they were able to disguise the panel to match the rest.

Heaving sighs that it was job done, they went home to large brandies apiece.

*

Le Mans was a highly dangerous place for the Resistanceards to operate. It was heavily populated by the Germans, bristling with military installations. Not only that, it was a junction for all kinds of traffic, road, rail and telephone. The Abwehr and worse still, the SD, the Gestapo secret police, had excellent networks and it was said that every café or restaurant had at least one paid French informer on the staff.

The Gestapo's ruthless control, imposing a brutal dictatorship and punishing any resistance savagely, made hiding arms and explosives in farm buildings and outhouses far more hazardous than normal. For Guy's Le Mans group, the quarry was heaven-sent.

The previous cache of arms, explosives and equipment had been blown along with the reseau, so fresh stocks were a priority.

On his next sked, Guy placed his order. The whole idea of a guerrilla force is to be highly mobile, to strike at the enemy then flee, not about pitched battles. Heavy weapons like machine guns are not on the agenda, but Bren and Sten guns, even light mortars which are portable, and naturally, ammunition, are the tools of hit and run. Plus explosives and detonators, grenades, limpet and land mines, wire cutters, torches and batteries all came in handy.

The dropping zone or DZ was to be a field about three miles from the quarry that belonged to Maurice, a local farmer. The Resistance often used horses and carts to carry their booty, but this was too great a distance to risk being on the road for so long, it had to be trucks. Maurice could supply one, two would come from Le Mans, courtesy of Alain at the Citroen garage. The drop would be 12 containers, a sizeable load and the plan was to take it all to the quarry cache in one run, returning the Le Mans trucks the following morning.

All the Le Mans network, now some thirty strong, volunteered to take part in the pickup. Thirty was too many, so Guy picked fifteen. The ladies would act as lookouts. The containers were pretty heavy and demanded brute force to lift them, not a job for the lightly built Yolande, Christel or new recruit Sabine. It so happened that the drop was scheduled for a Monday, the day the Auberge St Honoré was closed, so François could take part without arousing suspicion.

Two nights before the drop, the BBC broadcast the message 'Flaubert, your tweed jacket is ready at the cleaners' to confirm the arrangements.

Guy was like a cat on hot bricks throughout the day on the Monday, but he managed to hide it well and spent his working hours making sales calls and doing paperwork. The clock seemed to crawl round and its solemn ticking was reminiscent of a dentist's waiting room, but the sound wound up Guy's heart rate and he found himself sweating. Several times, he caught Yolande looking at him and she smiled to indicate she understood his tension.

André was duty cook, a pleasant meal of chicken and pasta, but Guy struggled to down a morsel, his appetite blinded by the thoughts of the night ahead. Nonetheless, he forced down some food, acutely conscious that the next meal was many hours distant.

Alain and his mate Robert were duty drivers. They would drive out of town and collect passengers in two different locations at 2100, well before curfew, then head chez Maurice by separate routes. Guy, André and François were in Alain's truck. On the dot of 2100, Alain hove into view and without any problems, they drove the eight miles south. Robert similarly had no difficulties. It all seemed too good to be true.

The drop was timed for 0200. Sitting at the farm, Guy found himself constantly looking outside at the sky, in case the clear weather should suddenly cloud in, but the bright moon glowed unabated, just the conditions for a supply run.

At 0100, the little convoy moved off, with a gap between each in case of problems. By 0130, they were in position by the field, parked on a side road, but not on the field in case of leaving tyre tracks. Guy looked at his watch.

It was 0145.

Despite the temperature, the cab windows were down to hear any untoward sounds.

Silence, total and utter silence. Then an owl hooted, an eerie, almost visceral sound.

It was Alain that heard it first, the faint whine of a Hanomag gearbox, swiftly joined by another as a patrol came down the lane. In an almost reflex action, Alain waved at the two lorries behind him, started his engine and heedless of the tracks he might leave, drove through the gateway and into the field to hide behind the hedge.

Scarcely had the tailboard of the third lorry swung into the field, than the patrol was upon them.

It was 0155.

Hoping and praying the patrol would just carry on, Guy's heart sank when a screech of brakes announced a halt about a hundred yards from where they lay concealed.

Slipping noiselessly from the cab, Guy walked along the hedge and listened. Voices, brief spurts of flame and the aroma of cigarettes announced a break. The Hanomags contained probably a dozen soldiers, who chattered as they enjoyed a smoke.

Guy's party was lightly armed with four Stens, two pistols and two Fairbairn knives, weapons he had concealed under one of André's trucks on a delivery run to an area where the Resistance had some arms. For every kind of reason, a fight was the last thing they needed. The Wehrmacht was sure to be better armed and trained, a firefight would blow their cover and if they did kill any Germans, the Gestapo would exact bloody revenge on the populace.

It was 0201.

Now Guy was beseeching two things, that the patrol would go and the Halifax would be late. The patrol stayed firmly put.

Guy crept back towards his companions.

He was a good ten yards away when the air was rent with a François flatulence fusillade and the noxious odour drifted down to Guy on the breeze. As he neared his group, the François garlic aura was plain as well.

'For God's sake François, put a cork in it,' hissed Guy.

'I'm bloody scared, I can't.'

Grabbing some sacks from the back of one lorry, Guy pushed François to the ground and wrapped a bundle around him as a primitive silencer.

Guy slid back to the Germans.

It was 0208.

A drone in the distance grew louder, a sound Guy identified as the British bomber as it approached at low level.

'Was ist's?' said a German voice.

'Das Flugzeug. Britisch oder Deutsch?'

It was the same voice again.

'Weiss nicht,' came another voice.

The Halifax came overhead, its engines at cruising revs. The arrangement was that if the plane could not see the welcoming lights on the ground, it would simply pass overhead and return fifteen minutes later. If still nothing, it would abort the drop and return home.

The hedge was very tall and obviously the patrol could not see the plane, thank God. So close to the coast, soldiers heard aircraft all the time and the fact it was low bore no relevance. They ignored it.

Just at that moment, a radio in one truck crackled.

'Nadel acht, Nadel acht, kommen.'

There was a scrabbling as one soldier climbed into the truck to answer the call.

'Nadel acht, Nadel acht, kommen.'

'Hier ist Nadel acht, kommen.'

Sensing action the soldiers began to talk, so Guy did not hear what base was saying, but almost immediately, a new voice was heard.

'Los, los, nach Bouloire.'

Engines burst into life, gears meshed and then they were gone.

It was 0220.

Swiftly, Guy ran to his group and scrabbling across the rough field, four of them arranged themselves in a line, torches shining upwards. The ladies kept watch on the road and the edges of the field.

It was 0222.

Now seeing the welcoming sign, the Halifax pilot throttled back and his approach was almost inaudible.

As the aircraft crossed over the hedge facing the group, parachutes blossomed and twelve containers made a near-perfect drop in fairly close proximity.

Well-drilled, the team sprang into action. Christel, Yolande and Sabine, each armed with a folding spade, gathered the parachutes and buried them in three separate holes at the edge of the field. Meanwhile, the men ran to retrieve the containers. With four men to each container, they proved heavy but fairly easy to manage. Backing one truck at a time into the road, they loaded up.

The tension was almost unbearable, the fear that the patrol would return or another would appear from nowhere, but once more, they seemed the only people abroad.

The little convoy proceeded gingerly to the quarry, Alain's truck leading. Briefed by Guy about the narrow, winding track into the workings, Alain nonetheless found it a challenge.

'Bloody hell!' he said with feeling, 'this is hairy. What's the drop, then?'

'You don't really want to know,' came the laconic rejoinder from the passenger seat.

All three vehicles reached safety without incident and reversed up to the double doors.

Guy and André did the honours, unbolting and retracting the panel, then hanging oil lanterns along the tunnel and around the cave.

Intrigued, the rest of the party followed my leader into the cave and in a trice, spotted the van and its bullet holes.

Guy and André had rehearsed how they would react to the inevitable questions.

'I found it like this,' said Guy in reply to Gabriel's enquiry.

'Who owns the quarry?' demanded Pierre.

'Isn't it some Italians, Bernard something? Haven't seen them for years.'

Had Guy not known that André was putting on an act, he would never have known, it was a consummate piece of theatre.

'Bernadini!'

Pierre's eureka was almost a shout of triumph.

'Bernadini, that's it. God, when did I last see old man Bernadini? '32, '33?'

The theatre continued.

As arranged, Guy cut through the speculation and brought them back to reality.

'We haven't time to yatter about what the van means, let's get the containers unloaded and checked. C'mon, let's get to it.'

Willing hands brought the precious cargo into its hidey-hole, then opened each in turn. Deliberately packed with mixed cargoes in case of a missed drop or a container breaking up on landing, the holders contained an eclectic mix of cargo.

Sten guns, magazines and ammunition; four Bren guns and ammunition; Colt pistols and bullets; a dozen Fairbairn knives for silent killing; grenades, sticky bombs, limpet mines, landmines; plastic explosives, detonators, shock cord, pencil timers.

Other booty comprised tents and sleeping bags, torches and batteries, overalls, boots, K-rations, wire and bolt cutters, hand axes, coils of rope.

All in all, a handy haul and a good night's work.

The group closed up the panel, replacing all the bolts. Guy rubbed dirt into the semicircular witness marks top and bottom of the adjoining frame. Then all the men exited the building while the ladies reversed out, deftly wielding birch brooms to erase bootmarks in the gritty dust. By the time they had finished, it all looked totally undisturbed.

Pierre walked to the top of the approach road to check all was clear. The lorries wended their way chez Maurice, eyes and ears straining for sounds of the Boche. Not a sign nor a trace.

Back in Maurice's kitchen, red wine corks popped and they toasted their night's success. Guy noticed that François was in a world of his own, staring into his glass as if he might draw inspiration or salvation from his libation.

When the rest bedded down in the salon and a couple of the bedrooms, to snatch a couple of hours before returning to Le Mans, Guy nodded at François. They found a quiet corner in the scullery.

Knowing what was coming, François tried to bluster it out.

'I know, I know, poor old windbag…

Guy slashed across the excuses, his tone absolutely icy.

'You could have got us killed out there, François, and you know it. If that patrol had been any closer, they might have heard you or smelt you. Do you realise that I could smell your farts ten metres away? And your garlic stench from three metres? Unless you cure your problem, you are banned from field operations, d'you hear me?'

Hanging his head like a dog in shame, François nodded mutely.

'Right,' said Guy, 'you have to cure the garlic habit. Don't do it suddenly, do it gradually. Blame Marie Claire if anyone asks, in fact get her to make a couple of remarks to you in public about how she can't take it anymore.'

Come the morning, the trucks made the reverse trip, dropping passengers on the outskirts of Le Mans. Bleary-eyed, they all went back to the day job and François to begin his gradual cold turkey on garlic.

Chapter 11

'My name's John, military intelligence.'

The young officer was very bright and breezy.

'Bit of a contradiction in terms, eh?'

The trainee SOE agents in the room at East Boldre laughed dutifully, guessing in an instant that he cracked the same joke on each course.

'Anyone keen on jigsaw puzzles?' enquired John.

Marianne raised her hand.

'Good, because piecing together intelligence is just like a jigsaw puzzle, taking lots of bits, deciding which bits fit and which bits don't, not trying to force together incompatible pieces. In your line of work, you are going to handle countless items of information and it's that ability to see the relevance, remember all the other items and make the connection that's really key to good intelligence.'

'And,' continued John, 'remember that the best intelligence will often come from the most unexpected source and you may not appreciate its significance immediately.'

The final piece of John's homily came home to roost as Guy sat in a bakers in Laval where he had just delivered flour. The rather grandly named 'Maison Hubert' was a bakery and patisserie with a café attached. Where the Hubert came from was a mystery, as the owner was called Thomas.

'You deliver again in two weeks?' asked Thomas.

Guy nodded.

'I'll need to up my order – I've got the dockets.'

The baker reached into his battered desk and produced requisitions bearing numerous stamps from the Mairie and the eagle of the Third Reich.

'The Dyna factory starts a night shift in three weeks and I've got the contract to supply bread and rolls for the mid-shift break.'

The name Dyna rang a faint bell with Guy but he could not quite place it.

'What does Dyna make?' he enquired.

'Batteries,' came the reply. 'You know, their logo is a lightning flash in yellow. They're on the industrial estate on the Le Mans road.'

Then it clicked where Guy had seen the flash, one of André's trucks had a Dyna battery. Guy's brow furrowed.

'With half the vehicles in France off the road for lack of petrol, I wouldn't have thought there was much of a call for batteries,' he said.

'True,' said Thomas, 'they've been ticking over on those since 1939, but their speciality is large batteries for trucks and aircraft and tanks and especially submarines. The factory manager, Georges, is a mate of mine, that's how I got the contract for the meal break. Apparently, the Germans have been getting all their batteries from two factories in Germany. Two weeks ago, the RAF got lucky and hit them both on consecutive nights, they'll be out of action for months. The Germans are desperate. They've been buying a few truck batteries from Dyna and discovered the plant's true capability. Some of the machinery for the big stuff was damaged when a storm broke some rooflights and the rain got in. The Boche are remanufacturing the parts in Germany and they're recruiting locally, mostly people who worked there pre-war. They reckon to have it all up and running in about two weeks, then begin the night shift about a week later.'

John was dead right when he said that the best intelligence comes from the most unexpected sources, but the significance to Guy was like switching on a light bulb powered by a large and freshly-charged Dyna battery. Annihilating the Dyna plant would be a major blow to the Axis.

Struggling to both contain his excitement and keep a poker face, he took his leave of Thomas, drove the truck towards the Le Mans road and parked it in a quiet square alongside other commercial vehicles. He always took Auntie on the back of the truck and now he retrieved the bike and pedalled off towards the industrial estate. With the need to conserve every precious drop of fuel, what he was doing was nothing out of the ordinary and nobody paid him a backward glance. When he neared the estate, Guy slipped down a small alley and making sure he was unobserved, he let some air from the rear tyre. As he reached the mouth of the road opposite the Dyna plant, he appeared to notice his soft tyre, so he stopped and leant the machine against a telegraph pole, then pumped air into it. By leaving the connector a little slack, most of the air escaped before it reached the inner tube, giving Guy the opportunity to observe the hive of activity that was now Dyna.

The Germans were fortifying the perimeter like there was no tomorrow, two layers of mesh and barbed wire fence, complete with a cordon sanitaire in between, no doubt for dogs. Arrays of floodlights were being installed to illuminate the site in case of intrusion and the main entrance gates made the Tower of London's seem wimpish. The Wehrmacht was out in force, checking anyone entering and leaving. Guy observed to himself wryly that what the Boche were doing screamed 'Very Important Installation' for what had until recently been an innocuous factory.

That factory was a long single-storey, brick-built affair with a comb roof. An office pod faced the road, with the factory proper stretching for several hundred feet behind. On the left hand side were three tall, black-painted tanks, two side by side and one further down. A service road led to the left of the plant, presumably wound around the back and re-emerged on the right so that delivery vehicles could just do the loop. Anxious not to attract attention by staying too long, Guy tightened the connector, pumped up the tyre and rode off down the estate road to the left of the factory.

The pair of black tanks bore warning signs and 'Concentrated H_2SO_4' in white lettering, but the third tank bore no markings, so Guy could not guess its purpose. His surmise was correct, Goods In was at the back, complete with a loading bay and from glimpses of machinery and benching through rather grimy windows, he could see that production was divided into various sections working frontwards from Goods In. Guy rode on down the estate road past several other factories before turning left to re-emerge from the complex further down and out of sight of the troops at the Dyna works.

Guy made haste towards Armand's. Armand was a self-employed accountant who made a comfortable living looking after the accounts of many a local trader or farmer. At year end there was almost a queue at Armand's door, each supplicant bearing a morass of receipts and invoices in boxes and bags. The ever-patient Armand would magically transform mayhem into a neat set of accounts. He was Guy's local officer in charge of the Laval cell.

Armand was alone when Guy walked in and as usual, was surrounded by piles of paper and hard-backed ledgers.

'Yes...' commented Armand when Guy explained about Dyna, 'I heard about this today, but my first thought was the same as yours, what's the call for car batteries in France. This puts a totally different complexion on it altogether. I only moved here in 1940, so I had no idea about the big batteries they can make.'

'Problem is,' said Guy, 'the Nazis have got it sewn up so tight, it would take a military assault to break through and we don't have that kind of firepower. And,' he added grimly, 'we've got about two weeks to get in there and flatten it before it's running 24 hours a day and packed with our fellow countrymen.'

'Leave it with me,' replied Armand, 'I'll scout around and see what I can come up with.'

Two days later, Guy returned to Laval. Taking Auntie on the train, Guy arrived mid-morning and cycled up to Armand's office.

'We're going to meet Jorge San Martin, he's an engineer. You can trust him.'

So saying, the accountant hustled Guy through a maze of sidestreets and stopped outside an office bearing a brass plate 'J San Martin, Civil and Structural Engineer'. The plate had been lovingly polished for years, so much so that the Victorian script had been almost buffed away and any black dye in the lettering had long since gone. Given the plate, Guy was expecting to meet someone elderly, but Jorge San Martin was in his thirties, the mix of Spanish father and French mother evident in his slightly paler than normal Mediterranean skin.

Jorge's large office was a typical engineer's, spartan and dominated by a big drawing board to the right of the cluttered desk. Plan chests, some almost two metres high, lined every wall and every available surface was covered in drawings and papers. What wall space that was visible contained photographs of factories and bridges. That slightly musty, dusty smell of paper pervaded the atmosphere.

Guy and Jorge shook hands.

'Christophe, because I am a relatively newcomer here, I asked some of my friends,' explained Armand.

The inverted commas around 'friends' was unspoken.

'One suggested Jorge, but I'll let him do the talking.'

'I am actually Jorge San Martin II.'

'My father moved to France on a construction job in the late 1800s, then settled here when he married Mum. He practiced in Laval into his 70s and no sooner had he hung up his slide rule than he died – 1935. Mum had died the year before and I think he just gave up. Being an engineer, he was a complete squirrel and he kept boxes and boxes of stuff in the attic. But for all that, he was an organised squirrel and he labelled the boxes and put a contents sheet in every one. I dug around and found these.'

With that, Jorge reached into one of his plan chests and hauled out several drawings and a brochure, which he proceeded to spread out on the tops of two plan chests.

'As I'll explain, Dad was more a civils man than structural, but he knew his onions on structures and he did the calcs on the Dyna factory. The master contractor was from Cherbourg and sub-contracted Dad, so very few people would know he had these.'

'These' were complete scale drawings of the Dyna factory, complete with all electrical and mechanical services. Better still, the brochure was for the official opening of Dyna in 1929 and the many pages bore photographs of each of the manufacturing sections and the complex machines within them. Guy could hardly contain his joy at this manna from heaven.

'Plus,' went on Jorge, 'I went to the opening with Dad, so I know the layout. By the way, the Boche hoiked all the drawings of Dyna from the Mairie as soon as they decided to put the factory back on full stream.'

'This is absolutely great,' exclaimed Guy, 'but how do we get in?'

Jorge smiled. 'I told you Dad was a civils man and his speciality was sewers, so much so that the majority of his work was designing systems in Northern France. We used to joke that he made a fortune from shit, but it's true. There's a real art to sewer design, getting the right size and the right fall. In the 1920s, Dad got the contract to install a new system for the industrial estate, to replace the crumbly Victorian system.'

A glimmer of light began to dawn on Guy.

'They left the old sewers down there and one comes right under the Dyna plant, in fact there's two manholes in the factory floor.'

Once again, Jorge delved into the plan chest and produced an ancient drawing dated 1898, the lines and the inked annotations in Gothic script beginning to fade. The drawing was covered in a spider's web of lines broken by small circles at regular intervals. Each line was marked with a number like a road map and each circle was annotated with a number, the annotations in newer ink and more modern script.

Jorge explained.

'Each sewer is given a number, the higher the number, the later it was built. Each manhole is given a number starting with the sewer number, then the direction of the sewer in degrees, then a serial number. The lowest number is at the head, the highest at the outfall end. So, 1932023 is Manhole 23 on Sewer 19 running in the direction of around 320 degrees, because sewers have bends and jink around obstructions. Every manhole has that number on a plate sunk into the manhole frame on the outside and inside and repeated in paint above the waterline on the sewer wall. If you have a complex system and old sewers still in place, it's all too easy to find yourself in the wrong one or going down the wrong manhole. Until meticulous old Dad appeared round here, they used to rely on old Charlie's memory, forgetting that old Charlie would retire or die. Dad perfected the numbering system and it's foolproof.'

'In case you're wondering if the Germans will make a connection to me, I have never done any sewers, my line is bridges and industrial buildings, so there is not a sewer drawing of any kind here.'

'What about the manholes in the factory? asked Guy.

'I went round the factory with Dad when it was being built. All they did was raise the finished floor level slightly above the manhole cover, then put a ¼ inch steel plate over the top so it fitted flush with the floor. All the floors are covered in thick bitumastic, so I doubt that the outline of the plate shows even now.'

Guy thought a bit. 'If we're going to get in by lifting the manhole covers, that's a heck of a weight. You've got a presumably cast iron cover?'

Jorge nodded.

'Then a ¼ inch steel plate welded in with bitumastic. Even with two strong guys at the top of the manhole access ladder, I doubt you'd be able to lift all that.'

Jorge grinned. 'Acro props,' he said.

Seeing Guy's blank look, he did a rough sketch of a Acro.

'Normally, these things are used to support a wall or an opening, so you just need to lock them up tight. If we put extensions on the adjustment handles, we can create powerful screw jacks and push the covers up that way.'

'Great, how do we get into the system?'

Jorge pointed to a manhole downstream of Dyna.

'That one is closest and it's hidden behind the next door factory. It's also outside the factory boundary, so no problems there either.'

'We need a recce,' decided Guy. 'Tonight?'

Jorge and Armand nodded.

Once again, weather was on their side. Strong rain and heavy cloud brought deep darkness and poor visibility. Wearing heavy boots and carrying overalls, gloves and torches, they made their way to the access point. They could hear the Germans on sentry duty at Dyna as their voices carried in the wind, but the ground behind the factory where they planned to enter the sewer was deserted. Jorge checked the serial number on the plate, it was correct. He had also brought manhole keys, but the cover had been undisturbed for some years and was stuck firmly in place with dirt and rust. It took twenty minutes patient scraping and tugging before the cover finally yielded. They decided that Guy and Jorge would explore the sewer, leaving Armand to replace the cover and stand as sentry. They could not risk leaving the cover off in case some German came wandering and they could not risk it jamming in place if all three went underground.

Guy and Jorge descended the ladder, but waited until Armand had replaced the cover before switching on their torches. Long disused, the sewer was the traditional ovoid shape, a brick-lined tunnel, dank, musty and still rank with the smell of old sewage. Guy caught his breath, feeling trapped and claustrophobic in the underground workings. The bottom of the sewer contained about 3 inches of rancid water from seepage and the two men began to splash through the slimy liquid towards the Dyna plant. The brickwork was in poor shape, with many bricks missing and the water peppered with lumps of rubble. It was really about a hundred yards, but it felt much longer. Their torches penetrated little distance into the inky, fetid blackness and there was the eerie sight of the beams reflecting off tiny red eyes as they disturbed the resident rats, which scuttled past squealing. Guy shuddered, he just hated rats. Jorge had identified that the two manholes were both in locations where nothing should have been placed over the top, so either or both could be used. Soon they were standing at the bottom of the ladder of the nearest manhole, confirmed by its serial number on the sewer wall. Climbing the rungs, they shone their torches. It was exactly as Jorge had said, the original manhole cover still in place. So it was with the second one, but Jorge looked worried.

'The sewer is taller than I expected. If we use very long Acros, they may bend under the strain. I'll have to devise a light steel frame to go under the prop.'

So saying, he pulled a tape measure from his pocket and handing the end to Guy, gestured to him to mount the ladder and hold the tape end against the underside of the manhole cover. The sewer itself was about six feet high, with a further six feet from the top of the sewer to the underside of the manhole cover.

Satisfied with their recce, Guy returned to their entry point, leaving Jorge at the first manhole. Guy flashed his torch in the agreed three flashes to see if the signal was visible to Jorge. Two minutes later, Jorge rejoined him.

'I didn't see your torch flash,' he said.

'We'll have to have a relay system if we need a signal to say that the factory is empty,' was Guy's rejoinder.

Then they tapped on the cover. A relieved Armand released them from their tomb and they made their way back to Armand's. Before leaving, they smeared dirt in the crevice between cover and frame to disguise its recent removal.

Jorge had been looking at all his father's calculations for the structure and poring over the drawings. With the exception of the storage area for finished batteries, every section of the factory led into the next using sliding doors. In several places, the steel frame of the factory doubled as crane gantries where needed. Jorge pointed out two things. One was that the factory was a weak-roof design. Neither Guy nor Armand understood this until Jorge explained that where explosion is a risk, the roof is made weak so that the explosion vents upwards, rather than hurling masonry and lumps of steel outwards. The second was that if explosive charges were placed on the steel uprights, he was pretty certain that the whole factory would implode.

Guy queried the tanks.

'I thought batteries were shipped dry-charged and filled with acid by the garage or motor factor?'

'Car batteries, yes,' said Jorge, 'but these are large and things like the submarine batteries contain many litres. Not only that, they go straight to the factory for installation, so it's more convenient for the factory if they arrive filled. Dyna ship in concentrated sulphuric acid, then dilute it in the filling shop. Those tanks are glass-lined and the filling shop has a pretty expensive system of acid-proof piping and taps.'

Jorge riffled through the brochure until he found a photo of the filling shop and its stations, then stabbed his finger at the relevant portions.

'The acid tanks have leakproof bunds, so you'll have to blow the bunds as well.'

'What's the other tank?' asked Armand.

'That's pitch, to seal the tops of some battery types,' replied Jorge. 'That tank is heated to keep the pitch liquid and so are the lines that lead into the shop. Very flammable stuff, liquid pitch!' He grinned again. 'You've got pitch, wooden benches, bitumastic or rubber flooring, plus concentrated sulphuric acid. Explosives and incendiaries in the right place, you'll have quite a party, eh?'

The three men planned the operation, working out quantities of plastic and incendiaries and the number of men required. One of

Armand's cell lived near the Dyna works and had surreptitiously watched the guards for several nights to check their routine. Mostly they stayed outside the building, but once an hour on the hour – God Bless the Germans' fascination for ordnung – two men checked inside. The routine never varied.

To blow the factory and plant incendiaries meant eight men, not only to carry Acro props, the weight of the plastic explosive and some satchel charges for the tanks and bunds, but to place all the explosive within the time available. They would enter the factory just after one internal patrol, plant the explosives and retrace their steps through the sewer. Guy and Armand would place the charges on the tanks and be the last to leave.

Guy returned home and radioed London. Because of the importance of the factory to the German war effort and the certainty of reprisals, he needed London's blessing: he got it, plus a drop to Armand in Laval. He particularly stressed the need for accurate timers, long a bugbear of this kind of warfare because they were so inaccurate.

London promised a drop in two days. Knowing that such drops were very much hit and miss affairs, Guy was on the qui vive. London knew they had only one chance. If the containers fell into German hands, it would point immediately to a raid on the Dyna plant and scupper any chances of success.

Guy slept not a wink the night of the drop, planned for a farm outside Laval. Once again, thick black clouds scudded across the night sky and visibility was poor. Standing at his bedroom window in André's, Guy visualised the aircrew trying to pinpoint a small field and some torches. Eventually, he gave up standing at the window and lay on his bed. The cold knot of fear gripped him once more.

Armand rang the next morning and included the word 'cherries' in his otherwise innocuous conversation. At this, Guy's heart sank. 'Cherries' was the word for a failed drop. Guy knew he had to transmit again and call London, even though the more frequent his radio calls, the more chance there was of the Nazis catching him. When darkness fell, he took André's car and drove some distance before plugging into the dashboard power socket and warming up his radio. London also knew the score about frequent transmissions and sent a message admirable for its conciseness and information.

'Thick cloud, no find DZ, Wednesday'.

So, Guy's qualms had been justified, the crew could not find the dropping zone in the thick cloud and would try again on Wednesday.

As Guy packed his radio, he began to worry about time going on and the ever-closer problem of the Germans working twenty-four hours a day to recommission the plant.

Armand acknowledged the new drop, now a few days away. He was back on the phone the following morning to report that 'the party's going to be on Saturday now'. Guy's heart jumped and began to hammer, because Armand's code meant that work on the recommissioning had been brought forward. If the drop was successful, the farmer would have to bring the explosives into Laval in one consignment on Thursday morning and the raid planned for Friday night. That gave them only the one shot at Dyna, it was shit or bust.

Again, Guy slept not at all on Wednesday night, even though clear skies presaged more chance of success and at the hangar next day, Guy almost jumped each time the phone rang. At long last it was Armand with news of some good apples. That meant not only a successful drop, but that the explosives had been delivered to one of the Resistance whose house overlooked the factory.

Guy now spent much of his time out of the office, so when he disappeared to Laval once more, Luc, Matthieu and the two millers did not even notice his absence.

Armand had arranged for the raiding party members to meet at the house near the factory before curfew. The house's owner, Gabriel, was a widower who lived alone. The men retreated to the cellar for a training and briefing session. It felt eerie being surrounded by enough explosives to start a minor war, even though all the incendiaries had yet to be fused and the plastic was as safe as houses. For three intense and intensive hours, Guy trained the party how to mould the explosive around steel girders and vital parts of the machines, using Jorge's excellent brochure to illustrate his point. Using the drawings of the old sewer and the scale drawings of the factory, they walked through and rehearsed the raid time and time again, memorising the layouts and the positions of windows and doors. All the windows were on the left of the building, the same side as the acid and pitch tanks. Fortunately, the side of each shop furthest away from the windows was designated as the access corridor and the only windows in this side were both small and high. The factory was kept in darkness when unoccupied, so the sliding doors between the shops were invisible from outside unless someone shone a torch.

Guy went through the plan step by step. They would leave Gabriel's house to arrive at the sewer entry point just before 2300, then enter the sewer. Gabriel would stay on the surface in a position to watch the wicket gate from Goods In. The guards making the internal patrol entered through the double doors into the office pod, then exited from Goods In, normally about 10 minutes past the hour. Whilst the guards were patrolling, Guy, Jorge and Armand would take the Acro props and the support frames and walk down to the nearest manhole to await the 'coast clear signal'. The remainder of the party were tasked with forming a human chain, each with a torch, to pass on Gabriel's' 'all clear' once he had seen the guards exit the building.

The explosives were of two types, plastic and incendiaries. The plastic was standard stuff and each man would have a number of fuses complete with detonator wires. The wire from each lump of plastic would be run back to a detonator box. With four main sections to the factory, this limited the number of detonator boxes and hence the number of chances of either a misfire or the timer going off at the wrong moment. When Guy arrived at Gabriel's and began sorting and checking the explosives, he had been handed a coded note from SOE HQ. Once decoded, it advised that the backroom boys of SOE had devised a new and very accurate timer using Swiss watch mechanisms. SOE's backroom boffins spent their days (and nights) inventing and perfecting all kinds of things from the strictly practical like timers to the esoteric such as rats and lumps of horse manure that were actually explosive anti-personnel mines.

The incendiaries were hemispherical, every one equipped with a sticky patch that when exposed, adhered to practically anything. Once fused, the incendiaries were set by rotating the dial of a clockwork timer. It was these that were unreliable and any time five to ten minutes either side of the actual was seen as punctual.

The satchel charges for use on the tanks were again plastic explosive and the timers similar versions to the detonator boxes i.e. accurate.

Detonation time was to be 1150, just before the next internal patrol and giving leeway for inaccuracies in the timers.

Guy spent Friday holed up in Armand's house, sweating and worrying about the operation to come. At last, it was time to make his way to Gabriel's, with all the party scheduled to arrive before curfew.

There they went through it all again and again. Once everyone was satisfied that it was all in the forefront of memory, Jorge burnt the incriminating drawings and the brochure to a dust.

At 2240, they began to make their way to the entry point. The very night they needed bad weather, it was clear, the whole area bathed in an unwelcome luminescence and they had to use the long way round and hug cover and shadows to remain unseen. Silently and swiftly, they raised the manhole cover, placing two lengths of wood on the bottom lip of the frame to prevent the lid jamming when Gabriel finally lowered it into place and joined them. As he climbed down into the chamber, Guy once again felt a clammy knot of claustrophobia as the rank, dank odour filled his nostrils. Guy, Armand and Jorge were carrying the Acro props and the supports and crept along the dank sewer, shining their torches and taking care not to hit the walls with the metal they were carrying. Rats squealed as they scuttled past them, eyes gleaming, but this time, Guy was far too preoccupied to notice them.

Once at the nearest manhole, located under Goods In, the trio very gently lowered their burden to the ground and sat back to wait the signal. The ten minutes dragged interminably, but as the flash of the adjacent torch flicked briefly in the gloom, they set to. Jorge had worked with one of the team, an engineering fitter. They had shortened a pair of Acros to the right length, with a short bottom section so that the adjusting collar would still be at the correct height to allow maximum purchase on the handles. Sections of six-inch diameter steel tube had had steel plates welded on top and bottom to create support pillars. Rubber sheet had been glued to the tops and bottoms of props and supports to stifle any noise when being assembled. Thoughtfully, Jorge had brought several pieces of timber to wedge under the supports to iron out irregularities in the sewer floor.

Swiftly, the impromptu jacks were placed under the manhole cover and two of the party climbed the ladder to steady the tops and swing open the manhole once the seal was broken. Much to their surprise, a few turns on the handles easily cracked open the cover and its plate, but once the jacks had pushed it up about four inches, it all jammed solid. No amount of pressure would shift the jacks further, so one of the men on the ladder lined up his eye with the crack where the cover was protruding and gingerly shone his torch.

His swift hiss of 'Merde' spelt trouble.

'Someone's parked a bloody fork-lift over the manhole, we'll never shift that!'

Conscious that every second was precious, willing hands dismantled the jacks and moved down to the next manhole. Guy's heart was now in his mouth, terrified that the other entry point would be blocked. If the first manhole was easy to crack, this one was a stubborn bitch. To gain added purchase on the short adjusting stubs of the well-greased Acros, they had packed pieces of thick-walled steel pipe and these were placed over the stubs. The two beefiest of the team heaved on the extensions, veins standing out on their necks and sweat pouring off them in spite of the chilly atmosphere. Still the cover refused to budge. Taking deep breaths, the jackmen gave it everything. Above their heads, there was a crack that seemed to reverberate around the building and the cover succumbed. Everyone stood stock still, convinced that the Germans must have heard the noise. Nothing stirred. The guys on the ladder eased the cover and plate fully open, then laid it down on another piece of wood provided by Jorge to prevent a noise and trapped fingers.

Watches synchronised, the raiders swarmed up the ladder and dispersed to their assigned stations to begin puttying plastic around machinery and steel girders and concealing incendiaries under flammable objects like wooden benches. Noiselessly, they slid back the well-oiled sliding doors to gain access, using just enough of a gap to shimmy through. The manhole had come up in the filling shop, Guy and Armand's assigned area, but Guy's first job was to move to the plate manufacture and assembly shop, where there was a wooden door leading to the tanks outside. A length of well-handled chain hanging on the wall near the lock spoke volumes about the previous security and the former location of the key. The Germans had instantly removed the key to a secure location after hours. Guy produced an oil-can and lubricated both lock and hinges before returning to the filling shop. The shop was full of fume cupboard type enclosures to allow the batteries to be filled without the highly toxic acid corroding the lungs of the workers and a travelling gantry overhead contained an electric hoist, the motor shrouded in rubber against the corrosive atmosphere.

A ducted ventilation system kept the environment reasonably clean during working hours, but the whole shop stank of sulphuric acid and both Guy and Armand gagged on the foul aroma. Swiftly, they packed explosive around the vertical support girders and in the interstices of all the filling equipment. Checking to see that no guards were in evidence, Guy shinned up the ladder to the gantry, blessing both the designer for putting the ladder on the tank side of the shop and whoever had last parked it on a section of the wall between two windows. He smeared plastic around the gantry beam near the hoist so that when the beam sheared during the explosion, the weight of the hoist would bend or topple the gantry beam. Armand meanwhile was peppering the area with incendiaries.

As Guy and Armand finished their tasks, the others began arriving back and all gave a silent thumbs-up before disappearing down the manhole. Guy and his companion slithered into the plate shop. Oh so carefully, Armand raised himself to look out of the window, then whispered 'OK' to Guy, who began to pick the lock on the outside door. The lock was in frequent use and combined with Guy's lubrication, easily succumbed. Again, Armand's 'OK' was the signal to ease the door open a crack, praying that the hinges would not give them away. Once more, Guy's foresight paid off and he and Armand crept towards the bunds carrying the satchel charges. Both bunds were over two metres high and they had to climb steel ladders to get inside. The high tanks gave them shadow cover and with ears straining, they glued the charges to first the acid then the pitch tanks and bunds, linking the charges with detonator boxes. Climbing the inner ladder of the pitch tank, they peered anxiously around, but the German sentries were nowhere in sight. Hearts pounding, they regained the sanctuary of the plate shop and relocked the door. As Guy worked the picks, they heard two sets of jackboots striding towards them as a pair of sentries made their rounds. A millisecond before a German tried the door to test that it was locked, Guy's nimble fingers engaged the tumblers. By now, Guy was convinced that the sentries must be able to hear the hammering of his vital organ, but they passed on down the side of the factory.

In a trice, Armand and Guy were back in the sewer, replacing the cover and plate, now glued to one another by rust and bitumastic. Now almost running, they sped back to the entry point. The rest of the group awaited them, carrying the Acros and supports. Cautiously, they inched up the manhole cover and made good their escape, scattering to their various homes and dropping the jack equipment in the deep river as they went. Guy made swiftly for his planned escape route, knowing that he had to be out of the area before the Germans sealed it off and that he had a long and perilous cycle ride back to André's house during that night.

Now secure in his own home, Gabriel climbed up to his loft and waited for the action to start. Barely had he gained his eyrie than a series of almost simultaneous explosions rent the air as the plastic detonated. The noise was surprisingly little, but the effects were anything but. Before the Germans' very eyes, vast sections of the roof blew off, windows shattered, millions of razor-like shards of glass were hurled outwards and holes appeared in the walls as the plastic not only sheared supporting girders, but blasted out sections of brick.

The NCO in charge hit the panic button, sirens began to wail and the floodlights went on, bathing the factory in a greenish-yellow glow.

A pair of guards began running down the left hand side of the factory. One was fleeter than his companion and his very speed was to spell his death sentence. As he reached the acid tanks, the charges blew, splitting open the tanks like cheap tin cans. The shock wave from the explosion hurled much of the acid straight through holes in the roof of the plate shop, but some of the wave went sideways, engulfing the soldier. His fellow watched in horror and disbelief as the man began to disintegrate before his eyes, the clothes and flesh dissolving in seconds. The screams of the hapless soldier were primeval, but almost instantly died as he fell unconscious to the floor, a ragged mass of flesh, bone and cloth being eaten alive by the fiery liquid. Transfixed by this horrific scene, the second guard did not notice that the acid had reached his feet, until the smoke from the dissolving soles of his boots struck his nostrils. Screaming like a madman, he fled the deadly stream, one second running on leather soles, the next on his bare and scalding feet.

At that moment, the first of the incendiaries erupted and with a succession of reports over the next ten minutes, its fellows joined in. Contrary to Jorge's forecast, the walls were made of stern stuff and despite sections collapsing as girders and beams tumbled, the structure remained largely intact. Fires sprang up throughout the building, feeding greedily on all the flammables. Flammables included many gallons of hot pitch which had been blown from the tank into the building through broken windows and holes in the walls. The gaps in the roof acted as chimneys, the rising flames and gases shooting out in long wicked tongues and gasping air into their insatiable maw through the many apertures in the walls to feed and amplify the fires. Now the fires began to crackle as they took hold and the heat intensified.

The plate shop had been engulfed by a savage, seething, sulphuric tsunami of almost 3000 gallons of concentrated acid, which consumed and destroyed virtually everything it touched. Once fine and delicate machines became misshapen lumps under the onslaught. The corrosive liquid streamed into every crevice, crack, nook and cranny, hissing and bubbling, devouring or eroding surfaces, wiring, controls and switches. Having swamped the machines, the deadly and destructive tide flowed on under the sliding doors to assuage its famine on anything in its path. And the sulphuric had another weapon in its armoury. Hydrogen gas spewed from the furious reactions with metals, either feeding the flames or gathering in pockets to explode in acidic fury whenever flames and gas coincided.

Summoned by the Germans, the local pompiers had turned out in force, but their chief knew only too well the perils of the battery factory, it had a five-star rating for danger in his risk assessments. Despite urging by the Boche, the chief instructed his firemen to stand well back and spray water on the pyre in a vain attempt to cool the blaze and dilute the acid. It was like a child peeing on a blast furnace. In any case, the incredible heat made it impossible to get anywhere near the building.

Truth to tell, the plastic had snuffed out the Dyna plant in an instant, but the fires and the acid made sure of the factory's total death. Temperatures were now at white heat and beyond, twisting and buckling steels and cracking walls. Three hours after the raid, the factory collapsed. Like a slow motion film, the main wall on the tank side began to sway gently, then it gradually bellied inwards in an S-shape before countless thousands of engineering bricks thundered to the ground in a mushroom cloud of dust, rubble and sparks. In quick succession, the remaining walls gave up and smashed inwards, thunderous roars and huge dust storms marking their demise. And still the fires raged on, flames licking and darting among the grotesque and twisted wreckage, pools of acid finding new routes in the rubble and fresh delicacies for their insatiable appetites.

During all this mayhem, Guy was pedalling as fast as he could for home using a carefully selected labyrinth of by-roads and paths to try and avoid patrols. The Boche had reacted but instantly to the sabotage and had saturated the locale with men in case anyone was trying to escape. On no less than five occasions, Guy had to dive for cover behind hedges and in ditches when he heard or saw German vehicles approaching. His luckiest escape was when cycling along a path behind a hedge. Only as he passed did he hear a German on the other side begin speaking to a mate. Guy was eternally grateful for having fettled Auntie so that she ran sweetly and noiselessly and the path was on hard soil, but it was a close call. Just before dawn's fingers clawed at the horizon, he slid unseen through André's back gate and into the house. André had lain awake all night on tenterhooks.

'How did it go, Christophe, everyone get away?'

Guy was exhausted both physically and mentally after the raid and the long, tense ride and needed a moment to gather himself before he could answer.

'If everything detonated as intended, then the factory is history, but I got away before the balloon went up. We'll have to wait a few days before we know for sure; my man won't dare phone in case the lines are tapped.'

Even dog-tired as he was, Guy did not let slip Armand's name, what André did not know he could not tell.

Although the pompiers took it in shifts and continually sprayed water to cool and dampen the blaze, it was four days before the chief satisfied himself the fire was truly out and stood his weary teams down. Another ten days were to pass until the fire chief was happy that the pile had cooled sufficiently to allow the Gestapo to investigate and even then, it was inch by inch progress in suits, rubber gloves and respirators. Every puddle was checked for acidity and concentration and many a suspicious pool had to be hosed away before the steel blade of the bulldozer could proceed.

The onslaught of the acid had obliterated the manhole cover and plate over the Resistance entry point and soon, the Gestapo were peering into the disused sewer. As the access ladder had been eaten as well, a wooden ladder was brought and a hapless Wehrmacht private ordered into the depths. Before he could descend, the fire chief stopped him, substituting one of his own men with protective clothing and a respirator. Even this fireman was not allowed down until yet more water had been sluiced into the empty sewer as a safety precaution. With a line attached to his waist and another suited and booted fireman standing at the bottom of the manhole, the pompier crunched his way over the rubble that had fallen in the manhole and along the tunnel, returning minutes later to report another manhole, but closed. He was unwilling to wander further in the impenetrable gloom as the atmosphere in the sewer was very suspect from the acid and he had no idea how far the drain extended.

Two Gestapo officers burned rubber on their way to the mairie's building department. Their demands for all sewer drawings were met with current drawings, but nothing as old as Jorge's 1898 plan. The manager of the building department hated the invaders like a poison and could have told them that old archive material was kept in a central repository in Le Mans, but they did not ask, so he did not volunteer the information.

By the end of the third day, the bulldozer party had reached Goods In. Protected by the now gaunt, twisted and almost unrecognisable hulk of the fork-lift, they found the first manhole, its cover and plate still protruding slightly above the floor. Now with proof positive of the raiders' means of entry, the Gestapo sent down a search party, which rapidly emerged onto open ground at the entry point manhole behind the adjacent factory.

The heat from the Dyna fire was but tepid compared to the wrath of the occupiers at the catastrophic loss. Jorge had been wrong when he said that nothing could be traced back to him. Whilst at the mairie, the Gestapo had found dozens of sewer drawings with 'J San Martin' in the right hand corner and were hotfoot round to Jorge's office.

The first Jorge knew that he had a problem was when Major Lutz and a lieutenant from the Gestapo burst through his office door accompanied by four soldiers. Unrolling a sewer drawing with 'J San Martin' on Jorge's desk, Lutz stabbed a finger at the name.

'This is yours, ja?'

It was a statement, not a question.

Jorge examined the drawing, dated 1929.

'No, my father's, he was the sewer engineer, I do bridges and industrial buildings. And I did not take over this practice until 1935.'

His reward for this information was a gloved punch in the face from Lutz, a punch so fierce that Jorge was thrown backwards in his chair to lie stunned on the floor, blood pouring from his nose and spitting out bits of teeth. He looked up to see Lutz and his lieutenant towering over him and before he could draw breath, they were aiming kicks at his torso.

'Don't lie to us, you French pig,' yelled Lutz, delivering another kick, 'we know it's yours.'

Jorge managed to move backwards sufficiently to take a breath and calm himself, even though his heart was in his mouth and the shock of the sudden onslaught made his pulses race.

'I am a bridge and industrial buildings engineer, I've never touched a sewer in my life. Just look at my drawings if you don't believe me.'

Lutz gestured to the soldiers, who immediately ransacked the plan chests, ripping out drawers and upturning their contents all over the floor. The fact that all the drawings were exactly as Jorge averred only seemed to incense Lutz even more and poor Jorge was dragged from his office, thrown into the back of a truck and driven to his home. There the Germans searched from top to bottom, ripping up carpets to check for hidden traps. They found nothing. Taking Guy's counsel, Jorge had systematically destroyed his father's old archives, assembling a large model railway from his youth on the floorspace previously occupied by the boxes. The presence of the railway also explained the cleanliness of the attic. Furious at having drawn a blank, the Gestapo hauled the engineer off to Rennes jail, which doubled as

Gestapo HQ.

Guy would not have recognised the Jorge who had stood by his side a scant three weeks ago. Huddled in a windowless cell, covered in blood, faeces and vomit, Jorge could scarcely see anything out of eyes so badly swollen from beatings, they were now mere slits. Barely a single square centimetre of his body was unmarked, boot marks, whip marks, baton marks covered him from head to foot and three ribs were broken. Tortured for hour upon hour, Jorge's genitals were red and scarred from being wired to a high-tension generator and innumerable shocks delivered in a vain attempt to make him talk. But Jorge was truly a man of steel and refusing to succumb to either his captors or the ceaseless agony, he maintained his innocence. Lying on the icy cell floor, he was delirious from torture, injuries, scant rations and the incessant chill and damp of his prison.

The cell door clanged open. Two guards dragged Jorge, every sinew screaming for mercy, back to the torture chamber. Four excruciating hours later, they dumped him back from whence he came, totally ignoring his screams from the broken ribs as they threw him on the filthy stone floor. With only darkness for company and almost out of his mind with pain, Jorge had no idea of time. The cell's massive steel door excluded any sound, it was total and utter isolation.

Jorge huddled his battered, broken and insanitary body into the foetal position and slept. He was awoken by the clang of the cell door being opened and once again, two guards heaved him to his feet, half supporting him, half dragging him into the corridor. Mentally bracing his psyche for yet more torture, Jorge suddenly clicked that they had turned left out of the cell, not the usual right. His eyes, so accustomed to darkness, blinked as he was propelled outside and into a courtyard. Even through the slits, he could make out a post in the middle of the yard and a mortal spasm of sheer terror hit him like an ague. Wordlessly, the soldiers tied his hands behind the post and blindfolded him. The last words Jorge ever heard were 'Leg an' and 'Feuer' before his indomitable heart was extinguished in a fusillade of bullets.

Jorge was the first of twenty-six citizens to lose their lives for the Dyna raid. Despite frenetic efforts, arresting half the population and pursuing any clue they could lay hands on, the invaders met a wall of silence and could not pin the raid on anyone. Their reaction was typical. Twenty-five people were rounded up during the Friday market and executed in the town square in full view of the public.

In reality, Guy did not have to wait long before visitors brought news of the havoc at the Dyna factory. His joy at the success was tinged with the regret for whatever retribution the occupiers would visit upon Laval and its townsfolk. When news of the mass execution reached him, he had to rush to the toilet, not only to relieve his bowels, but to wipe away the rush of hot, salt tears at the terrible sacrifice of ordinary people.

It was some weeks before he learned what had happened to Jorge. Once again in Laval, he walked in to Armand's. One look at Armand's expression told him that dreadful news was about to be imparted.

'Jorge's dead,' whispered Armand, 'they found drawings of sewers with Jorge San Martin on them. They wouldn't believe him that they belonged to his father.'

Armand's voice began to falter and tears welled up in his eyes.

'They… they took him to Rennes and… and *tortured* him for days on end.'

The accountant broke down into racking sobs, unable to go on. Recovering himself, he continued.

'Jorge was incredible, they wired his balls to a high-tension generator, they broke his ribs, they beat him senseless, but they could never break his spirit. When he refused to crack, they shot him.'

Once more, Armand was utterly beside himself, the hot tears flowing unabated. Guy found he could not hold back either and together, their tears became a mute and poignant requiem.

Chapter 12

Autumn's slightly icier fingers were at first a little weak, but gathered strength as September waned. Warm days still, but often frosty nights, and darkness drew her curtains across the landscape yet earlier each night.

Sometimes, God was on your side. In Jorge's case, God had not been, but fortunately, he chose that day to be on Guy's. If all had gone to plan, Guy should have been on the last train into Le Mans, but he finished earlier than expected with one of his farmer customers; rather than wait for the train, he cycled back. By now Guy's legs were in excellent shape and he could and did cycle for miles, pushing Auntie effortlessly across French farmland.

Rolling into Le Mans, the hairs on the back of his neck began to stand on end, for reasons he could not explain. He was taking a short cut through an alley, no more than a narrow defile between two houses and very dark. Just about to turn right into the street which housed François and Marie-Claire's restaurant, Guy had to stop for an oncoming MAN truck, a truck in Wehrmacht grey. Sitting in the back were a number of soldiers, but it was their prisoners which transfixed Guy –François and Marie-Claire and the nurse from the local hospital. All of them looked utterly terrified. The truck rolled on down the street, to stop at the dentist's. Sliding his left eye around the edge of the alley wall, Guy saw two soldiers barge their way into the surgery and emerge dragging the dentist in their wake. Guy's nape hairs stood utterly erect and an alarm bell somewhere in the back of his cortex began an insistent chime.

The alley was so narrow, he had to reverse Auntie down it, then he was off through a maze of similar alleys and backwaters to lead him out of town and into a fairly dense wood, where he holed up until dark. Making an educated guess that the Germans would be expecting him by train, he used the time available to him before the train arrived to work his way up to the ruined cottage. Each yard along the labyrinth of paths and tracks that he used, he was straining his eyes and ears for any signs of Germans hunting him, but apart from nearly flattening a small rabbit and putting up one very startled pheasant, he saw and heard no signs of life. Finally, he was opposite the cottage and spent nearly fifteen minutes 'getting the picture' so that any untoward movement would show.

Little cottonwool balls of cloud drifted languidly across the sky, occasionally masking sharp pinpricks of starlight, the only illumination with a scarcely visible moon. Jack Frost was astir and beginning to go about his business and any warmth had long since left the atmosphere. The leaves of the lime trees sent out an almost iridescent glow, flicking to the occasional zephyr. But that was the only sound and you felt you could cut the silence into blocks and take it away. Anticipating just such an eventuality, Guy had played Kim's game over and over again with the area surrounding the cottage so that he would know what should and should not be there. Nonetheless, he feared that at any moment, a bush would translate into one of Wippelmann's crack troops, ready to pounce on Guy and drag him off.

Using an infantryman's crawl, Guy elbowed and kneed his way closer and closer to the derelict building. A sudden rustling made him start, but it was merely a fieldmouse scampering through the leaves. Nerves at breaking point, Guy at last made it to the ruin and crawled inside. Still nothing happened, nothing stirred, nothing moved. Sidling along the walls, he reached the fireplace and fumbled inside above the lintel. To his astonished relief, he found the radio, a pair of night-glasses and another small package, which he unwrapped and transferred the contents to his jacket pocket. Departing as stealthily as he had come, Guy took the radio and concealed it in the bole of a fallen tree that was easily spotted, even in the dark. Then he retrieved Auntie and stole back towards the town.

Soon he was hunkered down opposite his goal, well-hidden and warm inside his coat and cap, but with a clear view of the target area. The alarm bell in his skull had grown to fire-engine proportions. By now, it was about 8.30pm and he had a long wait. Not until gone eleven was his patience rewarded, when a vehicle slowed and pulled into the cottage drive. Its driver stopped outside a small barn with the engine running, opened the double doors, drove the Citroen inside and switched off. The double doors were secured with a peg in the hasp and staple before the driver disappeared inside the cottage.

Guy's first instinct was to enter the cottage immediately, but something held him back and he kept his position. His instincts were rewarded when his sharp ears picked up the sound of another vehicle approaching, a vehicle which too turned into the drive in front of him.

Wippelmann alighted from the kubelwagen and knocked on the door, which was opened almost at once to admit him. Guy had scanned the cottage from all sides with his night-glasses and observed the lounge window being opened slightly to admit some air.

In ghostly silence, Guy slid under the window to listen. The first voice he heard was Wippelmann's slower, more measured French.

The second was Yolande's.

'Sorry, we had to rough you up a bit to make it look good' said the major apologetically, 'but we can now say we've questioned you thoroughly and are satisfied you were not involved and knew nothing of your lover's other activities.'

'How do I run the business now?'

It was Yolande's soft, semi-Spanish tones. Her question and its tone not only sent shivers down Guy's spine, but simultaneously ignited rage of a magnitude that he had last felt at the Gefreiter stealing his mother's rings.

'Give it a day or two, then I'll sign an order giving you control of the business and the bank account because Lavallois is vital to the food supply here. Once the war is over, I leave it to you to organise the legal side so that it truly is yours. After all, André Lavallois isn't going to be in a position to take any interest, is he?'

Wippelmann's hollow laugh once again ignited loathing and rage in Guy, but he kept stock still.

'Where's Courcy?' demanded Wippelmann, 'he wasn't on the train, I had men on from two stops before Le Mans and he didn't show.'

'I don't know,' replied Yolande, 'he may be staying with someone overnight and coming back tomorrow, or perhaps he's taken a bus.'

'Any chance he's been tipped off?' asked the soldier.

'I doubt it and you deliberately rounded us all up toward late afternoon and took in all the workers from Lavallois, so there was nobody to spill the beans.'

'Fact is, he's missing and I want him. I want him that badly, I can smell it – running a Resistance right next to my barracks, I'll be a laughing stock. We'll nab him though, there are two guards with a field telephone inside the hangar and André's house is staked out. We'll begin scouring the countryside again at first light.'

Guy almost screamed, 'Danke schön, Herr Major,' at these vital pieces of information, but hearing the officer beginning to take his leave, moved like a wraith back to his observation point.

Two things woke Yolande. One was a hand like a vice over her mouth. The other was the cold, blued end of a Colt silencer grinding into her left temple.

'One sound and you're history. Sit up very slowly and put on the bedside light.'

The ice and hatred in Guy's voice sent paroxysms of sheer terror through Yolande. Moving slowly, she sat up and reached over to the light switch. As she did so, the sheet fell from her bare breasts and instinctively, she snatched up the covers to hide her nakedness.

Guy had not the slightest flicker of interest in the woman's body.

'Put your hands where I can see them and make no sudden moves.'

Yolande complied.

'Why?'

The word was spat from between lips so compressed, they resembled two pencil lines and at such a velocity, it could have come from the menacing snout of the pistol in its enquirer's hand. Yolande's bowels turned to jelly and her normally dark skin paled at the intensity and hatred encompassed in that one short word.

Somehow, she summoned up a modicum of defiance and her eyes blazed as she declared

'It's us, the Communists, we're the ones who are going to run France after this war. We don't need the bourgeoisie, they'll simply hold us back.'

Instantly, Guy saw that his innate suspicions of Yolande had been absolutely spot on.

'And how long have you been a closet Communist?' he demanded.

'A long, long time,' was the reply, accompanied by a smirk that he longed to wipe from her treacherous face.

'And taking over a business, being a dirty capitalist, that's OK in Communist circles is it?'

Again, that smirk.

'We have to live and I've slogged my guts out for years for very little reward other than André regarding me as his bit of stuff. Well, not any more, now it's my turn.'

Yolande was neither the first nor the last Red to turn in their own purely on political grounds, but still Guy was aghast that Yolande could betray not only her lover but her Resistance comrades too. For a second, Guy was struck dumb.

'So, for the sake of your politics and material gain, you've condemned André to certain death and the rest of the cell to either death or the concentration camps. If you wait here, I'll go and find the twenty pieces of silver you think are so vital.'

The scorn in Guy's tone ripped into Yolande like a huge dart and all of a sudden, the enormity of her betrayal hit home and she began to weep uncontrollably.

'Did you give Wippelmann all the names?'

A nod.

'Bit late for crocodile tears, isn't it?'

Looking quickly round, Guy spotted a silk dressing gown hanging on the back of the door. Without taking his eyes off Yolande, he reached behind him, unhooked the garment and flung it on the bed.

'Put it on and get up,' he ordered.

Yolande shrugged into the dressing gown and stood up. Guy indicated with his hand that she leave the room and he followed her, jabbing the muzzle into her spine to accentuate the point.

Silently, they walked downstairs and into the kitchen, where Yolande obeyed Guy's instruction to unlock the back door. Checking that the coast was clear, Guy prodded Yolande towards the well in one corner of the garden.

'Turn round and face me.'

She did so. The Colt spat twice, the so-called SOE double-tap, and two spots of blood oozed from her left breast. Surprise and shock welled briefly in the woman's eyes before they glazed over and she sank inert and lifeless to the ground. A check of her neck pulse confirmed that Yolande was dead. Quickly, Guy heaved her shoulders over the parapet of the well, then grasped her heels and tipped her in. A momentary splash, then silence. Guy shone his torch, but it was a deep well and nothing showed. Taking a spanner from his pocket, he detached the wheels from Yolande's bike and threw those down the well. The wheels sank without trace, as did the frame. Anyone looking for Yolande would see her bike was gone and assume she was out on it somewhere.

Guy let himself back into the house and packed food and water into a small haversack he found in the understairs cupboard, before locking the house and depositing the keys in the well.

As night marched on, he found himself once more near the Lavallois hangar. Gaining the rear of the building and with nerves stretched in case Wippelmann had extra men camouflaged in the wood at the back, he almost buried Auntie and the radio beneath some fallen branches and a mass of leaves.

Wippelmann's unintentional but extremely kind intelligence on the disposition of his men in the hangar was vital, but only part of the story. Guy desperately needed to know how the guards were located in the hangar, the rosters and any external patrols. Plus, if they had a field telephone, that almost certainly involved some kind of regular check calls. Knowing the thickness of the steel doors, Guy was pretty sure he would not be able to hear anything through them, but he nonetheless sidled carefully up to them, his back pressed firmly to the hangar wall and listened. Nothing.

He decamped into the trees, from where he could observe the doors through night glasses. At twenty past the hour, the two guards appeared, locked the doors and did a circuit of the hangar, timing it to be back by half past. One of the men went inside again, leaving one door open, his mate staying outside for a quick drag. Just inside the door, they had set up a table from the office and two chairs. On the table was the field telephone. To one side, a Primus stove and kettle perched atop a small wooden crate. The soldier cranked the call handle vigorously, spoke a few words and replaced the handset. Difficult as it was to lip-read a foreign language at that distance, Guy thought that what he had said was 'Alles klar, alles gut'. At ten to the hour, the guards repeated their external patrol. When they next came out, Guy had repositioned himself where he could hear what the guards were saying.

'Fucking hell, it's enough to freeze your balls off,' remarked one as he marched round the hangar, probing with his torch but finding nothing.

'When do we get relieved?'

'0800,' replied his pal.

'Jesus, these eight hour shifts seem more like twenty-eight,' was the rueful rejoinder.

If Guy could have hugged the first guard, he would have done. The whole picture was now clear, but for what Guy had in mind, it left a very narrow window indeed.

As soon as Tweedledum and Tweedledee had gone back inside, he dived back to Auntie, grabbed the radio and scuttled to the rear of the generator room. The room was a single-storey blockwork lean-to on the side of the hangar. Like all generator rooms, it had been built so that the generator could be inserted into the building and if necessary, removed at some later date for major overhaul or change. At the rear was a kind of door and a half, one very large door and a smaller pedestrian entrance. When alone one evening in the hangar, Guy had taken pains to inspect the generator, not only to familiarise himself with all the controls, but also to check out this door arrangement which he had spotted when André gave him the ten cent tour on Day One. Instinct said another way into (or out of) the hangar might come in handy, so Guy tested the key in the lock. It was a bit stiff, but some oil from the bench did the trick and the lock turned smoothly and noiselessly. Fortunately, the doors were made of hardwood, so they were straight and true and did not stick, but Guy checked them nevertheless and oiled the hinges. Not being used to standby generators, Guy was at first puzzled why the room was so warm, but soon tracked down the built-in immersion heater that kept the engine warm so that it could deliver full power when fired up. He took away the key a couple of days later and had a duplicate cut which he placed on his ring.

Now that duplicate let him into the warm room. He dare not turn on the light, the door and a half were slatted to admit air to the generator. Using his torch, he located a power point and plugged in his radio. By now, it was time for another external patrol, so he let the guards make their rounds before running out his aerial on some bushes outside and calling London.

At his request, London replied, 'Call one hour.'

He did so.

'Pickup Sunday 0125, Z/R.'

Guy retrieved the aerial, locked the door and sat back to think.

He had chosen his hiding place for several reasons. One was that the last thing Jerry would expect was for him to hide on their doorstep. The second was the power for the radio and the third that the room was heated against the Autumn chill. Last, Guy figured that even if the power failed, the guards were unlikely to know about the generator and besides, the room was locked with a key held in the office. Fortunately, there was a turn-knob inside the room which released the lock. Some old flour sacks stored in one corner were transformed into a rough but passable bed and Guy settled down for the night. Nature's needs were satisfied by an empty 5-litre oil drum.

The next twenty-four hours seemed like a hundred and twenty four. Time after time, Guy heard the guards pass by on their patrol, the different voices and accents testimony to the roster changes. It appeared that the sentries ate before coming on duty, sandwiches and coffee on the Primus filling the gaps in between.

Guy's watch appeared to have stopped, so agonisingly slowly did it tick round. At 1155, he decide to sneak a look at the guard post whilst they were doing a circuit of the hangar, so gently turned the knob to release the lock to the door leading into the hangar. Guy's one fear was that Alphonse would be up and about and come to greet him, but the terrier must have been fast asleep in his bed and did not stir. Creeping around the edge of the mill building, the young agent satisfied himself that he had missed nothing, then crept silently back into his hidey-hole and locked the door.

By 0115, Guy was in position. Earlier, he had a scare when a heavy mist settled on the airfield and blocked out all vision. If this persisted, the pickup would be aborted. To his intense relief, a light breeze sprang up about 2230 and wiped away the clag. The guards always did a right hand circuit, it never varied regardless of who was on duty, so Guy hid just around the corner on the left hand side of the structure. Sharp at 0120, the two Nazis exited the hangar and Guy heard the door clang as they locked up. Heart pounding like a trip-hammer, he tensed and waited. Deliberately, he had been in position some minutes to accustom his eyes to the darkness, whereas the Germans had come from a lit room only seconds before. They never even saw him. As they appeared round the corner, Guy took careful aim and shot both of them once, then added a coup de grâce to make sure. A swift pulse check confirmed death, then Guy retrieved the hangar boys and raced to the office to find the torches he needed.

Walking out to that runway, he felt totally exposed and was straining his ears for the sound of the Lysander's engine, but nothing broke the stillness of the night. Now thoroughly panic-stricken, he laid out the torches in the required 'L' and looked at his watch. To his horror, it was within seconds of 0130. He ran back to the hangar and hands trembling, cranked the field telephone.

'Was gibt's' came the challenge.

Guy breathed very deeply and in his best German grunted 'Alles klar, alles gut.'

'Danke, wiederhören.'

The line went dead.

At that moment, his keen ears picked up a distant hum. He shot outside and onto the runway. Barely visible in the dark, he could just make out a silhouette on the horizon getting closer. There was a roaring in his ears and a pounding in his brain, knowing that if this was a Luftwaffe plane, he was doomed. Guy pointed his torch and flashed 'Z'. The Lizzie pilot immediately responded with 'R' using the landing lights in the undercarriage fairings and continued his descent. Whoever was at the controls was an ace. With engine throttled right back to minimise noise, the pilot deadsticked the aircraft onto the deck without a sound from the tyres and used his momentum to do the standard right turn around the top of the L. Guy stood to the left of the L, the SOP for pickups. Pilots were instructed to shoot anyone standing to the right of the L. As the aircraft turned once more and came to a stop facing down the runway, Guy scrambled up the ladder on the port side, slid open the canopy and flopped inside. If anything, the pilot's take-off was even more brilliant than his landing. Using the fall of the downhill runway to help his acceleration, he employed the minimum throttle to gain take-off speed, then gave it a brief burst through the gate in the final hundred yards. Almost as the wheels left the concrete, he reefed it hard right and disappeared behind the trees, the starboard wingtip barely clearing one tall pine. Once clear of the area, the pilot hugged the deck and made for La Manche and home.

Still as taut as a bowstring, Guy tensed himself for a night fighter or searchlights or flak, but all was strangely peaceful as they droned on over the French countryside. Suddenly, there were waves breaking on the seashore and the glint from the Channel below. Halfway over the strip of water, the pilot set a gentle climb. The height change slightly puzzled Guy, until he realised that it was so that the Lizzie approached the coast at an altitude where he could be seen on radar and the IFF – the 'parrot' in RAF jargon – would be visible on the plotter's screen. This gave at least a sporting chance of not being shot at by your own flak batteries. Soon, Guy could make out the Thames Estuary, then the Lysander made a slight left turn and began to let down into RAF Tempsford. The pilot clearly was an ace, his landing on the Bedfordshire tarmac just as skilful as in France. With not even a squeak from the tyres, he greased the aircraft onto the threshold and sank the tailwheel with nary a bump before taxiing to dispersal, where two erks in a Bedford awaited their arrival. So too did an RAF Hillman, which first took Guy to Hazells Hall before ferrying the pilot to the Officers' Mess. As the car stopped at the Hall, Guy shook his rescuer warmly by the hand.

'I can't thank you enough, a brilliant piece of airmanship,' he exclaimed.

The pilot, Tom Jefferies, was very modest.

'All in a night's work, just glad I made it and you're safe and sound, that's all.'

Guy walked into Hazells Hall to be met by the duty officer, who took him to a small bedroom, complete with en suite bathroom.

'I expect you'd like something to eat and drink?'

Guy nodded, suddenly worn out by recent events.

The bathroom contained razor, shaving soap and fluffy towels, so Guy made an immediate bath and luxuriated in a shave in real hot water. From walking armpit to human being was fifteen minutes and raised his spirits immeasurably. He emerged from his toilet to find a tray with a thick sandwich containing real butter and ham, a pot of tea and half a bottle of Johnnie Walker. He did justice to all three before collapsing beneath the covers. A knock on the door awoke him, it was a steward with a mug of tea.

'It's 0800 sir. I'll bring breakfast in fifteen minutes, your car leaves at 0900.'

The steward departed, to return on schedule with bacon and eggs, thick toast and another pot of tea. The aroma was irresistible and Guy demolished this feast before shaving and dressing. He suddenly realised that his clothes stank and it was an effort to put them on his clean body.

Prompt at 0900, the same Hillman appeared and he was driven to London. The Bedfordshire countryside looked not a lot different to peacetime, but as the car began to nose into the outskirts of London, the picture altered dramatically. Everywhere he looked, Guy could see the effects of war, from ack-ack batteries to barrage balloons, but it was the devastation that hit him most. Gaunt wrecks of buildings, rubble in the streets, grey-faced people trying to go about their normal business. The key thing was, they were succeeding. Battered they undoubtedly were, but bowed they were not and Guy marvelled at the doughty British phlegm that refused to allow the Nazi onslaught to defeat them.

The car pulled up outside a block of flats in Bayswater.

'Third floor, Number 19,' volunteered the driver.

Guy walked slowly up the stairs and rang the bell. It was answered by a man dressed in a grey suit, who showed Guy into a bedroom.

'Take off your clothes, there's a dressing gown on the door, then go across the corridor, you'll find all your clothes in there.'

Thankfully, Guy rid himself of his malodorous raiment, then did as he was bidden, finding all the garments he had left behind on going to France. Now in full fig, he emerged to be met once again by grey-suit, who directed him downstairs. The Hillman was parked outside and wafted him to a nondescript building at the back of Baker Street.

'The receptionist will look after you, sir.' was the driver's advice.

Reception was manned by an elderly janitor in a brown dustcoat, who barely looked up as Guy approached.

'You Mr Martin?'

Guy nodded, suddenly remembering his codename.

'Room 26, second floor. The lift works, just about. Follow the corridor to the left.'

The cage creaked slowly upwards and clanked to a halt. Guy exited the lift into a frowsty corridor with a haircord runner down the middle and cracked brown lino on either side of the threadbare carpeting. The whole thing smelt of cabbage and old polish. All the doors were solid, each numbered. Finding 26, he knocked.

'Come.'

Guy entered, to find Lionel seated at an oak table and flanked by two men, one either side.

'Welcome back, this is Jocelyn, Military Intelligence, this is Len, Air Force Intelligence.'

Lionel motioned Guy to a chair.

Of Jocelyn, Guy's instant impression was ex-public school woodentop, but five minutes of his sharp questions confirmed public school, delete woodentop. Len had clearly been a pilot, his limp testimony to the cannon shell over Duisburg that had wrecked his flying career. Even now, Len would wake up sweating, reliving the excruciating pain as the shell tore into his leg, the torrent of blood stemmed by his navigator and the long, long drag home with Len at the control column and his flight engineer on the rudder and brakes.

For two very solid days, they went through every last detail of his time in France, who he met, what he did, the names of all the various German regiments and Luftwaffe units he had spotted, the exact locations of all these military units, the morale and will to resist of the locals, the destruction of the Dyna factory. Len reached into his briefcase and slapped some photos on the table. They were vertical and oblique shots of the Dyna factory taken by a high-level PR Spitfire the week after the raid. They showed the factory in complete ruins, a pile of still smouldering rubble.

'Brilliant job that,' remarked Len and the others nodded their agreement.

In some ways, the debrief reminded Guy of the grilling he had received on first landing in Britain, but without the latent threat. Finally, they came to the betrayal of the cell. Guy gave them full details and that he had executed Yolande.

'What did you do with the body?' asked Jocelyn.

215

'Ding Dong Bell,' replied Guy.

'Ding Dong Bell?'

'Pussy's in the well.'

'Ah.'

'OK Martin, you're free to do what you want to do,' said Lionel, 'but let us know how to contact you, we may have another assignment soon.'

Lionel handed Guy a card with a number.

'Call that number twenty-four hours a day, they know where to find me.'

Lionel took Guy to one side.

'I guess it's Exeter, yes?'

A nod.

'Try the George Hotel, run by a friend of mine, Ken Hartwell, just mention my name. If you go to Room 10 on the ground floor here, they'll issue a rail warrant. Good luck, Captain Duplessis.'

He smiled at Guy's astonishment.

'Been gazetted six months, go and enjoy your back-pay.'

A clerk in Room 10 duly issued a first class warrant. Guy returned to the flat, and the following morning, took a taxi to Paddington. The train rattled its slow way south-west. He sat in the first class carriage, thankfully alone, and dozed. Lunch in the dining car was a tasteless affair, gristly mutton and grey mashed potato. He was awoken from his reverie by the cry of 'Exeter, this is Exeter' and grabbing his case, he alighted from the train. He was just in time to cash a cheque at Lloyds, where the kindly cashier gave him directions to the George.

A frock-coated Ken Hartwell beamed at Lionel's name and signed Guy into a large double room. The George was the epitome of a British small-town hotel, dark panelling, red plush and chintz, but comfortable for all its faded elegance.

'Dinner's at seven, breakfast seven till nine,' advised Ken.

Guy took his key and retreated upstairs. After unpacking, he rang Angela's number, but a guarded voice at the other end advised that Captain Walker was not available, but would return later. Guy left his name and number. Then, dog-tired, he settled down for a snooze. The insistent ringing of the phone jarred him back to consciousness. The excitement and utter relief in Angela's voice had him wide awake in a millisecond.

'Is that you Guy?' she cried, the joy in her voice unmistakable, then she just dissolved into tears, too overcome to speak.

Guy felt his own eyes moisten and the sound of Angela's voice brought a real lump to his throat.

'Yes, my darling, it's me, back and in one piece. 'I'm at the George, can you make dinner, 1930?'

Could a duck swim, Angela would have been out of her office then and there had not duty called.

By seven-twenty, Guy was in the foyer, so excited that he was shifting nervously from foot to foot. At that moment, Angela swung through the doors and there was a roaring in his ears. For several seconds, his body refused to obey his commands and he stood rooted to the spot, totally paralysed. Then they were in each other's arms, crushing each other in bear-like embraces and swamped in lip-pushing kisses. Guy had forgotten how good his beloved tasted, warm, soft, sensuous, slightly salty, absolutely and utterly delicious. Unseen at Reception, Ken smiled secretly, advised well in advance by Lionel of the lovers.

Dinner was good, some locally caught sole and fresh vegetables washed down with a Muscadet, but Guy and Angela ate mechanically, totally absorbed in one another.

'Can you stay darling?'

Angela nodded. They walked slowly out of the dining room, feeling all eyes must be upon them but in truth, nobody took the slightest notice. On a planet of their own, they drifted up the stairs.

Angela was still in uniform, looking trim and crisp. Slowly, Guy undressed her, marvelling anew at her slimness and beauty, then lifted her into the double bed. Sleep that night was the last thing on their minds and they lost themselves to passion, loving again and again, lying in each other's arms and blissfully unaware that the world was still rotating.

Angela was cradled in Guy's left arm, her dark soft head warm against his skin. He kissed her hair, marvelling yet again at how delicious she smelt and he squeezed her tightly to him.

'Guy, is that it or do they want you to go again?'

'Very probably.'

'Oh.'

The depth of feeling evoked in that one minute word was quite enormous and the next second, Angela began to cry, deep, racking sobs that revealed both her love for Guy and her fear that he would be torn from her by the war. Gently, Guy stroked and kissed her, calming the attack of fear.

'I'm a survivor, my love, always remember that. If I have to go, I'll return, I love you far too much to let the Nazis have me.'

The sobs gradually subsided and in minutes, the pair were asleep once more.

Guy was awoken by the bedside light going on. Angela was climbing into her uniform and brushing her hair.

'Got to be back by 0730. I'll call you later. You going to Jack and Mary's?' 'Can't wait to see Colonel,' said Guy 'I've missed him so much.'

'I've been up there quite a few times,' remarked Angela 'and he seems to cope, but he associates me with you and wonders that when I turn up, where are you. Tickle his ears for me, won't you?'

A long, mouthwatering kiss from her oh-so-kissable lips, then she was gone.

At 8 o'clock, Guy made his way to the dining room. The tea was a good British brew, but powdered egg and meat substitute sausage did nothing for the taste buds. The toast was really good, made from home-baked bread, so Guy feasted on that instead. Enquiries at the desk revealed a bus going to a village two miles from the farm. The bus left at 9.30. The elderly Bedford ground its way up the Devonian hills, dragging a coterie of local people and a couple of crates of squawking and rather smelly chickens.

An hour later, Guy stood up from the rock-hard bench called a seat and walked stiffly down the steps of the bus. An obliging local who knew Jack and Mary very well pointed him on to the right road and in a stiff Autumn breeze, the young man strode out towards the farmstead. With impeccable timing, he walked into the farm kitchen at elevenses. Colonel was standing with his back to Guy, trying the old soft soap to cadge a tasty morsel from Mary, but the scent of his adored master overcame any aromas of cake and he spun round. Colonel went berserk, his legs seemed to be like coiled springs as he bounded vertically three feet or more in the air, whimpering and whining furiously in his total euphoria. Guy caught him in mid-bound and the two hugged, with Colonel's little paws flying everywhere and a very wet, pink tongue covering Guy's face in ecstatic licks.

Everyone was in the kitchen, supping from large white china mugs and devouring seed-cake. Mary dissolved into tears and hugged Guy in a motherly way, Jack just looked delighted and shook him warmly by the hand. Letitia and Esme smiled very genuine smiles and welcomed him back. Jack could see the frown lines on Guy's face and wisely said nothing; Mary delivered tea and cake. Somehow, 50% went down Colonel's throat, but nobody cared. They talked about the farm, how well all the machines worked after Guy's attentions and the forthcoming Harvest Supper in the village hall.

'I guess you can't talk about it, but your face says it was pretty rough,' was Jack's opening remark.

'Right on both counts, Jack.'

'Back for long then, Guy?'

Jack had waited until the girls went back outside before asking the questions. 'Don't know Jack, I really don't. I could be back for quite a while, or I could be called upon very soon.'

'Have you seen Angela?'

Noticing the Duplessis blush, Jack added 'Damn silly question, really, of course you have. What are your plans?'

Guy thought for a moment.

'If Angela can wangle some leave, I'd like to take her away somewhere nice and quiet, do some walking, stretch Colonel's legs. Then, if I may, could I stay here and help on the farm? I'd pay board and lodging of course.'

Jack shook his head.

'You work, you live free and we'd be thrilled to have you back. Have you thought about Malvern for your little holiday?'

Malvern was an unknown to Guy.

'What's it like?'

'Very Victorian little town, surrounded by pretty villages and some really great walks over the hills – stretch anybody's legs, some of those climbs. Try the Feathers in West Malvern, I think they're still open and Mary and I have stayed there quite a few times.'

So saying, Jack dug into his crowded and untidy desk and after rummaging around, proudly extracted a dog-eared receipt from the Feathers.

'Here, take this, the phone number's on it when you want to call.'

Guy stuck the slip of paper in his pocket.

'Come and help me check over the sheep?'

Guy's wellies were still exactly where he had left them in the hall all those months ago. He slipped them on and with a euphoric Colonel leading the column, they strode off into the fields to look at sheep. It was almost a year since he had first set foot on the farm and the weather was shaping up for a classic russet Autumn, crisp air, a keen but not icy breeze, really fresh air and that marvellous sense of freedom at being safe amongst his friends and with his beloved terrier by his side. Guy inhaled deeply, savouring all those delights.

After a soup and ploughmans, Jack had business in Exeter and offered Guy a lift in the Jowett. Colonel riding shotgun, paws on dash, they rolled down to the city and back to the George. Guy had earlier checked that Ken allowed pets, but if Ken had any doubts, Colonel's party piece 'aren't I adorable' did the trick. Colonel snugged down on a rug in the bedroom whilst his master dozed in the armchair, to be roused by the phone and Angela announcing she would be round at 7 o'clock. She was on the dot, her reward that Colonel leapt excitedly straight into her arms and buried his muzzle against her soft neck. Angela cuddled him back, stroking the wiry fur and tickling the pink ears.

'What would you like to do darling?' enquired her man.

'I fancy a stroll, I think, and there's a nice pub at the end of it.'

'Done.'

In silent bliss, they walked hand in hand, with the dog covering at least twice the distance by running ahead and then circling back to make sure they had not gone away. The dark, shuttered streets were quite crowded in the city centre and every pub they passed noisy with military revellers sloshing ale, but the further away they walked, the quieter things became, their own silence even more pleasurable. The Crown and Cushion announced itself by the screeching of the hanging sign, in desperate need of both a repaint and some lubrication on the pivots, but the inside was warm and intimate, a small bar with a roaring log fire. Two local men sat at the counter, pint pots in hand and puffing contentedly at their pipes, but otherwise, the bar was empty. There were no beer pumps, all the ales were in barrels on stands at the back of the bar. Guy selected his brew and ordered a pint for himself, Angela joined him in a half. Never one to hang back, Colonel was already stretched out prone in front of the fire toasting his belly. Ensconced on a settle to one side and their backs to the puffers, they held hands and supped.

'I'd like us to have a holiday my love, what chance some leave?'

The firelight gleamed on Angela's dark, glossy hair and brought a huge surge of love and emotion in Guy. Angela wrinkled her nose.

'Hmm, things are a bit hectic right now, but give it a week or so, I might wangle a few days. I'll beard Colonel Grumpy in his den tomorrow.'

She grinned.

'Another pint?'

Neither had eaten for a while, so the alcohol took effect quite quickly.

Mellowed and warm, they retraced their steps to the city centre, finding themselves outside the same fish and chip shop they had patronised on that first, momentous date. The turbanned sisters still presided over the hissing vats and the zinc counter and the heat from the boiling oil mixed with steam to create an aromatic sauna. Gourmet supper that evening was cod and chips, the chips laced with Sarsons vinegar and a generous sprinkling of salt. Colonel did not partake of cod, but hoovered up his share of the spicy chips, a loud belch signifying his approval of this sumptuous fare.

By now it was time for Angela to return to barracks and they parted with warm, greasy, salty kisses. Angela's tongue flicked briefly inside Guy's mouth, bringing an instant desire that showed in his eyes.

'Down boy, there'll be plenty of time for that,' she teased. 'Tomorrow night, same time?'

Then she was gone, leaving Guy to his thoughts and a lonely night in the George. Probably against all the hotel's rules, the little dog retook his accustomed position on the counterpane against Guy's leg and with the familiar comfort of that furry head exactly where it was supposed to be, Guy slept like a log.

A crisp and quite frosty dawn mellowed into a passably warm day and saw man and dog striding off into the hills. Military activity was everywhere, vehicles and field guns on the move, aircraft overhead, whole fleets of jeeps, trucks, tanks and armoured cars lying in fields and swathed in camouflage netting. Determined to find peace and quiet, the pair took to footpaths and soon, the cacophony of conflict disappeared, bar the evocative, rolling sound of a supercharged Merlin V12 if a Spitfire or Hurricane flew past. They strolled companiably like this for over three hours, until breasting a ridge, they found themselves looking down on a small village, all stonewashed houses and thatch, a picture postcard.

'What'll it be, sir?' enquired the landlord of the village's sole pub.

With stone walls feet thick, tiny windows and a ceiling barely high enough to walk beneath without ducking, the taproom was dark and almost foreboding. A few locals were having a lunchtime beer and a game of cribbage. Guy had to accustom his sight to the gloom to see what was on offer. Here too, a row of wooden casks on stands at the back of the bar contained mild and bitter and even a stout. Guy chose a pint of one of the bitters, a dark but quite sweet brew that he found he liked instantly.

His enquiry about food was met with a wry look and an offer of bread, cheese and a couple of pickled onions. Guy took his tankard over to a seat near a window and sank gratefully onto a padded bench to ease his muscles. Minutes later his food appeared and after slipping a few titbits to Colonel, he sat back to enjoy his lunch, a coarse but moist home-made bread, a chunky Cheddar and the onions.

As he ate, he began to think. By now, his head had cleared from the stresses of his mission. The burning and so far unanswered question was how long he would be in Britain and when the clarion call would come, as come it surely must, to re-enter France and, more important, what for. If Guy was certain about one thing, it was that he treasured Angela and his utmost desire was to marry her, but he could not bring himself to enter marriage when the chances of coming back from a second mission were tenuous – and that was being polite. The attrition rates for SOE agents was 25% and the Yolandes of this world shortened the odds even further. But even with this proviso, Guy sensed that he would come out alive. Not only would he wed his sweetheart, but he would move to England, too. He loved France, but the memories of his parents' untimely death and the treachery of Yolande were as yet extremely raw wounds, wounds that time would assuage but never heal.

Suddenly resolute, he gulped the last of his pint, fed Colonel the final Cheddar morsel and set tankard and plate down on the bar. With a 'Goodbye and many thanks', he strode off towards Exeter and the George.

'Do you know any good solicitors, Ken?'

'Anything special?'

'My will.'

'Ah,' said the hotel manager, 'you know you can buy a will form from Smiths, it's just as good, you know.'

Guy thought about this, but concluded that with some of his estate in France and some in Britain, a spot of proper legal advice was the order of the day. Besides, he still had probate to sort out once the war was over. Ken directed him to Spillikin, Barnes, the firm Ken himself had used for many years. Despite the lawyer's duty of confidentiality, Guy realised that he had to do this in a way that covered the legalities but gave away nothing of value in intelligence.

If he thought the pub was gloomy, it was as night to day compared to the Spillikin, Barnes office, where they had cornered the market in chocolate paint, dark oak varnish and what seemed to be the cast offs from the smoking room of the local gentlemen's club in the form of rock-hard, overstuffed leather armchairs. The threadbare carpet only heaped sorrow upon sorrow of this dismal scene. Luckily, Ken had warned Guy not to be fooled by appearances, his man Spillikin was a cut above your average country solicitor. Mr Spillikin had an appointment free at 5pm.

'Trevelyan Spillikin.'

The solicitor proffered a hand. Guy's mischievous streak came to the fore and he had to suppress a giggle. Certain names conjured up certain visions and Trevelyan to Guy was some young, athletic rugger type. Probably nearing sixty, Trevelyan Spillikin was what bespoke tailors diplomatically classed as 'short portly'. Not that the lawyer seemed to have patronised a bespoke tailor, indeed any tailor, in the recent past. If the office furnishings were charity shop, then sartorially, Trevelyan was several orders below that. His pinstripe suit, whilst well cut, had not been even kissed by an iron since time immemorial and was shiny to the point of patination. One button was missing but the remaining threads still protruded from the cloth and the points of both lapels were worn away to reveal the lining. Guy's immediate worry was that Ken's judgement might be faulty, but a firm handshake and a pair of intelligent eyes suggested it might be premature to judge this book solely by its cover.

'I understand you want to make a will?'

Guy nodded.

'I am more than happy to take your fee, but one and sixpence at Smiths is a great deal easier and cheaper. But perhaps your own case is not that simple?'

He indicated to Guy to take a seat.

'I am a French national, over here because of the war. I was born of an originally English father and French mother. Father became a French citizen. Both my parents are dead, but I have no proof of this and any such proof will not be available until the war is over. I am an only child and as far as I know, the only living relatives are an aunt and uncle in France and an uncle in England. I believe all three are still alive, but my father and his brother had a big falling-out years ago and there has been no contact since. I wish to make a will in favour of a young English lady whom I hope to marry if I survive, but whom I want to inherit if I do not.'

Guy continued.

'The complication is that for security reasons, I cannot release to you all the detail you need. My idea is to make a will in favour of the lady, Miss Walker. All the detail you need will be written down and sealed in an envelope with you as witness, then put in a safety deposit box at Lloyds here in town. You will be given authority to open the box and the envelope in the event of my death. If I am killed, a friend near here will be told and will turn up here with the key to the box. I do not want Miss Walker to know of this arrangement, it might frighten her if she hears I am making a will.'

Spillikin sat back in his chair, steepled his fingers and mused for a moment. 'Mr Duplessis, let me tell you that until Herr Hitler became a little presumptuous, almost all my work was locally based and very rarely concerned matters without Great Britain. That still remains the case, but with the influx of troops from all corners of the globe, I find myself involved more and more in your kind of situation. Mostly, it is GIs marrying British girls then being killed. Some of them leave wills, many don't and I have to try and trace their estates in America and obtain probate. Since America is an Allied power and we almost share a language, it is not usually too difficult. By sheer coincidence, I have been handling two cases for French nationals in recent weeks and face precisely the same problem of being incommunicado until hostilities cease. And, of course, not knowing what records if any will still exist.'

'First, Mr Duplessis, a few questions. Is your late father's estate entirely in France or is any part of it elsewhere? Did he leave a will? Have you ever made a will? Are you engaged to Miss Walker? And whilst this may be a delicate matter, have you any children or any expected?'

Guy smiled to indicate he was not at all embarrassed by the questions.

'My father was very rich man who transferred much of his money to a London bank when war loomed. There are businesses and possessions in France and I will give full detail on how to trace these, plus the name and address of his lawyer in France who also holds the will. There is also a lawyer in England who can help. Until I found myself in the Army, a will was the last thing on my mind. And no, Miss Walker and I are not engaged. I know that there are those who take the view of snatching happiness when you can, like your GIs, but I don't want to leave a war widow who has been married just weeks or months, I don't think it's fair. I want to marry Angela – Miss Walker – when all this is over and we can lead a proper life together. I have no children anywhere and Miss Walker is not pregnant.'

'This is your first really serious relationship?'

Guy smiled.

Yes, a real coup de foudre.'

The solicitor nodded.

'Because of the two recent cases, I have formed an alliance with a French lawyer in London, we see more and more of this kind of work arising. My colleague had a lucrative practice in Lyon, but escaped to

England. Being Jewish… I am sure I do not need to go on? He has briefed me pretty thoroughly on the French laws of inheritance, so I have some idea, but please take what I say as a general indication, not gospel.'

'No action can be taken on your father's estate until the war ends, but when it does, his lawyer will have to obtain probate. Given the chaos likely to ensue after hostilities, that could take some years. If your parents' death cannot be proved, the major countries involved in this war are bound to bring in some special provisions to override the usual period of presumption of death. In this country, you may know that it is seven years. If we have to wait years to reopen cases that have long lain dormant on file, there could be widows desperate for monies in accounts that they cannot touch. The difficulty will be proving title to assets like a business or a building where the same has been abandoned because of the war. I would expect that any assets held outside France like the monies in London will be included in your father's estate. Any French death duties and taxes would be deducted before probate is finalised.'

'Once French probate is granted, then the work can begin on your English will. First, your estate may be subject to restrictions under French law.'

Trevelyan paused.

'This uncle in England, paternal you say?'

Guy inclined his head.

'I sense that this family rift was extremely serious and there is bad blood. Do you think your uncle will try to contest the wills?'

A wry smile flickered across Guy's lips at this question.

'I can see him wetting his lips right now,' came the reply. 'The two brothers hated each other almost from the moment of birth and the chance to get his revenge and his hands on my father's money would be irresistible.'

Trevelyan Spillikin continued.

'I have to assume that your father was well advised when he made his will and given the enmity, would have been extremely unlikely to bequeath anything to your uncle. Do you have any evidence of this feud?'

'The English lawyer can give you chapter and verse.'

'Good. Does your uncle have money?'

'Yes, indeed,' replied Guy, 'he is quite wealthy.'

Once more the steepled fingers.

'I doubt your uncle is going to contest the French will, given the circumstances, your primogeniture and that, without suggesting any impropriety, that a British plaintiff against a French national in a French court… The circumstances that dictate you make a will in England are manna from heaven for your uncle. Miss Walker is not rich, I take it? No, I thought not. So here you have rich uncle who can risk a court action knowing his opponent cannot and who will hire a top flight barrister who can make it seem credible that black is indeed white.'

'The attack will be on two fronts, in my opinion. The first will be an attack on you – young man, parents dead, away from his home country, the stresses of war, your vulnerability, first serious relationship, your state of mind when you made the will, etc, etc. The second will be to paint Miss Walker – who, if I may say, will be quite delightful if you are anything to go by – as the original scarlet woman, a siren who discovered her man was worth a small fortune and used her wiles to snare him into leaving her all his money. In some ways, if Miss Walker became Mrs Duplessis, it would strengthen her case, but even that could be turned against her. Not only did she snare you, but coerced you into marrying her as well so that she had a direct claim.'

Guy looked pained.

'As your lawyer, I am bound to point out the pitfalls. Let us hope it does not come to that. I have now developed a modus operandi in these cases. I will make enquiries as to the value of an estate and the potential ease or difficulty of obtaining probate. If the whole thing is worth tuppence ha'penny or what is there would be swallowed by my fee to obtain it, then I offer to withdraw. If the widow wishes to continue, then she assumes the liability for my fee. Is that acceptable?'

'Fine,' replied Guy.

'Well, then, I propose that you write down all the information you have that will assist me. We will then place it in an envelope together under my seal and witnessed by my clerk. Then we go together to Lloyds and deposit it in their vaults. Should you wish to retrieve it again, then it must be in the company of me or one of my firm, I can only do so after your death. Now to the details of your will. Do you want the entirety to Miss Walker or are there other bequests?'

Guy had thought about this and was ready. He left a portion of the estate to the two Hs, named as his only uncle and aunt in France and whose identities would be lodged with the bank. Jack and Mary also featured and were named as his executors. The balance went to Angela. If Guy returned the next day at 2pm, all the documents would be ready. He would bring the information ready to be sealed and deposited.

Angela turned up at 7.30, grinning from ear to ear.

'Old Grumpy turns out to be a bit of a sweetie under all that Eton and the Guards ramrod exterior. When I asked him for a week's leave, he looked at me and said, "I've got a daughter about the same age and just like you. Your eyes tell me you are madly in love and I'm guessing that your man's in town. Am I right? Give me the leave pass, please." 'And he signed it on the spot. I'm on leave from Sunday night for a whole week.'

Guy immediately dug out the bill Jack had given him and rang The Feathers in Malvern Wells. Luck was with them, the hotel had just one room vacant, which Guy booked for Mr and Mrs Duplessis. They went out to a restaurant for a meal, but it turned out to be nothing special, so they decided that what they really needed was a large helping of bed for afters. So they helped themselves, with a cherry on the top.

Angela slipped off around 10.30pm, leaving her man sound asleep. He woke the next morning, decided to have a lie-in, then after a leisurely breakfast, bought a pad of paper from Smiths and sat down to record all the vital information Trevelyan Spillikin might need in the future. Guy had a young person's photographic memory for names and numbers. All his father and mother's business details, their bank accounts in France and London, the names and address of the two Hs, Rhys Chapman's name and address, Angela's name, rank and service number and his own too, all these were written down. He added as much as he knew about the feud between his father and Henry.

Mission accomplished, he put all the sheets of paper into an envelope and tucked it firmly in his inside pocket before walking down to the station to check train times and buy tickets for Monday. With a little time in hand before his appointment with the solicitor, he looked at a few shops, gazing intently in their windows. A brisk walk and he was at Spillikin, Barnes, where Trevelyan had done a splendid job of both the will and the necessary documents for the bank. Guy signed, Trevelyan signed, the envelope was sealed, the clerk witnessed, they walked round to Lloyds, the envelope was deposited. Trevelyan shook hands with Guy outside the bank.

'I very much look forward to seeing you again, Mr Duplessis, I really do, take good care of yourself – and that dog!'

Having made up his mind whilst signing all the documents, Guy returned to the shops and made two purchases. One was quite large in every sense, as the local Gieves and Hawkes furnished him with a natty line in suits off the peg; he in turn furnished them with a wad of clothing coupons. The second was a very small but highly significant purchase.

'How about some sea air, Colonel?'

The terrier cocked his head to one side and grinned assent, so they took a bus to Exmouth and strolled along the front. The sea air was sharp and tangy and that seaside holiday noise of screaming gulls took Guy back to his childhood, La Baule and sandcastles on the beach. Everything was shuttered and barred, both because of Autumn and the war. An onshore breeze whipped the wavetops into a foam and the smell of rotting seaweed mixed with tar to produce that seaside aroma you could recognise instantly with your eyes shut. Grey clouds scudded across the bay, faint smudges of smoke on the horizon told of seaborne activity and little boats rocked gently at anchor in the bay. Virtually alone in the deserted resort, Guy enjoyed his solitude with his little chum and thought deeply about the unknown, that uncertain future yet so near and yet to come.

Leaving Exeter bus station on his return, Guy made a note of the phone number and opening hours of the town's smartest restaurant as he passed their door; a call at 6.30 saw a booking for two at 8pm. He managed to track down Angela and warned her to wear her glad rags.

At 7.30, his beloved appeared once more at The George, looking absolutely edible in a cream frock with matching shoes and handbag. Guy's heart nearly burst with pride when he saw her enter the foyer, she just looked unutterably lovely. She in turn looked at him in his new suit and silently reciprocated his emotions.

Taking Angela by one delicate hand, he led her gently into a small lounge.

'Where are we going, Guy? And why the posh frock tonight? And would you just look at that whistle,' she teased, running a hand over the lapels.

He put a finger to his lips to indicate that she should ask no questions, then closed the door firmly behind him. All at once, there was a lump in his throat and he struggled to form his words. Going down on one knee, he looked up and just managed to blurt out 'Angela darling, will you marry me?'

Her reply was to burst into tears and at the same time, furiously nod her assent. The couple just held each other gently, mutely communicating far more than a thousand words could ever do and savouring an historic moment in their love. Guy reached into his pocket and opened the tiny jewel box containing the diamond and sapphire engagement ring. Almost shyly, Angela proffered the appropriate finger and he slid the ring into place. Their joy was complete at its perfect fit. Giggling like naughty children, they took themselves off for a gloriously romantic engagement dinner.

Chapter 13

It was in every way idyllic, a quiet table, soft white napery, gleaming cutlery. The gently flickering candles brought warm reflections from not only the linen and the silver but also the flecks in Angela's green eyes. Best of all, they created starbursts from the diamonds and sapphires in her ring as she moved her hand around to let the facets catch the light. They held hands and gazed at each other in wonderment, suspended in a time warp, a dream that was almost a trance. Guy and Angela were locked in love.

Considering wartime constraints, the food was tip-top. For a night such as this, the chosen ambrosia could be only champagne, a bottle whose ruinously expensive price was a mere bagatelle to the enraptured young Frenchman. He gazed at his fiancée, scarcely crediting his good fortune; she in her turn had eyes for her man and her man alone. The rest of the world was totally immaterial.

'How long have you been planning all this, Guy?'

He had the grace to blush.

'Since I've been home, I've had a lot of time to think and to understand what I really want. I know that the most important thing is to marry you, but I'd like to do it properly, a church wedding with all your family there and mine too, a really joyous occasion. I don't want it to be just a register office do, I want it to be a day we'll both treasure forever.'

Angela smiled, a smile of deep happiness.

'I'd really like that,' she said and grasped his hand even more tightly than before.

The attentive but discreet waiter hove into view and Guy ordered coffee and brandies.

'Ready for the off on Monday, my darling?' he enquired.

She nodded.

'I'll be over on Sunday evening with my bag. Are you going to book me a room at The George?'

'Ken's very understanding and discreet, there'll be no problem about you sharing with me.'

Angela had wangled another night away from barracks and with

Colonel tucked up with Ken for the night, they drifted slowly, sensuously, deliciously into each other's arms, celebrating their union, losing themselves in deep, warm passion. That million volts sizzled time and again, cries of ecstasy spilling from their lips, then blessed sleep.

To clear her desk before her leave, Angela had to burn the midnight oil on Saturday, so Guy spent a lonely and impatient weekend doing very little, walking, trying out new pubs and snoozing in his room. Every timepiece he looked at seemed to move at a snail's pace, but at last, there she was, suitcase in hand, his for a whole week and no interruptions. Merveilleux.

The powerful Castle class locomotive could be heard as it drew into Exeter St David's, all clanking conrods and hissing valves, but wreathed in a huge cloud of steam, it remained hidden until the last moment. As the behemoth drew level, Guy could see the special blinds and the cover between loco and tender so that the glow from the firebox could not be seen in the dark. Like kids off to the seaside, they climbed into a First Class non-smoking compartment. Colonel got all excited about being on a train and bounced up and down like a dervish. The train was pretty crowded and before it left the station, the compartment filled. Seeking both comfort and solace from all these unfamiliar legs, the terrier climbed onto Angela's lap and curled up into a ball. The guard's shrill whistle was answered by the deeper note of the train's and with a flurry of wheelspin on the worn track, it set off towards Oxford. With the restrictions of wartime, the carriages but creaked along, but the clickety-clack of the wheels on the rail joints was soporific, the compartment was warm and soon almost all the passengers were asleep.

At noon, a stewardess announced the first sitting for lunch. Guy and his party roused themselves and wended their way to the restaurant car. Dreading an encore of the gristly mutton of the westbound journey, Guy was pleasantly surprised. Under the chef's hat was a lady who clearly knew how to cook, producing individual cottage pies with at least vestiges of toothsome meat, fluffy mashed potato and a nice cheesy crust. Washed down with a couple of beers apiece, it did more than fill a hole and they regained the compartment to slumber once more. The screech of brakes broke through Guy's reverie and looking out from the slowing train, he could see the outskirts of a city. After about twenty minutes stationary, the guard popped her head around the sliding door.

'Sorry about this, we're stuck just outside Oxford while they finish defusing a bomb near the line, a present from Jerry last night. Be about forty-five minutes.'

She disappeared. Looking at his watch, Guy began to wonder if they would make their connection to Worcester. The minutes dragged by and still they sat, immobile and helpless, steamclouds venting from the heating system. At the very point of no return, there was a loud whistle and the train dragged itself into Oxford station. Running across the bridge to the platform, they threw themselves in the door as the guard signalled the right away.

Catching their breath as they walked, Guy and Angela found an empty compartment and settled down for the next leg of the journey. Slower still than the so-called express they had just left, the train rumbled its way through Charlbury, Kingham, Moreton in Marsh – soon to become the inspiration for Much Binding – rolling on to Worcester's Foregate Street station. The countryside was new to both Guy and Angela and they stared excitedly at the autumnal vistas on either side of the tracks. Colonel, utterly unmoved – literally and metaphorically – remained as Angela's lap warmer and grumbled loudly at being disturbed when they detrained at Worcester. With three quarters of an hour to their connection to Great Malvern, they repaired to the buffet, now shrouded in blackout. The fug in the buffet could have been cut with a knife, a combination of heat and the smoke from the innumerable fags of the occupants. With their heavy outer clothes, they began to perspire freely and breathing was pretty difficult with oxygen in short supply. Guy ordered two teas, bringing them to the table that Angela had found, a table awash with seemingly more tea than in either of their cups. By mutual and unspoken consent, they drank up as quickly as possible and sought refuge in the non-smoking Waiting Room.

'Phew,' remarked Angela, sticking one brown tress under her nose as they escaped the buffet, 'I'm sure my hair reeks of smoke, I really hate it.'

Wartime trains were notorious for unpunctuality, but luck was with them, the local flyer depositing them at Great Malvern at 6.30. A cab took them to Malvern Wells and the Feathers, grinding asthmatically up the hill to the hotel. All that could be seen in the dark was a traditional black and white building with a thatched roof. Guy, Angela and Colonel squeezed past the blackout curtain into the reception area, but the dark wooden counter was deserted. Angela tinkled the small brass bell provided. A door slammed in the back somewhere and Marion Bennett appeared, wiping her hands on a pinstripe butcher's apron.

'You'll be Mr and Mrs Duplessis, you're in Number 6.'

The hint of Scouse in the Welsh lilt betrayed her North Wales origins. 'I believe you have a dog. He is well-behaved, isn't he?'

'Impeccably,' affirmed Guy, 'and although he sheds no hair, I've brought his blanket for him to sleep on.'

He forbore to add that the chances of that happening were nil as Colonel would be snuggled down with them on the bed. Marion came round the counter and was immediately enchanted by Colonel, stroking his head and tickling the small ears. Wily ol' Colonel worked out in a microsecond that he was on to a good thing here and that if he played his cards right, mucho tasty titbits were his for the taking. Shining eyes, head cocked to one side, tongue slightly hanging, he added yet another member to the Colonel fan club.

'He's *lovely,*' remarked Marion and Guy and his fiancée exchanged secret grins at this word and the accent.

Marion led the way up the broad stairs to Number 6. The Feathers was a deceptive structure. From the outside, it looked rather small; the interior belied that impression. Number 6 was a super room, dominated by a genuine four-poster with oak barley-twist supports for the cream silk canopy. The furniture suite was also oak and high quality. The walls were a beautiful neutral shade, somewhere between gold and light sand. The best bit was the carpet, pale blue, velvety and ankle-deep pile. Wall art was far from the customary stag at bay, six razor sharp photographs of wildlife, mostly birds, but also a fox cub and a badger.

'I'd expect you'd like some tea after your journey, have you come far?' asked Marion.

'Exeter,' replied Angela, 'and we'd love some tea, please.'

'There's lashings of hot water,' added Marion before disappearing towards the kitchen and the kettle.

Guy and Angela started unpacking. Angela took off for the bathroom, returning to find Guy bouncing experimentally on the mattress.

'Testing that it will stand the strain, are we?' she teased.

Guy responded by chasing her round the bed and they ended up scrapping on her side of the bed, squealing and giggling. Things were about to get more serious when there was a knock on the door. Sobriety was instantaneous, Angela standing up and smoothing her hair and her skirt, leaving Guy to answer the door. Outside stood a young girl of about seventeen bearing a tray with a pot of tea for two and some yummy shortbread.

'I'm Sarah,' she announced, setting down the tray on the coffee table by the window.

Realising they were famished, the young couple demolished the biscuits, but sparing the odd crumb for the hound. Then it was bath time, a shared soak in the tub. The bathroom matched the rest, being up-to-the-minute white enamel in a bathroom impeccably tiled in black and white.

Suitably refreshed and coiffed, they descended to the bar for couple of pre-prandial G&Ts, served by the ubiquitous Marion. Guy had brought down Colonel's dishes and Colonel was soon ensconced by the inglenook with a dish of chicken and vegetables, his rather indelicate smacking of chops indicating his satisfaction with the local cuisine. Dinner of carrot soup, succulent chicken complemented by fresh vegetables al dente and an apple lattice and fresh cream brought home to Guy that although not spared from the problems of WWII, the locale was geared to producing and consuming its own food. Wartime had changed that centuries-old pattern but little. The hotel was full, with one pair of guests obviously American and a man and wife talking in what Guy surmised was Polish. Certainly, his fractured English bore a heavy East European accent. Marion triumphantly announced that coffee was back on the menu that evening, thanks to Mr Silver and Mr Horowitz. The two Yanks grinned and waved their thanks when the assembled clientele raised their glasses in tribute to this generosity.

The last delicious morsel consumed, they donned anoraks and strolled along the narrow lane to walk off the feast and give Colonel his constitutional. After being cooped up in trains all day, the crisp night air was very welcome, clearing their heads. Arm in arm, they followed the white scut of the dog's tail as he tracked along enjoying all those new smells. From time to time, they paused to hug and kiss, savouring each other and these blissful moments together. Having covered a mile or so, they backtracked to the warmth of the bar, where Dave Bennett was now in charge. Two guests sat warming themselves by the fire, so Guy and Angela perched on two of the leather-covered bar stools, ordering single malts from a fine display behind the bar. Dave turned from pouring the spirits to find the third stool now occupied. Amused, he leaned across the bar.

'Good evening, sir. And what'll it be? Another single malt?'

Colonel just gave his best doggy grin and was rewarded with a tickle under the chin and a soupçon of cheese.

'I'm Guy, this is my wife Angela. This place is a real gem, absolutely spot on.'

Dave was pleased with the compliment.

'I was born here in Malvern Wells, my dad worked for Morgan. I've spent all my life in hotels, trained in Birmingham, did a few stints at some of the big London ones, then moved out to the provinces. That's how I met Marion, I was managing The Beaulieu in Aberystwyth and she was Head Housekeeper. Problem about big hotels is you never seem to have a minute to yourself, especially in the season. We found that many days, we saw each other at the morning staff meeting and snatched a few words as we passed in the corridor, it was no life at all.'

The accent was a softer version of Brummagen.

'Saw this advertised for sale in the Caterer a few years ago and bought it. It was pretty good, but we've gradually changed it to the way we want it to incorporate all our own ideas. All the bedrooms have an individual theme, all the bathrooms are state-of-the-art and we've replumbed so that there's plenty of hot water. So many hotels we find can manage a tepid trickle and that's the last thing guests want. There's a good kitchen garden at the back and a local old boy tends that for me, so we grow all our vegetables and herbs. The orchard provides fruit and two dozen hens scrat around in a big cage, so we've eggs too. Local butcher rears and slaughters his own meat, but fish is a problem now there's a war on. We can sometimes pick up local trout, but a chap from Bristol used to call daily with sea fish. Not now though. What we can get comes by train and sometimes, it's been sitting on ice for days. Has that grey look, you know?'

Dave wrinkled his nose in disgust.

'Who took the pictures?' asked Guy, having seen more around the bar and in the dining room.

'Hobby of mine, when I get a bit of spare time, it's ideal round here, all kinds of birds and animals right on your doorstep.'

He smiled modestly.

'I'm a very patient chap.'

Guy felt his eyelids beginning to droop and he could see his fiancée's head lolling. Draining their glasses, they bid mine host goodnight and retired to bed. Barely had they wrapped their arms round one another than they were in the land of nod. Satisfied that there would be no carnal cavortings, Colonel plumped himself down at the end of the counterpane and nose in paws, joined them in slumber. For a little dog, he actually made quite a noise, whistling through his nostrils, snoring, nose and paws twitching as he dreamed about whatever little dogs dream about. But nothing short of a volcanic eruption would have disturbed Guy and Angela.

Guy woke slowly, at first not sure where he was. He looked down at Angela, her dark hair spread on the pillow, limning her face. Oh so gently, he leaned over and kissed the end of her nose. Like Sleeping Beauty, she awoke, stretching languidly like a cat. Then her eyes flamed with desire, a flame swiftly quenched before descending for breakfast.

And what a breakfast. Thick rashers, eggs plucked from the straw scarcely an hour since and fresh-baked bread. The piece de resistance had Angela's eyes out on stalks, a whole pat of yellow, creamy butter.

'I haven't had real butter since I can't remember when, all we get is marge,' she remarked to Marion.

'Oh, we do that ourselves as well. Dave went to a farm auction a few years ago and picked up all the kit, so I do it.'

The temptation to spread it thick on the bread was too strong to resist so they made pigs of themselves. Guy had to admit that he actually preferred the British salted variety to the paler French unsalted.

'Are you here to walk?'

It was Dave. They nodded.

'We've got some local maps of the hills in proper map cases you can borrow and we can do you sandwiches and a flask of tea if you like.'

They did like and armed with a pair of walking sticks from the collection in the hall, set off to climb to the top of the hill. The ancient volcanic eruptions that had formed the Malvern Hills created a kind of steep sided spine. With months of pounding Auntie around French byways, Guy's muscles were like whipcord, but poor Angela was soft from days spent behind a desk. Within minutes of starting the climb, her legs were protesting and she was gasping for breath. Guy just slowed the pace, took her arm and with plenty of rest stops, they gradually achieved the summit.

It was a real russet day. The sun was shedding the final vestiges of her warmth before retiring for winter. On top of the hill there was a slight breeze, but on both the Worcestershire and Herefordshire sides, the air at ground level was calm and still. As the couple walked, they could see glimpses of cottages nestling at the base of the hills, lazy tendrils of smoke drifting straight up from their chimneys. Golden browns of the brackens and leaves contrasted with the yellow flowers of the gorse. Colonel had a great time with the gorse, darting in and out of the clumps, playing hide and seek and jumping out in front of the lovers. They walked steadily, sometimes taking the direct route over the top of a hill, sometimes the long way round on the paths that ran either side of each peak. There were a few other walkers, but in the main, the hills were pretty deserted. The view towards Worcester and Evesham was especially clear. Toy tractors and farm carts went about their business in the fields below, the odd cough from an exhaust making its way into the hills.

One slightly baffling sight was a Lancaster bomber which arrived in a roar of Hercules engines, then flew parallel tracks up and down, repeatedly throttling back each engine in turn, then lowering and retracting flaps and undercarriage before finally opening the taps and thundering into the distance. When the same thing happened a couple of hours later, their curiosity was aroused further.

'What do you think he's doing?' enquired Angela.

The same question had been exercising Guy's mind, then it dawned.

'We're not far from Brum, my guess is they're air-testing planes from the factory before delivery to the squadrons.'

They found an ideal spot for lunch, a bowl surrounded by gorse, a real suntrap. Happily, they munched cheese and pickle sandwiches and apples, sharing the flask of tea, before lying back to soak up the rays. Overhead, a hawk circled lazily on a thermal, watching below for his own lunch.

'Guy?'

'Mmm?'

'You know when you were talking about the wedding the other day? You said "Now I'm home." 'Did you mean that?'

Guy rolled over and kissed her gently on the lips.

'Freudian slip, my love, but that's exactly what I meant. Home's where you are and that's England. Quite apart from that, the vision of finding my parents dead the way I did, that will stay in my mind forever, plus there's... there's the war,' he added a touch lamely, nearly spilling the beans about Yolande. 'I love my France, but for me, it can never be the same again, it just can't.'

'What will you do?'

'For a living?'

'Mmm.'

'Open a garage or two, that's what I love.'

'What about your father's businesses?'

'God alone knows what I'll find when this war ends. I think I told you that the Boche requisitioned most of his trucks. Where they all are and in what condition is anybody's guess. They may end up as wrecks or be destroyed by a retreating enemy. So restarting the freight business could be tricky and take a lot of capital, even assuming there are trucks to buy. But there'll be plenty of business carting goods around to rebuild the economy, so I'll have to take a view. The garages, well, what will be left? I simply can't hazard a guess. The main thing is, my darling, that I don't want to find myself stuck in France for weeks on end rebuilding the businesses and you hundreds of miles away on your own. I'd happily take you along, but it would be a lonely existence with me at work and you with just a few words of French. Plus it pains me to say that many of my countrymen are chauvinistic and will refuse to speak English on principle.'

'The way I see it,' went on Guy, 'is that France has been occupied, families have been torn apart, many have fled as refugees, thousands have been dragged off to concentration camps or simply disappeared. The country is divided by factions, those who collaborated, those who didn't, those who sat on the fence and finally, the Communists. God knows what they want. The fabric of society has been seriously damaged. The first thing that will happen is that there will be old scores to settle and rebuilding that fabric's going to take a long time. Britain has taken a pasting and thousands of men will never return, but there's been no invasion and society's fabric is largely intact. Britain's economy is in a far better position to stage a recovery than France's. Probably the only good thing about war is the way it accelerates technology development, so all those new materials, better fuels, improved lubricants, they'll be poised to be absorbed into the car industry. I foresee a large demand for cars and I plan to be there to supply it.'

'Thank you, Professor Duplessis,' said Angela mock seriously.

'Sorry, was I waxing a bit lyrical?'

'Just a touch, darling, but you've obviously given it considerable thought and it makes good sense. And I'll be honest, I don't want you miles away in France for weeks on end either.'

They cuddled.

Having planned their day's walk carefully, late afternoon found them descending towards Malvern, a steep lane leading to the main street, where they found a tearoom open. The scones contained enough bicarb to set your teeth on edge, but the tea was an honest brew and revived flagging corpuscles sufficiently to fortify them for the walk back to Malvern Wells and The Feathers.

Poor Angela's leg muscles were screaming for mercy, so a hot bath and some more tea were prescribed. Thus medicated, they descended for aperitifs and dinner. A coarse pâte followed by locally caught trout from the reservoir at the British Camp, then some concoction somewhere between custard and zabaglione. A chunky Pouilly Fuisse was a fine accompaniment and they toasted Jack and his choice of hotel.

For the next two days, they wandered the hills, once with a packed lunch, then taking the chance on a pub in the host of tiny villages clustered around the base of the Malverns. Angela's legs found their second wind and the walking was so relaxing, so therapeutic, that all their stresses and strains just vanished. Overall, the war was passing the Malverns by. In Exeter, every window had the telltale criss-cross of tape; in the Malverns, nobody bothered.

On Thursday, they took a bus to Worcester, where the market was in full swing. Happy as larks, they browsed through stall after stall of bric-a-brac and found some good pieces of silver at quite reasonable prices. A late lunch in a pub, a stroll along the banks of the Severn, afternoon tea and then the early showing of a silly American comedy before catching the last bus back to Malvern.

Friday was their swansong, the trains dictating a return to Exeter on Saturday. They awoke to a thick hoar frost and that hint of snow in the air. The sun had finally packed her bags and hibernated for the winter. A steel-grey sky was matched by an icy wind that keened over the hills and the higher they climbed, the colder it became. Even Colonel was swaddled in his little coat. But somehow it did not matter one jot, the weather was irrelevant, even though at one stage, it appeared to be sleeting upwards. They set themselves a tough schedule for the day. First they struck out for Wyche and West Malvern, turning back through Colwall to end up at the pub at the base of the British Camp, an Iron Age fort. A couple of pints and a sandwich or three regenerated their energy and permitted icy skins to unfreeze. Angela wiped a dewdrop from the end of her cute nose.

'Bit of a change from Tuesday, this,' she commented.

Guy nodded.

'Even Colonel's feeling it a bit, I think,' came his reply.

Sure enough, the small blaze in the grate was virtually invisible behind a small dog catching every watt of heat available.

'Come on boy, we're off again.'

Colonel gave Guy a look that said eloquently "Do we really have to?" but bounded out of the door.

Now it was actually snowing, large flakes that melted rather than settled, but swirled around in eddies from the wind. The trio began the steep climb towards the fort's summit. This side was in the lee of the wind, so was not at all bad, but when they reached the crest, a howling gale was blowing, stinging icy flakes and sleet into their faces. Pulling hats lower and scarves higher, they set their teeth against the wind and carried on. The conditions unfortunately obscured the usually splendid panorama. They continued along the Shire Ditch, Colonel back to his usual brisk pace, Guy and Angela hand in hand, just savouring being together and the freedom. Gradually, the little party worked their way downhill into some woodland, where the wind abated and they could speak without their words being snatched away. As dusk was hovering, they climbed once more up the side of the camp, passing the reservoir and regaining the car park opposite their lunch-time pub. Back on the road, they tramped downhill to Malvern Wells, pushing for the final time through the blackout curtain and into the hallway of the hotel. Bodily they were warm from their exertions, but the couple's faces were brick red and frozen into a near rictus from the cold and the wind. Marion emerged from the kitchen as they walked in, took one look and about-turned to the tea-kettle. Gratefully, they sank into armchairs by the inglenook and allowed themselves to be fussed. The log fire thawed the outside and the hot drink the inside, so within twenty minutes, all numbness had gone. As he had done in the funny little cottage in France those many months ago, the terrier exposed his chest to the flames and rocked soporifically in the heat.

The piping hot bath a deux was bliss, soaking away the aches and completely rejuvenating the extremities.

'Happy my lovely?'

Angela smiled a very wide smile that demanded and received no words and reached out to hold Guy's hand. Hotel towels were of the thick, white, fluffy variety, warmed on the rail, and the two dried each other, a little service and a token of their love. With an hour before dinner, they slid beneath the quilt and dozed.

Matched to the climate, the starter was carrot and coriander soup, the rich glow being matched by the fire it spread in the entrails. How the Bennetts got hold of the entrée could only be guessed, but the roast beef, pink, rare and juicy was a sight that neither Guy nor Angela had seen in a long while. The remainder of the dining room was also pleasantly surprised and all that could be heard for some minutes was the intake of succulent slices.

'Have these on the house,' was Dave's offer when they chose their concluding nightcap and for an hour they sat, whiskies in hand, and talked to Dave and Marion about their holiday, the scenery, the fun they had had, in fact anything but the war.

Their room felt very snug against the gale that lashed outside, rattling a loose piece of mesh on the thatch and hurling sleet at the windows. Cradling Angela in his arms, Guy had a feeling of déjà vu, when that little French cottage in the wood felt safe, a sanctuary against the war and not to be left. Come 8 o'clock the next morning, booted and spurred, replete with the full Feathers breakfast and thanking Dave and Marion profusely, leave it they did and the same Austin rumbled to the station.

At Worcester, there was over an hour until their connection.

'Of course darling, you just can't wait to sample that buffet again, can you?' To which Angela stuck out her tongue is a most unladylike fashion.

Depositing their cases at left luggage, they wandered into the town. As they left the station concourse, the wind slashed up the street like a razor, taking their breath away. Setting their teeth against the gale, the trio found interest and shelter in a gaggle of antique shops within a stone's throw of one another. In wartime Britain, antique dealing was not exactly big business. The best value was furniture, not something on Guy and Angela's shopping list, but Angela struck lucky when she found a solid silver photo frame lurking under a pile of junk. It looked promising, but was heavily blackened with verdigris. A surreptitious wipe of one corner with the hem of a curtain in another pile revealed a deep lustre, so Angela bought it.

'That will be just the thing for your photo on my desk,' she said happily.

Time was by now getting on. The last emporium was most unprepossessing, long, deep and so dark, you had to let your eyes adjust to the gloom to be able to see. The grimy front window was no help to the illumination. Whilst the sign over the window proclaimed 'Antiques', only a proportion could truly claim that particular fame. The pluportion was better classed as bric-a-brac and much as just plain tat. Now with his night sight, Guy's eye was caught by a flash of red in a glass case at the back and he navigated a course around an Edwardian pram, piles of records and a stuffed bear, closely followed by his co-pilot.

'What is it, Guy?'

He stared at the model, a rakish Italian sports car.

'An Alfa 1750 Zagato, we used to have one of those.'

Angela turned to the proprietor.

' Could we see this please?'

Tugging a shabby cardigan tighter round his shoulders, he shuffled across in his carpet slippers to open the case. Guy examined the model carefully. It was a fine thing, a proper diecast, with lustrous paint and good detailing on things like the radiator and the wheels.

'Would you like it, I'd like to buy it for you.' She turned to the dealer. 'How much is it please?'

'£3.'

'That's an awful lot of money for a model.'

The elderly man's tone was querulous, as though he was totally unused to anyone questioning his prices.

'It's an excellent Italian model, not a toy and in very fine condition. I even have the original box.'

Angela fell to bargaining until honour was satisfied at £2 12/6d. The spoils wrapped in brown paper, they resought the station, arriving ten minutes before the puffing billy drew in.

The Cotswolds were dusted with snow, adding to their considerable charm as the train tootled Oxfordwards. Many of the GWR stations like Charlbury seemed little changed since they had been built, all Hansel and Gretel-ish in weatherboard and chocolate and cream paint. Guy recalled that it had been nicknamed 'God's Wonderful Railway'. Where the Cotswold Line had been quiet, the lunchtime train to Exeter was heaving, with a contingent of Scottish troops intent on topping up the levels of usquebaugh from the night before. Despite the fact that they were further down the train, their drunken revels echoed and all attempts by the lady guard to quieten them down were as straws in the wind. Concerned at their potential behaviour towards his delicious fiancée, Guy did a recce to the restaurant car. The bar was packed with the soldiers, many of them braw lads at the aggressive stage of drunkenness and the two stewardesses were fighting a losing battle to serve whatever alcohol that had not already been consumed. As the soldiers quite obviously had ample stocks of liquor in their kitbags, why they felt the need to buy more was a mystery. Deeming discretion the better part of valour, Guy beat a retreat. When the train stopped at Bristol, he did a quick dash to the buffet trolley for sandwiches. The disturbance took the edge off their journey somehow, probably because they had become so used to peace and quiet, such behaviour was a rude awakening.

But, justice was done and seen to be done as the train drew into

Cullompton. The platform was deserted, save for a cohort of redcaps spaced out at regular intervals, each toting a baton. And one other. The RSM. In the true traditions of the Scottish regiments, he was built. In fact, not so much built as hewn from Grampian granite. Over six feet tall, erect as a ramrod, he was immaculate in full Highland uniform topped with a glengarry. The snow-whiteness of his gaiters was positively dazzling. He looked both magnificent and menacing. Guy prodded a dozing Angela.

'Come and look at this, it should be fun.'

The pair leaned from the window, as did a large number of other passengers intrigued by the welcoming party. The revellers began to spill from the train, most of them from the buffet car, carrying their kitbags. What had appeared a large number in the confines of the train was actually about thirty. Two of them, utterly sozzled and incapable, tried in vain to reach the platform, but a combination of drink, the high step and the weight of their kitbags proved too much. They tumbled haplessly down the steps and collapsed face down on the concrete. The remainder took one look at Authority in a glengarry and scrabbled frantically to put on their hats and fasten belts and buttons. During World War I, it was said that some men went over the top because they feared the RSM more than the enemy. From what Guy could see, history was about to repeat itself.

From the moment the Sergeant Major opened his mouth to the moment he left the station, Guy understood not one word of what he said. Either the soldiers did, or it was a reflex action in response to a tone of voice, much like a dog. The RSM marched up to the two prone squaddies and bellowed at them to stand up. Stentorian did not get anywhere near doing justice to that voice, a truly thunderous parade-ground bellow that reverberated clearly for hundreds of yards. When even this verbal onslaught brought no action, the RSM detailed four of the less inebriated to get the drunks vertical. This was achieved, the pair swaying like saplings in a wind and threatening to topple once more.

'Gef'n thr' r'nks,' came the command and like well-ordered puppets, they fell into three ranks, even the swiftly sobering saplings, then dressed off when ordered and placed their kitbags beside them.

'AH-ten-HUAH!'

The Cullompton canopy concatenated to the explosion of thirty pairs of ammunition boots crashing to attention. He gestured to the redcaps, who, moving as one man, searched every bag, confiscated every drop of booze and smashed every bottle into a station dustbin requisitioned for the purpose. This scene was watched in its minute detail by the NCO, himself now rigidly at attention facing the parade.

'Mo' t' the r', riiight TAHN!'

More explosions from ammunition boots. The glengarry executed an immaculate left turn.

'By the r', quiiick MARCH!'

Trooping the Colour standard it was not, but the men broke into quite a regular cadence, kitbag in left hand, right arm swinging to shoulder height, RSM in the van, kilt swinging, pace stick tucked under left arm at precisely ninety degrees to his torso, right arm reaching shoulder height.

Seeing this fitting retribution, the watching ensemble on the train let out a ragged cheer. The response was immediate and on the command, thirty-one pairs of eyes snapped left, accompanied by a dazzling salute from the RSM as they passed up the train, off the platform and towards the cooler. Guy and Angela were by this time hysterical with mirth.

'Going to be a long line outside the CO's office in the morning,' said Angela. 'Be the most sparkling latrines in Devon County, I shouldn't wonder!'

The patter of the wheels on the rail joints seemed to be saying 'We're going back, we're going back' and as the express screeched to a halt at St David's, they felt rather down. The weather might have been fractionally warmer in Exeter, but it was a points decision. Ken welcomed them back to the George like long-lost souls, despatching the luggage via the porter and thrusting large gins into their hands.

'Tell me all about your holiday,' he demanded and within minutes, the conviviality had completely restored their joie de vivre. They showed him their toys and Ken at once disappeared out back, returning with Silvo, a duster and a damp rag. A gentle wipe with the damp cloth removed the coating of dust from its time in the showcase and returned the pretty Alfa to its full glory. The more Guy looked at it, the more he found that Angela had collared a bargain. The detailing was excellent, right down to the suspension and working steering. But there was no doubt, Angela's frame was the bee's knees. It was one of those things that filthy dirty, it did not look much. Five minutes with the Silvo and it was transformed into a real beauty, with that soft, deep lustre of quality silver.

'Hang on a minute,' said Ken, 'I think I have a book on silver somewhere.'

He dived off to the bookcase in the lounge, returning triumphantly with a small book and a magnifying glass. After scanning the hallmarks, he worked his way through the book to announce that the frame had been made in 1781 by Matthew Boulton, a prominent Birmingham silversmith.

'If it's not a rude question, what did you pay for it?' Ken asked.

'10s.'

'Then I think, my lovely, that you've picked yourself a bargain.'

Without their noticing, refills had magically appeared and with only a sandwich apiece all day, they were starting to feel decidedly squiffy. Half an hour's fresh air with Colonel blew away the cobwebs and the Gordon's fumes, returning in time for dinner. Ken treated them like royalty, pressing a bottle of an AC Cotes de Rhône on them and refusing any payment. By bedtime, they were extremely Brahms and Liszt and feeling mellow, and their lovemaking that night was like a couple of happy puppies, just relaxed fun, pure enjoyment.

All the booze took its revenge next morning when both awoke with thick tastes in the mouth and some swine playing the Anvil Chorus fortissimo in their skulls. It took several libations of tea and some aspirin before normal service was resumed. About 11 o'clock, Angela took a taxi to the barracks to collect the little car she had borrowed for their first tryst and they spent the rest of the day gently swanning around the lanes before making tracks for Jack and Mary's. Guy was driving and he could sense Angela tensing up in the seat beside him; so could Colonel, who sat on Angela's lap and leaned his body comfortingly against her. Unspoken yet completely understood was that their relationship had entered another phase. Guy searched in his mind for a suitable word. The nearest he could find was 'consolidation', but it was far from being the mot juste. It was simply that they were now a real couple, as one, who often sensed or anticipated the other's thoughts and who just wanted to be together.

The little Morris braked smoothly to a halt in the farmyard. Guy held Angela close, caressing her hair.

'Don't worry darling, we'll see each other regularly, you know that.'

Between tears and sniffs, his fiancée nodded.

'Don't mind me, I'm just being silly.'

Then she climbed into the driver's seat and shot off.

Unbeknown to Guy, Jack and Mary had been watching from the window and cautioned Letitia and Esme from saying a word. Supper was a fairly silent affair followed by ITMA, then bed. Dawn, or more precisely, the alarm, came all too soon and at first light, Jack and Guy were tending sheep and mending a gap in a dry stone wall. Jack was a dab hand at walling and soon taught Guy the basics.

'Match the space to a stone and once you pick up a piece, make sure you place it in the wall. Havering costs energy.'

After breakfast, Guy started checking out all the machinery. Letitia in particular had listened to Guy and had done a sterling job in keeping things shipshape and Bristol fashion. The two Fords were in good shape and over the next couple of days, Guy checked and fettled everything else. He was pleased to see that Letitia returned everything to its marked place in the racks and kept the workshop spotless.

Sitting on the tractor ploughing, Colonel perched on the passenger seat, it all revived memories of a year ago. And, thought Guy somewhat ruefully, it was just as bloody cold.

Petrol had become in very short supply, so taking the Jowett to Exeter was to be an occasional treat. Guy asked Jack if there were any other form of transport.

'There might be an old bike in the hayloft,' said Jack 'you'll have to root around.'

Root around Guy did, finding an old sit up and beg bike covered in grime and wedged in a dark corner. A bit like Angela's picture frame, it looked rather desperate covered in muck, but scrubbed up quite well. Best of all, the tyres, whilst not in their first flush, had a reasonable amount of tread and held pressure when inflated. Rubber was critical and any kind of tyre rather like hens' teeth. Guy stripped the bike down, lovingly reassembled it and produced a workmanlike velocipede. Given his French wanderings, ten miles each way to see his beloved was as nothing and three or four times a week, he made the trip to Exeter. Their pleasures were simple, a meal, the pub, the cinema, the theatre, passion at the George. Just being together was enough, regardless of what they were doing.

One Thursday, Guy cycled down as usual. They had arranged to meet at the cinema and duly enjoyed a Western complete with the standard neverload guns issued to all Western heroes. Enjoying a post-celluloid pint, Angela announced that they were invited to dinner on Saturday.

'Where?' asked Guy.

'Colonel's residence, so best bib and tucker, eight pip emma prompt.'

Having established that best bib and tucker was lounge suit, Guy asked the Colonel's real name, as Angela always referred to him as 'Colonel Grumpy'. Angela was hard put to suppress a giggle.

'You'll never believe this, it's actually Clarence Magdalen-Humphries-Beckington – hyphenated naturally, one of a long line of Army officers. The guests will be some of my fellow officers and local bigwigs, Clarence is very hot on local relations.'

Guy met Angela in the foyer of The George at 7.30, giving them time for a quick snifter before the taxi arrived. Guy was every inch the tall, dark handsome man in his suit; Angela was clad in a figure-hugging blue silk dress and Guy's heart leapt about a foot as he caught sight of her through the glass of the revolving doors.

Colonel Clarence was housed in an old villa on the outskirts and prompt at eight pip emma, Guy and Angela presented themselves at the substantial front door. It was opened by a batman, who took their coats and ushered them into the drawing room. Guy had expected a very formal affair and was pleasantly surprised when the colonel and his wife Marjorie greeted them with genuine warmth.

'Clarence and Marjorie, this is a social occasion, so please call us Clarence and Marjorie.'

Angela introduced Guy to her colleagues and between them, the colonel and his lady effected introductions to the mainly local councillors who made up the balance of the guests. Everyone was geared to wartime and asked no awkward questions. In a country where champagne was in short supply, the colonel seemed to have no difficulty and hovering waiters topped up their glasses at frequent intervals.

Dinner was announced by a tail-coated butler, who led the way into a dining room replete with long oak dining table, spotless napery, crystal glasses and a good proportion of the regimental silver. Candles reflected off both polished oak and the beautiful silver, bringing a warm glow to the room. Guy and Angela were seated next to one another, their fellow guests to either side and opposite an eclectic mix of military and civilian. Lubricated by the champagne and the assortment of white and red wines that followed, conversation flowed. The food was well up to the mark. In true mess tradition, the ladies retired after the pudding, leaving the men to coffee, brandies and cigars. The conversation was centred around the war. One of the local men was by now well-oiled.

'What do you do?' he demanded of Guy.

'I'm an Army officer,' replied Guy equably.

'Yes, but what do you actually do?'

'I can't say.'

At this, chummy became a bit obnoxious and tried to draw Guy, who stonewalled manfully. All of a sudden, Clarence was there, skilfully diverting the questioner by manoeuvring him to another guest. Inwardly, Guy sighed with relief and sipped his brandy. Clarence reappeared once more, decanter in hand, and topped Guy up. He smiled a genuine smile at Guy.

'Can't tell you how happy you've made my young officer, but I'm sure you know that without me telling you, what?'

He was still very much old school tie.

'You going to marry the gel?'

'I certainly am,' said Guy, 'but not until the war's over and we can be properly together. We are engaged, but with the no-jewellery on duty rule, Angela keeps her ring on a gold chain round her neck.'

Guy was suddenly gripped by a sense of foreboding, that his halcyon days in the comparative safety of Britain were strictly numbered.

'Clarence, look after her when I go away again, won't you?'

Clarence took one of Guy's hands warmly.

'You can bet on it, my boy,' was his response.

The ladies rejoined them. Sitting in one corner was a Steinway grand piano at which Marjorie seated herself and gave some good renderings of classical numbers, passing a very pleasant hour before it was carriages.

Guy and Angela were once more chez the understanding Ken, and a taxi delivered them safely to the George for midnight. As Guy had to be back in the Jowett for 5.30am, it gave little time for sleep, but sleep was the last thing on their minds. Unable to chat in the taxi, mindful that careless talk cost lives, they waited until they were alone before speaking.

'Old Colonel Grumpy is actually rather human underneath the Sandhurst veneer. Got a real soft spot for you, my darling.'

Angela smiled.

'I think it's part of the standard military defence mechanism,' she said, 'keeping your distance from your subordinates, that kind of thing.'

'Misses nothing, though,' commented her fiancé. 'Got cornered by some councillor with too much wine in his belly, kept trying to pump me, it was all getting a bit embarrassing, when in comes Grumpy on his charger and rescues me.'

As they talked, they were undressing. All of sudden, his beautiful lady was standing there in her skimpies. Not for long, the flames of lust and passion engulfed them and both got very little sleep that night.

Scraping the frost from the windscreen, Guy cranked the van to life and made his way back to the farm, arriving just in time for milking. He quite liked milking, a quiet time apart from the cows lowing in the yard outside as they waited their turn in the shippons. Mary had taught Guy how to gently tease the liquid from each udder and sitting on a stool, milk hissing into the pail and the warmth exuded by the cow taking away the dawn chill was really therapeutic. Mucking out afterwards was not, but got the circulation going and gave you an appetite for breakfast.

The key job that day was repairing a barn roof whose slates had been damaged in a storm, the same one that had struck the Malverns during the little holiday. Jack kept a stock of spare slates; in this exposed location, such damage was not that rare. Once it was light, Guy and Jack secured ladders to the guttering, hooked two roof ladders over the ridge and secured a box attached to a rope and a sandbag. The sandbag acted as a counterweight on the other side of the ridge, leaving the box to hold the slates. The barn was over thirty feet high and Guy did not like heights, so it took a little while before he felt comfortable working up there. The slates had been ripped off in twos and threes rather than large patches, so they had to work along the roof and up and down it. Held in place by nails, each slate had to be winkled out using a slate ripper to guillotine the nail heads, then replaced. Up there, exposed to the wind, it was a freezing job and for safety, they came down every half hour or so to thaw out and return feeling to numb fingers.

On a farm, there was always something to do and at times, Guy felt a bit like King Canute. As fast as you thought you had cleared all the jobs, another stack magically appeared to prove you wrong. Preparing fields and planting were actually the easier jobs, whereas hedging, ditching, fencing, walling – depending on whereabouts on the farm you were – were physically tough work that went on regardless of the weather. The West Country might have had a reputation for a softer climate, but Guy saw scant evidence of that. Muffled up to the hilt, he and Colonel earned their daily keep in support of the war effort.

On Wednesday evening, Guy biked once more into Exeter. By a process of elimination, they had found that The Three Tuns served excellent bitter, had a warm and cosy snug and best of all, was not on the beery boys circuit. Once seated, Angela dug in her pocket and produced a letter bearing a Worthing postmark.

'I wrote to Mummy and Daddy and told them about the engagement. They are planning to come down by train on Saturday and meet you, if that's OK?'

Gently, Guy clasped his beloved in his arms and kissed her firmly on her forehead.

'Of course it is, they want to check that you haven't fallen for some gay Lothario, so would I if you were my daughter. What's the form then?'

Angela read the letter once more.

'They're on the 3.30 into St David's, so I've booked them and us into The George for Saturday night. She smiled ruefully.

'Separate bedrooms for us, I'm afraid, Mummy's real old school and the mere thought her little girl had tasted the sins of the flesh before walking up the aisle, well...'

'You mean chaste, not chased,' teased Guy.

'I booked with Ken himself and gave him the full intelligence, so he'll make sure that there's no careless talk.'

'What are your parents like really?'

'Daddy's been with Barclays all his life, manages the town centre branch, your archetypal bank manager, I suppose. Leading light in the local operatic society, plays social golf but with a huge handicap. Strangest thing is for a banker, he loves horseracing and a flutter. Nothing out of his depth, but he's a regular at Goodwood and Lingfield Park and would think the world had ended if he missed the Derby. Bit like Colonel Grumpy really, a lot more under the pinstripe suit than first meets the eye. Mummy's, well, Mummy. Never worked, family was everything, a bit bewildered by this war and seeing two daughters in the ATS. I think joining the WVS has been the making of her, she's seen what real life is all about, as opposed to a kind of false world of dinner parties and bridge mornings and whist drives. She did say once, though, that she found some of the women in it 'rather coarse'. Only Mummy could say so much with just two words. Loves me and Joyce to bits.'

'What have you told them about me?' was Guy's next question.

'Simply that you are an Army officer who spends his leaves with friends on their farm. I said that you can't talk about your work, so they won't ask. They haven't the slightest clue you're French, not that it would bother them, so you're safe on that count too, and your English is pure Southern.'

They arranged that Guy should arrive at the George at teatime. Smartly but casually dressed, cuticles scrubbed with bleach and with his suit in his luggage, he threaded the Jowett into the hotel car park prompt at 4.30. Ken winked conspiratorially when he checked in, then handed him the key to a single room.

'Not even on Angela's floor,' he whispered, 'you'll just have to keep it in your trousers tonight, boy!'

It took him all of two minutes to unpack, then he wended his way downstairs for inspection. His mental picture of Mr and Mrs Walker conjured up chalkstripe suit for Mr and the fashionable box suit for Mrs. Absolutely and utterly wrong. Both in their early fifties, Graham Walker was in flannels and quite a loud sports jacket, Penelope Walker in a soft blue silk dress. She and Angela were so alike, they could have been taken for sisters, albeit some years apart. Penelope had an air of slight unworldliness about her. He summed them up as Mr and Mrs Middle-Class England, but this was a compliment, not pejorative. They were one of many thousands of families from all walks of life who suddenly found their way of life and freedom threatened by Adolf Hitler and had summoned up an inner strength they did not realise they possessed. The Third Reich would be resisted to the last by such as Graham and Penelope and if the Boche ever did invade, they would get a far tougher time than they envisaged.

Guy had also surmised that if Angela were anything to go by, they would be very warm. In that, he was 100% right. Graham and Penelope's greeting told him at once that this was no inspection, merely a genuine desire to know the man their daughter had chosen.

'Mummy, Daddy, this is Guy.'

'Delighted to meet you,' said Guy, 'good journey?'

'Is any journey good in this wretched war?' asked Graham. 'Air raid hit the tracks at Redhill last night, we only just made the Exeter train. And the food...'

His wrinkled nose spoke volumes.

'Not gristly mutton?'

'How did you know?' demanded Penelope.

'Seems to be a speciality of theirs on this route, assaulted my digestive system a few weeks ago.'

That comment and Guy's infectious grin broke the ice and from then on, the evening was a roaring success. Replete with tea and scones, they all retired to dress for dinner, reconvening in the bar for G&Ts and a schooner of sherry for Penelope. Ken's maitre d' hove into view to apologise for a slight delay, so more G&T and a second schooner not only filled the time, but mellowed the imbibers. By the time dinner was served, they were feeling no pain. Unbeknown to the diners, Ken had threatened his chef with dire consequences if the food for his favourite couple on this special occasion was even a smidgen off. It was not.

'Do you have any wedding plans, Angela?'

Guy squeezed the hand of his gorgeous fiancée under the table at the inevitable question from a doting Mum.

'Mummy, we want to wait until the war ends. We don't want to get married until we can do it properly and be with each other.'

'Quite right too,' snorted Graham and returned his nose to another of Ken's seemingly endless supply of Cotes de Rhône.

They retired to the lounge for coffee and liqueurs. Angela and her Mum started catching up and discussing wedding dresses, Guy and Graham talked about anything and everything. Certain that Penelope was engrossed, Graham spoke quietly to Guy.

'I'm a major in the Home Guard, so I know that you can't talk about what you do and I'm not even going to ask you. All I can tell you is that Angela and Joyce are everything to us and we're frightened all the time that something will happen, one of them will be caught in an air raid, you know what I mean?'

An emphatic nod.

'I can see and so can Penny that you two are, well, you're so right for each other. Whatever it is you do, come back safe and marry my daughter, that's all we ask.'

A little tear appeared in the corner of Graham's right eye.

'You can bet on it and I'm told you're a betting man?'

'God Bless you, Guy.'

The little party broke up at eleven. Guy bid his fond farewells, explaining that being part of a farm, crack o'dawn was de rigueur. He received a warm kiss on both cheeks from Penelope and an equally warm hand clasp from Graham, coupled with an invitation to Worthing when he and Angela could wangle some more leave. Tactfully, Penny and Graham departed to bed so that the lovers could be alone. They walked up to Angela's floor and her room.

'Guy, I love you so.'

Angela's arms were around him and they kissed, long and passionately. All of a sudden, for reasons she could not begin to fathom, hot tears coursed down her cheeks and she rushed into the room and closed the door behind her.

Guy left the hotel at 5am, meandering slowly towards the farm. He arrived before the house was up. Lying on the table next to the phone in the hall was a simple message which sent Guy's heart beating like triphammer.

It said 'Ring Lionel tomorrow at 0900.'

Guy was on milking again. Try as he might, he could scarcely concentrate on the task in hand. On the dot of nine, he rang.

'Sorry Guy, get on a train today, be at Orchard Court 0900 tomorrow, say your au revoirs. Stay at the flat, Walter will expect you.'

For almost a minute, Guy stood transfixed once he had replaced the handset. This could mean only one thing, a return to France. His blood ran cold and a shadow passed over his grave. Suddenly that warm family dinner party of last night and the promise of a future yet to come were a million miles away. He rang St David's. There was one train, leaving St David's at 1.30. Where was Angela? At 10.30, he tracked her down to the Officers' Mess. Over and over again, he had practised what he would say.

'Darling, I'm sorry, they need me again, I've got to go to London at 1.30.'

The answer was deep, racking sobs, sobs that spoke of love and fear and separation. They arranged to meet at the station.

The train clanked into the platform. Desperate to be with each other to the last second, they clung together until the guard's whistle forced Guy to entrain. As the train pulled out, he leant from the window and gave Angela one last kiss. Then he was gone, obscured by clouds of steam. It mattered not, Angela's vision was obliterated by hot salty tears.

Chapter 14

The train pounded its way east towards London. Guy felt so low and miserable, the fun and joy of the past few weeks as nothing as he contemplated an unwelcome return to France.

On arrival at Paddington, he took a taxi to the flat, where Walter was expecting him, then spent a sleepless night, his imagination running riot as to what lay in store. Orchard Court in Portman Square, at the end of Baker Street, was a typical 1930s edifice, all white stone. On the dot of 0855, Guy presented himself at the desk. The concierge looked up 'Martin' on his list, then dialled a number. Minutes later, the lift doors clanked open and Lionel stepped out. He escorted Guy back upstairs.

'For the moment, I'm going to keep the details to myself, but you're off to Wales for a week. Here's your rail itinerary and warrants, pack good warm outdoor clothing. You'll find Walter has laid in some useful items in your size.'

'What am I going to Wales for?'

'You'll find out when you get there. Once you arrive at Bangor, ring this number and ask for Chris or Roy, they'll come and pick you up. Oh, and start growing a beard.'

Guy's train to Bangor involved a long, tedious route, first to Crewe, change again at Llandudno Junction. As his connection to Crewe left at 1100, he stepped lively back to the flat, where Walter had all kinds of heavy trousers, sweaters, socks and other paraphernalia for some patently outdoor activity. The journey to Bangor was not good and that was being kind about it. The further north the train steamed, the harder the rain, pouring down the windows and blotting out most of the grey, dismal landscape. At least the Crewe train had heating; on the connection to Llandudno, the system was not working and the inside of the train was tomb-like. The only food available was a sandwich on the Crewe leg, so by the time our hero finally made it to Bangor at around 7.30, he was tired, cold, hungry and pissed-off to the eyeballs.

Guy duly rang the number and spoke to Chris.

'You're at Bangor Station, I take it?' said Chris, 'we'll be there in about forty minutes.'

The phone went dead. Guy retreated to the waiting room. Almost an hour later, a sandy head poked around the door.

'I'm Chris, you must be Martin?'

He stuck out a strong calloused paw. Outside in a Vauxhall sat the driver, Roy. Guy threw his kit onto the back seat and climbed in. The car left the car park, the worn blades of the wipers flap-flapping ineffectually, trying to disperse the torrential downpour. The view out of the windows in any direction was grey – grey stone, grey slate, grey walls, grey pavements. Neither Chris nor Roy said a word.

'Now I'm here, perhaps you can tell me why?' asked Guy.

'You mean you don't know?' replied Chris, turning towards the back seat.

Guy shook his head.

'You're going to learn rock-climbing and caving. Have you ever done any climbing?' With his blood sugar low, Guy's temper was at flashpoint.

'Thankfully, no.'

The heavy sarcasm was not totally lost on Chris, but his next question lit the blue touch paper.

'Why is that?'

'Because I'm terrified of heights, that's why. If I wanted to be a human fly, I'd have done it long ago. Instead, some chinless wonder in Whitehall has decided it's a good idea to send me to this godforsaken hole.'

Not surprisingly, this killed conversation stone dead and the rest of the journey passed in stony silence. On the outskirts of Llanberis, the car pulled into a complex that had once been a farm. The farmhouse was flanked by a number of barns converted to living accommodation and storage. Chris and Roy led the way into the hall of the farmhouse. Roy was the first to speak.

'Have you eaten?'

'I had a sandwich at lunchtime, that was the last time.'

'Fancy a bacon sarnie?'

At this, Guy practically slavered.

'Give me five minutes,' said Roy and the young blond man disappeared into the kitchen, to return with the aforesaid sarnie and mug of sweet tea. Guy fell on these like a starving dingo. Thus refreshed, he looked up at his two hosts and suddenly felt mightily ashamed of his outburst in the car.

'Sorry, guys,' he began, 'I'd had a really rough day, but I had no right to take it out on you. Please accept my apologies.'

Roy and Chris just grinned and Roy consulted his watch.

'Fancy a pint?' he enquired.

'Best offer I've had all day,' said Guy.

They climbed back in the car and drove for ten minutes to a local pub.

'These,' said Guy very firmly, 'are on me.'

He fetched three foaming pints of Brain's Best Bitter. In Guy's case, the first never even touched the sides, but the second slipped down more slowly. Over the drinks, they chatted.

Guy apologised once more for his loss of temper.

'Think nothing of it,' said Chris. Roy and I are outdoor instructors. I do rock climbing and mountaineering, skiing and sailing. Roy does the same, except he does surfing not sailing.'

Looking at the two fit and strong instructors, ruddy faced from their outdoor life, he could well believe it.

'We get paid to do what we love doing and you can't ask for more than that, can you?' said Roy.

It was Chris again.

'In peacetime, we get people here who want to be here, who love outdoor sports, but this is war and we get quite few like you, who need the skills but are pressed men, not volunteers. We'll look after you, never fear.'

They drove back to the training centre, where Chris presented Guy with a key to Room 9.

'There are quite a few military here training, but they are in the barns and won't bother you. Breakfast is here at 7 o'clock, we'll meet you in the hall at eight. OK?'

Guy nodded, then went upstairs to his room. The Hilton it was not, bare limewashed walls, wood floor, a small rug. The radiator was tepid, but only if you were prone to exaggeration. The bed looked like a cast-off from the local hospital, all cast iron and chipped paint. The sheets were grey and rough, the thin blankets greyer and rougher still. Having found the bathroom two doors down, Guy prepared for bed. He donned a sweater against the cold and climbed in, to find that the mattress had more peaks than the hills outside. Sighing, he set the alarm and tried to sleep.

He awoke from a long tunnel of slumber. It was 6.30. The water was good enough for a shower and shave before descending for breakfast. Bacon, powdered egg, cardboard toast, strong tea. It filled a hole. Prompt at eight, Chris and Roy appeared and led the way to the stores to draw ropes, karabiners, pitons, an axe-cum-piton hammer and a belt with various loops to carry the items. For the next hour, they briefed Guy on all the kit and its uses, taught him various knots then let him practice them, concluding with a safety briefing.

After that, it was out into the endless rain once more, stopping by the kitchen for flasks and packed lunches. A twenty minute walk brought them to a wall of rock, a pitch about thirty feet high and with a slight slope. Roy took the easy way up and dropped safety ropes, which he secured firmly. Chris knotted the ropes round himself and Guy.

'Right, I'll climb this and talk you through it, you observe, then I'll come down and you do it. Our sherpa will keep a tight hold on you, you'll be quite safe. OK?'

Guy nodded. Chris climbed quite slowly and deliberately, talking about the handholds and footholds. This pitch was clearly one they used often for basic training. Guy could but admire Chris's smooth economic style, an expert that made it look easy.

'OK, now you.'

Mimicking what he had seen and with his safety rope taut to give him confidence, Guy climbed the face. His legs were in good shape, but he rapidly found that his upper body was not and hauling himself up on a handhold was much tougher. On this first foray, he consciously avoided looking down and reached the top in fairly short order and quite pleased with himself. He returned to ground level the easy way.

Roy shifted himself and his ropes along the face.

'Now it's your turn,' said Chris, 'find your own way up. Remember that the key is looking two or three holds ahead, that makes for the easiest and fastest progress and demands least effort.'

Tentatively, Guy scanned the face, picked a route and commenced his second climb. Following someone else's route was fairly simple, finding your own was not. He made a couple of wrong choices and had to gingerly backtrack, but reached the summit without too much effort. He did find that the concentration needed made him forget all about the height. They stopped for a cup of coffee before walking further into the hills to a bigger and steeper pitch, where the process was repeated. Guy was certainly gaining his sea-legs, but he was finding muscles that he did not know he possessed and all of them hurt. He had been taught the art of jamming, putting his hand flat into a crevice, then creating a fist that jammed securely. It worked well, but was pretty tough on the knuckles. Using a more difficult pitch on this face, Chris and Roy began teaching him how to climb using pitons and belays. About 12.30, they stopped once more, sharing soup from the flask and chewing spam sandwiches.

With the torrential rain unabated and no shelter, they could not stop moving for long for fear of muscles stiffening, so pressed on. The afternoon's exercise was to climb a two hundred foot sheer face. Guy was about half way up, a spout of icy water streaming with pinpoint accuracy from the face into the back of his collar, when he glanced down. Instantly, fear gripped him, his stomach started to churn, his head to buzz and his limbs to become immobile. Like some fly, he clung desperately to the rock, totally frozen and unable to move an inch.

'Come on Martin,' called Roy from above.

Guy could not even speak. Realising immediately what was wrong, Chris worked his way up beside Guy.

'Take very deep breaths, don't look down. Roy has you secure, there's no way you can fall.'

Gently, he soothed the young Frenchman until inch by inch, he galvanised his leaden limbs back into action and crawled upwards at a snail's pace. They reached the top, but Guy was mentally strung out and they called it a day.

Guy was concerned at his freeze, but his two instructors were completely unfazed and took it in their stride. They had seen it happen time and again. As they walked back, Guy asked, 'If it's not a question you are forbidden to answer, how come you fellers have not been called-up?'

Chris grinned.

'If you look on War Office records, Roy and I are actually PTIs in the Marines, but we've never put on a uniform or been on parade. We spend our days instructing, mostly here, but we move around to various locations.'

When they reached the school, all the equipment was cleaned, checked and put away.

'Supper's at seven, then there's a film in the rec hall at the end of the larger barn. Oh, and you'd better have this,' said Roy, digging in his pack and producing a bottle of embrocation. Roy and Chris took their leave. To his intense relief, the water was hot and plentiful and Guy soaked away some of his aches. The embrocation smelt foul and reminded him of the school changing rooms after rugby, but he ladled it on before crashing onto the lumpy mattress.

Supper was just another variation on the spam theme, satisfying rather than nutritious. At 7.45, the film began in the recreation hall created at one end of the barn, a Tom Mix cowboy classic. It passed some time, but the hard wooden chairs did nothing for Guy's sore muscles and once the credits had been shown, he hit the sack once more.

Over the next three days, he honed his skills under the tutelage of his expert guides, learning such techniques as chimney climbing. With due care, they put him in the lead on various occasions and bit by bit, his confidence grew. The rain never stopped, just an endless deluge from grey skies.

'Does it ever stop raining?' enquired Guy.

'Yes,' came the reply from Chris, 'just long enough to draw breath!'

On Friday, they stopped at 2 o'clock. Guy queried this.

'We're back out after supper, we're going to do a night climb,' came the answer, striking fear once again in Guy's heart.

'OK, listen in,' said Chris. 'Night climbs are much more difficult unless you get clear weather and moonlight because you can't see ahead. Once you have experience, you can make educated and pretty accurate guesses about what lies above you, but you have no experience. We'll just teach you the basics.'

Half an hour's walk from the school, then it was an ascent of a sheer face about 150 feet high. Contrary to expectations, the rain stopped and a moon appeared, if somewhat fitfully, so the climb was a little easier than envisaged. Nonetheless, it was indeed groping in the dark and it took a long time to scale the face.

They sat companiably in the equipment store, wiping down the gear.

'Well' said Roy 'you've spent a week going up, now you're going to spend the weekend going down. Caving starts tomorrow, here at 0800.'

Prompt at 8 o'clock next day, they were once more drawing equipment, but this time it included helmets, lamps and batteries. After a full briefing to Guy, the trio drove for about ten miles before pulling into a car park at the base of the hills. Roy leading, they walked a short distance before halting at what appeared to be no more than a rabbit burrow.

'Here we go.'

With that, Roy dived head first into the burrow and Chris indicated to Guy to follow. If he thought that rock climbing was very frightening, in a pico-second, Guy decided that caving was utterly terrifying as he was struck by an enormous bolt of claustrophobia. Despite the fact that the soles of Roy's boots were moving steadily ahead of him, Guy felt trapped in a dank, damp tunnel scarcely big enough to squeeze through and he felt panic beginning to rise in his chest. Having been warned that panicking would cause his body to swell and thus should be avoided, he took deep breaths and squirmed in pursuit of Roy. In any case, the presence of Chris hard on his heels drove Guy onwards. About forty feet later, they emerged from the tunnel and stood upright. Roy took a large torch from his bag and shone it around the walls and ceiling.

Guy had no idea if the caves ever dried out completely, but right now, everywhere you looked there was moisture or water. It ran down the walls, dripped from the roof, splashed from cracks and ran as a small but fast-flowing beck across the floor on one side. For the next six hours, Guy wondered extremely seriously how anyone could have caving as a hobby, as he squeezed through tunnels and crevices, climbed over large rocks and rockfalls, waded through streams, small rivers and sumps. If it were possible to get any wetter, he could not imagine how. And he loathed being underground, he felt trapped. Roy and Chris were extremely safety conscious, roping up whenever necessary and especially when crossing streams and rivers. During the briefing, they had warned Guy that in weather such as now, a minor stream could become a raging torrent in seconds as water from the surface emerged many feet underground. And Roy constantly checked his watch to ensure they made the return ETA notified to the school before departure. They hit the ETA on the button and Guy made a beeline for the shower, emerging several degrees warmer and his spirits several notches higher.

The next day, they taught Guy cave climbing.

'Thing is,' said Roy, 'instead of always going up, on the way in, you're always going down. Plus you need to plot your route back and if necessary, leave things like pitons in place to help you.'

A combination of shorter pitches and the dark somehow made it easier and Guy acquitted himself well on the cave climbing.

Like pit ponies, they emerged from the caves blinking in the afternoon light, then set sail for the school and that oh so welcome shower. Supper that night eschewed the limitless variations on spam so far offered, roast Welsh pork and all the trimmings, followed by spotted dick and custard. Guy felt both full and at peace with the world. Seeing his instructors at one of the tables, he walked across.

'Fancy a few beers on me?'

'Is the Pope a Catholic? Thank God this bit of Wales isn't dry on Sundays.' was Roy's cheery reply.

Leaving the car behind, they ambled down the road to the pub to consume perhaps excessive amounts of Brain's. Settled with their drinks, Guy asked

'OK, so what's the verdict?'

Chris and Roy looked one another.

'We both agree a B- for the climbing and the caving. Truth is, you would never choose to come here. You've done very well to conquer your fear of heights, but you still spend much of the time wondering if you are going to fall off, so it doesn't come naturally to you,' said Chris.

'If anything, you hate caving even more than climbing,' went on Roy, 'claustrophobia is a serious issue for you and you spend all the time underground wondering how soon you can get out. But ten out of ten for trying. You are now a very competent rock climber and caver, well done.'

'Thanks for putting up with me,' said their pupil, 'it can't be easy when you have someone like me that would rather be a million miles away!'

Now well into their second pint, the atmosphere became very convivial. In peacetime, Chris spent most of each winter in Switzerland as a ski instructor and regaled them with tales from the mildly risqué to the downright bawdy of goings-on in the chalets. All too soon, the landlady was clanging the ship's bell to signal closing time, time to weave a slightly unsteady path back to base.

On Monday morning, Chris drove Guy back to the station at Bangor. They shook hands warmly and wished one another good luck before Guy boarded the train to Llandudno Junction. The seemingly endless rain was back with a vengeance, obscuring any vision of the mountains and countryside. That weather sensed the day to come. The short hop to Llandudno was fine, but the journey from then on was a nightmare. For two hours, the train sat outside Crewe. The guard walked the train to explain that Crewe had been blitzed the night before and considerable damage inflicted. When the train eventually crawled forward at walking pace, the signs of devastation were all too clearly visible through the windows. Many buildings were still ablaze, defying the strenuous efforts of the firefighters to quench the flames. Loud crackling could be heard, even with the windows closed, and acrid smoke and the smell of burning timbers drifted into the compartment. Above the sounds could be heard the clanging of bells from emergency vehicles. Some buildings were gone, only gaunt skeletons remaining, wisps of smoke still emanating from the wreckage. As they neared Crewe Junction, Guy saw some ARPs bring out a body from one shell, to be laid alongside the other four lying rigid on the pavement. Suddenly he felt sick, as the sight brought back still fresh memories from his discovery at his former home and he leaned from the window and retched.

The damage from the raid similarly affected the London connection, which left three hours late. With no phone number for Walter, Guy could not call and advise his delay. He had both eaten at Crewe and stocked up on sandwiches, but it was past midnight before Euston hove into view. To cap it all, there was not a taxi to be had and he ended up walking to Bayswater lugging his suitcase. It took four long rings on the doorbell to rouse Walter, who opened the front door clad in a tartan dressing gown. Probably between 60 and 70, Walter had that deferential air of a former manservant, but said only the minimum he had to and never but never asked difficult questions. He took one look at Guy and led the way to the kitchen, producing cheese on toast, hot tea and a mega tot of Johnnie Walker Black Label.

'Trains were terrible, Crewe got blitzed last night,' volunteered Guy and received a sage nod in reply, coupled with another stiff JW.

'Orchard Court at 1000, sir,' advised Walter before leaving Guy to catch some shut-eye.

Bleary eyed, Guy walked round to Portman Square, where Lionel was summoned and led him upstairs to a locked room. Once he had admitted them, Lionel secured the door once more.

'Before I brief you, I have to impress on you that this is very hush-hush, the top end of Top Secret.' Having received Guy's affirmative nod, Lionel walked over to a board on an easel and rolled up the cloth which covered it. Pinned to the board were a number of aerial shots, the lower set clearly taken later than those at the top. The photographs were of a curious rock formation dominated by a short, narrow crevasse in the centre. To the left of the crevasse, the mountainside rose quite steeply. To the right was a vertical rockface which climbed several hundred feet into the air to point peaks with chimneys in between. The strangest feature was a dam-like ridge of rock stretching across the crevasse at its open end. An oblique frame showed an arch-like opening at the base of the dam and leading into the crevasse. In front of the dam was a small, grassy plain.

The later shots gave a very different picture in terms of human activity. The earlier shots were devoid of any signs of life; the later set contained a hutted camp on the grassy plain, wheel-tracks into the crevasse and just the cab of a truck visible at the inner end of the defile. A number of quite large trucks were parked in the camp area and two more could be seen driving up a rutted track from the valley below. Soldiers in grey uniforms and a number of figures in plain clothes were visible around the huts.

Lionel allowed Guy to absorb the detail before speaking.

'We've got wind that the Germans are up to something here, but exactly what we don't know. We're told that there is a honeycomb of caves in this area and that there is very probably a cave entrance at the far end where the truck is parked. That camp supplies electricity to the cave – have a look at those two huts.'

He handed Guy a magnifying glass. Peering at the huts, Guy could just make out two exhaust stacks, each protected by a flap at the top which opened under exhaust pressure.

'What do you think they're up to?' asked Guy.

'That's why we want you to go in, we simply don't know, but we suspect some kind of weapon, possibly to be launched by a new weapon called a V1. Jerry knows that he's losing the war and is getting desperate. The Geneva Convention will not even feature on the radar, so expect something radical and nasty.'

'And what's a V1 when it's at home?'

Lionel consulted a piece of paper in front of him. 'Stands for Vergeltungswaffe Eins, apparently. My German up to the mark?'

Guy nodded affirmation.

'Jerry knows it's only a matter of time, so he's been developing the V1, which apparently has a jet engine and is pilotless. They'll launch the things from Northern France and our guess is, the target will be London.'

'If it's pilotless, how will it know when to descend and strike?' asked Guy.

'The boffins' best guess is some kind of timer based on speed and the distance it would cover, or a distance measuring device that cuts the engine at a pre-set point. Their guess is distance measurement, so the strike pattern is going to be pretty random.'

'And,' continued Lionel, 'there's strong evidence of an even bigger and better version called a V2 which will be rocket-powered.'

Guy was deep in thought.

'What do you think's the purpose of the camp, Lionel?'

'Living accommodation is our guess, for both the soldiers and what we also assume are civilians. Part of your job is to find that out, too.'

'When were the last set of photos taken, then?'

'A couple of weeks ago, we've not had the resources to take more, or when we have, the weather's clagged in.'

Lionel was almost apologetic.

Guy studied the photos in minute detail, using the powerful magnifying glass. Even to his untutored eye, the trucks coming up the hill were heavily laden, tails down and belching exhaust smoke as their motors laboured up the steep incline. Some of the parked trucks were also down at the back, whilst others sat level and empty. Nothing was visible that would give the least clue as to their cargoes, all the tilts that were visible were firmly shut.

'Any chance of an update before I go?' Guy lifted a brow.

'Probably not,' came Lionel's reply.' You're off in four days, which is when the weather is forecast to clear so that we can take you in by Lysander.'

At the word Lysander, Guy let out a sigh of relief at not having to parachute in.

'That area looks familiar,' remarked Guy.

Lionel suddenly found his toecaps extremely interesting and did not glance up as he replied.

'That's your turf, about forty miles from your home town. Good news is that your house is exactly as it was after the raid, so your cover is still intact. We're sending you because you know the area backwards and you have proved yourself extremely resourceful and effective. We couldn't ask for anyone better. Get in there, find out what's really going on and obliterate it. You'll have A1 priority on any resources you need, but you have to go in alone and pick up with the local cell.'

'Is that why I've had to grow a beard?' A nod. Guy expressed his displeasure at what he was being asked to do.

'This is going to put me in real danger, you know. I know so many people, who probably – almost certainly – think I died in the house alongside my parents. Now I appear like a rabbit from a hat after all this time. It could blow my cover in a jiffy.'

'By the time our disguise artist has finished with you,' replied Lionel, 'you won't look at all like the young Duplessis they knew. You'd be amazed at what really simple alterations, like a change of hair colour or glasses can do. Your beard has made quite a difference already. And,' went on Lionel, 'maintaining the disguise will be easy, you won't need the experts to keep topping it up.'

Guy and Lionel returned to the photos. Guy sat opposite the board and played Kim's game to memorise them. He would turn away at regular intervals and Lionel would fire questions at him on features and locations.

'How far back does the crevasse go and how deep is it?' demanded Guy of Lionel.

'The PI experts reckon about 50 yards front to back and about 200 feet deep,' came the answer.

By the time Guy was satisfied that he had the scene indelibly printed on his brain, it was lunchtime and the two repaired to a pub in Baker Street for a pint.

Post-lunch, Lionel briefed Guy about the mission, where he would be landed, the composition of the local cell and the details of its French leader, Raoul.

'Raoul's a quantity surveyor with the local mairie,' explained Lionel, 'which gives him the opportunity to find out what's going on and also to wander about supposedly checking things but in reality, gathering intelligence. The local cell are well-trained, but are largely sleepers, waiting to harass and impede the enemy from moving north to reinforce the Channel coast if we invade.'

'Age, Lionel?'

'About 42-43, but pretty fit by all accounts, used to be a useful amateur boxer, I understand.'

'And the rest of the group?'

'Usual motley collection, professionals, craftsmen, artisans. Raoul will brief you.'

'What about Communists? After last time, I could really do without that.' Guy's tone of voice gave Lionel no doubt as to the young man's depth of feeling.

Guy's answer was a wan smile.

'As far as we know, there is no problem in that direction, but you know from your own experience how wrong that can be. That's why we debrief all our agents so heavily when they return, they know the real picture as opposed to the one we believe is true, Problem is, the information has a pretty short lifespan in a war.'

Lionel sighed heavily.

'I wish we had better intelligence, but getting it is pretty difficult and if we ask our operators to pack transmissions with detail, we put them at risk of discovery. Not an ideal situation, really.'

First covering up the photos, Lionel reached for the phone and dialled.

'Yves, we're ready now.'

'Yves's doing your cover story again, Guy.'

'Excellent, he was spot on last time and from the sound of things, I could do with something cast-iron.'

There was a knock on the door and the tall, spare figure of Yves loped into the room. Mid to late thirties, dressed in slacks and an English tweed sports jacket, he was one of those self-effacing figures that you would pass in the street and never even notice, let alone remember. His thin physique was matched by an equally thin face, hawkish nose and grey eyes covered by a pair of wire-rimmed spectacles. Guy thought he looked an academic and would have been startled to learn that the intelligence officer came from the unlikely background of La Poste, the French post office. During his career, Yves had managed a number of postal regions and thus possessed an almost encyclopaedic knowledge of France right down to minutiae. This cornucopia of facts he used to the utmost effect in creating highly credible cover stories for the agents. At the outbreak of war, he had had a spell in the French Army before escaping to England.

'Bonjour, Martin.' Yves shook hands with Guy, who recalled instantly Yves's southern accent, probably Nice or thereabouts in Guy's estimation.

'We want you in and out quickly this time,' began Yves, 'so you're not going to be employed. You're going to have a fiche de demobilisation from the French Army on the grounds of asthma and you are just wandering around picking up casual work. You'll need to be A1 on your Army life, so I am going to coach you on that and your regiment.'

They settled down to a long afternoon of regimental detail, army slang, layouts of barracks and HQs, the history of the regiment in WWII – it went on and on. About 4pm, they called it a day. Guy was instructed to go back to the flat, go over and over the story to get it fixed in his mind, then come back the following morning for a test by Yves.

Yves and Guy descended in the lift and the receptionist signed Guy out. 'Blowing half a gale out there,' remarked the man on the desk and as Guy opened one of the double doors, an icy wind whipped into his face and he put his head down instinctively as he negotiated the steps. Just as he gained the bottom step, a figure, head similarly bent against the blast, hurried around the stone balustrade and crashed headlong into Guy. The man clearly spent a small fortune at his tailor and his bootmaker. The classic Oxfords were polished to a mirror finish, the chalk-stripe trousers visible below the hem of the worsted wool overcoat patently bespoke tailored. Snow-white cuffs and silver cufflinks peeped from the sleeves, echoed by an equally snowy wing collar at the neck, complete with dark tie. An expensive Homburg covered most of the now greying hair.

Guy's recognition of his involuntary assailant was instantaneous, his assailant's took a fraction longer, probably because of the beard and the thirteen years since they had last met. When recognition dawned, the effect was astonishing. The man went chalk white and a look of absolute horror appeared in his eyes. For a subliminal moment, he stared at Guy like a rabbit caught in headlights before recovering his composure.

'Uncle Henry!'

'Guy!'

The passage of time had altered the civil servant but little, middle-aged spread and flabbier jowls the sole evidence of passing years.

'What are you doing here, Guy?' demanded his uncle.

The peremptory tone brought Guy's hackles to attention in an instant.

'I'm in the Army now,' came the simple reply.

Henry made no attempt to enquire further, but his next question set his nephew's pulses racing and shivers down his spine.

'And how are your father and mother?'

From anyone else, this would have been a natural and totally innocuous question, but it set Guy's every nerve and sinew tingling. Without hesitation and a straight face, he replied, 'They're fine as far as I know.'

'Good, give them my regards when you do see them next, won't you?'

Guy nodded. Henry reached inside his coat, pulled out a half – hunter on a silver albert and consulted it.

'Well, nice to bump into you after all these years, must dash.'

With that he shook Guy's hand rather limply and strode up the steps of Orchard Court. The young agent watched Henry's retreating back, a whirl of thoughts cascading through his mind. The first was that Henry's pretentiousness was undiminished, that only he would continue to sport a fob watch when almost everyone else carried a wristwatch. The remaining thoughts revolved around what Henry now did. Undoubtedly he would have risen to high rank, but his very presence at Orchard Court indicated that he was involved in clandestine war and top-level secrets. And that made Guy feel more uncomfortable than he ever thought possible.

Mind still buzzing like a beehive with a plethora of thoughts, he wandered down Baker Street and into a Kardomah Café, where he drank a fine brew of tea and munched his way through a slightly stale 'wad' as the British forces termed the fruit bun. Foremost in his mind was Henry, even from that brief encounter, still the self-important, loathsome bully that Guy remembered from his childhood. Although his father Robert rarely said anything derogatory about anyone, he was always vituperative if the subject of his younger brother chanced into the conversation. For that reason alone, Guy and his mother alike studiously avoided the subject. Guy knew that asking Lionel about Henry would produce the standard 'Need to know' reply and commonsense told Guy that Lionel must know about Henry and the family tie; patently, Henry was unaware until now that his nephew was connected with clandestine warfare. Guy reasoned that if Lionel knew the SP, it must be OK, but a little bell was ringing somewhere in the darkest recesses of Guy's psyche.

Suitably refreshed, Guy wandered back to the flat to mull over his cover story. With the sudden realisation that it would be his last chance for a decent meal in the foreseeable future, or indeed, ever again, he rang the Savoy Grill to request a table for 8 o'clock. Robert had been a regular at the Grill for some years and even after all this time, the Duplessis name registered instantly with the maitre d', who seemed to have been there longer than the panelling. The two hours before setting off for his rendezvous Guy put to good use in going over and over the cover story.

Leaving himself ample time in case he had to slum it on the Tube, Guy was actually lucky and caught a cab. As the taxi moved slowly down the forecourt of the famous hotel, Guy dredged up from his store of little-known and useless facts that it was the only street in Britain where traffic has to keep to the right. With half an hour to spare before taking his table, he strolled into the bar and indulged in his favourite cocktail, a Manhattan. Guy's taste buds inclined towards the dry rather than the sweet, so his recipe was rye whiskey not bourbon and all French vermouth, not a mix of French and Italian. Even in wartime, the Savoy was not about to have its reputation tarnished by lack of ingredients or a barman who did not know his trade. The drink was perfect, exactly as Guy liked it and the alcohol mellowed him into a nicely relaxed frame of mind. A refill slipped down effortlessly and with impeccable timing, a tailcoat and white tie padded into the bar to announce his table as the last delicious drops were extracted from the glass.

Guy followed the tailcoated captain aboard the good ship Savoy Grill, which unchanged and unchanging, sailed calmly and serenely across the storm-tossed waters of a world war. The panelling glowed, the carpet's pile was still deep and the only sounds to disturb the stillness were those of muted conversation and the clink of silver against bone china. Wartime was reflected by the combination of mufti and military of many nations. The large sprinkling of broad rings of blue and gold and heavy pips led Guy to muse that a bomb in the Grill could do incalculable damage to the war effort. The menu looked very much as it had done when Guy last dined, all those years ago after his grandparents' funeral. As the maitre d' pulled out Guy's chair, so his waiter glided alongside bearing menu and wine list.

'Any recommendations?' enquired our diner.

'The smoked salmon is especially good today, sir.'

That was one decision made. Torn between lamb cutlets and rare roast beef carved from the trolley, he plumped for the best of both worlds with two cutlets and some beef. The delicate starter based on smoked salmon primed the taste buds for the piéce de resistance, lamb cutlets grilled pink and juicy, rare beef of the same hue accompanied by fresh vegetables al dente. With the need for a clear head on the morrow, Guy satisfied himself with just a half bottle of a fine Bordeaux, but did indulge in a cognac with his coffee. It was truly a delicious meal, but much as he enjoyed it, looking at the vacant seat opposite gave him huge pangs of loneliness and his dearest wish was to wave a magic wand and somehow materialise Angela in front of him. Realising magic wands were in short supply, he called for the bill and a taxi.

Mellowed by good food and wine, he fell asleep as his head touched the pillow, to be brought back to consciousness by the shrill clangour of the tinny alarm clock. At nine sharp, he and Yves were together again; for three hours, they went at it hammer and tongs, first testing Guy on his cover story. With a keen memory, Guy accurately recited names, dates, regiments, descriptions of barracks, the thousand and one details so vital to maintain his nom de guerre. Inevitably, he slipped up on some minor details, to be jumped on by Yves.

'Do you want to end up in front of a firing squad? he demanded roughly, 'because that's exactly what will happen unless you're 110% on your cover. Those Gestapo bastards are far too bloody good at winkling out the slightest slip. Now, let's do it again.'

Two and a half hours of sweaty palms and Guy was 120%.

As the session came to its conclusion, Yves managed a wry grin and said, 'You'll do. Bonne chance, we won't be seeing each other again for a while, but see each other again we will. Perhaps we can crack a bottle together when all this nonsense is over, eh?'

'Very gladly,' came the reply, 'and I'm buying.'

'I'll hold you to that and you'd better bring your chequebook,' was Yves' signoff.

He picked up the phone and called Lionel, who duly appeared and took over. Yves shook Guy's hand warmly and left.

'Right, you're going down to Hamble House by car now,' explained Lionel. 'The disguise artist will work his magic, then you'll have the best part of a couple of days to relax before you take off from Tangmere. I'll be there to see you off.'

With that, he dialled a number.

'Your car will be outside in five minutes, take you back to the flat for your personal kit, then the New Forest.'

The pair chatted desultorily for a few minutes before the phone rang to announce the car; Lionel escorted Guy to the foyer.

As Guy descended the steps of Orchard Court, the FANY driving the black Rover stepped briskly from behind the wheel to open the rear passenger door. Guy slid into the leather-trimmed interior. After a brief sojourn at the flat to collect his few belongings, he sank back and relaxed as the car sped through the southern environs of the metropolis and down the A3 towards the south coast. Central London had ample evidence of bomb damage and seemingly miles of criss-cross tape on every pane, but the further into the suburbs they ventured, the more normality returned, with only the odd flattened or damaged building from strays dumped by Jerry as he ran for home. His imagination ran riot as he pictured the devastation that might be wrought by V1s and V2s. Little did he realise that in a few scant months, his imagination was to become stark reality.

Before too long, he was gazing at the luxuriant ferns he remembered so well those many months ago. The Rover was a comfortable barge and without realising it, he dozed off. He was rudely awakened by his nose slamming into the back of the driver's seat and the squeal of rubber on concrete as the FANY executed an emergency stop, the car slewing sideways as the rear brakes locked up. Unseen and perfectly camouflaged in the half light, the errant pony that had trotted from behind some trees and insouciantly crossed the road oblivious to vehicles, now cantered off into the bracken, completely unaware of the near mayhem it had just caused.

Recovering her composure, the driver let in the clutch and rolled away. By now, there was that tang in the air that told of being near the sea and gulls wheeled and screamed overhead. Twenty minutes later, they pulled up at some imposing gates set in a high brick wall, the gate uprights still gleaming with black paint and gold tips on the spear points at the top. A uniformed sentry checked the driver's papers, then swung back one cast iron portal to admit the car. The drive curved to the left, so the house was initially hidden from view, but two hundred yards later, the full majesty of Hamble House was revealed. In truth, the house was one of the lesser stately piles of the New Forest and as far as Guy could make out in the gathering darkness, had none of the WWII appendages of his first training billet. The stonework was almost entirely covered in creeper, adding warmth to the building. An imposing set of steps led up to the double entrance doors. The young driver opened Guy's door, then moved to the boot for his bag. Guy walked up the steps and let himself in through the blackout curtains. The receptionist seated at the desk looked both formidable and forbidding, all big bosoms and scraped-back hair.

A warm smile, a handshake and an, 'I'm Muriel, anything you need whilst you're here, you only have to ask,' soon dispelled any misgivings about her personality.

Hefting the bag brought in by the driver, Muriel led the way up the stairs. Whereas that first house had boasted a wide, sweeping staircase that bifurcated at the first landing, this was lesser treads, although the number of trees that had been used to fashion the oak panelling was considerable. Guy noticed that there were lighter patches and vacant hooks on the walls where family portraits had been removed for safe keeping. Muriel took him along a landing and showed him into his room. Thankfully, the oak panelling was not evident in the room, which was decorated in an expensive green and cream wallpaper.

'The bathroom and toilet are here,' advised Muriel, pointing to doors just along from his room and emblazoned with the appropriate symbols on discreet enamel signs. 'Please come down to Reception as soon as you have unpacked.'

Guy nodded acquiescence. His room was at the front of the house and overlooked the drive. In daylight hours, it would offer a nice view.

Unpacking took all of two minutes, then he descended the stairs. Muriel guided him towards the back of the house, where a pantry had been set up with theatrical makeup mirrors and chairs. As they

271

entered, two men put down their newspapers and rose to greet Guy.

'I'm Luke, this is Laurent.'

Luke was in his forties, black hair, slightly paunchy even at that age; Laurent in contrast was tall and scrawny. The most noticeable thing was his long, pale fingers. He and Guy exchanged pleasantries in French before reverting to English.

'I'm the disguise artist,' said Luke, 'Laurent is a hairdresser. We're going to alter your appearance, mostly your hair. We'll keep it simple so that you can maintain it all yourself.'

Laurent indicated a chair and Guy seated himself in front of the mirror. Laurent's slim fingers began to skilfully manipulate comb and scissors, turning Guy's now rather straggly locks into a French-style cut but with a right-side parting. He trimmed the new beard. Then he and Luke died the light brown locks and beard to a much darker shade.

'Much of disguise is about making you look different to the way people who know you expect you to look,' explained Luke. 'For example, if you normally wear a suit, white shirt and tie to work, then just putting you into an open necked leisure shirt can produce sufficient difference that at the very least, people not used to seeing you like that are not sure it's you. It's a kind of whole picture they're used to and if you alter some of the picture, it can fool them. We've chosen dark brown for your hair so that if for some reason you can't redye the roots, the lighter brown is less obvious. By the way, the dye needs solvent to remove it, so washing your hair or getting it wet won't affect it.'

Guy looked in the mirror and was startled at the transformation. As he sat there, Luke reached over from behind him and set a pair of glasses on his nose. The thick horn rims did even more to alter the appearance and plain glass lenses had been provided so as not to obscure his vision.

'Here's a spare pair as well.'

Looking at himself once more, the young agent had to admit that he bore little resemblance to the person that had entered the pantry half an hour before.

'Where did you learn your trade, Luke? I'm fascinated,' said Guy.

'In more peaceable times, I'm a makeup artist at Elstree Studios,' was the perhaps unsurprising reply. 'For many of the thrillers and horror movies, disguising the heroes and the villains is all part of the job, so I've become an expert in that side of things. I've worked on all the big productions for the past twenty years.'

He picked up two bottles, both French.

'This is more dye and this is solvent, just in case. From experience, you'll have to touch up your roots about every two weeks.'

'Suivez moi,' commanded Laurent, taking him to a small room set up as a photographic studio.

Laurent proved as deft with a 35mm Kodak as his scissors, and turning on the photofloods, swiftly took a series of ID shots. He disappeared through a door marked 'Darkroom', reappearing with some still wet ID photos of Guy. He blotted them dry, then placed them in an envelope. He and Guy walked back to Reception, where the FANY that had driven Guy to Hampshire waited. She took the envelope and drove off back to London, where as Guy knew, the pictures would become part of his French papers.

Muriel smiled once more.

'Dinner's at 7.30 in the Dining Room over there.'

She pointed out a door on the other side of the hall.

'Bar's over there, I expect you'd like to freshen up first.'

Guy climbed the stairs once more and taking towels from his room, immersed his corpus in a long soak in the cast-iron tub. Thoroughly refreshed, he dressed and headed for the Bar. Half a dozen 'Joes' like himself were already in residence as he walked in, supping everything from British beer to meaty French reds. Everybody was speaking French. As per SOP, he introduced himself as Martin and the others responded with their code names. Nobody made any indiscreet enquiries of identity or the reason for being there. Guy had no idea whether these were agents waiting for the off or whether they were resting. Intriguingly, the bar walls were decorated with old motor racing posters, photographs of 1930s racing cars and a couple of cord-bound steering wheels that had probably graced some voiturettes that had pounded the banking at Brooklands or drifted beneath the bridge at Donington. Muriel announced dinner and they trooped into yet another panelled room. Dreading a repeat of the first house's cuisine – well, culinary disasters – Guy was delighted that the food was excellent and very, very French. 'The condemned man ate a hearty meal' was his wry inner thought as he savoured the fine dinner. Everyone ate French style.

Coffee was served in the bar and within a few minutes, there was a card school going with poker being played for small stakes. Guy was no great player, but acquitted himself not badly, ending the evening a few pennies up. The party broke up at eleven and in the silence of the country, Guy slept like a log.

When he awoke, he immediately went to the large Georgian window to see if his theory was right. It was, the view from the room was in the foreground, Hamble House's neatly manicured lawns, extending out to picturesque New Forest brackens and ferns, now golden brown, almost glowing in their still autumnal hues. The sun cast but a weak yellow glow over the landscape, but was very welcome nonetheless after the endless rains in Wales.

Glancing at his watch, Guy found it was only 8 o'clock so with breakfast at nine, he made a swift toilet and stepped out into the grounds. Hamble House was built in the classic mode, with an elegant façade and steps at the front and stables and outbuildings at the rear. Whilst many of the fine houses requisitioned by the military had suffered GBH, this one was immaculately kept. Fresh paint on the outbuilding doors told of good maintenance. Guy meandered into the stable yard, his shoes echoing on the shiny cobbles. Most of the stables were intact, but one side of the square block had been converted to a motor-house, with four sets of double doors to admit the vehicles. The only windows were in the doors themselves and set too high to allow a view of the interior. Hearing footsteps behind him, Guy turned to find a military figure walking towards him.

'Captain Rigby, I'm OC Hamble House,' announced the newcomer.

'Martin,' replied Guy, offering his hand.

'Charles. See you're wondering what's in there, you keen on cars?'

'A real enthusiast, just love the things,' countered Guy, 'I take it they're interesting, then?'

'You betcha. Come on, I'll show you.'

So saying, Charles led the way back into the main house through a service entrance and fetched a key from his office. He strode along a corridor beside the kitchen which Guy saw linked up with the motor house. At the end lay a stout oak door; Charles swung the key in the lock. The motor house was well-lit, the actually large windows in the double doors were complemented by even larger glazing in the back wall. But it was the contents that excited Guy. Shrouded under cotton covers lay four cars, two clearly open tourers or racers, one a large saloon and the fourth a small two-seater. With Guy's help, Charles peeled back the nearest cover to unveil a Bentley 3-litre. Subsequent unveilings revealed a Derby Bentley; a Rolls Royce 20/25 with a Hooper body; last but not least, a racing MG Midget, complete with fish-tail exhaust. All four cars were resting on blocks with their tyres clear of the floor. Charles explained.

'The house belongs to the Honourable Martin Raglan. He's living on the outskirts of London in a flat, so he left these here with the agreement that we look after them and run them up from time to time. Problem is, we just don't have the manpower to do that, so we keep the batteries on charge over there, but that's all.'

He gestured to a bench at the rear containing four batteries connected to chargers.

He spotted instantly the gleam in Guy's eye.

'You fancy having a twirl in these, don't you?'

The emphatic nod in reply told him all he wanted to know.

'I've worked on Bentleys and Rolls Royces,' said Guy, 'and the MG is a pretty simple affair. Sitting here and never moving isn't good for a car, all the oils drain off the surfaces and if you're unlucky, rust can form in the cylinders. I can assure I do know what I'm doing, so it would be a pleasure for me to run them up and give them a canter round the estate.'

'Fine,' said Charles, 'there's a workshop at the end, lots of tools and I can lend you some overalls. Why don't you have a crack at them after breakfast?'

They walked back into the warmth of the house, where our mechanicien fortified himself with coffee and croissants before donning the borrowed plumes and getting stuck into the cars. The workshop had a number of tools, but not the selection he would have expected with such a collection to fettle. A can of engine oil lay on a shelf above the bench. He placed it on an old tin plate he spotted in one corner, then gently warmed it on a gas ring doubtless used by the chauffeur to brew up. Starting with the 3-litre, he unscrewed the spark plugs and poured a teaspoon of warm oil into each cylinder. Then he checked the dipstick and radiator, 100% for both. Five minutes later, he took the starting handle and inserting it between the dumbirons, gently leaned on it. To his relief, the engine moved easily at quite a moderate pressure, so he cranked it slowly, checking for any high spots; there were none. He cranked the car about twenty turns to pump the oil into the system and prime the bearings. Next, he laid the spark plugs on the tin plate and heated them. Whilst the plugs were cooking, he retrieved the battery from the bench and reconnected it to the car. Turning the key and pressing the starter produced a healthy effort from the starter motor, so he carried on cranking until oil pressure showed on the gauge. A pair of old chauffeur's gauntlets offered protection to his fingers as he took the hot plugs and reinserted them. Removing the gloves, he crossed his fingers, set the controls and pressed the starter once more. Nothing. He tried again and was rewarded by a spit from one cylinder. At his third attempt, two cylinders ignited, following which the remaining two joined in in sympathy and the engine roared into life. Trimming back the controls to reduce revs, he had to rush to open the doors in front of the car to avoid being suffocated by a cloud of black fumes as the cylinders cleared their throats.

As the engine warmed up, he cautiously engaged first gear and released the clutch. The gear engaged with a loud grating sound despite his care, but the rear wheels obediently turned. Five minutes further on, he ran through the gears and tried the steering and brakes. Everything worked and an underbonnet check showed no leaks. He switched off and using the screw jack lying in the workshop, reacquainted the Bentley with terra firma. Bulging tyre sidewalls announced sterling efforts with a stirrup pump before at last he could slide behind the wheel and awake the Bentley once more. The clutch was pretty fierce at first, and he kangarooed into the yard, checking the brakes once more before venturing onto the estate roads.

After three years or more of total inactivity, the old girl had very stiff joints, so Guy eased her around for the best part of half an hour until her circulation improved. The clutch eased off and the brakes, initially pulling to the left, once more pulled up straight and true. Bentley gearboxes needed a skilled touch, but he gradually retaught himself the technique of silent changes. Hamble House might not be that big, but the estate was vast, with miles of metalled or gravel roads and Guy was able to really get a good run. Thankfully out of sight of anyone, there was a long straight with a right-hand bend at the top, covered in gravel and with a wide sweep of grass on the outside as runoff. Grinning like a Cheshire cat, Guy, now at one with his steed, pointed the long green snout into the apex and flexing his right foot, slid the car through the curve on opposite lock.

Back in his mechanical heaven, our hero spent a blissful day repeating his tricks on the remaining three cars. The Midget was very reluctant to fire up, but cleaning the carburettor cured that. Racing exhaust barking, the little car proved surprisingly quick and was even more fun than the Bentley to drift through the gravelled corner. Charles Rigby appeared near lunchtime and enjoyed himself in each of the cars. As dusk was falling, Guy elevated the motors back onto their blocks and recocooned them. Turning the key on that oak door into the house had an air of finality about it. Charles was still at his desk when Guy returned the key.

'You really enjoyed yourself today, didn't you?' remarked the officer.

'It's therapy for me, I forget everything once I get my nose under a bonnet and it stops me fretting about what might be to come.'

Charles just nodded sagely, no words were necessary.

The evening was almost a carbon copy of the first, aperitifs in the bar, a good dinner, then a gramophone appeared from nowhere complete with a selection of French records, metaphorically hoisting the tricolour once more.

Guy slept barely a wink that night, his mind a whirl of thoughts about his mission in France. He had no hesitation in admitting to himself that he was bloody scared.

The weather held, so he spent the day exploring the estate on foot, striding over the grass, crunching leaves in the spinneys and putting up a startled pheasant or two in long grass. The thing he wanted to do so much it was like a physical pain was to phone Angela, but he knew it was strictly forbidden. A couple of times, he found himself standing in woodlands with tears streaming down his face. A message at Reception at breakfast time advised him that Lionel would arrive about 4 o'clock, so at three, he wandered back to his room and wrote Angela a letter. There was so much he wanted to say, but somehow the words simply were not there and he contented himself with telling her how much he loved her, how much their time together had meant. He looked at his words and somehow they seemed inadequate, yet try as he might, he could not coax more from his embattled brain.

Prompt as ever, Lionel bowled up to the steps prompt on the dot of four, bringing all Guy's French clothes, papers and his radio.

'How are you doing?' enquired Lionel as they ensconced themselves in Guy's room, only too aware of the tension in the young man's eyes and body language.

'If you want it in plain English, I'm shit-scared,' replied Guy, 'I've got a nasty feeling about this one, nothing tangible I can put my finger on, just gut instinct.'

Lionel shifted uncomfortably in the armchair.

'You know the score, this is a big one and it needs you or we wouldn't be sending you. All we can ask is that you do your best and I know you will whatever your feelings. Shall we get down to business?'

Yet again, they went over the briefing, the codewords, the poem

Guy had chosen as security in his radio skeds, the skeds themselves, the frequencies for his broadcasts. Thoughtfully, Lionel had arranged for dinner to be served in Guy's room. The knock at the door brought coq au vin, some excellent Brie and a good claret. As he was driving, Lionel indulged in just one glass. Guy handed over his letter to Angela.

'Right, time for your glad rags.'

All of the French items were in another room and Guy revisited the same routine as before, stripping out of his British clothes then walking into the next room to don his new identity, Gerard Arcachon. Once dressed, he was checked by Lionel for any stray item that might betray him, but he was clean.

'Your field code name will be Hugo,' instructed Lionel.

'I'm sure it works, but I take no chances,' said Guy, opening the radio.

Everything appeared to be in order, the day and night crystals were there plus a spare. By now it was 8 o'clock. Lionel checked the time.

'OK, time to roll.'

Guy picked up his luggage and with not a backward glance, climbed into Lionel's Rover.

With poor headlights and no signposts, the drive to RAF Tangmere was almost three hours, even though Lionel knew the way. Sitting at dispersal was a Lysander which had flown in earlier from Tempsford and was now fuelled to the eyeballs for the run, which was near the limit of its operational radius. As Lionel's car drew up, the pilot finished his groundchecks. Guy fetched his cases from the boot. Never one for long goodbyes, Lionel just shook Guy's hand and was gone.

'Take-off's timed for ten minutes,' advised the pilot, a flight lieutenant clad in battledress and an Irvin fleece. He lit a cigarette, offering one to Guy.

'I don't smoke, thanks.'

'God, couldn't manage without the weed,' responded the flier. ''Kay, let's do it, you'll find a headset up there so we can talk to one another.'

He gestured towards the passenger cockpit and Guy obediently climbed the ladder and sat down in the forward facing of the two seats. In Special Duties configuration, the Lizzie could carry two comfortably, three at a pinch and four in dire emergency. He donned the headset as the pilot settled in his seat, tightened his straps and called for start-up clearance. The traditional whirling finger to the ground crew, then the Mercury engine cracked into life with a brief spurt of flame from the exhaust. After running up the powerplant for a couple of minutes to warm it through, the pilot waved 'Chocks Away' and taxied towards the edge of the pan. Setting the plane crosswind and standing on the brakes, he gradually wound open the throttle and the airframe shuddered as he satisfied himself all was in order. Taxi clearance was given, the little plane rolling over the concrete of the perimeter track and bouncing gently on its tyres, the beams from its landing lights illuminating the way ahead and washing over the frosty grass to either side.

It pulled up on the threshold.

'Peter Able, request take-off clearance.'

'Peter Able, cleared for take-off, have a safe trip.'

This was the part Guy hated. Once more, the pilot braced his toes on the brakes and gradually wound open the throttle. Once more the whole plane shook and shuddered, the prop torque shaking the airframe and the wash from the prop rippling over the fuselage skin. Then the brakes were off, the Lysander rolling. In mere seconds and a few yards, the tail lifted, then they were airborne, the landing lights extinguished and England was no more.

Chapter 15

The Lysander climbed away from Tangmere and turned left towards the Sussex coast. Guy's final view of England for some time was the phosphorescent glimmer of waves breaking on the beach at Selsey Bill. Skimming the surface of the Channel to avoid the radar, they made landfall over the French coast. The sky was clear of aircraft, both friend and foe and there was no flak.

'Good show so far,' came over the intercom, 'now we get down to some serious flying.'

Guy knew that behind this typically jocular comment lay a hard road ahead. One of their briefings had been from a pilot with 161 Squadron. There was simply no room for a navigator, so the pilot had to both fly low level in darkness, itself no mean feat and requiring intense concentration, and navigate a course which dog-legged around built-up areas, ack-ack installations and any other known hotspots to find three flares in some field in the middle of nowhere. On time. The pinpoint navigation demanded – and received – many hours of careful planning for each run.

Like some oversized bat, the Lysander flitted above the French countryside, almost trimming the top branches of the trees it seemed. Just how low they were was brought home in a millisecond, when a sharp burst of full throttle and a swift backwards yank on the stick were all that saved them as they pole-vaulted over pylons and high-tension cables. To the east, distant pencil-beams from searchlights and the starbursts of flak cast a weak glow in the skies as the defences probed yet another of Bomber Harris's forays to soften up the German populace. In the Lysander's part of France, they were utterly alone.

The plane droned on, altering course according to the data on strips of paper on a clipboard strapped to the pilot's knee. There was one heart-stopping moment when a lone Me110 appeared above them, but it flew on, oblivious to the enemy beneath its wings.

Guy's headset crackled.

'We're about 10 minutes from the RV. I'm going to climb a bit to get a better view, so keep your eyes peeled.'

'Wilco,' replied Guy, that dentist's waiting room feeling suddenly and painfully back with a vengeance. Pupils straining to make out anything other than the black and indistinct shapes over which they flew, Guy stared through the plexiglass. Nothing.

'Should be there by now, according to my DR.'

'OK.'

Then he spotted it, Guy's keen young eyes picking up the near pinpricks of light from the three flares.

'Over there, 2 o'clock.'

'Got it,' came the laconic reply as the plane was reefed round in a steep bank to the left.

With deft precision, the airman lined up the nose directly in line with long side of the L. Ahead in the distance, one of the welcoming party flicked a Morse-code challenge with his torch; the aircraft's landing lights winked their reply. Not wishing to attract unwanted attention, the pilot flew straight in. To Guy, the ground was rushing up to meet them at a frightening rate, but the 'driver' had things well under control. Turning on his landing lights at the last second, the pilot swooped onto the rough turf. The wheels cut swathes into the grass, hurling twin rooster tails of frost-flecks high into the air and past the cockpits, whilst the airscrew picked up its share of frozen moisture and contributed to the snowstorm. Turning quickly inside the top of the L, the aircraft made its way back to the first flare and turned 180 degrees once more to line up for take-off. Leaning out of his cockpit, the pilot began winding up the engine against the brakes even as Guy descended the ladder and as his feet touched French soil, the brakes were released and the monoplane began its take-off run. Within seconds it was airborne and as the tiny contraption of aluminium, steel and fabric disappeared into the night sky, Guy felt that his umbilical cord to Britain had been severed.

'Welcome.'

The reception committee was small, just three people. They had snuffed the flares just as soon as the Lysander departed and then showed Guy the hidey-hole in the trees, a skilfully concealed trap over a wood-lined cavity, where flares were hidden for next time. Simple but effective, the flares were old commercial size bean tins part-filled with paraffin. Wicks made of webbing had their upper ends supported by a wire frame, with the bottoms submerged in paraffin. A 5 litre drum of fuel took care of top-ups. Guy took bearings from nearby trees to be able to find the cavity again if needed.

In a kind of déjà vu, he spent the night in yet another chilly farmhouse, yet another breakfast of bread and ersatz coffee, then a cycle ride with the farmer's wife to catch the bus to Clermont Ferrand, some 20 miles south. The Renault bus was running on borrowed time, plumes of smoke from the exhaust and the rattle of worn big-end bearings ample tocsin of its imminent demise. The passengers all looked grey, drawn and undernourished and Guy was glad of his beard, it hid a rather better-fed face than his companions. Several crates of chickens and rabbits shared the passenger compartment. Of most worry to Guy was his suitcase, the hiding place for his radio. A thorough search at a checkpoint would guarantee at least a seat in Ravensbruck or Auschwitz, if not a dawn appointment with a solitary pole. Sure enough, on the outskirts of the town, the bus was halted at a checkpoint and a posse of feldgrau climbed aboard to check papers. Guy had slid his case under the seat, then allowed the skirt of his coat to conceal it. As the soldiers advanced up the bus with their usual 'Papiere, bitte', a knot of icy fear gripped him. The young soldier leaned over towards Guy.

'Papiere – schnell!'

Trés vite, Guy proffered his identity. The private flicked through them and satisfied, thrust them back into Guy's hand. A few shopping baskets were rifled through, but Guy's suitcase was not spotted and checks duly completed, the patrol allowed the bus to continue.

Ten minutes later, the Renault ground into the main square and Guy alighted. Raoul was there to meet him, an easy figure to recognise, big-built, a square jaw and a nose broken at some time from his pugilism.

'Cold even in Nice,' was Raoul's challenge.

'But still warmer than Brive,' was the reply.

'Pleased to see you again,' said Raoul, keeping up the old friends theme of Guy's cover. 'I've scrounged you a bike.'

It was a ringer, or at least a close relative of Auntie's, a stove-pipe special, solidly built with an oil-bath chaincase. This not only prolonged the life of the chain, but made for silent running, something that had saved Guy's neck on the run back from Laval all those months ago. Strapping his suitcase to the rear carrier with some thick string wound round the seatpost, Guy rode after Raoul for about ten minutes as he wound his way into the northern suburbs. Guy has been to Clermont Ferrand a number of times but not for several years and his knowledge of the environs was scant.

Part way down a wide avenue flanked by plane trees, Raoul swung to the right and dismounting, wheeled his steed through a wrought iron gate in a low brick wall. Behind the wall stood an imposing Victorian villa. The structure and woodwork were still in basically sound heart, though the paintwork had not seen a decorator's brush for some years and, reflected Guy, was unlikely to do so for some years to come. The dark green paint was either missing or peeling, what remained hanging off in curls and strands. Almost all the heavy wooden shutters were closed. To the left was a wide concrete drive leading to the rear of the house and protected by a pair of high gates. The front garden not only had that dank, soggy-brown look of all gardens in winter, but was unkempt and neglected, with patches of leaf mould blotching the lawns. The dominant garden ornament was a complex sphere of cast iron, rather like an astrolabe, mounted on a truncated Cleopatra's needle of the same material. Its silvery finish was now somewhat tarnished and flaking in several places.

'This will be your lodgings,' said Raoul. 'I've known the old lady, Violette Peugeot, for years. I used to work for a local firm of builders and we did a lot of work here. That was when Charles, Violette's husband, was alive. He ran a furniture factory here and one in Brive, pretty well-off. The old chap died about ten years ago and as Violette's got older and more infirm, I've been coming round here two or three times a week to do her shopping and a few things round the house. Just follow my lead, she knows nothing of who you are, just a friend of mine looking for lodgings and work.'

With that, Raoul marched up to the peeling front door and tugged the old-fashioned bell-pull. Somewhere in the bowels of the villa, a bell clanged. It was some minutes before Violette shuffled to the front door, the thump of her walking stick clearly audible through the stained glass door panels. The door creaked open to reveal an elderly lady clad in clothes of yesteryear, all purples and blacks. Now diminutive with age, she still managed a straight back, but the painful, creeping gait and grotesquely swollen knuckles telegraphed arthritis without her saying a word.

'Violette, this is my friend Gerard, the one I was telling you about, he'd like to rent your garden flat.'

Violette proffered a gnarled hand and gestured them to come inside. The vestibule was icy cold, but Violette led the way down the corridor to a small salon where a wood-burning stove kept the room cosy and warm. To one side of the stove was a large built-in locker, its lid open to reveal billets of wood for fuel. Lying with its back to the warmth was a large cat, entirely black save for a white blaze on its chest and one front paw in the same colour. The cat half opened one eye and glared balefully at the visitors. Deeming them unworthy of any attention, the animal clicked shut the eye, stretched its paws and returned to the far more weighty matter of snoozing. The room itself was crowded with dark mahogany furniture, much of it overstuffed and hard, the arms and other wear points shiny or threadbare. The carpet was high quality but very uncared for. Practically every surface was hidden under ornaments or framed photographs, most in sepia and the majority in stiff, formal poses. Violette and Charles were easily recognisable on their wedding day standing by a brougham drawn by a pair of black horses, shiny and resplendent with plumes.

The salon had french doors leading to the large walled garden at the rear and through the doors, the weak afternoon light filtered into the room. Violette creaked to an armchair near the stove and sank painfully onto the cushions.

'Well, Gerard,' she asked, 'and how long do you intend to stay?'

Despite her years, Violette still possessed a melodious voice, full of warmth and kindness.

'I'm not sure' replied Guy, 'it depends on whether or not I can find some work.'

'Do you have any skills?' enquired Violette.

'I'm a good mechanic, but there's not much call for that in wartime,' said Guy, 'I'm willing to turn my hand to anything as long as it pays. I do have some money, so I can live for a while until I do find something.'

Violette smiled, it lit up her face.

'Just pay me 50 francs a month for the utilities, it will be good to have the flat occupied again.'

The little catch in her voice and a touch of wistfulness in her tone raised immediate question marks in Guy's brain, but he stored these until he and Raoul could be alone.

'Raoul, there's bedlinen in the armoire on the first floor, help yourselves.'

Raoul led the way back to the vestibule and up the wide staircase, dusty banisters and treads either side of the staircarpet evidence that upstairs had lain unused for quite a while. On the landing at the top stood a huge mahogany cupboard, the inside an Aladdin's cave of linen of every kind. Raoul selected a pile of sheets, blankets, pillowcases and teatowels, then led the way back downstairs to the kitchen at the rear, where he rummaged through cupboards for dishcloths and dusters. Taking some keys from the mantelpiece, he unlocked the back door and walked into the garden. Opening a wooden door set in the high wall to his left, he continued through the arch into a paved courtyard beyond. On the left was a wide motorhouse with black painted wooden concertina doors and two windows set in the wall above. On the far side of the building were two high wooden gates leading to the drive that Guy had seen on approaching the house. A personal door in the gates offered pedestrian access to the drive. Guy looked to his right over the jungle that had once been the potager, some fruit trees at the end the only reminder of what had once been. A wooden door in the wall at the bottom led outside the property, but some cypress trees and the height of the wall concealed what lay beyond.

Raoul used a Yale key on the ring to open a personal door into the motorhouse and Guy followed him in. Light filtered into the gloom from panes set high in the leaves of the concertina doors. The dominant occupant of the garage was a 1920s Renault, its coachbuilt landaulette body stretching towards the ceiling. Covered in a thick layer of dust and with extremely flat tyres, it had not turned a wheel in years. Even if it had been roadworthy, it could not have moved anyway, its exit blocked by a monster pile of logs. Beside the pile was a chopping block, an axe and a wheelbarrow, also a heap of old fruit trays being gradually broken up for kindling. The rest of the space was fully occupied by furniture shrouded in dustcloths, seemingly endless suitcases and sundry other junk. Raoul jinked and weaved his way around the obstacles to an open wooden stairway at the back. Climbing to the top, he opened a door onto a small landing and switched on the light. Guy noticed the door had no lock. Raoul crossed the landing, opened the door into a galley style kitchen and walked straight over to the window. He unbolted the internal wooden shutters and folded them onto a recess to the left of the sash window. The frosted glass admitted enough light to see by, but it was not exactly the brightest spot in Clermont Ferrand.

Immediately to the left of the door was an Aga-style cooker and beyond that, a painted wooden worksurface, a pot sink and draining board. Above and below lay cupboards. The only loose furniture was a deal kitchen table and two chairs sitting against the right-hand wall.

'Have a look around and open up the other shutters while I fetch wood for the stove,' ordered Raoul. 'Sitting room, bedroom, bathroom.'

His hand swept over the three doors on the landing as he spoke, then he was off back to the garage. Guy started with the bathroom – bath, basin, toilet and an airing cupboard in one corner complete with hot water cylinder. The only natural light was borrowed through a fanlight above the door. A downside was the colour of the walls, a hideous shade of green, but what the hell? The bedroom contained a single bed, a wardrobe and a dressing table. Guy swung back the shutters and opened the window trying to get some fresh air into that indefinable odour of a long-empty room. It was not at all damp, just that shut-up smell. The sitting room was similar, well furnished with a settee and a couple of comfy armchairs, even an old wind-up gramophone complete with His Master's Voice trumpet. Guy repeated the shutters and open window routine. He had noticed that the bedroom had a cast-iron radiator below the window and the sitting room had two radiators, so what supplied them?

Raoul reappeared with arms full of billets of wood and kindling, then proceeded to fire up the stove in the kitchen. Once satisfied that it had caught, he emptied the contents of the small haversack that he had been carrying since collecting Guy from the bus. A tin of acorn coffee, some rather dense bread and a tin of soup.

'Sorry, that's all I could muster. Milk's impossible to get now, what little there is the Germans collar, so get used to café noir, there is no other.'

So saying, he ran the cold tap. After sundry rumblings and a water hammer, the water ran clear and he filled the tin kettle sitting on the stove. A two-ring gas burner on the work surface was ignited and the kettle boiled for a cup of warming liquid.

'OK,' said Raoul, 'let me fill you in on Violette. Charles died about ten years ago from a stroke and she sold the business. I think the shock of his death aggravated the arthritis and it's steadily got worse. For years, she and Charles had been looked after by Edouard, who lived in this flat.'

His sweeping gesture encompassed the little home.

'Edouard was killed in 1938, a bus skidded on the ice one winter, mounted the pavement and crushed him. He'd been everything – cook, butler, housekeeper, chauffeur, gardener –and Violette never got over his death. Edouard was like a son, she refused to have any domestic help after he died.'

Now Guy grasped the catch in her voice about the flat.

'I take it she's not blown away for a bob?'

'Absolutely not,' came Raoul's answer.

'So why not move to the Riviera, it would be much kinder to her arthritis?'

'I did gently broach that when she asked me to oversee the

286

conversion of one corner of the house to a little flat, but she said that she'd lived in the house all her married life and she intended to die there. Besides, she had her friends Elisabeth and Gretchen then, they used to come round almost every day and play cards, do the crossword, bring her shopping. Both of them died a couple of years ago within three months of each other. Despite you being here, I'll continue to come round. That way, the neighbours won't see anything different and you'll be free to do what you need to do.'

'Does she have any other visitors?' probed Guy.

'No, she lives like a recluse. Her sister Clothilde lives in an old folks home in Bordeaux. I don't know if it runs in the family, but Clothilde's arthritis is even worse than Violette's. There is a daughter, Anne, she and her husband Jean-Paul live in Geneva. Used to be regular visitors, four or five times a year, but the war put the kybosh on that. Charles has a brother, lives in Bordeaux, I think, but I don't even know his name and I've certainly never seen him.'

By now the stove had a real heart. Raoul stood up and leaned over a wooden casing to the right of the stove. He flicked a switch on the top and a pump in the casing began to hum softly. Within minutes, the long dormant cast-iron pipes began to emit loud cracking noises and sundry trapped pockets of gas gurgled from their lairs. Taking a bleed key from a hook on the mantelpiece, Raoul bled each radiator in turn, the rank smell of long-trapped air being swiftly replaced by dribbles of rusty brown liquid as the radiators filled. As warmth began to permeate, Guy spread the sheets and blankets over all the radiators to air. Raoul unearthed two stone hot water bottles and placed them in the bed. Gradually, the flat warmed up and began to feel like home.

Raoul showed Guy the manual distribution valve, which could be set to either hot water or central heating only, or halfway between the two.

'Your only real control is the damper,' advised Raoul, 'but get it right, you can control the temperature and keep it in all night.'

'And what about you?' asked Guy, 'all I know is that you are a QS for the mairie and that you used to be a boxer.'

'Divorced.'

The bitterness and emptiness in that single word made Guy wince inwardly, but he made no outward sign of what he felt.

'I grew up here,' said Raoul, 'not really any good academically, but I excelled at sport, took up boxing in my teens. Got really good at it, became middleweight champion of the département, then South-West France. I was Jack-the-lad, a few beers with the boys, played the field. I trained as a QS, became contracts manager with a local building firm. My sister asked me to help out with the local church fête, that's where I met Annette.'

At the mention of her name, a kind of dreamy look came over Raoul's face.

'The only knockout I ever suffered, we were married within a year, deliriously happy. I took part in a boxing match in Brive. That's where I met Carole. You ever been to a boxing match?'

Guy shook his head.

'Mostly a man thing, but a few women do come along. Some are really knowledgeable, but some find it a turn-on – rippling muscles, sweat, a bit of violence. Carole was brought round to my dressing room after I had won. I still don't know why, but we started an affair. My marriage was idyllic, our love life was great – I just don't know what possessed me. Problem was, we had a contract to build a large hotel in Brive and the client was hell, so I was spending two or three nights a week away. It just offered the ideal opportunity to pursue Carole. After about four months, I realised it was all sex, and pretty poor sex at that, so one night I took Carole to a restaurant and finished it. What I didn't know was that one of our neighbours was at a corner table and he blew the gaff to Annette. She confronted me when I got home. I couldn't deny it, but I did tell her it was over. She packed her bags and walked out, I never saw her again.'

'Funny.'

There was irony is his tone.

'My Dad was a bit strait-laced, but he could be very pithy at times. I remember him saying when we talking about the birds and bees one day "Never forget, Raoul, a straight penis can be a crooked ruler." How right he was. About a year later, I came home to a letter from some lawyer in Toulouse and the divorce papers. I wrote back saying how much I wanted Annette back and enclosing a sealed letter to her. I told her it was all my fault, how much I loved her and missed her. She never replied, even though I wrote several times and eventually, I had to sign the divorce papers. I couldn't bring myself to attend the court hearing, my lawyer went.'

'Life had fallen apart. My boss was Annette's uncle. He sacked me. I started looking at life through the bottom of a glass and scraped by on the tools as casual labour. The boxing went out the window. It took a year to see sense, then the divorce began, but I was determined to come back. I went to the gym again, stopped boxing myself and began bringing on promising youngsters. I landed the job at the

288

mairie. That's me in a nutshell.'

'Not married again?'

It was the gentle Duplessis interrogation once more. Raoul dropped his gaze and stared at the floor. There was a silence, a silence Guy did not break, knowing that Raoul would be compelled to speak. Raoul lifted his head and his composure regained, looked straight at Guy.

'Once the divorce was settled, I began to recover a bit, thought I'd begun to get over Annette, so I plucked up courage and started dating again. Problem was, it went wrong every time. The relationship would start off OK, then at some stage, I'd begin comparing the girl to Annette. It was nothing I said or overt, but every girl must have sensed it and nothing lasted. So, I'm destined to be the eternal bachelor.'

He indicated two keys hanging from the mantel.

'That's for the drive gates' personal door, that's for the garden door at the bottom. I oiled all the locks and hinges in readiness for you coming.'

Guy was beginning to really take to Raoul, he was on the Duplessis attention to detail wavelength.

Raoul glanced at his watch.

'Gotta go, be back about seven, take you for a beer and a tour of Clermont Ferrand.'

He shot off.

Guy's immediate priority was to conceal the radio and where Raoul knew nothing of its whereabouts for both their sakes. Guy went back down to the motorhouse clutching his torch. The Renault had been parked close to the back wall, but with enough space on the left-hand side to open the doors part way. Now with flat tyres, the chassis was close to the ground and it needed a slim and determined person to slide underneath. Helping himself to two screwdrivers and a rag from the bench, Guy sidled round the boot of the car and using the rag to avoid disturbing the dust on the handle, cracked open the rear door. The interior of the car smelt of leather, a touch of oil and grease and that indefinable aroma of unused car. The seats were dark blue leather, the carpet a midnight blue bordering on black, deep-cut pile edged in blue leather piping. Guy ran his fingers around the pile at the edges and was rewarded by screwheads at regular intervals. He shone his torch to find the carpet secured by japanned metal woodscrews and cups. Taking care not to let the screwdriver slip, he undid enough screws to allow him to fold back about a foot of carpet. Below lay the floorboards, not just cheap plywood, but tongue and grooved elm boards about six inches wide. These were in a well and fastened by steel screws. Hefting the large screwdriver, he set about loosening them. Undisturbed for years, they proved stubborn, screeching as they turned, but eventually, they succumbed. Teasing the boards from their bed, he revealed the chassis below. He was delighted to find cross-bracing at exactly the right place to rest his radio. Not wanting grease or depressions in the leather of the case from the chassis, he needed a suitable tray in which to lay the radio. Casting round the garage, he seized upon a fruit tray made of very dark wood. This was laid on the cruciform and the radio placed in it. The boards and the carpet were reinstated with a dab of oil on the screws.

The next task was to bring his bike round from the front. Sure enough, the lock and hinges on the personal door slid like silk and his precious bike was quickly parked in the motorhouse. With dusk falling, he set off down the garden path towards the door at the bottom. The path was cambered to disperse water, covered in moss and lichen and extremely slippery. Picking his way gingerly over the concrete, he reached the portal. Once more, Raoul's ministrations proved their worth. Cautiously, Guy swung back the door, to find himself in a tarmac passageway dividing the villas. The tarmac was neglected but sound. Best of all, the passage was wide enough to admit a car. A quick foray proved revealing. The passageways were arranged in the form of a cross, a bit like a Battenburg cake in plain view and thus divided the villas into four blocks. Each end of the passageways gave onto a different street and there were no obstructions like bollards to impede free access. All the villas seemed to have been constructed around the same time and to a pattern, with high walls shielding both houses and passageways from view. Unless he met anyone en route, Guy could come and go unseen and had a choice of routes to follow.

Regaining the warmth of the little flat, he cleaned and polished it, then rewarded his endeavours with a hot bath. Ah, bliss! The soup and some of the bread filled a bit of a hole before Raoul appeared in the courtyard below and called softly to Guy to admit him. As they pushed their bikes across the yard, Raoul pointed out that the villa overlooking the drive was now boarded up, its occupants riding out the war in Spain, so nobody overlooked the flat or its environs.

Companiably, they tootled into Clermont Ferrand, taking a tour of the prominent landmarks like the Mairie, the station and all the bars and cafes frequented by the Germans. Raoul was very clued up on the set-up and unspoken rules about officers, NCOs and other ranks and pointed out which café or bar was which. At Guy's request, they ended up at a café frequented by the other ranks. The atmosphere as they entered was reminiscent of that evening in Exeter when Guy first met Angela – hot bodies, beer and more smoke than oxygen. The good news was that the beer was quite passable. Finding a corner near the bar, they surveyed the scene and made for a table near the middle as two squaddies swayed off into the chill night. Remembering Norman's wise teachings, Guy listened in to conversations without appearing to do so, but everything he heard was just soldiers' gossip, who was due leave, who was managing to get his leg over a French bird and who had got a dose. Not a word about transporting machinery up into the mountains nor anything else of any consequence. Well before curfew, Guy and Raoul made for their respective homes. A little woozy on even the weak French beer, Guy pedalled homewards, set the tinny alarm by the bed and was out like a light.

The next morning, he sloped off to the shops and wrested what was available, which was not much, to at least partially assuage his keen hunger. Returning home, he made himself breakfast, then took to his bicycle to reconnoitre the locale. On each occasion he had left the flat, he had deliberately used the bottom gate and a different exit from the network of passages behind the villa. Now he wheeled his way around the town, reinforcing the knowledge of the night before and learning the maze of boulevards, avenues and rues that was Clermont Ferrand. He surreptitiously took particular notice of the Gare, but saw and learned nothing of interest from his observations. Meeting Raoul outside the Mairie at 1830, they once again frequented the other ranks' bars, drinking beer in four or five, but again drew a blank on intelligence. As they made to go their separate ways once more, Raoul drew Guy into an alley. Making sure they were unobserved, he slipped Guy a map of the roads in the area, a gesture for which Guy was truly grateful. Clermont Ferrand might have been only 40 miles from home, but the fact was, he knew the main and some of the side roads , but lacked the crucial knowledge of the byroads and tracks he might need in extremis.

'One other thing?'

'Yes, Raoul?'

'How good is your German, really?'

'Good but not perfect,' replied Guy. 'I can understand one-on-one conversations, but I can't filter when a group is chatting, especially if there are thick accents and they've a had a few beers. Provided I get the gist, I think I'm doing well.'

The night was pretty cold, the two men's breath emerging in clouds.

'Look Raoul, time is short. I have to have some good intelligence and PDQ if we're to knock out whatever Jerry is planning. Call your cell together and let's see what they have.'

'D'accord', came the reply, 'I'll set up a meeting for the day after tomorrow, before curfew.'

The next two days Guy spent cycling the highways and byways of the Clermont Ferrand region, with an emphasis on the tracks and byways leading to the landing ground, as he knew instinctively that this would prove vital to his very survival. The evening was spent once more supping beer and earwigging; third time lucky, he found himself within earshot of a transport driver whose commonsense had been overcome by the beer.

'Thank Christ for that,' remarked the German, 'the last of all that bloody machinery delivered. It's been hell, taking trucks up through all that bloody ice and snow, hairy stuff. Anyway, we delivered the final load yesterday.'

Guy was all ears, but nothing showed on his face or in his body language. Leaving the bar, Raoul took Guy to his home, a modest semi in a quiet suburb.

'Tomorrow night, 1830 here,' said Raoul, 'bonne nuit.'

Next day, Guy once again did 'The Knowledge' of Clermont Ferrand before taking to the hills and tracks leading to the landing ground. Rounding a corner on a D road, he found himself heading towards a Nazi roadblock. Heart pounding, he squeaked to a halt and presented his papers. London had done an excellent job, he merited no more than a cursory inspection before being released. Nonetheless, his heart was beating like a triphammer as he pedalled into the distance. The roads and byways he travelled were a complete mix, from good tarmac and smooth surfaces to rough, stony ribbons cut into the very soil, jarring the spine. Mindful of his tyres, Guy took it easy, steering slowly and carefully over rut, ridge and runnel until he had memorised the spider's web to the town's north-west. He duly found the landing-ground and taking care that he was unobserved, homed in on the concealed pit that contained the flares to light the way for the Lysanders.

Dusk was falling as he picked his way back to the town. Sliding carefully down the passages, he saw nobody and let himself through the bottom gate and into the flat. Bathed and shaved, Guy made his way to Raoul's. The nearer he got to the semi, the more his heart beat faster and faster; it was a reprise of Le Mans, exposing his identity and purpose to those who quite literally, held his life in their hands. One wrong word, curtains.

Raoul answered the door and ushered him inside. There were already three men in the salon, introduced as Philippe, Antoine and Georges, shortly to be joined by Marcel, Albert and Simon.

Guy was introduced as Hugo, his new field codename – all of them knew the score about security.

'Right,' said Guy, 'we all know that the Boche are up to something up in the mountains, the burning question is what. Anyone got any ideas?'

Albert nodded.

'I work at the gare as a shipping clerk, so I get to hear and see a lot of what's going on. The Boche have been bringing in equipment by the ton, then trucking it up into the mountains. All terribly hush-hush, unmarked crates, guards everywhere. All I know is that the last lot came in yesterday and was hauled off in several trucks. In three days' time, there's supplies coming in. The Jerries took over an old flour mill in the station yard as a warehouse, it has its own siding. They're going to use it for transit and haul the supplies away at regular intervals. I was in there yesterday and they've set aside one room – steel mesh cages, top-class lock on the door. The whole place is guarded twenty-four hours a day.'

Albert's information on the equipment matched exactly what Guy had gleaned in the bar the previous night. Clearly, the plant, whatever it was to produce, was near coming on stream. Time was short.

'Anybody add to that?' asked Guy.

All the others shook their heads except Antoine, who it transpired, worked as a roadmender.

'I can't really add to what Albert has said, but they sure as hell have shipped a lot of kit up there, I've seen convoy after convoy go past. Must be something big.'

Top of Guy's agenda was to identify the supplies, presumably chemicals of some kind if what Lionel had told him was true.

'It was good to meet you all, now I must talk to Albert. I am going to need you all once we find out what's afoot, so thank you, I'll certainly be calling on you very shortly.'

The cell took their congé and left. Guy, Albert and Raoul settled down for a chat.

Albert was nearing sixty, a veteran of the railways whose

knowledge of the system was matchless.

'Albert, is there any way you can find out what those supplies are?'

Albert shook his head, his shoulders indicating resignation.

'They guard everything, keep it hidden, keep us out of the way when they unload the wagons, there's no chance. We don't see any shipping documents either. Your only chance is to break in to the warehouse and sneak a look.'

'Any chance I can do that?' asked Guy, 'what about alarms, that kind of thing?'

Once more, the elderly railwayman shook his head.

'There are no alarms, they rely on the round-the-clock security. But there is a way in through the lift motor room at the top. I'll show you. Raoul, I need a paper and pencil.'

Raoul obliged and Albert drew rough sketches of the plan and elevation views of the former mill. They showed a rectangular block some twenty-five metres high. At the front of the building were two roller doors, side by side. One gave access to the ground floor, the other covered the entrance to the sizeable goods lift.

'It has lattice gates at front and back so that you can wheel loaded trolleys or barrows straight in or out,' explained Albert. 'All the floors are open plan and the Boche have built their cages on the second floor.'

Being French, Guy immediately understood the continental system of calling the ground floor the first floor, so the cages were at first-floor level. Albert sketched in the lift motor room, essentially a shack on the roof. Guy peered at the drawing.

'How do you reach the motor room normally, Albert?'

The man added the symbol of a trapdoor to the left side of the main building roof.

'Up a steel ladder and through that trapdoor, but Jerry's put a steel bar and a padlock across the inside, so no chance that way.'

Guy was puzzled. 'So how do you access the mill through the lift motor room, then?'

'Simple,' came the response, 'there's a trap below the lift motor. If the motor ever needs changing, the trap allows the old motor to be lowered and a new one hoisted into place. It's only happened once in my time here, about ten years ago and I helped the lift engineer swap them over, so that's how I know about the trap. You can't see it from below unless you climb on top of the lift cage and it's so dark and greasy in the motor room, the trap's virtually invisible. It's held down by four bolts in circular recesses in each corner.'

Guy's engineering brain clicked in immediately.

'What make is the lift?'

Albert looked at him strangely, not seeing the relevance of the question.

'Some French make, but why's it important?'

Because if it's French, the bolts will be metric. If it were American or British, they could be American or British threads and sizes.'

'Ah.'

Comprehension dawned.

'How do I get on the roof? I've seen the building,' said Guy, 'and there's nothing nearby to use as a jumping-off point.'

'You climb,' was the chilling reply, turning to an instant jelly the young agent's guts.

'How, I can't use pitons and so on because of the noise.'

Albert sketched once more, detailing the stonework at each corner, showing the large blocks and the grooves in between.

'There you are,' he joked, 'a nice ladder straight to the top! You'll be the King Kong of Clermont Ferrand.'

Guy smiled politely at the humour, but the dread fear of climbing like some spider up the side of the mill clawed at him; but there was simply no other way, he had to know what the cages held. Albert confirmed that the motor room door had just a cheap mortice lock and promising to report back to Raoul once the supplies had arrived, he made for home.

Raoul broke the silence that followed Albert's departure.

'Christ, Gerard, you'd have to be a shit-hot climber to scale that mill. You ever done any climbing?'

'Part of my training,' replied Guy reassuringly.

'Rather you than me, I'm used to being on scaffolding, but that's pretty safe and you've got handrails. Ugh!'

Raoul shuddered at the very thought.

Next morning, Guy scouted the mill, outwardly nonchalant, but with all his senses at key pitch. He needed to avoid the north side where moss and lichen would tend to gather, not only because they would be slippery, but he might dislodge bits of green onto the sentries beneath. The side next to the road was his selected route. When evening fell, he returned with Raoul. Concealing themselves in an alleyway that gave a view of the warehouse, they observed and timed the guards. Or at least, they tried to time the guards, finding that with only a small area to cover, the sentries' beats were totally irregular. Guy would have to take his chance and shin up the first pitch like greased lightning and in complete silence. The need for silence dictated gym shoes. Raoul's feet were a fraction larger than Guy's, but a thick pair of socks made the vital footwear a snug fit; Raoul lent his knapsack to carry all the tools and the rope that Guy would use during his breaking and entering.

Two days later, Albert confirmed the arrival of the shipment. With no time to lose, Guy decided to go in that very night. Sitting in Raoul's house, he was almost paralysed by fear at the thought of what lay ahead. What made it worse was that it was pouring with rain, so the stonework would be slippery. His stomach churned and churned and he had to go into the bathroom to retch. When he emerged, Raoul was checking his watch.

'Time to go, Gerard.'

In total silence, they flitted through the deserted streets to take up position where they could observe the warehouse once more. In the distance, a loco whistled mournfully, an almost eerie sound. Guy checked the contents of the knapsack before strapping it firmly in place at waist and chest. He blacked his face and the backs of his hands with burnt cork. Leaving their observation post, Guy and Raoul slid across the road and against a convenient fence which hid them from the sentries' view. As soon as the sentries crossed on their way round the building, Guy sprinted into position and scrabbled up the jutting stonework. To his relief, the grooves between the stones proved deeper than expected, but the facings were treacherous with the rain. He made good progress, stopping as the guards passed by again. Inch by inch, he scaled the face until he was about fifty feet up.

Moving his right leg to the next groove, he slipped. For a brief but interminable moment, death stared him in the face as he fought to regain his balance, nails clawing grooves in the stone in his desperate attempts to survive. Completely petrified, he froze just as he had done on that Welsh rockface scant weeks ago and for a full five or six minutes, he just clung there, completely unable to move a muscle. He gulped down huge breaths of air, but still felt as though he were suffocating. Apart from clinging on, he had lost all motor action in his limbs, which steadfastly refused to obey his brain. Oh so slowly, he regained control and checking for the noise of the guards' boots, he completed his climb.

The incredible sense of relief at gaining the parapet could not be put into any words, he just inhaled breath after deep breath, elated to still be alive. Then he padded over to the motor room and began picking the lock. Rusty with disuse, it resisted him fiercely, but some oil from the can in his bag eased the tumblers and he was in. The motor room smelt of grease and that frisson of ozone that surrounds electrical installations. The lift mechanism was contained in a bulky steel frame. Above the motor, a lifting eye on a girder stood ready for a motor change. Guy shone his torch below the motor, but initially, could see no sign of any trap, such was the thickness of dirt covering the floor. Working out where the edges of the trap were likely to be, he dug around carefully with a spoon until he located the first indentation containing a securing bolt. Spooning out the encrustation, he placed it carefully to one side before repeating the exercise on the other three. To his delight, each bolt contained a flush-fitting grab handle that swivelled upwards. With so much greasy dirt keeping moisture at bay, the bolts turned smoothly using just the grab handles. Once loosened completely, each bolt was prevented from coming out fully by some kind of pin or retainer so that the grab handles could be utilised to lift the trap. At least, that was the theory. The trap was jammed firmly in place and Guy's mind switched in an instant to that night below the Dyna factory.

Passing his rope through the lifting eye, Guy fashioned a cradle secured on all four handles, then hauled the cordage downwards. This did the trick and the trap swung gently above its aperture. Tying off the rope on the frame, once more Guy delved into his stock, this time locating four pieces of wood. Very carefully, he slid the trap onto the chocks. Then it was time to climb down into that pitch-black liftshaft. With extreme care, he secured his climbing rope to the lifting eye. The rope had knots at regular intervals to assist his passage. There was not enough space for Guy to fit through the trap with the knapsack on his back, so he had to resort to hanging it round his neck. Taking yet another deep breath, he swung into space.

At first, the rope was quite stable, but the lower he climbed, the more it oscillated and he had to cling on for dear life and slow his descent. By now, his eyes were accustomed to the darkness and he could see the lift gates at second floor level. One thing Guy did know about lifts – the only thing, he reflected –was how the safety detent on the gates worked to keep the gates shut unless the lift was at that floor. The lift cage pushed a lever above the doorframe upwards or downwards to release the gate lock. Guy's knowledge had come from being trapped in a lift in a Nancy department store and being rescued by the pompiers. Guy also knew that each lever had a pin that could be engaged to lock the detent open for servicing. As he neared the gate, he wrapped the rope securely round himself and shone his pencil torch. The chain on which the pin was stored was there, but no pin! Looking upwards, he could see a pin on the next level, so laboriously climbed upwards once more. By now, he was tiring and longing to put his feet on something solid. The pin was held by a keyring arrangement and it took five minutes before he prised it free and descended once more to push and lock out the detent. He prayed that the lift gates would not screech and cracked them ajar fractions at a time so as not to make a sound.

The cage was a strongly-constructed affair, thick welded mesh from floor to ceiling and a steel plate door with a chunky lock. Guy's dexterity had proved a godsend when learning lock-picking, even earning him the grudging soubriquet of Raffles from his instructor. Taking a pouch of lockpicks from his bag, Guy set about the Fatherland's finest. Albert's description of 'special' was an understatement and it took twenty minutes before it surrendered. Conscious that the Wehrmacht were scant feet the other side of the wall, Guy was listening constantly for any untoward noises. Nerves stretched in case Albert's intelligence on alarms proved false, he inched open the door. Nothing went off.

The cage contained wooden crates piled six or seven feet high. Apart from the German eagle, their only markings were the letters A-E, obviously an identification code for those in the know. In one corner of the cage, brown hessian sacks were piled layer upon layer. These too had the eagle stencilled upon them, plus the chemical shorthand 'NaCl'. Even a chemistry ignoramus like Guy knew the name for common salt. Concluding that they must be associated with the contents of the crates, Guy climbed to the top of one of the stacks marked 'A'. He had been expecting to have to jemmy off each lid, but Herr Hitler's boffins wanted the crates to be reused, so each lid was held down by screws. That those screws had been recently inserted was evident from the bright witness scratches on the heads. Guy suddenly grinned, he would not have to disguise his own efforts.

Each crate held tightly packed drums of chemicals. By drawing out one drum from each of the series A-E, Guy could see the contents labels. But the labels had only the maker's name – IG Farben – and a chemical formula. None of the formulae made the least sense to Guy, but he carefully wrote down each one before sliding the drums back into place. Checking his watch, he found he had been in the cage for an hour and a half. Swiftly, he secured the final screw, exited the cage and swung home the tumblers. Then through the lift gates, pulling out the locking pin and the long climb back to the motor room. Somehow, sixty or so feet seemed like six hundred and he gained the top breathless and exhausted. Reinstalling the trap was the work of but seconds, disguising his handiwork on the securing bolts took several painstaking minutes. Finding some more oily dirt behind a stanchion, he smoothed over the cups and any scratches in the top's encrustation. Even some dust on the inside face of the lifting eye was added to complete the disguise.

Once more, fear, near panic seized Guy as he approached the parapet to begin the long climb down. The rain had stopped, but a useful wind was blowing to carry away any noise. He feared the descent more because he would be feeling for the next groove below, unable to see his target. Much to his surprise, nay absolute delight, he developed a rhythm as he did his spiderman impression down the warehouse face. But Sod's law struck when he was ten feet from the ground – the guards stopped for a chat. Clinging to the stonework and wishing himself invisible in case they should glance up, it seemed an aeon before the soldiers ceased their smutty innuendo about some girl in Clermont Ferrand and marched on. Guy was at ground level in seconds and back in the alleyway, where an obviously relieved and ecstatic Raoul greeted him. They stole back to Raoul's, where a stiff brandy followed a thorough clean-up for Guy.

Raoul knew from the broad grin that the mission had been a success.

Chapter 16

'Welwyn, this is Welwyn.' The cry was still lost somewhere in the mists of the steam from the train as it rolled into the platform. Having taken this route many times, Lionel knew only too well where he was, but at a time when all station signs had been removed or obliterated to confuse any invaders, the announcement would be all the welcome to an unfamiliar traveller.

Striding purposefully through the station concourse with its all-pervading odour of soot, Lionel spotted a uniformed FANY waiting at the exit. There was instant and mutual recognition, she had driven him on numerous occasions. Smiling and with a discreet 'Welcome, Sir', she opened the kerbside door of the khaki Hillman; he sank into the rear seat and was borne away through Home Counties suburbia. It was a slow and careful ride, the town had caught the tail end of a Luftwaffe raid on London the previous night and wherever you looked, there were stricken buildings and debris.

The car stopped outside the imposing doors of what in more peaceful times had been The Frythe Country House Hotel. Now it was an hotel no longer, now it was known in SOE at Station IX, the very heart of clandestine research into anything and everything that might aid guerrilla warfare. Smaller and yet smaller radios, folding bicycles, a pistol that separated into its parts for concealment, exploding rats or horse dung – all of these were the brainchild or brainchildren of some febrile mind at Station IX and manufactured just up the road at Stevenage.

Lionel showed his pass and was admitted to the vestibule. The security guard signed him in, offered him a seat and picked up the phone. A minute later, John Gough was shaking Lionel's hand and leading him upstairs. John was an ex-colonel in the Royal Engineers, press-ganged from retirement to bring the voice of sanity to his coterie of boffins. Combining an engineer's logic with strong man-management skills, he piloted the station through the maelstrom of a world war, celebrating its triumphs and smoothing over the inevitable disasters. Overall, the enterprise was a resounding success.

'I gather you need to see Erik urgently?'

Lionel nodded.

'We'll go straight to his office, he's expecting you.'

John knocked at the door marked 'Erik Knutsen'.

'Come in,' filtered through the panelled door and they entered what looked at first sight like the aftermath of last night's air raid. Despite the unceasing efforts of Erik's secretary Marion, not an inch of the broad desk was visible beneath sundry piles of papers, files and books. Bookcases lined the walls on both sides of the room, each volume bearing the title of some esoteric chemical subject. Erik himself looked, sounded and acted like the archetypal Englishman, even his English had a North London accent. The chemist had come to Imperial College from Bergen in 1919 to study organic chemistry. He romped to a First, swallowed whole his PhD and took up a research fellowship. Somehow, he had shown no inclination to leave his alma mater despite tempting offers from countless universities across the globe and had risen to Head of the Chemistry Department. The papers he had written or co-authored would have filled a small library by themselves. Lionel's initial meeting with Erik was when they served on a working group to improve the unreliable pencil fuses then in service. Thanks to Erik, the detonators had improved beyond all measure. It was Lionel who was responsible for Erik's recruitment to Station IX, moving the professor lock, stock and library to Welwyn.

Erik woke each day with at least a million ideas in his head; by day's end, he had had a million more. The trick was to focus Erik, something John had learned to do, although not with 100% success. Once started, Erik was unstoppable. He would go into a kind of Cloud Nine mode, where he saw and heard nothing of what was going on around him. Lost in his musings, he would frequently work all night. The security staff recognised his Wee Willie Winkie moments and would phone his wife Eugenie to warn her not to expect him home. On a number of occasions, staff had found Erik slumped over bench or desk, spatula or pen still clutched in his hand, out to the wide. John had recruited Marion to attempt to bring at least some order to Erik. Somehow, she managed to keep him more or less on the straight and narrow, filing papers, making sure he was on time and prepared for meetings, that letters and memos were answered. Marion often remarked that her surname of Jackson should have been Canute.

Under John's guidance, Erik had specialised more and more in explosives. His latest offering added 60 to 70% more power to the existing plastic explosive.

Erik waved them both to chairs.

'OK, Lionel, so what's the flap?'

Lionel grinned, Erik was too sharp to take this as just a routine visit.

Lionel unlocked his briefcase and pulled out a piece of paper containing a list of chemical formulae decoded from Guy's radio transmission. Holding it down on his lap, he briefed Erik.

'We've got word that the Nazis are working on a secret chemical weapon, airborne delivery. We have a man inside, he's come up with this list of the chemicals they plan to use. Means nothing to me, my chemistry begins and ends with H_2SO_4.'

He proffered the single sheet and its handwritten notations.

Erik took the list, then hunted through the piles on his desk before he unearthed a pad and a pencil. In seconds, he was in brown study mode. You could hear the cogs whirring and the invisible shield come between the chemist and anyone else around him. He was completely unhearing and oblivious, to the extent that a bomb going off in his ear would have been unnoticed. The pencil flew across the pad, formula after formula. Clearly he was getting nowhere, the formulae crossed out time and again. Suddenly, he downed both pad and pencil, walked swiftly over to one bookcase, selected a blue tome and regained his seat. The book was well used, but Lionel snatched a glimpse of 'Chemical Dictionary' on the faded gold embossing on the cover.

For several minutes, the Norwegian riffled through the entries and a look of triumph came into his eyes as he found what he was seeking. The pencil flew again and formulae streamed over the page.

After several minutes, he reached a conclusion, but the look on his face had changed from one of triumph to one of total horror – grey, drawn, terrified of what he had now to reveal. Even the circle he drew round the final formula on the page was a slow, fearful figure.

There was a long silence.

Lionel and John sat mute, waiting for Erik.

At last, he raised his head and spoke, but when he did, it was a hoarse whisper, pregnant with fear.

'It's Eisenmann 22.'

Another silence. Lionel could wait no longer

'Ei...?'

'Eisenmann 22. It's a nerve gas, completely paralyses the respiratory system in ten seconds.'

Seeing their enquiring looks, he continued.

'Friedrich Eisenmann is a professor of chemistry at Heidelberg University, always inventing new compounds. They're all Eisenmann something or other, he just gives them the next consecutive number. One of those formulae you gave me – he tapped Lionel's paper – rang a bell. I found it in the dictionary. It was one of his early ones, Eisenmann 6. He sold it to IG Farben, it has lots of commercial uses, funds Eisenmann's research. IG Farben call it Ammonite. Eisenmann is a true academic, just wants to try things. He got into an argument with a neurologist about what it took to stop the nervous system and from that came 22. Eisenmann knew what he was doing, produced the stuff under tight conditions, zoot suits, all that. Tested it on rats and mice, then a few dogs. Worked like a charm. Then, would you believe, he actually published a paper on the stuff in 1936. The University took exception, even in those glory days of the brownshirts, and told him to cool it. I actually met Eisenmann at a conference in Berlin in 1937, nice guy, brilliant, but strictly with the fairies.'

The three men stared at one another, trying to absorb the import of what Erik had just revealed.

The Knutsen cogs were at full throttle once more.

'Airborne delivery, you say?'

He directed the enquiry at Lionel.

'Can't be by aircraft then,' went on Erik.

'How do you fathom that?' asked John.

'Think about it – you'd have to use a number of squadrons and the more you spread the gas deliveries, the more chance there is of a leak or an accident. More storage, more bombs to be filled. Ground crew dying, perhaps most of an aerodrome wiped out, that'll do wonders for Luftwaffe morale, I don't think. Then there's the aircrew. One leak and it's goodnight Munich. A hit from flak or a fighter, same thing. Even the iron men of Goering's tribe are not too likely to rush to volunteer, in fact in their present demoralised state, the word mutiny could enter even the German dictionary. Besides, how many aircraft now get through? If we get a few hits, it will frighten people, but the whole thing could be suppressed. What it needs is a constant stream of hits. Unless it's raining, the gas could cause hundreds, perhaps thousands of deaths from one strike. Drop it on a building or in an enclosed space like a market square, it will be mayhem.'

Lionel decided to come clean.

'We've strong intelligence that Germany is just about to introduce pilotless drones, a jet-powered one called the V-1 and then a rocket called the V-2. They could do exactly what you envisage.'

Erik nodded sagely.

'Makes sense, you stockpile the stuff, then shift it in one, perhaps two consignments to minimise risks from leaks and attacks. It gets delivered to a few sites, stored securely, all the personnel wear protective gear, so they're safe. You launch it in a jet or a rocket. If it fails on take-off, the launch site people are protected. Once it's airborne, you're home and dry. Some may drop short, but you have to count on most of them hitting built-up areas. Imagine it, an endless stream of missiles which don't explode on impact but kill thousands without leaving a mark on them.'

He was in his scientist stride now.

'Formulated to be about the same weight as air, the gas will hang around and not sink or float away, so in still conditions, it could last for hours. People won't dare enter a strike zone for fear of hidden gas pockets, whole districts could become no-go areas, bodies left rotting in the streets. It'll create wholesale panic, Londoners fleeing in droves.'

He paused, then threw up his hands in an expressive gesture.

'Jesus Holy Christ, this could cripple morale and completely alter the course of the war!'

Once more silence reigned, a completely stunned silence, the absolute enormity of Erik's words stilling any conversation. It seemed a lifetime before Lionel broke that stillness.

'What's the significance of rain?'

'Oh, didn't I say?'

The academic was re-emerging.

'Eisenmann 22 dissolves harmlessly in water, so in heavy rain, its effects would be far less. One more thing....'

Lionel and John looked at him expectantly.

'The whole production cycle is very slow, it takes a lot of chemicals to produce a little gas. The final part of the process involves electrolysis, passing a 30,000 volt current through a solution. Mark my words, it will take several weeks at least to build up sufficient gas to begin the strikes.'

The atmosphere in the office was funereal, laden with menace, latent threat, impending disaster. Lionel was suddenly on his feet.

'Sorry, Erik, can you write down the 22 formula on the bottom of the list I gave you, then shred your calculations?'

Lifelessly, Erik rose from his chair, wrote the 22 shorthand on the paper and returned it to Lionel. Then he ripped his jottings from the pad and dropped them into a large shredder in the corner near his desk. A brief whirring, then the pages were gone, sliced neatly into illegible tendrils.

Lionel hurried back to London, willing the train ever faster, willing the train ever slower.

Mere hours after leaving Welwyn, he was sitting across the desk from a familiar figure dressed in siren suit and puffing on a large cigar.

'Sir, what do we do with this?'

Lionel indicated the piece of paper containing the formula. The man opposite him merely grunted to show that he had heard what had been said. Then he spoke.

'You're worried that this might leak out if I put it to Cabinet and then we'll have wholesale panic before Jerry's fired a shot, yes?'

A nod.

'Your man inside –it *is* a man, I take it?

A second nod.

'He's good?'

'The tops.'

'Then this remains entre nous unless he fails in his mission. After that, it's out of my hands, we'll have no choice but to examine options. This has top priority, refer anyone who gets in your way to me. Good night.'

Several hundred miles further south, Guy was lying wide awake, trying to fathom how to get sight of the secret plant and more to the point, how to destroy it. Switching on the bedside lamp, he retrieved the map from its hiding place in the housing for the central heating pump and studied it in minute detail with a magnifying glass, taking particular note of the contour lines of both the plant area and the mountains opposite. Fifteen minutes later, happy with his findings, he returned the map to its concealment.

Raoul had watchers reporting on the disposition of troops protecting the site. His intelligence was that they were concentrated on the approach up into the mountain area, with a mere handful elsewhere. Such was the terrain that any approach, let alone an attack from other than the road leading directly to the plant, was nigh on impossible.

A day later, Guy and Raoul threaded their way into the hills opposite and overlooking the site. At this altitude, thick snow lay everywhere and they had to use a circuitous route through the trees not to be observed. Guy dipped into the knapsack and pulled out a monocular. Never in his life had he handled an optic like this one. So powerful was the magnification, you would swear that you could see the pimples on a gnat's bottom at a thousand yards. It took some manoeuvring, including climbing halfway up a pine tree, before he could focus the objective lens on the doors to the plant. The detail through the monocular was crystal-clear, superb in its clarity. As he watched, a truck rumbled into view. Using the turning space hewn from the rock by the Germans, the vehicle reversed up to the doors, stopping short to allow an electric fork-lift truck to drive up to the tailboard to unload crates, crates which were very familiar to Guy. Positioned thus, the lorry did not impede Guy's view of the doors. Resting his monocular on a branch and careful not to let any light reflect off the lens, Guy focused on the doors. Double doors made of steel and as they swung open, he had a clear shot at the edges. He estimated their thickness at about three or four inches, built to keep any escaping gases in check, rather to withstand blast. Thick black rubber gaskets on each door confirmed their task as sealing the plant from the outside world. Nonetheless, a formidable obstacle. Which led Guy to speculate as to an inner wall, forming an airlock.

Above the doors, two stacks rose upwards, one much longer than the other. They appeared to be the intake and exhaust for the ventilation system, with presumably the exhaust the higher to avoid suckback of anything nasty. On the left wall of the defile, he could make out the thick black placenta of the mains cable.

By climbing slightly higher up the tree, Guy could refocus on the hutted camp, an enclave of wooden buildings. Lowryesque figures swathed against the chill moved between the huts and a number of trucks, kubelwagens and half-tracks were dotted around the edge of the encampment. In the far left corner lay the two generator buildings Guy had seen on the aerial shots. Black smoke from only one exhaust and the rainflap jiggling in the pressure from the pipe confirmed that only one was online at any one time. A stout welded mesh fence and matching gates guarded against intruders.

OK, so now he knew the layout, but the means of destruction was still a million miles away. It would take a whole battalion to storm that redoubt, which could be held against many by very few for months on end.

Chastened, Guy and Raoul travelled back to Clermont Ferrand for a council of war, but it proved a fruitless council.

Three days later, Raoul appeared at the flat, scarcely able to contain his excitement.

'I've found somebody who I think may be able to help, one of my farmer contacts mentioned him, so I took a chance and went to see him. You're at his place tomorrow, he lives in St Nectaire, about five miles from the site. His name is Gilbert Montigny.'

Later the next morning and several Tour de France ascents into the snowladen mountains, Guy found himself outside a comfortable house in the town of St Nectaire. He knocked at the oak front door. It was opened by a man in his early sixties. The word 'rangy' probably described him best. About Guy's height, he was big-framed, no spare meat, pretty fit. A tanned, weather-beaten complexion spoke of years working outdoors and crinkles around the eyes of many hours spent gazing at a thousand horizons. He could have been a mariner.

'Hugo?'

'Gilbert'?

They shook hands and Guy was ushered inside to a cosy sitting room with a wood fire blazing cheerfully in the grate. A small white kitten lay in front of the warmth, toasting its sleek belly on the welcome flames. Guy tickled the cat's tummy, for which his reward was his finger grabbed by the tiny creature's front paws and his palm assaulted by the twin pistons of the back paws moving in a blur.

'Coffee?'

Guy nodded. Gilbert returned from the kitchen minutes later with the customary acorn brew and Guy allowed the liquid to soak the chill from his bones before starting a conversation.

'Raoul tells me you can help?'

Gilbert nodded and leaning forward, picked an envelope from the low table in front of him.

'Just to make things clear, this is where we're talking about?'

He tilted the brown manila and four photographs dropped onto the table. They were sharp images. One showed the cave entrance before the Nazis had installed doors; the second the archway into the defile, the third a view of the defile and the cave entrance from the slope to the left of the crevasse and the fourth a view of the archway from the defile itself. Inwardly, Guy smiled hugely, these were an intelligence dream. He was surprised to see that the photos were quite recent, the paper on which they were printed still fresh and white, not yellowed with age.

Gilbert sensed the inward smile.

'Do you know anything about me?'

Guy shook his head.

'I was, I guess still am, a geologist. My father was a master shotfirer for a local quarry company. I left school at 15 and joined him, learned the trade, but I was bored, realised I could do better. But

307

I loved rocks, so I went to college, studied as a geologist. Then I joined a French oil company. I got headhunted by an American outfit and spent many years in Texas and Louisiana. I can say 'Y'all be careful, d'y'hear' with the best of them.' His Texas accent was pretty good and made Guy smile once more.

'Know much about oil exploration?'

Guy shook his head once more.

Gilbert himself smiled, but it was a rueful smile.

'Unless someone discovers oil under the Champs Elysée or Piccadilly or Times Square, then all the exploration and drilling will continue to be in the land God gave to Cain. I've travelled the world, from having my nuts frozen off in Siberia to being roasted almost black in Arabia. You think this is cold?'

His gesture indicated the white landscape beyond his living-room window.

'This is a very warm day in Siberia. In winter, you get minus 50, minus 60, even minus 70 out on the steppes. It's so cold, either you work 20 minutes out, 20 minutes in, or else you stop altogether. It's so freezing, steel changes its crystalline structure and snaps. In the desert, you can be talking 40 degrees, too hot for anyone to work, so you start before sunrise, pack it in around noon until late afternoon, then get stuck in again come evening. I'll tell you, if the world had piles, they'd have them in most of the places I've explored and drilled. Weeks on end in some godforsaken spot miles from the nearest civilisation. When you do reach civilisation, you spend all you've just saved pissing it up against a wall.'

Gilbert paused.

'I retired in '38. I'm pretty fit, but that kind of life takes its toll and I figured that I'd made a tidy pile, so why not enjoy it?'

'How old are you now?' enquired Guy.

'Sixty-five.'

'OK, so how can you help, Gilbert?'

'My love of rocks extends into caving, I'm a speleologist. I learned all the local caves as a boy, now I spend my retirement exploring them all over again. I think I have the answer to your problem, but I need to show you. Those photos, incidentally, were taken in 1941, long before Fritz was here in any numbers.'

Gilbert rose and gestured to Guy to follow him. In the back porch lay two white snowsuits. Seeing Guy's quizzical expression, Gilbert explained.

'We were drilling in Siberia. The locals took exception to the

Yanks, thought they were stealing their birthright, so they started taking potshots at the crew. We bought the snowsuits as camouflage. Then we got lucky, their school and the church next door got burnt down, so we built them new ones of stone, all mod cons, and spread some baksheesh, problem solved. But I kept the snowsuits. Stick yours in your rucksack for the moment.'

So saying, he handed Guy a rucksack. Guy peered inside. It contained a caver's suit and helmet, a lamp, several batteries, some lengths of rope, pitons and a hammer. Guy stuffed the snowsuit on top.

After donning boots and outdoor clothing, Gilbert led the way outside and they began to climb into the mountains. For the first few miles, they could keep to woodland and concealment, but as they neared the target area, it became more open and they stopped to don the suits. Then Gilbert was once more leading them higher and higher, but to the east of the target. Fit as he was, Guy had to work hard to match his leader's pace cross-country. Part way up a mountain, Gilbert stopped and laid down his pack.

'Take off your snowsuit and hide it in that rock crevice,' he instructed. Guy did as he was bidden, then followed Gilbert's lead in wriggling into his caving suit, putting on his helmet and light and plugging in a battery.

'Follow me.'

It was a command, not an invitation.

Before Guy's eyes, Gilbert dived into a crack in the ground seemingly no bigger than a rabbit hole. Once again, fear gripped as claustrophobia took over, but Guy did as he was told and pushing his pack before him, slid after his guide. The fissure was actually bigger than it looked and some twenty metres later, Guy found himself in a cavern. The walls were white and encrusted with calcium, water dripped everywhere and stalactites and stalagmites abounded.

For the next hour or so, Gilbert led Guy through cave after cave, apparently impenetrable crack after impenetrable crack. Some of the caves were like the first, rimed with a glistening whitewash of calcium, some were quite dry. Guy initially worried how he would get out if his guide was injured or, God forbid, had a heart attack, but his fears were groundless. At the far side of each transit, Gilbert hammered in a miniature piton with a green luminous disc attached, so that the luminescence would be easily seen in the total blackness and guide towards safety.

'Right, we won't be able to hear ourselves speak in a minute, so just follow me, take it all in, then we'll come back here, OK?'

Guy nodded assent before trailing Gilbert through yet another labyrinth. The further they penetrated, the louder the noise became, until they emerged into a small cave reminiscent of a box at the theatre. Except that theatre was not the right description, a Metro or Tube station was much nearer the mark. About five metres below them, a torrent emerged from one tunnel mouth, screamed through the precipitous cavern and rocketed out through a near identical tunnel at the downhill end, a frothing, threatening floodtide in the beam of Gilbert's powerful handlantern. Guy estimated the width of the river at about six or seven metres and unable to be heard above the noise, held his hands one above the other in the time-honoured 'How deep?' gesture. Gilbert responded with five or six fingers, waggling one palm to indicate approximation.

The cavern was just like a Tube station, but with no platforms. Steep, near vertical sides led down to the surging waters. Above their heads, the sides rose another two metres. Above each tunnel was a near vertical wall. Gilbert pointed back the way they had just come and they retreated. Once away from the deafening noise, Guy could speak and be heard.

Now in the peace of a dry cave, Gilbert took a map from the side pocket of his rucksack and spread it out on a convenient piece of rock. Setting the lantern as illumination, he stabbed his forefinger at the crevasse that housed the Nazi plant.

'That's the target, right?'

'Yup.'

'This is our cavern, where we've just been.'

His finger pointed at a spot almost opposite the far end of the crevasse.

As soon as he had entered the cavern and seen the boiling spate, Guy had clicked instantly what was in Gilbert's mind. The question was, how to divert those onrushing waters from their subterranean main into the defile and even more important, how to flood the nerve gas plant. Those doors looked pretty chunky, built to withstand attack.

Guy spoke. 'Your idea is to use the river to flood the crevasse and the workings, isn't it?'

'Got it in one,' replied Gilbert. 'I'll explain.'

'I've been fascinated by this underground river ever since I saw it for the first time over twenty years ago. When I retired, I started coming here regularly with a lightweight rope ladder and all the climbing kit. I hooked up the ladder so that I could get down to water level. The river's about seven metres wide, five or six deep, so let's say 35 cubic metres of water if you take a slice. I've measured the depth using rods that screw together in sections and pitons hammered into the rock to steady them as I lowered them into the current. I was intrigued how fast the waters ran, so I measured the speed as well. I brought up some chunks of wood I'd painted white. Then I rigged pitons and a boltrope for my feet so that I could walk along one wall of the cave and I used my rods to calculate the length between the tunnel mouths – it's thirty metres, give or take. I shone my torch on the downstream tunnel mouth, dropped a piece of wood at the upstream one and used a stopwatch to time how long it took to transit the cave. It's a very short time, so I repeated the wood trick several times and averaged the times I got.'

Gilbert's scientific approach was impressive and Guy said so. Gilbert inclined his head to acknowledge the compliment, then tugging a pad and pencil from his backpack, he began to write and sketch.

'So, 35 cubic metres of water. The speed is 40kph, eleven metres a second, so about 400 cubic metres per second, 23,000 cubic metres a minute. That's one heck of a lot of water.'

'Do you know the dimensions of the crevasse?' asked Guy. The older man raised his eyebrows in mock horror as if insulted that he might not know these vital statistics. With his face lit from below by the lantern, he looked a little ghoulish anyway.

'110 metres long, eight metres wide on average, eighty metres deep, so around 70,000 cubic metres in all.'

Guy's maths were never a strong point, but even he did not need a calculator to work out that the water would flood the crevasse in just about three minutes.

'Knowing you Gilbert, you'll have the formula for the water pressure at ground level once we flood the crevasse?'

A slightly wolfish grin reminiscent of André's played briefly over the geologist's face, then a quick calculation on his pad.

'About 7.5 bar.'

As a Frenchman brought up and educated in France, Guy could only do maths in French, not English, but his maths teacher had teased him about his English side and had taught the whole class about gallons, pounds per square inch and all those 'funny measurements les rosbifs insist on using' as his teacher put it.

'Can I borrow your pad?'

Gilbert obligingly handed over the pad and pencil. One cubic metre of water was 220 gallons, so translated to English, 23,000 cubic metres became 5 million gallons per minute. The pressure of 7.5 bar became around 110 psi. From Guy's observations through his monocular, comparing the height of the soldiers to that of the doors, he guesstimated the doors and frame to be four metres wide and three high. He scribbled furiously. The final figure for the pressure the doors would face staggered him – about 900 tons. It seemed incredibly high, so he passed the pad to Gilbert to check the calculations.

'Seem spot on to me,' was Gilbert's response. 'Question is, how thick the doors are and how they're anchored?'

'I could just see dog-bolts on the hinged edges, so probably on top and bottom as well. The doors are about 75-100 millimetres thick,' said Guy, then explained how he and Raoul had observed the site through the monocular.

Guy was deep in thought, very deep.

'So how do we divert the river to flow into the crevasse, then?'

'I've actually scaled the far wall of the cavern as well, bit hairy, but possible.'

Guy had a mental picture of tumbling into that maelstrom, either drowned in seconds or more likely, dashed to a pulp on the walls of the tunnel.

'You like living dangerously, don't you?' he remarked.

That incline of the head once more.

'I found a small fissure showing daylight. You can only see it from a certain angle. I took over my rods and fixed a luminous disc to one end, then pushed them up the aperture and jammed them in place. By taking compass bearings inside these caves, I had a fairly accurate picture of the location, but when I went out onto the slope the next day to find the fissure, it took me over two hours of a square search to locate it. I lowered a weighted line down the hole and gave it plenty of slack to make sure it reached the bottom, tied it off at the top, then went caving again.'

Guy found the amount of effort Gilbert had expended to satisfy his curiosity quite astounding.

'The answer to your question is that the rock is around five metres thick, but only for a distance of ten metres from just this side of the upstream tunnel mouth. After that, an outcrop at least doubles that. If we can block the exit tunnel then blow that far wall, you'll have a French Niagara to give Fritz wet feet.'

Gilbert stared at Guy, his eyes almost burning into Guy's very soul.

'What are they doing that's so damned vital to destroy. Come on, tell me, please.'

Guy stared back.

'I can't, I simply can't. All I can tell you I that if we annihilate those workings, we'll save thousands of lives. You have to trust me.'

A deep sigh, then Gilbert was sketching again.

'As I told you, I was a trained shotfirer in a quarry. That wall is limestone, not that strong. If we place charges here, here and here...'

The pencil dashed across the paper.

'...We can bring down the walls and roof and block that exit tunnel. Then here, here, here and here, that'll blast open the wall and release the water. How are we going to crack open those doors?'

Which, Guy had to admit, was the $64,000 question. His brain mentally ranged across the whole target area. When it reached the natural dam at the end nearest the encampment, a light suddenly came on in his little grey cells.

On arrival back in Blighty after his escape from Le Mans, all the papers had been abuzz with the success of the Dambusters raid and how they had used the water to magnify the percussive effect of the bombs to create a water hammer. If the steel doors could take the water pressure from the flood, they surely could not withstand the force of underwater mines if placed close enough. But placing those mines would be extraordinarily tricky with a torrent hurtling down the mountain.

'Gilbert, let's go back,' said Guy. 'I have an idea, but we need to check if it's feasible.'

Map, pad and pencil were stowed, then it was backtrack, backtrack, backtrack. Gilbert's little beacons stood out in the blackness of the caverns, guiding them to that final rabbit burrow and safety. Dusk was falling as they emerged, blinking like pitponies, but even so, they still used the snowsuits until they reached cover.

Back at the ranch, Gilbert cooked a simple meal and with vim and vigour restored, they fell to planning.

Guy outlined his idea about the mines, explaining the Dambusters raid and the principle, but Gilbert's immediate reaction was the same as Guy's, how to place the charges accurately with a massive waterfall gushing downhill. When they had kitted up to go caving, Guy had seen pile upon pile of old newspapers in a small pantry near the porch.

'We can use your photos to make a model of the area, then pour water down it to simulate the flood. If we dye the water, we can see the effect and the currents and so on.'

Gilbert disappeared to his shed, to emerge with a large sheet of thick plywood. Like nursery school kids, they fell to making papier-mâché in a couple of tin buckets. There was something quite satisfying about plunging your hands and forearms in a bucket of grey, sticky gloop. Gilbert laid out his photos on the kitchen table and inch by inch, they created a scale model of the mountain and the crevasse. It took a lot longer than they anticipated and it was gone midnight when they put the finishing touches, scrubbed the bits from their paws and hit the sack. The model was deposited by the fire to dry it out. Despite leaving the fire well stoked, it took until the following afternoon before it was dry enough to varnish against the water to be poured on it.

Anticipating he might be with Gilbert for a few days, Guy had packed both clothes and some food, so he could supplement Gilbert's rations.

By next morning, the model was ready. The Montigny garden hose provided a controllable water source, set to fill the mock crevasse in about three minutes. Coffee grounds were mixed with water to provide a dye and with Gilbert on water and Guy observing, they experimented. Two key findings emerged. One was that the as the water naturally ran downhill, away from the cave end of the defile, it created a calmer area immediately above the cave mouth. The water outside the cave doors was similarly tranquil. The second was that if they blew a slightly smaller gap in the wall of the cavern and left a section of the cavern wall nearest the upstream tunnel intact, the outfall streamed away from the cave mouth and the doors. By using rubber dinghies on tethering lines firmly secured to the slope above and to the east of the cave mouth, they could lower the mines down to the target.

But, Guy still was not satisfied. He needed those mines as close to the doors as possible. He put his problem to Gilbert, who scratched his head and went to make coffee.

'Fancy a dram in that?' he asked. 'I still have a drop or two of bourbon from my time in the US of A.' He turned to the sideboard and lowered the flap to reveal a smattering of bottles.

'Got it!'

Guy's eureka moment came out as a shout of pure triumph.

'What?'

'Look at your cabinet. What secures the flap?'

'Ah, magnets!'

'Precisely. If we can magnetise the mines, we have a good chance of them actually sticking to the steel doors.'

'Electromagnets would be better still,' remarked Gilbert. 'Any chance you could get hold of some?'

'Dunno,' replied Guy, 'the boffins in England come up with better and better gizmos all the time, I'll just have to ask.'

'And the explosives?' enquired Gilbert, 'it would take a stack of dynamite to do what we have in mind.'

'We'll use plastic. You ever used plastic explosive, Gilbert?'

'No, dynamite and jelly were my tools. We used dynamite for the seismographs.'

'Can you explain, please?' was the rejoinder.

Gilbert outlined that since the early '30s, geologists had been using seismographs to more accurately locate oil-bearing strata. Dynamite was embedded in the ground at pre-set points, then set off. The waves from the explosion reflected off the ground beneath and were recorded by a seismograph. Reading the plotted lines gave a much clearer picture of the best place or places to drill.

'But like most things, it's still more of an art than a science,' remarked the geologist. 'We drilled less dry wells for sure, but the instincts of some of the wildcatters for the right spot saved us a heap of dry holes.'

By late afternoon, Guy was back in the flat. He had never transmitted from the flat or the garden in case the German detection system locked on to him. What he had done was to locate several empty houses within easy reach of the flat. Taking the radio on the back of his bike was a risk, but by using the network of alleyways, he could travel quite a distance in relative safety. He would then pick the locks on the houses, hook up to their electricity supplies and call London. That could be quite risky if the electricity company has removed the main fuse, but he got used to jumping the incomer using crocodile clips.

Now his Morse key rattled as he outlined his needs. London told him to call again in two days, so he concealed the set in what appeared to be firewood on his bike carrier and pedalled home, to stash the transmitter in the Renault once again.

Two nights later, Guy had another sked. London would arrange a drop of mines fitted with timers, not barostatic switches, and some electromagnets that hung from the bottom of each mine on a chain. Each magnet was quite powerful, each energised by an internal battery that switched on automatically as the magnet was immersed in water. But – and it was a big but – the high current demanded to energise the magnets meant the batteries lasted ten minutes at most, less in cold water where the batteries were less efficient. Sufficient plastic of the latest Knutsen genre, together with the detonator boxes used at Laval, many yards of shock cord and three inflatable dinghies, one as a spare, would be included in the drop to a farm south of the target area.

That evening, Guy sought out Raoul.

After a couple of wind-down beers, they retreated chez Raoul, who was agog to hear the latest. Slowly, carefully, Guy went through the plan, blowing the cavern, flooding the crevasse, blasting open the doors and inundating the works.

Raoul's nose wrinkled in concern.

'Will that release poisons or something nasty into the locality?'

'No,' affirmed Guy, 'it won't.'

'How many will it take to do the job?' asked Raoul.

'Good question. I think four to lay the explosives in the cavern. They'll need to chisel out the holes, so it's quite a few hours' work and they have to be out to confirm that they've been successful before we gear up to do our part.'

Guy was in planning mode.

'We'll need two in each dinghy, the mines weigh 25 kilos each and the magnets 10 kilos each and there will be three mines per dinghy. Then we'll have to have three men ashore to pull us back in against the current once we've planted the mines. Hmm, four in the cavern, four for the dinghies, three ashore, so eleven in all. I suggest you and me in one boat, you're pretty strong and we'll need that kind of strength. A similar pair in the other boat. And the cavern guys, Gilbert will lead, but climbing above that torrent is not for the faint-hearted, knowing that one slip is curtains.'

Raoul's mind was also in overdrive.

'Twelve.'

'How so?'

'One to cut the telephone wire to the camp. We spotted the cable on our foray and you said that with the flaky radio reception in the mountains, the Nazis were bound to rely on a landline to call the cavalry.'

'Bless you,' Guy's voice was warm with gratitude at Raoul's foresight.

'OK, Guillaume and Robert in Dinghy 2, Jean-Paul, Helene and Philippe in the cavern with Gilbert. Both Jean-Paul and Helene are mountaineers, so they know how to climb and they won't be fazed by the risk. Philippe can't climb, but he's a strong lad, so he can help carry all the gear and sort out the food and drink to keep them going. Jean-Michel to cut the cable, he lives not far below the camp.'

'Can you arrange the pickup from the drop and we'll need to meet to plan the operation.'

'You betcha, see you tomorrow night,' came the enthusiastic response.

Two nights later, a Halifax throttled back over a DZ south of Clermont Ferrand, flying along the line of torches on the ground. Three containers drifted earthwards, where very willing hands buried the parachutes and bore the booty away to a secure hiding place.

Twelve figures sat around a scrubbed deal table in the kitchen of the farm where the drop had taken place. Guy looked round at a mix of excitement, fear, anxiousness, perhaps dread. He cleared his throat.

'The mission we are about to undertake is vital to the war effort. For security reasons, I am bound to keep from you the true nature of what is going on in that cave, but I do assure you that if we destroy the operation, it will mean the difference between victory and defeat.'

Eleven pairs of eyes were out on stalks at his words.

'Right, let's start planning.'

Guy pulled a sheet from the model and began his briefing.

'We are going to flood the Nazi plant to destroy it. There's a huge underground river in the mountain above this crevasse and there's a cavern in the mountain that provides access to the river. We plan to block the downstream end of the cavern, blow out one wall and flood the crevasse. Then we plant electromagnetic mines to blow the doors to the plant and the inundation will do the rest.'

'Jean-Michel, you cut the wire at 1155 precisely. The cavern will have its first explosion at midnight, that will block the exit tunnel and the water will fill the cavern. A minute later, the cavern wall will blow and we calculate the Niagara will fill the crevasse in perhaps two minutes, maybe three. We've deliberately set the explosion to leave a relatively calm area over the doors. The cavern team will be Gilbert, Jean-Paul, Hélène and Philippe. That team have to report to us before we go to Stage 2, blowing the doors. Then the dinghies will be launched to plant the mines. Raoul and I will be in Dinghy 1, Guillaume and Robert in Dinghy 2, Albert, Yves and Marcel on shore to pull us back in once we signal that the charges have been laid.'

Helene had a question.

'There's the entrance to the crevasse, surely that will let the water out?'

'Yes, some,' said Guy, 'but we're talking millions of litres a minute and that tiny gap will be like a little boy peeing compared to the influx. And,' he continued, 'it's almost certain that lumps of rock will jam the opening anyway. That underground river is just awesome.'

'All of you,' directed Guy at the dinghy crews, 'will carry pitons, a hammer and some rope. If you do get thrown out, your chances are slim, but at least it gives you a chance to get clear if you do make the shore.'

Again and again, they studied the model and Gilbert's photos, discussed and rehearsed the timings, looked at possible difficulties. Yet again, Guy had to reassure them that nothing harmful would spill from the plant once the doors were breached.

They arranged that Albert, the farmer, would provide the truck to carry the explosives, equipment and most of the personnel to the target. Guy had driven up to the farm with Raoul in a Citroen provided by Raoul and this would be their transport to safety once the job was done. Officially, Raoul had la grippe, so was not expected at work.

They examined the explosives and equipment, familiarising themselves with it prior to H-day, set for the evening after next.

Much as the day before the raid at Laval all those months ago, Guy's stomach was turning catherine wheels all the day before the raid. How were the cavern party getting on, that was the key to the whole thing.

Using Gilbert's home as a base, the party set out at 0530. Whipped on by Gilbert, they had force marched across country to make the RV before dawn and the need for snowsuits, as Gilbert possessed but two. Albert, helped by Philippe, had humped all the gear to the entrance. The party moved all the equipment into the first cave, then portaged it to the cavern, but there was a great deal to move and it took over two hours. Then Gilbert, Jean-Paul and Helene built a rope bridge above the upstream tunnel mouth and similar contraptions on both walls. The rock might have been limestone and in rock terms, quite soft, but hacking out the holes for the explosive was an Herculean task and progress was very slow. Even the fit Gilbert found that an hour was the maximum he could manage before taking a rest. Philippe manfully provided soup, coffee, sandwiches and encouragement.

The underground team had started work at 0900, but it was 2100 before the explosives were packed and tamped, the maze of shock cord wired and the timers set. Then an hour to clear the caverns and forty minutes hard slog to yomp over the mountains to the waiting inland mariners.

Chapter 17

The would-be matelots lay concealed on the slope overlooking the crevasse. At 2030, they had checked all their equipment for the umpteenth time, cross-checking each other and at 2100, had moved stealthily to the target site. Piled beside them lay six mines, six magnets and two spares, three black dinghies and their gas inflation bottles, yards of rope as tethering lines for mines and boats, pitons, hammers, ropes and razor-sharp sheath knives. The weather was at its worst, a snowstorm driven hard before a knife-like wind. Visibility was practically non-existent, the temperature well into the minuses.

Guy peered through his night glasses, trying in vain to see the cavern party. All he could discern were snowflakes. Both he and his party were covered in whiteness, bereft of shelter from the violent storm. Again and again, he looked at his watch, willing the caverners to appear and report success.

Unseen in the murk, the cavern party suddenly appeared at 2340.

'Bingo,' was Gilbert's cryptic but oh-so-vital comment.

'OK, now for the big one,' was Guy's equally cryptic response.

With frozen fingers, everyone lent a hand to inflate all the dinghies, attach the tethering lines to boat and shore alike and place the mines and magnets aboard the little craft. Each sailor wound a rope around his chest and buckled on a belt carrying pitons, hammer and sheath-knife.

As if on cue, the snow abated, offering a clear view of the mountain where lay the cavern wall.

Guy stared at his luminous watch, the seconds to midnight like aeons. Midnight came and went. Now everyone was in agonies of apprehension. Was it all going to be for naught? At precisely ten seconds after midnight, there was a dull thud and the ground beneath them shuddered. At midnight plus fifteen seconds, a far bigger explosion vibrated through the rock and the whole mountainside rocked. Strung up like a taut bowstring, Guy focused his nightglasses on the snowbound slope. Nothing but nothing moved, it was just an unruffled carpet of white flakes. Then without warning, the patch of snow began to heave and a thin jet of water spurted upwards. Slowly,

slowly, the bulge intensified and more water jets blasted skywards.

What happened next was spectacular. With a sound like a cannon exploding, a massive lump of rock weighing many tons was catapulted into the air and hurled into the night chill, to land further down the slope and rumble into the canyon at its base. A monster fountain of water jetted skywards, so high it disappeared from view, to fall into the crevasse with unerring accuracy. As the party watched, the crevasse filled at an unholy speed and within three minutes, water was beginning to flood over the top of the dam at the forward end. Such was the volume of the torrent, a pool began to form below their feet and the dinghies were launched, complete with deadly cargo.

Out of their sight, events occurred at lightning speed. At the archway, the flood fired out a rock weighing over half a ton as though it were a pea from a peashooter. The missile struck the bonnet of a truck parked near the offline generator, spinning it like a top and smashing it into the generator's diesel tank. The diesel tank split asunder, as did the truck's petrol tank, mixing the two volatile liquids. Torn from its tray, the battery shorted and emitted a November 5th display of sparks, igniting the fuel mix with an explosive 'Whoosh'. Anyone who has never witnessed the heat, smoke and fumes that even a few litres of a petrol/diesel mix can blast out would have been staggered at the magnitude of this conflagration. Now the deadly river poured beneath the huts immediately below it, to then dart hungrily across the narrow road to the huts on that side. With very limited space, the Nazis had been forced to allow very narrow breaks between buildings and now the flames vaulted greedily from hut to hut, grasping the flammable wood into their fiery maw. Within seconds, all the buildings were ablaze, their occupants emerging with clothes and hair on fire, to find only a sizzling lake without. Some dived through windows, but in vain, the whole site was engulfed. The colonel in charge did somehow make it to the field telephone in his office, but his frantic crankings produced nothing, Jean-Michel had performed. Rooted to the spot, the officer was hurled through his own office window by a fireball from the orderly office next door to die an agonising death, burned to a crisp. But the online generator, unscathed above the burning lake, purred contentedly, pumping volts and watts as intended.

Eighty metres above the conflagration, the two dinghies jostled to position themselves. The three onshore rope handlers, Albert, Yves and Marcel, supplemented by the cavern crew, hauled manfully on the tethers. The model that Guy and Gilbert had crafted was fairly accurate and indeed, the current above the cave mouth was less, but the powerful suction from the torrent sweeping down the mountain threatened to snatch the little ships and hurl them over the dam above the camp. The waters, disturbed and choppy, bounced the dinghies like balloons at a funfair shooting gallery. The raiders quickly found that pulling the boats together and acting as one was far easier on the occupants and helpers alike and with a great deal of to-ing and fro-ing, they finally inched into position.

Guillaume and Robert worked in concert, clipping on the magnets, setting the timers and then one by one, carefully lowering their mines into the void beneath their keels. Guy and Raoul held the boats steady by adjusting the tethers in unison with the shore party. Then the compliment was returned, the stocky Raoul using all his strength to place his charges as near the doors as he could. But, it was blind fishing and lady luck had to play a considerable part if the doors were to be breached.

Raoul was lowering the final mine into position when it snagged on a rock in the crevasse. Playing it like a fish and acutely conscious that the clocks were ticking, Raoul winkled the sphere free and began to lower once more.

At that instant, the mine exploded. Now some fifty feet down in the crevasse, 25 kilos of Erik's finest blew its top. Trapped by the sides of the crevasse, the enormous force vented upwards, producing a spectacular column of water like some giant whalespout and a shockwave like a monster steamhammer. The waterspout rocketed the two dinghies in the air and for a split second, both craft were supported on a column of liquid before the tethering lines snatched at both vessels, turning them turtle and spilling the occupants into the freezing maelstrom.

Down in the camp, the few survivors of the inferno had been praying for water to douse the flames. Their prayers were partly answered when the waters flooded over the wall of the dam, but the unwanted effect of the growing tidal wave was to wash people, huts and vehicles down the steep mountainside. The explosion from the mine created its own tsunami, which like a colossal surfing wave, curled over the dam and smashed onto the camp below. The waters snuffed out the generator in a trice as the humming engine sucked incompressible liquid into its iron lungs. Rising pistons met immovable water and in a welter of bent conrods and snapped crankshaft, the engine self-destructed.

Now the might of the flood swept away not only charred timbers, scorched bodies and blazing vehicles, now it unseated even the generators from their concrete bases, tumbling them downhill like giant footballs. One German technician, horribly burned, bruised, shocked and disorientated, found himself five metres up in a pine tree on the mountain slope. He had not the slightest recollection or idea of how he came to be there. Sensing an object above him even in his traumatised condition, he glanced upwards. The cartwheeling generator was the last thing he ever saw, as it careered into the trunk below him, snapping it like a giant matchstick and catapulting the hapless tree-hugger from his eyrie towards the valley floor and a violent end hundreds of feet below.

Inside the gas plant, a young Wehrmacht sentry stood guard. Horst Kring was twenty-three, now miles away from his home on the Bodensee and Helga, his new fiancée. Dressed in a zoot suit complete with hood and a self-contained air supply from a backpack tank inside the suit, he was totally petrified. The first indication of trouble was when water began to pour from the outlets and intakes for the ventilation system and in seconds, the waters began to rise above his ankles. Then the doors began to creak ominously and although the massive dog-bolts held, the gargantuan pressure from outside forced the doors from their seatings. Water was now gushing into the airlock in which he stood. Horror rooted him to the spot, but with superhuman resolve, he dived for the field telephone connecting him to the camp. Vigorous cranking produced no response and had he known of the devastation beyond the archway, he would have been still more panic-stricken if that were at all possible.

Even though the sixth mine's pre-emptive detonation was 50 metres above the doors, it sent a mighty bolt of energy through the inundated crevice. A hand of supernatural power pushed against the doors, bending and stretching the dog-bolts and their operating rods, bulging and bowing the massive doors inwards like sheets of tinplate. Still the doors held, snapping back into shape, but as they bulged, so water cascaded through the openings. The creaking and groaning from doors, frames, hinges and bolts intensified as they entered their death throes.

Now composed as he faced inevitable death, his ears detected a faint clang on the outside of the doors. Although commonsense would have told him that help was totally impossible, his brain was miles away from being logical and walking to the doors, he tried to turn the wheels that undogged the bolts. With such pressure, they budged not one jot.

His one ray of hope was that the lights were still working, suggesting that the camp and help were still in business. Then the lights were snuffed out, leaving only an eerie greenish glow from the emergency system.

Clamped limpet-like to the steel by their powerful magnets, the first two mines detonated, setting off the third in a sympathetic explosion. One moment, Horst was a living, breathing human being; the next, he was an insignificant blood smear on the concrete as the doors and frame were wrenched from their mountings and punched into the chamber to squash the young man like a beetle underfoot. The fifth mine exploded, but it was superfluous.

'Awesome' and 'stupendous' were simply grossly inadequate words to describe the lethal, malevolent, cataclysmic force that fired its gigantic water cannon into a natural tunnel around four metres in diameter. The very constriction of that tunnel magnified the pressure to unimaginable levels. Ironically, it was the Germans' own equipment that did the most damage. To move heavy crates and equipment up and down the twenty metre tunnel to the cave housing the plant, the Boche had installed roller trackway on trestles. Each section of track hooked on to its neighbour, each section weighed in at 90 kilos. The onrushing liquid thunderbolt snatched the rollers, punching the sections into the tunnel until they met the steel wall separating plant from tunnel. Constructed to provide a gas-tight seal not impregnability, the steel was annihilated by over two and a half tons of flying metal, which punctured the skin as though it were tinfoil. Driven by the torrent, the track sections whirled and snaked around the cave, pulverising people, lacerating lines, razing retorts.

The staff of the plant had been suffering identical traumas to young Horst. Their first indication of trouble had also been water flooding in via the ventilation system and they too had jumped to the phone, to find only deathly silence at the far end of the line. All the staff were dressed as Horst, in hooded zoot suits with internal air supplies from backpack bottles. To avoid carrying too much weight, each bottle had to be changed every four hours in a positive-pressure room built in one corner of the cave. The next change time for every staff member was chalked on a stateboard and as an extra precaution, a gauge on a flexible pipe was held in a celluloid pocket at the front of the suit. Rather like a nurse's watch, the faces were upside down so the user could see his or her own gauge, but a red section indicating that the bottle was near exhaustion was clearly visible to colleagues.

Thus the inrush of water did not immediately drown the fifteen scientists and technicians on shift, but within a matter of seconds, all bar three had been crushed, pulped, decapitated or torn limb from limb by 90 kilo steel lumps being hurled willy-nilly around the cave. One man was sliced neatly in two by a section of trackway that arrowed at him like some horizontal guillotine; another was macerated against the rear wall of the cave by two sections that hit him broadside.

Only the four electrolysis machines stood up to the onslaught, largely because of their position out of the line of fire. Everything else was smashed or torn from its mountings by the lethal combination of whirling steel dervishes and pulverising water scour. True, dented but unbowed, the pressure vessels into which the nerve gas was pumped did withstand the onslaught, but all the feeder pipework was split and ruptured and the deadly vapour seeped harmlessly into the floodtide.

But, unknown to those both above and below, fate had one last card to play. Mine four had failed to detonate, lying like some ominous, oversized cricket ball near the cave mouth. The explosion of the other mines removed its tethering line but not the electromagnet. With the path now clear of any obstructions, it was swept into the cave by the onrushing waters and slammed against the back wall with a savage impact. That shock re-awoke the somnolent timer that had caused it to hang fire and the backwash from the cave walls rolled the deadly sphere under the second electrolysis machine, where it fastened itself resolutely to a steel stanchion.

For the final time in this sketch, Erik's chemical magic took centre stage. The mine erupted. With the hammer effect provided by the waters, the explosion was intensified and the machine immediately above the sphere splintered into a million pieces of shrapnel. The machines either side were shattered and destroyed to unrecognisable metal fragments and any remaining life in the cavern was snuffed out by the enormous pressure wave from the detonation.

With the cave now flooded, the torrent was spent. An underwater observer would now have been able to see a slightly uneasy soup, a vile broth whose recipe was a suspension of bodies, bits of bodies, a snowstorm of paper, a laboratory stool now devoid of three of its four legs, but bizarrely with its cushion still attached, shattered planks from equally shattered crates, empty chemical drums, bits of protective suits, a peasoup of animal, vegetable and mineral flotsam and jetsam. Somehow, God knows how, some of the emergency lights had survived the devastation and cast their ghoulish glow through the troubled waters. Das Fabrik war ganz kaput.

As the dinghies tipped over and spilled their passengers into the water, Guy was vaguely aware of his three companions tumbling through the air. He never saw them again. All three were swept to their deaths, fired over the dam wall and down the mountainside. Guy survived simply because he was holding on to a tethering line to keep the dinghy in position for Raoul, the rope snaked around his right wrist. When the boat was thrown skywards, he was still attached firmly to it by one arm, to land back on the water with the underside of the dinghy between himself and the surface. The impact drove all breath from his body, but whilst it did cushion the fall, it also tore the line from his grasp as he landed; he was swept away by the current.

The water was spectacularly cold, full of ice spicules. With his breath driven out by the impact, the shock of the cold sucked away any last vestiges of oxygen from his lungs. Borne away by the riptide, he knew with the utmost clarity that he was but mere seconds from the same violent death as his companions. Inhaling deeply to try and galvanise frozen, flaccid limbs, he could just make out the foam and spray where the torrent plunged over the dam. A mere second before he was hurled over the edge, he duck-dived under the maelstrom. Head down, body vertical, back to the dam, he was slammed against the rockface, an agonising impact that punched every breath from his body. The incredible water pressure pinioned him to the rock and with lungs now bursting, a red mist began to appear as he neared drowning. Groping frantically for some kind of purchase, his right hand found a rocky outcrop. Using every reserve in his armoury, Guy inched his body clockwise from head down vertical to head up vertical. And all the time, despite being in extremis, a warning bell clanged loudly in his brain of the imminence of the mines' detonation.

Inexplicably, the waters relaxed their pressure momentarily and he bobbed to the surface, spewing liquid and gulping in huge draughts of oxygen. Refreshed, he pulled himself along the dam and began hauling his body up the adjacent cliff face. His legs were barely clear of the water when the first two mines exploded, engulfing him in a tidal wave that did its utmost to scour him from his haven. Somehow, just somehow, he clung on grimly and summoning the last vestiges of adrenaline in his tortured system, he scrambled clear just as the third mine erupted. The wave from this explosion was smaller, but even so, it kissed the soles of his boots as it tumbled past.

Two matters now concerned Guy. One was his impending climb up the sheer face, the second was whether or not the attack had breached the entrance to the gas factory. As part of his preparation for the mission, Guy had memorised every detail of their target area and knew he had about 150 metres to climb, mostly sheer rock, but with a convenient chimney for part of the way. It would have been a tough ascent if he were dry and warm, but soaked to the skin and frozen to the marrow, it was sheer purgatory. He was about ten metres up the cliff when he sensed a vibration as mine number four wreaked havoc on the electrolysis machines. Glancing down, he saw various flotsam break the surface as the pressure expelled it from the cave. Despite the horrors of what he knew must lie below and the savage deaths of his companions, the young agent knew that the job was done and many thousands of Allied lives saved. A little smile of elation played across his blue lips.

The detail of his ascent became no more than a blur. The water in his clothes began to freeze, he was so icy cold, so chilled, he did not think he could ever be any colder. Hypothermia began to set in. That he began to laugh inexplicably told him that. His goals became the next hold, possibly the one after that, because his brain and his corpus could not take any more at one time. The howling wind screamed unabated, exacerbating yet further the extreme temperature and making his climb more dangerous. Many of the holds were themselves icy, treacherous to hand and foot and he lost count of the times he slipped and nearly fell. The chimney offered some respite. To say he enjoyed that part of the climb would have been a misnomer, but he made steadier and faster progress.

Getting out of the chimney was another matter, there were just no holds within reach. Had it not been for his prescience in carrying pitons and a rope, he would have been stymied. Wearily, he hammered pitons into the rock to establish hand and footholds sufficient to haul himself to an outcrop above his head and thence back onto the cliff face and the final lap. Pausing to bang ice from his clothes, he sent tinkling shards into the depths below. Inch by inch, he dragged his shattered frame to the apex of the ice-covered ridge. Standing on the ridge was almost impossible, the violent wind threatening to peel him from his eyrie and driving snow and hail against his face, itself now almost a frozen mask.

Keeping to one side of the ridge to avoid being silhouetted against the skyline, he trudged back to where he had hidden his car in a small copse on a byway. This was some distance from where the other vehicles had been parked. The idea was that he and Raoul would make their own way back to Clermont Ferrand. Now he would make the journey alone. There was no sign of anyone else. Believing that everyone had died when the dinghies turned turtle, the shore party had made good their escape. In the car were dry clothes, towels, brandy and chocolate. Numbed fingers made simple things like buttons a trial, but gradually, the young agent stripped off his frozen togs, towelled himself as vigorously as present energy levels would permit and drew on fresh, dry garments. He immediately felt 100% better. A whole bar of Cadbury's Bournville with raisins and two stiff slugs of brandy made that 200%. Then he picked his way across country and back to Clermont Ferrand. By now, the Boche were in full cry, trying to mop up after the raid – a forlorn hope – and catch the perpetrators. Predicting this would happen, Guy knew that trying to drive back into town would be far too dangerous and had reconnoitred a spot about 5 kilometres outside where he could hide the car in an old farm. Before leaving the vehicle, he took off the rotor arm and the king lead from the coil to immobilise the engine.

Now came the really tricky bit, to steal quietly back to the flat avoiding the patrols. Entering Clermont Ferrand proved no problem and he thought his luck might hold as he flitted from shadow to shadow. No chance. He was half way along one street when he heard a foot patrol rounding the corner. Frantically, he scanned his environs for cover. Two doors away from where he stood was a house with a high front hedge. Running on the balls of his feet, he raced towards sanctuary, vaulted the gate and pressed his face into the inside of the hedge, praying that the patrol would not sweep the garden. His luck held, they marched imperiously on by. Twice more he was to evade patrols, once by diving into a convenient alley and standing stock still, then by using the porch of a villa. The porch wall was not very high and he squeezed his body into the tightest ball he could muster. To his horror, the soldiers swept their torches over the front of the house and feeling sure he was visible, he willed himself into a yet smaller bundle; the patrol moved on.

The final, agonising, lap was the broad alleyway at the back of Violette's house and he crept down it feeling extremely vulnerable and exposed. Reaching the back gate, he cautiously pushed it open, then stood, watching and listening for any movement. Satisfied that the coast was indeed clear, he moved up to the personal door to the garage. The smear of grease he had deposited in the keyhole mouth was intact and there were no signs of the door being forced. He moved into the garage, again nothing. Mounting the stairs, he found the hair he had placed over the gap between door and frame was still there; the kitchen was as he had left it, a chair blocking the way into the room, a pan handle sticking out and in the way. Similarly, the pillow left slightly awry in the bedroom had not been touched.

He put a match to the previously laid stove, set a pan of vegetable broth and a kettle of water to heat, then slipped back down to the garage. He and Raoul had installed two stout bolts on the inside of the personal door, which opened outwards. Now he set the bolts as added security against surprise attack.

Returning to the safety and sanctuary of the flat, he waited for the kettle to boil then took it into the bathroom.

'My God, Guy Duplessis, what would your mother say?' he asked himself as he gazed into the mirror.

He was not a pretty sight. Dirty, hair and beard unkempt, a raffish bump below his right eye from hitting it on the cliff face during his climb. The eyes that stared back at him were gaunt, hollow, rimmed with black circles, reflecting the torments of his ordeal. His hands, grazed and raw from climbing, his nails broken and looking as if he had been ploughing a field. Every part of his body ached abominably, to the extent that he wondered if he had cracked a couple of ribs when he struck the dam.

Fifteen minutes later, toilet complete, he felt a new man. Like a starving wolf, he devoured the whole pan of broth and at least a partial thaw of his icy frame had begun. Setting the damper on the stove, he boiled another kettle, filled the two hot water bottles and retired to bed.

With the shutters closed, he had no idea of time when he finally awoke from the long tunnel of sleep. The clock told him he had been spark out for 18 long hours. He was stiff, but at least some of the aches had gone and careful probing of his ribs confirmed severe bruising but probably no broken bones. The flat was now warm and he luxuriated in a hot bath, soaking away yet more aches, pains and stiff muscles.

Sitting in the bath, his brain in overdrive, Guy was utterly focused on escape. How long before the Germans tracked down his lair? Hours? Days? There was the comfort that Clermont Ferrand was a large town, but there was simply no way to tell. It was almost a déjà vu of Le Mans when the network was blown and he had but scant time to evade the Boche. The plan discussed with Lionel pre-mission was by Lysander, but that was utterly dependent on clear weather. Guy towelled himself vigorously, swathed his body in warm clothes, then stole away, radio in hand, to one of his safe houses. Before leaving the flat, Guy had encoded the briefest message he could, knowing that the

Nazi RDF network would be on maximum alert after the successful annihilation of the nerve gas plant.

Lionel was also on maximum alert, whiskers twitching as his sixth sense told him that the attack had taken place and had briefed the operators to be on the top line. 'Ripe cherries' was exactly the news Lionel wanted to carry to Churchill. God was in his heaven for Guy, too. With a clear forecast, Lysander pickup would be 0200 next morning.

Guy's decision was that he would make the break entirely unaided, not only to keep other Resistanceards safe, but for total security for himself. Knowing where the flares were hidden, he would arrive at the landing ground in good time, set up the flare 'L' and be gone.

Another decision was to keep the shutters on the flat windows closed so that anyone watching would assume that is was shut up – as were many buildings in wartime – and pass it by.

Now warm and well-fed, Guy passed the day snoozing, although he was on the alert for anything untoward and at regular intervals, slid down to the personal door and listened for sounds that might presage danger.

To give himself plenty of time, Guy aimed to leave at 9.30pm, and calculated that if he left to collect the car at 8pm, he would be in good time. Still exhausted from recent events and the battering he had taken, he dozed off and came to with a start to find it was 8.25. Hurriedly, he dressed in dark clothing, moved unseen out of the back gate and made his way to where the car was hidden. In seconds, he had refitted rotor arm and king lead. Heart in mouth, he pressed the starter. The Citroen purred into life. Oh so carefully, he drove back to town, parking the car in the alley at the rear of the villa.

The gate slid open at his touch and he made his way to the garage and took the stairs to the flat. As he walked into the hallway, Guy flicked the light switch, but nothing happened. Silently cursing that the bulb had blown, he felt his way into the kitchen for a spare ampoule. The second he pushed open the door, he was blinded by the beam of a powerful torch, below which menaced the muzzle of a silencer.

Sitting behind the kitchen table and grasping the torch, a voice in English, cold as the pistol's muzzle, greeted him.

'Good evening, Dinny, just put your hands in the air, very slowly.'

The tone was gloating, triumphant.

Guy did as he was told, sweat beginning to trickle between his shoulder blades.

'That was a really fine job you did up there in the mountains, I take my hat off to you. And now you are going to pay.'

The voice behind the torch had a rasping quality that rang distant bells in Guy's brain, a voice he had heard before. And then it clicked, even though the speech was English, not German. Obersturmbannführer Wägner!

'Lower your right hand, very slowly, and turn on the light.'

Even as he obeyed, Guy was calculating a riposte. Wägner's torch beam jinked to illuminate Guy's right hand.

His left hand lay temporarily in shadow. In one lightning movement, he lowered both hands to waist level and using the door frame as purchase, drop kicked the kitchen table with all his might. The solid deal table weighed 40 pounds and catapulted by the twin pistons of the Duplessis legs, slammed the German against the back wall with such force, Guy heard ribs cracking and the man's breath smashed from his lungs. The torch arced upwards, clattered to the floor but remained alight. Wägner's right hand jerked upwards, there was a phut! as his finger tightened involuntarily on the trigger and a bullet sang past Guy's left shoulder to bury itself in the ceiling plaster. Regaining his balance, Guy hurled himself across the table, grasped the Nazi's skull and twisted hard. There was a tearing, snapping sound, then Wägner's head lolled to one side, his neck broken.

Guy switched on the light. Wägner lolled in his chair, his head at an odd angle like some broken marionette. On the floor lay the torch and pistol, soup bowl shards, the spoon, Wägner's felt hat and a small key with a grey metal tag. Guy cleared the floor, then looked at the key. Once more he was to thank Germanic thoroughness, the tag was stamped 'Citroen' and the car's registration number.

For a second, Guy stared at the corpse then shook with sudden panic. At all costs, he had to protect Violette. Who else knew where Wägner had gone and would come looking when he failed to return? The body had to be dumped – fast.

Taking the Citroen key, Guy first slipped away to the back alley and moved his own car to the courtyard, he could not risk it being parked out there for too long. Next, he carefully walked the neighbouring streets and as expected, found Wägner's motor not far away. After checking there was nobody in the car, Guy took it back to the courtyard and closed the gates.

Entering the garage, he navigated the wheelbarrow to the bottom of the staircase. For the second time in this war, Guy found himself dragging a German corpse, the fleshy Gestapo officer even more of a strain than the Gefreiter. Wrapping his arms around the man from behind, he hauled Wägner to the top of the stairs then heaved him down to the bottom, flaccid heels bumping and clattering on the bare treads, before depositing him in the barrow.

Grunting with the effort, Guy wheeled the improvised hearse to the car and propped the body upright in the front passenger seat, pulling the hat low over the eyes. Then he placed his bike and a broomstick in the back.

Eyes peeled and senses on 110% alert, he drove out of town, windows down to hear any patrols or vehicles better. A wise precaution, he heard the noisy gearbox of a Hanomag truck in the nick of time and heart in mouth, dived into a side road, killing engine and lights and praying the patrol would not spot him. They did not.

Once outside town, he drove into the steep hills and two miles further on, braked to a halt. Some yards ahead lay a hairpin bend with a gap in the guard wall where some other unfortunate had plunged over the edge.

With considerable effort, he slid Wägner's body into the driver's seat. In winter's chill, rigor was already setting in, making the task more difficult still. Bike and broomstick were retrieved from the back seat and the velo parked against the wall. Guy was moving as fast as he could, conscious that someone could appear at any moment even on this remote byway. Despite the cold, he was sweating profusely.

First he smashed the driver's window with a stone, then gritting his teeth, he forced himself to perch on Wägner's ice-cold lap. It was a horrible sensation, sitting on a dead man and forced a shudder of revulsion. Leaving the driver's door open, Guy pulled away, changing up to second at walking pace. Grabbing the broomstick, he jumped out of the vehicle, slammed the door and ran alongside. Leaning in through the window, he steered with his left hand towards the gap. With scant yards to go, he jabbed the accelerator with the broomstick and rolled his body clear.

He regained his feet just in time to see the car clip the wall with its right-hand wing as it disappeared from view and he ran to see what would happen. In all the movies, cars that plunge off mountains inevitably catch fire: this one did not. The black Citroen was invisible in the inky blackness, but Guy could hear the sounds of it somersaulting and bouncing into the ravine before finally coming to rest. He knew that the bottom of the valley was thick with bushes and scrub, so hopefully, the car would be difficult to find.

The downhill ride back to Clermont Ferrand was interrupted for a brief moment as he discarded the broomstick over a hedge, then more patrol dodging to reach the villa.

The contretemps and impromptu funeral had put him way behind time, now the clock said 1130. Pausing only to snatch his precious radio, he made his final exit through the web of alleys and side roads. God was truly his guide that night and soon he was clear of the town and making his way on remote tracks towards the landing ground. Nerves keyed like banjo strings, the clock ticking and the lights of his own Citroen almost useless, he took a wrong turn. Quickly consulting his map, he could see that this byway rejoined his original route further on. Invisible in that dark, the deep runnel at right angles to the track had been gouged out by countless winter rains. The car's left-hand front wheel plunged into the trap with sickening force. A screech of tortured metal, then the revs soared and all drive was lost. Guy knew the answer before he lifted the bonnet and he gazed transfixed at the shiny, raw break in the driveshaft and at a car that was now utterly useless. With about 12 miles to go and his bike still at the villa, his chances of making the pickup were zero.

Still his brain continued to function in secret agent mode and he looked for somewhere to hide the car from view. About 50 yards down the sloping track he found a gate and used gravity to roll into the gateway and behind a stone wall.

That gateway seemed in some way familiar despite the darkness. As he climbed out and looked up the field, he was almost mesmerised as he recognised the barn where he and his father had incarcerated the Bugatti.

Salvation was at hand, or rather behind a stone wall in that barn. The if – and an almighty if – was whether he could disinter the racer in time.

The Citroen's toolkit contained two stout tyre levers with chisel ends and a hammer. Within seconds, he was attacking the mortar around one piece of stone, but the stone was deeply embedded and he had to loosen the mortar around a second before they surrendered. It took him nearly half an hour to make a hole big enough to climb through.

Crawling into the Bugatti's wartime garage, he smelt immediately that familiar tang of rubber, leather, metal, overladen with the smell of castor oil from the lubricant. Anticipating that many things post-war would be like gold dust, Robert and Guy had put everything they would need in with the car. Petrol, some aviation gasoline with a high octane rating, antifreeze, new sparking plugs, a screw-operated trolley jack, a tyre pump, all these were just part of the backup to rouse the Bugatti to life once again. Hammers and tools for dismantling the wall sat beside two oil lamps, a jerrican of paraffin and Swedish waterproof matches.

Perched on axle stands, the car sat on several sheets of thick ply to keep it level. Guy lit one of the oil lamps, its yellowish glow illumining the delicate blue of the dusty coachwork. For one fleeting moment, Guy was back at Monthléry and that sunny, victorious afternoon so long ago. He pictured his father, blackened face, shining eyes, and his mother, dressed as if for a garden party, hugging this dirty husband. He wiped away a tear.

Condensation is the bugbear of any car laid up for a long period and the pair had taken as many precautions as they could. The petrol tank had been drained to prevent fuel turning to jelly and a light coating of preservative oil sprayed inside the tank. Sparking plugs had been pulled, some oil poured into all eight cylinders, then threaded alloy blanking plugs screwed into each plug hole. The sump had been filled with fresh oil. The radiator was empty, so Guy filled it with neat antifreeze

Guy lit the second lamp, grabbed the plug spanner and withdrew the blanks. The 35TC had a built-in starting handle, so Guy leaned gently on it. Initially, there was some resistance, then at a firmer pressure, the stiff engine yielded and began to turn smoothly. Guy cranked it over about 20 or 30 turns to loosen it off and build up oil pressure. Then he pumped up the pressure-feed fuel system.

Before fitting new spark plugs there was another vital job to do. Torch in hand, Guy peered anxiously into the jerricans of petrol and AVGAS. To his relief, both looked pretty clear and sludge-free, so he sloshed half of each can into the tank before cranking vigorously once more to pump fuel into the carburettor.

Plugs in, ignition advance/retard and throttle set, time for an enormous deep breath and every finger crossed. Even fully fettled, the 35 could be the very devil to start. He grabbed the starting handle and cranked madly. His reward was sweet nothing, not a chirp. A smell of petrol suggested that fuel was getting through and pointed to a lack of spark. Ever mindful that time was pressing, he pulled off No1 plug lead, connected it to a spare plug from the stock and set it with its nose against a cylinder head bolt. Sure enough, cranking produced no spark.

Feverishly, Guy removed the magneto cover and taking a piece of spark plug box, inserted the slip between the points and worked it back and forth like an emery board.

Now he had a spark, but the stubborn engine refused to fire. Desperation and fear were now writ large across the young man's face.

Spinning the T-handled plug spanner in a blur, he whipped out all eight plugs, poured a measured amount of AVGAS into each cylinder and reinserted all the bougies. A slight adjustment to the advance/retard and the throttle. Crank like a whirlwind.

With a deafening bellow, the straight eight roared into life, hurling a blue haze of fumes from its exhaust as the cylinders cleared. Guy sprang towards the cockpit, setting the controls to a fast tickover before placing a piece of sacking over the exhaust outlet to absorb some of the fumes.

Some frantic effort with the tyre pump rejuvenated the tyres. The engine was now warming, but the fumes were choking and Guy's eyes streamed.

Totally focused on his escape, he wielded the sledgehammer like a maniac, coughing with the fumes and scarcely able to see for the tears. Stones flew at the crack of the hammer until there was a gap just wide enough to squeeze the car through.

Before reuniting car with the soil, Guy tried clutch and gears, which crunched home but appeared to work. Scorning the jack, he pushed the Bugatti off its stands, put both oil lamps and the radio on the passenger seat, engaged first and manoeuvred the little car through the gap.

The Bug was a racer, so no headlamps, but a silencer had been fitted for road driving. A prod on the brakes evinced some action and with the hands of his watch now at 0120, Guy steered towards the landing ground and freedom.

Somehow, despite the circumstances and the danger, driving the thoroughbred once again was a thrill, its delicacy and fine engineering a bouquet to be savoured as it stretched after its long slumber.

Guy bumped along tracks as far as he could, but the last five miles had to be on public road. With his night sight now perfect, Guy was cracking along at up to 80mph on straights and drifting the car around curves.

Too late he spotted the roadblock as he slid round a fast bend, a half-track on one side of the road and a truck on the other, leaving a slit between the two like a chicane. With no lights and a dark car, he was almost invisible to the Germans, but they heard his engine and turned towards him.

At unabated speed, Guy hurled the car at the gap, the soldiers diving to either side on his approach. Flicking the steering to the left, he realised he was travelling far too fast and stabbed the brakes in a last-ditch attempt to lose some speed. The rear of the Bug skidded to the right, responding instantly to a touch of opposite lock but careering through the gap slightly sideways. The pointed tail bounced off the rear mudguard of the truck, then they were away, foot to the boards and weaving from side to side to put off the gunners.

The Wehrmacht leapt to its feet and began firing at their now almost invisible quarry, one soldier clambering up the half-track towards its searchlight. Guy could hear bullets whistling overhead, then the racing screen to his left starred as a round punched a hole in it.

A second later, he felt agonising pain as a bullet smashed through his left shoulder, driving all the breath from his body. In the intense pain and shock, he almost left the road, recovering as he approached the next corner. Just as he entered the bend, the searchlight caught him briefly in its glare.

Blood was soaking into his clothes, the agony made him almost faint and his vision blurred. Now on the limit, he let the right-hand rear wheel drift onto the gravel in the verge. Instantly, the car whipped sideways, the wheel sliding onto the grass. He never knew how he got it straight again, the car sliding for thirty yards before snapping back into line.

Initial pain and trauma began to subside, his brain to work again. With five miles to run and the Germans in slower but inevitable pursuit, getting away was looking marginal – and that was being optimistic by any standards. Any delay by the Lysander...

Guy arrived at the site at 0145. Parking the Bugatti behind a hedge, he dived towards the flare cache, sprinted down the 'runway' and ignited the markers in the classic 'L'. In the night's still, he could hear the clatter of the half-track and glimpsed the occasional flash of its searchlight.

It was 0155.

Ears straining, Guy picked up the faint hum of an aero engine. It was heading straight for the flares!

He raised his torch and flashed the recognition signal.

Chapter 18

The Lysander pilot could see the approaching lights of the Nazi patrol, especially its probing searchlight on top of the armoured vehicle, sweeping from side to side across the fields, stabbing menacingly at dark grass and hedgerow in search of its prey. The enemy seemed to be moving towards Guy at a far greater speed than they actually were.

Yet again, Guy marvelled at the skills of the Lysander aviators as the pilot toggled the landing lights' switch. Twin swathes illuminating the frosty turf, the Lysander hurled itself onto the deck and round the top of the L in the aviation equivalent of a handbrake turn. As the plane retraced its path back towards the bottom of the L and the waiting Guy, the pilot leaned out of the starboard side of his cockpit, shouting and gesturing. Guy could understand not a word of what was being said, but the airman's body language was transparent – 'I'm not stopping, just hop on as I slow'.

Engine bellowing, the Lizzie did indeed slow, the pilot's head now out of the port side and watching Guy. Desperately, the young agent leapt onto the ladder as the aircraft swept past. No sooner had he seen Guy's feet on the bottom rung than the pilot banged the throttle through the gate and began his take-off run. Treacherous with ice, the rungs offered scant grip and the jolt as the taps were opened, the sudden rush of propwash and a hop as the tailwheel danced over a rut threw Guy backwards. First his feet were dangling in the air, then his right hand lost grip. For a second or two, his sole contact with the plane was his left hand. Dangling by his fingertips, body almost parallel to the fuselage, his wounded left shoulder screamed in utter agony. Such was the pain, he almost let go, but survival is a primeval instinct. Every sinew and tendon afire and screaming 'Enough', he somehow clawed his way back onto the ladder. Feet scrabbling for grip as the plane accelerated, he fought to the top of the ladder, grabbed the passenger cockpit canopy and cracked it open. Such was the slipstream, it threatened to pluck him from the ladder and hurl him back to the ground. With a final, superhuman, do or die effort, Guy jackknifed his body into the matt-green sanctuary of the passenger space. As he tumbled haplessly to the floor, his left shoulder struck the frame of the forward seat. The searing bolt of pure torture made him almost faint and he huddled on the floor, powerless to move.

The Nazi gunners now had the searchlight bathing the aircraft and were throwing everything they possessed at stopping it. Bullets zipped through the air like angry hornets. One passed through the canopy of the rear cockpit, a second through the cockpit itself, so close to Guy's back that despite being semi-conscious, he felt a burning sensation in his back. Later, he was to find a scorch mark on his jacket where the shell had missed his body by mere fractions of a millimetre.

Unnoticed by its passenger, the plane had unstuck. Free in its true environment, it came alive in the pilot's hands, hugging the deck and turning its tail to the enemy to minimise the size of the target before disappearing from sight behind a clump of trees. Now safe from immediate danger, the pilot levelled out and began his home run.

It was to be nearly fifteen minutes before Guy's level of consciousness regained anything like normality, triggered by a faint crackling above his head. Fighting to concentrate, it penetrated his scrambled brain that it was coming from the headset on the hook above him. Groggily, he pulled himself into a sitting position, suddenly conscious of the howling gale coming through the canopy opening. He knelt on the seat and slammed the cover shut before pulling the headphones on.

'You OK?' came the enquiry over the wires.

'Just about,' was the rather weak reply, 'I've been shot in the left shoulder, they winged me when I crashed their roadblock. The bullet's gone through, I think, but it hurts like hell.'

'Not surprised,' was the rather laconic rejoinder, 'there's a first aid kit under the forward seat, help yourself.'

Dragging the metal box from its clips was easy, but divesting himself of his top clothing in that tight space to tend the wound was excruciating and several times, he nearly passed out. Finally, he dragged off his bloodsoaked shirt and very gingerly felt the entry and exit wounds. In the dark he could see virtually nothing, but the holes, although oozy, seemed fairly clean. Snapping open the kit, he found rolls of cotton bandage, gauze, surgical tape and some scissors. Figuring the exit wound the easiest place to start, he made a pad of gauze and bandage, then applied tape round the edges. This makeshift dressing he pressed carefully onto the wound. Repeating the exercise on the entry wound was a damn sight harder and it took three or four attempts before he managed to fix it in place. Now feeling a little better, he abandoned the shirt and teeth gritted, pulled his sweater back over his head and donned his coat. The redundant shirt he put to good use, cutting off strips with the scissors and taping them over the bullet holes in fuselage and canopy. The freezing darts of air that had been coursing into his space magically ceased and bit by bit, the cabin heater began to make headway. One other essential medicament in the first aid kit was a half-bottle of brandy and he poured the spirit down his throat, gagging as the fumes caught him and fire crept through his frozen veins.

For the first hour, Guy was rigid with fear, expecting at any moment a Messerschmitt or a Focke-Wulf night-fighter scrambled by the patrol to materialise from the cloud above and intercept them. But the tiny monoplane was close to invisible as it picked its way over the French landscape and they never saw another aircraft.

Now sitting on the forward seat, Guy's mind sprang back to that moment in the kitchen at the flat, the stark, chilling, split-second when Wägner uttered that greeting 'Good evening, Dinny.' *That* was the part that sent icy rivulets down Guy's spine, the use of his childhood nickname.

It began in 1925 when Guy was just four. William and Constance were celebrating their ruby wedding and organised a big party at their home. Robert, Madeleine and Guy were invited and Henry turned up from London. By mutual and unspoken consent, Robert and his brother maintained a frosty truce for the long weekend. Young Guy was allowed to attend the early part of the festivities, given some ice-cream and pop then despatched to bed. William simply adored his grandson and the following morning, presented him with a large tin drum. To any four year old, a drum was manna from heaven and true to expectations, he beat seven bells out of it. As he entered the drawing room where the adults were enjoying a pre-prandial sherry, his grandfather hoisted the little drummer boy above his head, proclaiming 'Dinny, dinny on the tinny.' Like any small child, Guy repeated his elder's words, crying 'Dinny, dinny, dinny, dinny'. From then on, William always referred to Guy by the nickname of Dinny, although only within the family.

Gone were William and Constance; gone too were Eric and Mary Thornthwaite, who had retired to Canada to live with their son when the house in Halifax was sold; Guy's parents would never speak again. The two H's in St Malo had never even met William and Constance and in any case, only Hugo spoke English. There was one person, just one, who knew that nickname.

Henry.

Muzzily, he began to piece together the jigsaw of evidence. First and foremost, apart from Raoul and Violette, nobody in the Clermont Ferrand cell knew the nom de guerre on his papers, he was just known as Hugo. That way, everyone was safeguarded. For Wägner to have been sitting there in the flat waiting, he had to have known where to find Guy. No, Wägner had been fed Guy's alias, Gerard Arcachon, but how had he found the address?

It had to be Henry; the burning question was why he should have betrayed his nephew. Was it significant that Wägner had appeared after the mission to destroy the nerve gas plant was complete? The answer in Guy's head at this stage was 'Possibly'. Whilst he had no clue as to how Henry communicated with the Axis powers, he certainly could not just pick up a phone and call, so any messages had to be by some intermediate and uncertain route – unless Henry had a wireless operator secreted in Britain. Certainly, Henry himself was extremely unlikely to risk being his own wireless op.

Was it that Henry feared that if an ultra-secret operation was blown before it happened, some mightily awkward questions would be posed in Baker Street? Then again, agents being blown before they even left British soil or within days of landing in France were all too common. With Guy dead, as he surely would have been if Wägner had captured him, Henry would have been fireproof. The fact that Wägner had come alone and without a couple of soldiers as backup was very pertinent, strong evidence that it was more personal than official.

Parking this conundrum at the back of his mind for the time being and with a little adrenaline now sharpening the concentration, Guy's thoughts drifted back to one lazy summer Sunday afternoon in his late teens. His mother was at the restaurant and Guy and Robert were lounging in the garden, sharing a particularly fine red unearthed on a trip to Bordeaux. Somehow, the conversation meandered round to the subject of Henry. Soothed by the wine, Robert talked about his brother in a way that he had never yet done. He recounted to Guy the almost constant bickering and open warfare of their childhood and separate schools, then moved on to Henry's days at Cambridge. He described how his younger sibling had spent all his vacations abroad and the succession of postcards soliciting money. At that moment, a phrase his father had used, almost forgotten in the mists of time, hit Guy forcibly between the eyes.

'Most of them came from towns in Germany,' Robert had remarked.

Robert continued with his tales, recalling the episode in Rhys

Chapman's office after the reading of William's will.

'What really made my blood boil,' said Robert, 'was when Henry remarked that I'd probably put my share in the petty cash tin. Bloody cheek.'

It was at that moment that the scales fell from Guy's eyes. That look of absolute amazement, horror and fear that had blazed for but an instant in his uncle's eyes when he saw Guy, followed by the immediate question about Robert and Madeleine. The Germans had clearly told Henry that all the Duplessis had been killed when the house collapsed; seeing Guy was like seeing a ghost. Ideological Henry might be, but his betrayal of Guy was for one reason and one reason alone.

Money.

Insanely jealous of his older brother, of what he saw as favouritism by William, of Robert's success and huge wealth, the envy had gnawed at Henry like a cancer. When he heard that the family had been killed, he knew that he could at last wreak his revenge by getting his hands on his brother's fortune. Finding Guy alive completely shattered that dream. Blowing him to the Gestapo was a heaven-sent opportunity to reawaken the dream and no questions asked.

If Wägner had not used Guy's nickname, he would have been none the wiser about his betrayal; the Nazi officer's gloating, convinced he held all the cards, provided the crucial evidence. Obviously too, the closeness between Henry and Wägner was far more than spy to spymaster.

Where did they first meet and what was the relationship? Even those brief orders to Guy from Wägner had been in clear and accentless English.

Cambridge perhaps?

The mole that Lionel had mentioned when he first recruited Guy. Henry?

For sure, Henry was about to see a ghost transmogrify for a second time into flesh and blood. That anger that had seized Guy when the Gefreiter was stealing his mother's rings reached white heat once more. The day of reckoning was nigh.

A short time later, Guy was to help unravel at least the London end of a very tangled web, but had he known what lay in the villa during his confrontation with Wägner, his execution of the Gestapo officer would have changed from a cold-blooded act of war to something very personal. And his deduction that Henry knew his nom de guerre was entirely wrong.

'Horror' barely described Henry's feelings on meeting his nephew outside SOE HQ. Convinced he was now the sole heir to the Duplessis fortune, Henry was panic-stricken at seeing his pot of gold snatched from under the rainbow. But, coldly calculating as he was, as Henry walked away from the encounter, he instantly surmised Guy's current role, a profession unlikely to register as low-risk on any actuarial table. But, and it was a big 'but', Henry knew his sole chance of eliminating Guy was to blow him in the field. In doing that, the civil servant faced two obstacles. The first was that knowledge of operations was on a strictly need to know basis and despite Henry's very senior role, asking questions would meet not only with a stony silence, but also unwanted suspicion. The second was that Lionel had this ultra-secret mission sewn up tighter than a drum. As a result, Henry did not even know whether Guy was in England or on a mission.

Fate, as ever, played a hand. Cypher clerk Alistair ffitch-Lewis, threatened with the exposure of his homosexual affair with a Cabinet minister, had succumbed to Henry's blackmail and was feeding him a regular stream of intelligence from SOE's radio HQ. Alistair just happened to be on duty the night Guy was sent the confirmation signal about the explosives drop for Operation Cherry and actually saw a plain language version of the message. Knowing that Clermont Ferrand was Guy's back yard, Henry risked putting two and two together and alerting Wägner.

From a previous operation in which he had played a part, Henry knew Raoul's name and job. Because activity in Clermont Ferrand was pretty mundane, Henry decided to leave Raoul undisturbed as a potential sprat for a much bigger mackerel; now came his chance to use that bait. Again a but – Henry had to pass his coded message through two cutouts and Operation Cherry was history by the time Wägner decoded it. The Obersturmbannführer had to act unofficially and alone. A key part of the coded message offered 20% of the Duplessis megabucks for Guy's elimination. First, Wägner visited the Mairie. On finding Raoul off sick, he went immediately to Raoul's house, to find it cold and empty. Furiously and in vain, he searched the house from top to bottom, but found nothing that would lead him to Guy. Frustrated, Wägner sank into an armchair in the lounge. Sitting on the dresser was a large silver-framed portrait of a lady in a garden and in the background, a curious spherical ornament. Instinct told Wägner that this was the key to finding Guy and he vaguely remembered seeing such an ornament somewhere in the town.

Fate was again clearly a strong influence on events. After two days driving round Clermont Ferrand, Wägner spotted the astrolabe. Dressed in plain clothes, he parked in a sidestreet opposite the villa and observed the house. Nothing moved, so he walked around the alley at the back, but could see nothing over the high walls. Wägner decided to wait for darkness before making a move; his move coincided with Guy's foray to recover the car.

Herr Obersturmbannführer rang the bell and like Guy some weeks before, heard the tap-tapping of Violette's stick and her painful progress down the hallway.

'Wägner, German Police,' he announced when the door opened, 'I need to ask you some questions.'

He trailed Violette down to the salon.

'Do you have a lodger?' he demanded.

Violette nodded.

'How did he come to you?'

At this, Violette recognised imminent danger, but the hesitancy before she replied and her dropped gaze were ample proof that she was lying.

'He knocked at the door and asked if I had a room to let.'

Her reward was a back-hander that left her dazed and battered, with blood oozing down her chin from where her teeth had split her tongue.

'Don't you lie to me, you bloody French whore,' raged Wägner, 'he came to you through Raoul Vicomte, didn't he?'

Violette was petrified, the calm of her genteel existence shattered by a blitzkrieg of terror, violence and pain. Shock and hurt sprang into those eyes, then resignation as she realised that she had told the Gestapo officer all he needed to know.

'Where is he?'

'He lives in the chauffeur's flat above the garage. I don't know when he comes and goes, I can't see the flat from here.'

Glancing around the room, the Nazi spotted a phone.

'Is this the only one in the house?'

Painfully, Violette nodded once more. Wägner strode over to the instrument and ripped the wires from the wall, then placing his nose inches from Violette's face, he screamed, 'Don't even think of moving until I get back. How do I get into the flat?'

'Through the kitchen at the back, the keys are on the mantelpiece.'

Quietly and carefully, Wägner slid through the back door, cracked open the door in the wall and let himself into the courtyard. For several moments, he stood, watching and listening for any signs of activity in the flat. Taking an automatic from his jacket, he screwed a silencer to the end of the barrel. Then he let himself into the garage. Casting the beam of his torch, he spotted the staircase, which he mounted with his feet to either side to avoid creaking treads. Silently, he let himself into the flat, rapidly establishing that it was empty. The glowing stove, a soup bowl and spoon laid ready and a packed haversack beside the chair told him all he wanted to know. As quietly as he had come, Wägner stole back to the salon, pistol in hand. Violette was still sitting in her chair, bolt upright, clawlike hands grasping the arms, staring at the fire.

But those once bright, beautiful, luminous eyes stared at nothing, snuffed out by the massive heart attack brought on by Wägner's brutal terror. The man's lip curled in a sneer and a flash of annoyance in his own eyes revealed his disappointment at missing his revenge. Then he stole back to the flat, careful in case Guy had returned. Loosening the bulb in the hall, Wägner started his vigil behind the kitchen table.

Chapter 19

Exhausted by the battering from the mission, the mental strain of being on the run and his narrow escape, the shock from the bullet wound and the effect of the brandy, tiredness swept over Guy like a tidal wave. Leaning forward in his seat, he rested his head on his arms and slept.

The little dog was snuggled against the back of Angela's knees as she slept in the bed that Guy normally used when at the farm. The night was completely still, not even an owl or a fox broke the silence. A chance zephyr rattled the slightly open casement. Instantly, the dog was on his feet. Padding silently across the floor, he jumped onto the blanket chest below the window and nosing between the blackout curtains, jammed his snout firmly in the window opening. He sniffed hard. Nothing. He inhaled again. Still nothing. Then another minute draught trembled against the window. The terrier drew in air deeply, his brain absorbing not only the oxygen but also the ethereal message that it carried. With a soft thud, he climbed down from the window and resumed his place on the bed. Satisfied that his beloved master was now safe, he rested his head on his paws and slept.